Praise for Claire LaZebnik's Previous Novels

The Smart One and The Pretty One

"Winning...moments of real depth combine with witty dialogue as LaZebnik deftly spins each turn convincingly to avoid easy answers." —*Publishers Weekly*

"This sparkling novel about two sisters is both witty and stylish. You won't be able to resist LaZebnik's charming take on modern relationships. Read it!"

—Holly Peterson, *New York Times* bestselling author of *The Manny*

"A funny and endearing novel that truly captures the devotion and rivalry between sisters...whether they relate to the smart one or the pretty one (or both), readers will find this book irresistible." —*Booklist*

"Another alluring tale of two seemingly different sisters...Recommended for fans of intelligent chick lit." —*Library Journal*

"A deliciously intimate portrait of sisters."

—W. Bruce Cameron, author of *8 Simple Rules for Marrying My Daughter*

"A fun novel...perfect for reading on a beach."

—WomansDay.com

"Claire LaZebnik explores the sister bond with warmth, wit, and honesty. I loved this novel."

—Jill Smolinski, author of *The Next Thing on My List*

"Sisters everywhere will recognize themselves in *The Smart One and the Pretty One*. Claire LaZebnik has written a touching take on love, longing, and the ties that bind."

—Heather and Rose MacDowell, authors of *Turning Tables*

"Claire LaZebnik has written a wonderfully smart and funny novel about the complexity of love and friendship between sisters. Filled with real warmth and astute observations, it made me wish I had a sister of my own. You'll enjoy every heartfelt page."

—Leslie Schnur, author of *Late Night Talking* and *The Dog Walker*

Knitting Under the Influence

"At turns hilarious, at times heartbreaking, and so, so honest about life, love, and friendship. I loved it." —Melissa Senate

"Charming…smart, engaging characters, each of whom is complicated and real enough to be worth an entire book on her own." —*Chicago Sun-Times*

"LaZebnik juggles periods of personal crisis while maintaining her characters' complex individuality. Social knitters, especially, will relate to the bond that strengthens over the click-clack of the girls' needles." —*Publishers Weekly*

"[A] funny and heart-tugging story about three twenty-something Los Angeles women who drink, cry, and, of course, knit together whenever they can." —*Arizona Republic*

If You Lived Here, You'd Be Home Now

Claire LaZebnik

five
spot

NEW YORK   BOSTON

5 Spot
Hachette Book Group
237 Park Avenue
New York, NY 10017

www.5-spot.com

5 Spot is an imprint of Grand Central Publishing.
The 5 Spot name and logo are trademarks of Hachette Book Group, Inc.

Printed in the United States of America

First Edition: September 2010
10 9 8 7 6 5 4 3 2 1

Library of Congress Cataloging-in-Publication Data
LaZebnik, Claire Scovell.
   If you lived here, you'd be home now / Claire LaZebnik. —1st ed.
      p. cm.
   ISBN 978-0-446-55501-2
   1. Single mothers—Fiction.   2. Single mothers—Family relationships—
Fiction.   3. Domestic fiction.   I. Title.
   PS3612.A98I34 2010
   813'.6—dc22

                                                        2009041379

For Julie, Alice, Nell, and Ted, with love and gratitude

If You Lived Here,
You'd Be Home Now

I.

The heat wave that had tortured us for most of September finally broke and Tuesday morning was cool and overcast, so I volunteered to take Eleanor Roosevelt around the block. My mother thanked me a little too enthusiastically, effectively conveying the message that her expectations of me were so low that she was bowled over by a simple offer to walk the dog.

I was trying to get Eleanor Roosevelt's leash on, dodging her happy dancing legs and scolding her to hold still, when my cell phone rang. I dropped the leash so I could get the phone out of my jeans pocket. Eleanor Roosevelt stopped wiggling and looked at me, confused. This wasn't how the game went.

"Hey, Rickie," said a male voice on the other end.

I breathed in sharply. "Ryan?"

"Yeah."

I gave a delighted bounce and Eleanor Roosevelt jumped and barked with sympathetic excitement. "Are you back in town?"

"Yep. Just got back a couple of days ago."

"It's good to hear your voice."

"Same here. Sorry I didn't keep up with your e-mails the last month or so."

"No worries," I said. "Have you seen Gabriel yet?"

"Last night. We talked for a long time. I still can't believe it—I leave home for six months, and they decide to get divorced? What's up with that?"

"It's a mess."

"Want to come over and discuss it with me?"

Just nine words, but they were enough to make every inch of me tighten with desire. I kept my voice casual, though. "Right now?"

"I'm not doing anything. You?"

"Nah, not really." I glanced down at the dog and whispered, "Sorry, girl." Into the phone I added, "Half an hour good?"

"Perfect. See you."

I gently nudged Eleanor Roosevelt away from my leg and hung the leash back up on its nail in the coat closet. The dog whined and followed me as I headed toward the kitchen, where my mother was working on her laptop.

"I thought you were taking her on a walk," she said, looking up.

"I just got a call. I'm going to meet a friend for lunch."

"Can't you walk the dog first?"

"I said I'd be right over."

"You're breaking her heart."

I looked back at the yellow Lab. She ducked her head down but kept her eyes pinned on my face hopefully. "She's just a dog," I said, even though I felt bad about disappointing her. "She'll be fine."

"Just run her around the block—"

"I don't have time. I promise I'll walk her later."

My mother rose from the table, heaving a dramatic sigh. "Come on," she said to Eleanor Roosevelt, who immediately raised her head, her eyes gleaming with sudden joy. "I'll take you." Eleanor Roosevelt gave a leap of pure happiness and trotted ahead of Mom out of the kitchen, toward her leash and the walk she loved so much.

I went the other way, toward the garage, and got in my car. I drove past them on the street. Eleanor Roosevelt was hauling my mother along, practically pulling her arm out of its socket in her delight at being out and about.

I didn't slow down and Mom didn't wave.

Ryan worked on movie shoots as a production assistant. He was always traveling to different countries. Sometimes I'd be at a movie and see his name in the credits, and I'd feel a funny burst of pride even though he hadn't told me anything about it and his name was always buried way at the end.

We met when his brother, Gabriel, and my half sister, Melanie, first got engaged. I was sixteen, moody and insecure and far more excited about being Mel's maid of honor than I would ever admit to anyone. Ryan was five years older, just finishing up college, and, as Gabriel's brother and best man, my official partner in all ceremonies and table seatings. He was tall, cute, mildly roguish, and so far out of my league that I immediately developed a major crush on him and proceeded to spend way too much time trying to figure out what relation Mel and Gabriel's children would be to ours when Ryan and I got married in turn.

Ryan winked at me and squeezed my arm when we walked back down the aisle together after the ceremony. Feeling grown-up in my strapless silver bridesmaid dress, I thought that meant he was finally seeing me as a woman, until I took a sip of champagne in front of him a little while later and he said, "Don't be in such a rush to grow up. Being a kid is more fun." I thought he was just being patronizing, but over time I came to realize he meant it—the guy was in no rush to become an adult. Me, I was in too much of a rush, although how much too much only became evident about three years later.

Anyway, when Ryan left his seat at our table to flirt with Melanie's former college roommate who was twenty-four and gorgeous—or at least so blond and tall that she passed for gorgeous—I surrendered the fantasy that I could ever be anything other than Mel's little sister to him.

Our paths continued to cross through subsequent years of family holidays and celebrations, but Ryan was never more than civil and distantly friendly until a couple of Thanksgivings ago at our house, when my mom seated us together and something just clicked. The timing was finally right, I guess. He was a footloose twenty-eight-year-old and I was a twenty-three-year-old with responsibilities. Made us almost the same age.

We talked to each other the entire evening, mostly about our families. We both knew what it was like to be the younger and less successful sibling—maybe that was what bonded us, made us similarly sarcastic, similarly vulnerable, similarly determined not to let anyone see through the sarcasm to that vulnerability.

Ryan was actually better-looking than Gabriel. His features were smaller and more even and he was a lot thinner, but he lacked Gabriel's charm and exuberance. Gabriel was a chubby teddy bear of a guy whose overgrown beard and mustache made him look like he'd taken refuge in a cave for a number of years, but wherever he went he took up a lot of space in a *good* way. He made every room feel a little warmer and homier and more welcoming because he was in it, whereas Ryan hovered around the edges wherever he was, always an observer, always a visitor, never at home. It was no surprise he took jobs that let him travel all over the world: he liked being rootless and independent.

We surreptitiously exchanged phone numbers that Thanksgiving night. A few days later he called me, and we met at a restaurant for dinner and ended up back at his place. From then on, whenever he was in town, he got in touch with me.

Neither of us told our families. They might have thought it was meaningful when it wasn't.

I would be the first to admit that I hadn't ever completely gotten over my crush on Ryan, but the more I got to know him, the more I realized he wasn't a guy you could pin a lot of hopes on. The second you tried to grab on to him in any way, he turned slippery and slid right through your fingers. The reason he liked me was because I was smart enough to leave him alone most of the time.

It was harder than it looked.

He greeted me now at the front door of his small apartment building, in answer to my intercom call. "The lock's broken," he explained as he gave me a brusque kiss on the cheek. "I can't buzz people in anymore. Have to come down."

"Can't you get them to fix it?"

He shrugged. "I'm only in town until the next job. Someone who lives here all the time can deal with it. Come on."

He led me upstairs and I studied him from the back. He looked good: a little thinner than the last time I'd seen him, and his wavy light brown hair hadn't been cut for a while, but both things suited him. The guy could still pass for a college student even though he was over thirty.

The last time we'd gone out for drinks together, we had both been carded.

We entered his apartment. It looked exactly the same as it had six months ago, when I'd last been there: an IKEA sofa, a couple of framed generic prints on the wall, a large-screen HD

TV. Not much else. "So you already have another job lined up?" I asked, turning toward him as he closed the door behind us.

Ryan nodded. "Yep. With Jonathan Bluestein." I must have looked pretty blank, because he added, "He directed that movie I worked on a few years ago, *Coach Class*. I'm not sure you ever saw it." He didn't bother to wait for my response. "Anyway, I leave for Turkey sometime early or mid-December for a three-month shoot."

"Really? Turkey? Wow." I tried not to sound disappointed. I thought he'd be in town longer than that. "You'll miss Christmas."

"Yeah and it's so meaningful to me," he said. "What with my not being religious or having kids. I care as much about missing Martin Luther King, Jr. Day." There was a slight, possibly awkward pause. "Take off your shoes, stay awhile," he said then with a sly grin. "You want something to drink?"

"It's not even noon yet."

"I'm still on European time."

"Yeah, well, I'm not. I'll have a glass of water, though." I followed him into the kitchen, where he opened the fridge, which was empty except for a bottle of wine, a few take-out packets of soy sauce and hot mustard, and a six-pack of Evian water. "Do you *ever* eat at home?" I asked as he handed me one of the waters.

"Never."

We went back into the other room and sat next to each other on the sofa, a little stiff and awkward the way we always were when we hadn't seen each other for a while, and he told me about the shoot he'd just been on, which had taken him first to Paris and then to London.

"You're so freakin' lucky," I said. "I want your life."

"You can't have it. I still use it." He flicked at my hair.

"What's going on with this? I remember when you first did this green stripe thing, but now it's looking kind of faded and putrid. And then there's some red dye over on this side—"

I moved my head away from his touch irritably. "I don't know. I'm just growing it out, I guess."

"Then dye it all back to normal," he said. "It just looks like a mess. And then there's the piercings and the tattoos..."

I self-consciously reached up and touched the ring in my eyebrow and the stud in my nose.

He shook his head. "Honestly, Rickie, when are you going to clean yourself up? Let yourself look like a pretty girl for once?"

I crossed my arms. "So you're saying I'm *not* pretty?"

"You're pretty," he said and, leaning forward, carefully uncrossed my arms like he was peeling a banana.

That was enough of a cue for me: I fell back against the sofa cushions, eagerly pulling him down on top of me. This is what I had come to see him for, after all.

I was twenty-five years old and rarely had the opportunity to have sex. Lust ruled my body. I couldn't even look at a men's jeans ad without getting aroused. So, once the dam had burst, I started grabbing at Ryan like some kind of crazed *thing*, eagerly sliding my hands over his chest and then tearing off my own shirt to offer up my small breasts to his touch.

Everything he did felt so good I could have screamed—my whole body, all of my skin, every inch of me responded to the slightest touch from his fingers. When we finally moved to his bed, both of us stripping off our jeans a little frantically before climbing up, I pushed him down and straddled him and he laughed and let me do whatever I wanted until he was breathing pretty hard and then he rolled me over onto my back and took charge.

I wondered at some point whether I was the last woman

he'd slept with or if there had been another—or others—since then, some Parisian girl, or maybe a British one. I told myself it didn't matter. But I couldn't put the question completely out of my mind.

Afterwards, we lay side by side, catching our breath.

"We've got to stop meeting like this," I said eventually.

"Never," Ryan said. "We have to never stop meeting like this. Promise me that when you're married and all settled down with like ten or twelve kids, you'll still meet me like this."

"You don't think my husband will object?"

"Nah. He'll be grateful. How could one man ever keep up with you, Rickie?"

"I'm really not such a major nympho," I said. "I only seem like one because I get it so seldom. I mean, this is it for me until you come back to town again."

"I'm here for a little while this time. There'll be time for more."

"Good." I curled up against him so I could nuzzle at his neck.

"Why don't you have a boyfriend?" Ryan asked, pushing me away so he could look at my face. "Every time I come back to town, I think, 'This time Rickie will be with someone.'"

"Are you relieved or disappointed when I'm not?"

"Do you really have to ask?" He pushed my overgrown hair back over my shoulder and studied the effect. "From a purely selfish standpoint, I'm thrilled you're available. But as your sort-of-not-really older brother, I worry about you."

"Don't. I'm fine. And please don't refer to yourself as my brother when we're still in bed together."

"You should be doing more with your life," he said. "That's how you meet people. When are you going to go back to school?"

"I take classes online." Only one easy course at a time, but I always kept myself enrolled so I could tell people I was working on getting my bachelor's degree. Otherwise, they acted all judgmental—like Ryan was right now.

Unfortunately, he had heard that line too many times. "Oh, please. That doesn't get you out and meeting people. If you're not going to get serious about your education, then you should get a job. How long are you going to keep mooching off your parents, anyway?"

"I don't know," I said. "How long are you going to keep living like a college student and running away to other countries to avoid making any long-term decisions about your life?"

"Ten more years," he said calmly. "At least."

"You'll be over forty by then."

"So? And you still haven't answered my question. Do you think about the future at all, Rickie?"

I rolled onto my back and glared at the ceiling. "Leave me alone, will you?"

"I'm just trying to help."

"Don't need help," I said. "Sex. I need sex." I sat up and made a grab for him. He caught my hand in his.

"Give me a few more minutes," he said. "I'm not as young as I used to be. Let me recharge."

"Now that's romantic," I said and sat back against the headboard with a pout.

"So how's Melanie doing?" he asked, playing with my hand a little. "She okay?"

"Not really. I could kill your brother."

He dropped my hand. "It's hardly all his fault."

"He cheated on her," I said. "With that stupid actress. How is that not all his fault?"

"She didn't have to throw him out so quickly. She could

have given him another chance. People sometimes do things that they regret. They don't deserve to have their lives ruined because of one bad moment."

I pulled the blanket up over my body and pinned it across my chest with my arms. "You probably don't know this because you've been away and Gabriel's not going to rush to tell you, but he's been going around publicly with that woman and totally throwing it in poor Mel's face that he's in love with someone younger and prettier. He doesn't give a shit about saving the marriage."

"You're wrong," Ryan said. "Melanie broke his heart when she threw him out."

"*He* cheated on *her*."

"She could have forgiven him."

"Some things are unforgivable."

"Nothing's unforgivable."

I scowled. "That's what cheaters always say."

"I've never cheated on anyone in my life."

"Yeah, well, you can't cheat when you don't commit."

He gave an indifferent shrug. "Maybe. But my point still stands: your sister could have saved the marriage if she'd wanted to."

"God, I hate men!" I slid out of the bed and reached down for my underpants, which were still caught in my jeans. "You can behave like total assholes and then find a way to pin the blame on everyone but you."

"You're not listening to me," Ryan said. "And why are you getting dressed already?"

I turned to him, wearing only my underwear. "Because Melanie is the only truly decent person I know, and your brother screwed her over and broke her heart and you're defending him."

He put his hands up. "I'm sorry. Look, I don't want to fight with you, Rickie."

"I know," I said dully. "You want to have sex with me."

"Right. Is that so bad?"

I considered for a moment and then I sighed. "Nah. That's why I'm here." I crawled back into the bed next to him. "But let's not talk about them anymore, okay? We're not going to agree on this one and it makes me too angry."

"Yeah, okay," he said. He held out his arms and I moved into them and against his chest. He gently rubbed my arm and my shoulder, and then his hand slid down to cover my left breast. He cupped it in his hand while his thumb lightly played with the nipple until I made a little involuntary noise of pleasure. "There," he said. "Now are we back in sync?"

"Depends," I said. "Are you recharged?"

"Getting there," he said with a grin. "Definitely getting there."

"I'm hungry," Ryan said a little while later. "You want to grab something?"

I sat up and looked at my watch, which was the only thing I was wearing at that particular moment. It was a good one, too, a vintage Hamilton that my parents had given me for my twenty-fifth birthday. I had taken it as my mother's not-so-subtle way of suggesting I keep to a schedule. "I should get going."

"What time is it?" he asked with a yawn. "I'm still so jet-lagged I never know whether it's morning or night."

"It's past two-thirty. I have to pick Noah up from school at three."

Ryan propped a pillow under his head. "How is the little guy doing, anyway?" he said in the affable but remote tone he always used when the subject of Noah came up.

I leaned over the side of the bed to snatch up my clothes. "He's fine."

That satisfied him: it wasn't like he really cared. "Great. Hey, there's this new place about three blocks away I want to try. I think it's Lebanese. Something Middle Eastern, anyway. You sure you don't have time to just run over for a few minutes?"

"I'm worried about traffic."

"What would happen if you were a couple of minutes late? I mean, they don't throw him out on the street, right?"

I shook my head. "He freaks if I'm late."

"Too bad. I really wanted to try this place with you."

I didn't say anything, but I was bummed too. It would have been nice to have lazily gotten dressed and wandered out to that restaurant and eaten there; we probably would have had the place to ourselves at this time of day. Instead I'd be fighting traffic all the way back to the Westside just to sit in car pool for half an hour with my little car heating up in the sun and people cutting me off with their enormous SUVs and Noah complaining as soon as he got in the car about something his teacher or one of the other kids had said to him that had hurt his feelings and ruined his day, his week, his month, his year...

"Maybe we can have dinner one night next week," Ryan said.

"I'll have to check with my parents." I made a face. "And beg them to babysit. You know how I love to owe them favors."

He yawned again. "No wonder you don't get out much."

"Yeah." I got off the bed and pulled on my pants. "Having a kid at nineteen really screws up your dating life," I said, trying to sound lighthearted about it.

"Well," he said, closing his eyes sleepily, "you'll always have me."

2.

On my way back down the stairs, I fished my cell phone out of my purse and saw, with a sick feeling of guilt, that I had missed a couple of calls from Noah's school. This couldn't be good. I called back and was immediately forwarded to the nurse, who informed me that I should come as soon as possible because Noah wasn't feeling well. "Don't worry, Mom," she said in a carefully cheerful voice that meant he was in the room with her. "He's fine." I resisted a familiar urge to point out I wasn't her mom and told her I'd be there as soon as I could.

The drive across town felt endless. Traffic was bad, and even when it cleared up for a few blocks, I'd get stuck behind someone slow.

Car pool had already begun by the time I got to school. I parked out on the street and raced inside, taking the stairs three at a time as I headed up to the administrative offices on the top floor, where the nurse's office was. Noah was sitting on the edge of her sofa, his shoulders hunched forward and his arms folded tight across his stomach like he had to protect it from an incoming fist.

"Mom!" he said, raising his head as I ran over to him. "Where were you? We were calling and calling." His face was pale and he had dark circles under his eyes.

"You okay?" I asked. He shook his head. I knelt down on the floor next to him, holding my arms out, and he collapsed against my shoulder. "What happened?"

"Caleb gave me a brownie," he said into my neck.

"And you ate it?"

"He said it was gluten free."

"Noah—"

"Really, Mom!" He sat up and looked at me with big, earnest eyes. "He asked me if I wanted a brownie and I said I'm not allowed to eat it unless it's gluten free and he said it was and that his mom got it specially for me. So I ate it and then my stomach hurt and then I threw up and he started laughing and so did the other boys. They high-fived him."

I looked over at the nurse, who was sitting in her desk chair watching us. "Did he tell you this?"

She nodded and smiled complacently. "I reminded him that he should only eat the food you pack him."

"He's *six*," I said. "He believed Caleb."

"He'll be all right," she said calmly. "He already looks a lot better."

"Why did it take you so long?" Noah said to me. "I've been here forever."

"I'm sorry. I didn't hear my phone."

"You *never* hear your phone!" He burst into tears. For some reason, eating gluten not only made him sick to his stomach, it also made him emotionally fragile. I hugged him, not bothering to argue the point, just wishing he didn't have to deal with this thing.

It hadn't occurred to me for the first few years of Noah's life that there was something weird about how small he was until Melanie gently pointed out that he was still wearing size two clothing at the age of four and said that maybe I should make sure he was okay. I checked with the pediatrician and, long (miserable, painful, boring) story short, a few months later Noah was diagnosed with celiac disease. The GI doctor said that he'd make up all the height he'd lost so long as we kept him on a strict gluten-free diet, but here we were, two years later, and he was still really small for his age. It was possible

I wasn't careful enough about his diet. Or that he was simply doomed by his genes to be a ninety-nine-pound weakling.

I mean, by the genes he got from *me*, since I was a shrimp. But his dad was pretty tall. We used to joke about how his too-tall genes and my too-short genes would cancel each other out and our children would be normal.

"Normal" was the last thing anyone would call Noah.

The worst of it was that because Noah went to this exclusive private school that my parents insisted on (and paid for)— and, yes, the same one that I had gone to not that long ago *and* the same one that his cousins currently went to—all the other kids were like these huge athletic beasts. I don't know what parents fed their kids on the Westside of LA, but it was clearly high in nutrients. Or human growth hormone. The infamous Caleb was the worst, a kid who could already be described as "hulking" at the age of six, and who managed, through an apparently irresistible combination of charisma and brute force, to convince half the boys in the class to join him in torturing the other half.

A few weeks earlier Noah had come home crying because Caleb and his friends hadn't let him sit at their activity table during class free time, so I asked his teacher if she could do something about their behavior. Ms. Hayashi's response was to ask me if I'd been adequately "encouraging" Noah to make more friends. "You'd be surprised at what a difference it can make for a child to feel like he's made a connection or two in his class," she said. "You really should try to set up more playdates."

Like it was my fault the kid was ostracized. Like it had something to do with the fact that his mother was at least a decade younger than all the other moms and didn't have a single friend among them, that she dropped him off quickly in the morning and picked him up even more quickly in the afternoon and never talked to any of the other mothers or made plans with them or scheduled playdates with their kids. Like *that* had something to do with Noah's problems.

Personally, I blamed Caleb.

I always kept a plastic bag or two in my car. Noah was so sensitive to gluten that the smallest crumb made him throw up a half hour later, so he frequently vomited on the way home from restaurants. We were both so used to it that it didn't faze either of us—he'd just ask for the Bag and I'd toss it back at him and he'd throw up into it and that would be that.

I asked him as we got in the car if he needed the Bag, but he shook his head. "Nah. I'm done barfing."

"Good to know." I started the car.

"Can I watch TV when I get home?" he asked as we drove off.

"Not until your homework's done." He had a few minutes of homework every night, usually a worksheet and a list of vocabulary words to study for each Friday's spelling test.

"But I'm sick."

"You're not sick," I said. "You ate some gluten and that made you throw up."

"The brownie was GF. Caleb told me so, so I think I might have the flu."

"Caleb was lying."

"No, he wasn't. I think the brownie was GF and I threw up because I'm a little sick."

"You're not sick. Caleb tricked you into eating something he knew you weren't supposed to have."

"No, he didn't," Noah said. "Caleb's my friend."

"Caleb is a little—" I stopped, realizing that anything I said would only make Noah feel worse.

He knew as well as I did that Caleb was no friend to him and that he had been the butt of a mean prank. But if it made him feel better to pretend otherwise, I didn't have the heart to take that away from him.

To my frustration, he was crying *again* two days later when I picked him up in car pool. The teacher who was helping him get into the car leaned forward and whispered to me, "I don't know what's wrong. He wouldn't tell me," before cheerily singing out, "Have a good one!" and closing the door.

As Noah struggled to buckle his seat belt through his tears, I twisted in my seat so I could look back at him. His nose was running and his hair was sticking up with sweat. His T-shirt was on backwards; I hadn't noticed it that morning when I'd dropped him off, but we'd both slept late and had been rushing.

All around us were perfect moms with perfect hairdos picking up their strong and happy little kids and their playdate friends and hauling them off to play at a park or have private tennis lessons—and then there was Noah and me.

I sighed and shifted the car into Drive. "So what's up, Noey?"

"It's all Coach Andrew's fault. The whole class was mean to me and it was all his fault."

I was about to swing the car out of the car-pool lane when some woman in a black Mercedes tried to pull in front of me, cutting the line and breaking all the school rules. There wasn't enough room for her car so she got stuck at an angle, which left me just as stuck until the cars up ahead moved out of the way. I suppressed the urge to swear at her and contented myself with a glare. She blithely played with a strand of her blond hair and stared blankly off into the distance, like she had no idea someone in my car wanted her to die. "Coach Andrew?" I repeated through gritted teeth. "Who's that?"

"God, Mom. He's the new PE coach. Don't you even know that?"

"Sorry." I didn't keep up with much at school. "So what did he do?"

"He was making our class run up and down the stairs because the sixth-graders were using the field. He said we had to do it ten times. It was so hard." Noah's voice got uneven. "I did it a couple of times but then I couldn't even breathe anymore and I told him so, but he just pointed up the stairs and said I had to keep going. I started crying and then everyone made fun of me and he let them."

My stomach hurt. The driver in front of me inched forward with a lurch and then braked hard again. I was still blocked from moving. God, I hated the rich blond women at that school. They all thought they owned the universe and taught their big blond kids to think so too. I took a deep breath. "How did they make fun of you, Noey?"

"I had to crawl up the stairs because I couldn't walk anymore and they called me a baby and then some of the kids started kicking me." A strangled sob. "But Coach Andrew didn't care. He just said I'd have to go see Dr. Wilson if I stopped trying." Dr. Wilson was the school director, a tall, angular man in his mid-sixties with gray hair, whose vaguely humorous geniality toward the kids did nothing to diminish their terror of him. "The other kids were kicking me and he didn't say *they'd* have to see Dr. Wilson, just *me*. It wasn't fair."

"I'm sorry," I said. Had the coach really let the other kids kick him? Noah could be overly dramatic. But his misery seemed genuine. And I'd believe that Caleb and his pals were capable of anything.

"You have to write a note, Mom. Please. Please write a note saying I don't have to do PE ever again. *Please*, Mom."

"I'll talk to Dr. Wilson about it," I said. "He's very smart about these things."

"Maybe he'll fire Coach Andrew," Noah said hopefully.

Louis Wilson sat in an armchair at a forty-five-degree angle from where I was sitting in another, lower armchair, and smiled his careful smile. "I must say, there's something very moving to me about seeing you in here as a parent, Rickie."

"I feel like I'm in trouble." I gave a little laugh, but it was true. I had never actually been called into his office when I was a student there, but it still had that effect on me.

"Don't worry," he said. "I rarely give my parents detention." We both smiled, but I felt his eyes taking in the stud in my nose, the eyebrow ring, the tattoo that ran around my left wrist, the tight jeans and worn T-shirt I was wearing, and I felt eleven years old again. Only a lot less confident than I was back when I was eleven and a total teacher's pet.

I cleared my throat. "It's about Noah," I said. As if he hadn't guessed. "He was pretty upset about something that happened in PE."

"Yes," Dr. Wilson said. Every time he spoke, I could practically see a subtitle floating in front of him. His "yes" was really *I'm well aware of the problems your son has been causing in our PE class.*

"I know he's not the best athlete—"

"We don't care about that," he said calmly. *It's his attitude that concerns us.* "All we ask is that our students engage and make an effort to enjoy themselves."

"He's trying," I said. "But it's hard for him. He's so small and he has this autoimmune disease—"

"The PE coaches are all aware of Noah's health issues," he said. "As am I." He leaned back in his chair. He was wearing a dark wool suit with a tie. I had been acquainted with Dr. Wilson for close to two decades and had never seen him without a jacket and tie. "They take that into account when they're working with his class." *Trust me, we don't want any lawsuits.*

"Not always." In an effort to look relaxed, I crossed my own legs, but that exposed the hummingbird tattoo on my right ankle and I quickly uncrossed them. "Yesterday he said that the coach—the new guy—had made him run up and down a flight of stairs a bunch of times, and it was just too much for him."

"Hmm," he said. "He found that difficult?"

His skepticism angered me, which was good: my anger buoyed me up, made me less afraid of this man who had been the ultimate authority throughout my childhood. "Noah told me he was so tired he had to crawl up the stairs and some of the other kids started kicking him. And the coach *let* them."

Dr. Wilson contemplated me, eyes narrowed. "You're sure about this?"

"It's what he told me."

For a moment he studied my face hard, like he was trying to probe through to my brain to see if there was any deception going on in there. Then he sighed, stood up, and opened his office door. "Barb?" he said to his assistant. "Would you please locate Coach Andrew and have him come right to my office?"

He closed the door. I had risen to my feet when he had, so we were face to face when he turned around again.

I dropped my eyes first.

"How are your parents?" he asked abruptly.

"They're fine." I realized I was fidgeting like a little kid, shifting from one foot to the other. I forced myself to stop.

"I'll be seeing your mother next week at the board of trustees meeting," he said. "It's such a pleasure working with her."

"Oh, good," I said and kind of meant it. My mother was president of the board, which made her, in a certain sense, Louis Wilson's boss. I wondered if Dr. Wilson was thinking about that now. I hoped so.

"Excuse me," he said. He wandered over to his desk and shuffled through a few papers while I rocked on my heels and looked around the room. There were a bunch of plaques on the wall, including one my mother had designed that said, FROM THE SIXTH-GRADE CLASS OF 1998, which was my class.

"It feels like yesterday to me," Dr. Wilson said from over by the desk, looking up.

"It feels like forever ago to me."

"Time passes more quickly at my age. Too quickly." He went back to the papers on his desk.

There was a knock on the door, and the coach came in. He was wearing sweatpants and a blue T-shirt and a baseball cap. He looked younger than I expected. His shoulders were slightly stooped and he was more skinny than muscular. "You wanted to see me?" he said, addressing Dr. Wilson but glancing at me, clearly trying to place me—I didn't look like the kind of teacher Dr. Wilson was likely to hire but I didn't look much like a parent, either.

"Andrew," Dr. Wilson said, with a brisk clearing of his throat, "this is Noah Allen's mother. Rickie Allen."

"Ah." He nodded slowly. "Hi. Nice to meet you." He held out his hand and, as we shook, his eyes strayed to the tattoo on my wrist. As he raised them again to my face, I could see they were dark—almost black—and unreadable. "So what's up?" He looked back and forth between us.

"Rickie?" said Dr. Wilson with a gallant little "go ahead" kind of a gesture. *You wanted to complain. So complain.*

I swallowed. I wasn't a confrontational kind of person. I was more of a hide-in-your-room-and-sulk kind of person. But I was Noah's mom and dealing with this was just something I had to do. I raised my chin. "Noah said you made him crawl up the stairs and let the other kids kick him."

"Whoa, whoa," Coach Andrew said, putting his palms up. "I don't let anyone kick anyone in my class."

"He said kids were kicking him."

"They weren't," he said emphatically. "I was right there at the foot of the stairs, watching. No one was kicking anybody. But it is true that Noah chose to crawl up the steps, even after I asked him to stop, and it's possible someone might have bumped him by accident on their way back down."

"He said he was too weak to climb anymore. He's not very strong—he's got an autoimmune disease."

"I know. The school nurse said it shouldn't affect his ability to keep up."

"It obviously did the other day."

"Noah needs to run around more," he said. "Build up his stamina. He's not weak because of his disease, he's weak because he doesn't get enough exercise."

Could he have been any less sympathetic? "You don't know anything about his health or how much he does or doesn't exercise," I said tightly. "You pushed him too hard. And when he tried to tell you it was too much, you wouldn't even listen and let the other kids make fun of him. He was still crying about it when I picked him up."

Dr. Wilson had been watching our exchange with his arms

crossed as if he were hoping we would work it all out without him, but now he said with patronizing gentleness, "Noah *does* resort to tears fairly often, Rickie, which sometimes makes it hard to know how seriously to take them."

He had a point, but I wasn't in the mood to hear it right then. "Whatever," I said. "I just don't think PE class is working for him right now. Can't he go to the library or something while the rest of the kids run up stairs and beat each other up for exercise?"

"You can't take him out of PE," the coach said. "Noah needs more exercise, not less. The more he can keep up, the more fun he'll have."

"Oh, right, because climbing stairs is such fun."

He flushed. "We were a little restricted yesterday because we didn't have access to the field. But the other kids liked it—we made a game out of seeing how many times they could go up and down."

I turned to Dr. Wilson. "How about we make a deal? I'll make sure Noah climbs a flight of stairs five times a day if you let him skip PE."

The principal shook his head. "As long as Noah goes to Fenwick, he'll take PE with his class. It would be doing him a disservice to single him out by excusing him."

I stepped back, flinging up my hands in disgust. "So, in other words, nothing is going to change."

"I'm not ignoring this, Rickie," Dr. Wilson said. Years of managing parents had made him smooth as silk; anger slid right off of him. "We'll put our heads together and figure out some way to offer Noah some extra support during class. Right, Andrew?"

His face was impassive. "Of course."

I looked back and forth between the two of them. Dr.

Wilson was smiling his bland fixer smile at me, and the coach wouldn't even meet my eyes. I wasn't going to get anything more out of either of them. "Fine," I said. I grabbed my bag and left the office.

3.

When I brought Noah home from school a few hours later, Melanie's car was parked in front of our house. It often was those days. A few months earlier, when she and Gabriel had first separated, they agreed that their kids' lives should be disrupted as little as possible. So instead of uprooting Nicole and Cameron or making them shuttle back and forth between two homes, they took turns living with them in their old house.

My mother invited Melanie to stay with us on the nights Gabriel was with the kids, and Melanie gratefully moved some clothes in and took over my mother's office. Mom carried her desk and files down to the family room. Mel kept saying that she was going to find an apartment, that she shouldn't impose, but we had the space and her heart wasn't in the search, which was probably just as well. She needed company to distract her from worrying about whether Gabriel had remembered to give Nicole her antibiotics or to pack Cameron a sack lunch for his field trip and stuff like that.

She kept her cell phone on and within reach at all times and dove on it the second it rang.

If you passed by her room at the kids' bedtime, you'd see her all curled up around her phone, singing and chanting her way through some bedtime ritual with them.

When she was away from her own kids, she poured a lot of her frustrated maternal impulses into Noah. She'd spend hours baking gluten-free cookies for him and searching out books at the library she thought he'd like.

Noah wasn't the kind of kid to go around saying "I love you," but if he had been, I think he'd have said it to Mel way before he'd have said it to me or even to my mother, whose relationship with him was always a little distant, a little judgmental. "He's *your* child," she liked to say whenever a decision had to be made about something to do with Noah.

I don't know why she felt the need to remind me of that so often. I certainly never thought of him as anything else.

Sometimes it struck me as ironic that both Melanie and I had ended up living at home with my parents. It was clear why *I* was once again living in my childhood bedroom. But Melanie had done everything right—gone to a good school, taught at a school for kids with special needs, married a guy whom we all adored, and then devoted herself to raising two of the sweetest, most lovable kids known to mankind—so why was she, like me, unhappily wandering my parents' hallways at two in the morning?

You'd think I'd have felt a touch of satisfaction in our ending up in the same place. I mean, Mel was the family golden girl and my whole childhood was spent watching her soak up admiration and love and attention. I should have been delighted to see her brought down to my level, right? But that just wasn't how things were with me and her.

It probably helped that we didn't actually grow up together. She mostly lived with her mother and only visited us on the weekends, and I was still pretty young when she went off to college. So we never had to fight over rooms or toys or who got the car or anything like that. No sibling rivalry because there was no reason for any.

But it wasn't just that.

When I was a little tiny girl and Melanie was a teenager, she'd come over to our house and curl up with me on the bed and read book after book after book—whichever one I put in her hand, she'd read to me. If she got bored, she never said so. I remember carefully piling up all my picture books the moment I heard her voice downstairs, getting them all ready to present to her because she never said "Enough" or "Leave me alone."

When I was the teenager and she was in her twenties, she'd let me come stay at her apartment whenever I wanted, which was a lot because I often felt like I was going to explode under my mother's constant scrutiny. On days when the world of cruel girls and indifferent boys was too much with me, I'd call Melanie and she'd say, "Come stay with me this weekend," and then all weekend long there would be popcorn and manicures and stupid girly movies and no questions asked—which was why I always ended up telling her everything, all about the cruel girls and indifferent boys. "It sucks now," she would say, "but I promise you, Rickie, it gets better," and I'd believe her because she wasn't old like my parents or stupid like everyone else in the whole world.

When Noah was born, she left her toddler daughter and husband at home together so she could spend the night at the hospital with me, curled up on the hard, narrow fold-out chair that was meant to be used by the new baby's father, whispering to me whenever I woke up that Noah was the cutest, the sweetest, the best little boy who had ever been born and that we were going to have so much fun bringing him up together.

She kept me from being alone when it would have hurt the most.

So you see, there was no way I could ever resent Melanie or rejoice in her marriage falling apart or anything like that.

All I could do was love her.

Melanie was waiting for me and Noah in the kitchen with a beautifully arranged plate of cut-up fruit. Noah grabbed a handful of grapes off the plate and left, probably to go play on the computer, which he wasn't supposed to do until he'd finished his homework, but on days when I wanted a break I followed a strict "don't ask, don't tell" policy.

That was most days, admittedly.

"How was your meeting with Dr. Wilson?" Mel asked. As far as I knew, she had never had to meet with the principal about either of her kids.

I described it to her and she said all the right sympathetic things but then ruined her supportive streak by adding, "They might have a point, though, Rickie—I mean, about Noah's needing to get stronger. He can't keep up with Cameron on the scooter and Cameron's a year younger. He always complains when he has to walk a block, and he never wants to run around or play a game outside. If he stopped doing PE, he wouldn't be getting any exercise at all and—"

I waved my hand impatiently, cutting her off. "I know, I know." I edged toward the doorway. "I'm going to go run and check my e-mail. We have to leave again in half an hour."

"Where to?"

"Noah has a doctor's appointment. Blood test."

"Want me to go with you?"

"Nah, I'm good."

"You sure?" She looked crushed. Melanie never had anything but time on her hands when the kids were with Gabriel.

My mother kept saying she should get a job, for her own sake, but Dad said to give her more time.

Seeing her disappointment, I quickly added, "But it would be nice to have company."

Her face lit up.

It went badly. Sometimes it just does. First they kept us waiting forty minutes, which gave Noah time to work himself up into a state of anxiety over the blood test. But that wasn't the bad part. That came in the examining room when the nurse couldn't find the vein right away and had to keep wiggling the needle around under Noah's skin. He was sitting on my lap—the good thing about his being small for his age was that he still fit there—and I tried to hold him steady, but, god, it looked like it hurt. He had been so brave at first, too, resigned as the needle went in, just intent on reminding me that I owed him a treat afterwards, but then when the nurse started poking around for the vein, he turned pale, then he moaned and then he screamed and the scream ended in a sob. I looked at Melanie, who was standing across the room, and there were tears in her eyes but she mouthed, "It's okay," like *I* was the one close to crying. I just nodded and held Noah's clammy, shaking body against my chest and closed my eyes so I wouldn't have to see the sharp tip of the needle moving around under his skin and murmured over and over again, "I know it hurts but it helps, I know it hurts but it helps" until the words didn't mean anything to me at all.

Mom was cooking something on the stove when we got back. "How'd it go?" she asked, glancing over her shoulder at us, still stirring.

"They couldn't find the vein," I said. "Had to go into the second arm. Took a while with that one, too."

Noah held up his arms to show her the gauze and Band-Aids on the inside of both elbows and Mom clucked sympathetically. "It'll bruise," he told her. He was calm now, having informed me in the car that he would never submit to another blood test. I didn't bother arguing the point. When he had to, he would. "Mom got me candy," he added. "Two kinds because it hurt even more than usual."

"I can see that," Mom said. "There's chocolate all over your mouth. And something blue."

"That was Fun Dip." He turned to me. "Can I play on the computer?"

"Get your homework done first."

He groaned and headed out of the kitchen.

"Dinner will be ready in about half an hour," Mom called after him.

"I'm not hungry," he said over his shoulder. "I had *candy*." He left the kitchen and I sank into a chair. Eleanor Roosevelt was lying under the table, snoring. I absently rubbed my foot against her shoulder and she thumped her tail against the floor without opening her eyes.

"That new nurse is awful," Melanie said. "She doesn't know what she's doing. I told the doctor she wasn't allowed to take Noah's blood again ever." She went to the sink and washed her hands. "Want me to make a salad, Laurel?"

"That would be great," Mom said. "There's lettuce and carrots and red peppers."

"Don't put peppers in," I said. "I hate them."

Mom said, "I know. You can pick them out."

"How about she just doesn't put them in?"

"The rest of us like red peppers," my mother said. "You can pick them out."

"Noah doesn't like them either."

"Noah doesn't eat salad."

"I'm just saying it's not true the rest of the family likes them."

"Your logic is unassailable," my mother said dryly. "But I still want peppers in my salad."

"And it's your house, so you win."

"Not everything is a war, Rickie."

"*Now* she tells me." I got up and left the kitchen and went upstairs and checked on Noah, who wasn't doing his homework, although to be fair it wasn't like he was doing anything else. He was just sitting on the edge of my bed, fingering a tiny hole in his pant leg, gazing down at it with eyes that had gone dreamy and unfocused.

He didn't even notice when I came in. I said sharply, "Noah? What are you doing?" and he started nervously and looked up at me.

"I don't know," he whispered.

I believed him.

When Mom called us down to dinner half an hour later, the table was set and Melanie was putting down a vase filled with freshly cut roses. "Aren't they pretty?" she said with a satisfied sigh. "They're just starting to bloom again."

"They're beautiful," said Dad, who had just come into the kitchen. He made a slight noise as he sat down. He seemed to be doing that more and more: grunting every time he sat down or stood up. He had gained a lot of weight over the last ten years, and I suspected it put a strain on his back, but he wasn't the type to complain. Or to go on a diet.

"There's a bug in there," Noah said, pointing to the center of one of the flowers.

"Oh, sorry." Melanie grabbed a tissue from the box on the counter and brought it down toward the bug.

"Leave it alone!" Noah said, grabbing her arm. "It's just a beetle. It won't hurt us or anything. Leave it alone."

"On the dinner table?" said my mother as she put down a dish of polenta.

"Why not?" my father said, winking at Noah. "Bugs gotta eat too."

"Exactly," said Noah with a serious nod.

Dad and Noah understood each other. They both looked at the world from some kind of sideways angle that no one else could get to. Especially not me.

I loved my dad, but he could drive me crazy.

When I was in seventh grade, I came home devastated one day because some of the girls had made fun of the brand-new sweater I was wearing, telling me the black and white stripes made me look like a fat skunk. My mother wasn't home, so I vented to Dad. He listened, patted me on the shoulder, and said calmly, "The skunk is an unfairly maligned animal."

I stared at him for a moment and then gave up and trudged off to my room to wait for my mother's return. He just didn't get me. And vice versa.

Fortunately, he had made his career in academia, where his single-minded devotion to his studies and social awkwardness were both considered pretty normal, and he became a full professor at an unusually young age. He had been teaching biology at UCLA since before I was born.

Sometimes when I looked at my father, his eyes would be vague and distant and his train of thought indecipherable. At those times, he reminded me so much of Noah. And I loved him the way I loved Noah: with frustration, loyalty, impatience, and the realization that the two most important males in my life would always be a complete mystery to me.

Melanie got a call from one of her kids just as dinner was ending and left the room to talk. Dad disappeared into his office and Noah went upstairs, but not before he'd informed me that he couldn't do his homework without my help so I had to come up too.

"I need to talk to Grandma," I said. "Get started without me and if you get stuck, I'll help."

"I already know I won't be able to do it without you," he said. "Can I just play on the computer until you come up?"

I was too tired to argue and just waved my hand in a gesture that was more surrender than actual assent. He ran off.

"What do you want to talk to me about?" Mom asked, stacking some plates and moving toward the kitchen.

I grabbed a bowl and followed her. "I'm mad at Dr. Wilson," I said.

"Why's that?"

I put the bowl down on the kitchen counter and told her about the PE class, throwing in the story about Caleb and the brownie for good measure. "I think Noah's being targeted for some real teasing and bullying and no one will do anything about it. Dr. Wilson just says vague, unhelpful things like how he'll 'look into it.'"

Mom scraped some scraps of salad off a plate into the sink. "He doesn't like to commit to anything concrete with parents. Used to drive me crazy when I was in there with a complaint."

"You used to go in there to complain?" That surprised me. She was so madly in love with Fenwick as a school that I couldn't imagine her ever complaining about anything there.

"Of course I did. Every parent does at some point."

"Why? What happened to me?"

She reached for another plate. "Oh, who knows? I was a typical first-time mother, always worrying that something would go terribly wrong if you weren't treated like glass."

"And yet look how well I turned out," I said with heavy sarcasm.

"You haven't 'turned out' yet. You're still a kid."

"I'm not. I live at home like one, but I'm not one." There was a pause. She stacked up the plates in the sink. Her bobbed, dyed-blond hair was a little rumpled in the back. "Maybe you could talk to him about the Noah stuff," I said, leaning back against the counter, trying to make it sound like the idea had just occurred to me, like it was just a passing thought.

She looked over her shoulder at me. "To who? I mean whom. Louis Wilson?"

"I want to make sure he doesn't blow it off."

She shook her head. "I trust Louis to handle these things appropriately."

"I think he's more likely to if you get involved."

"Rickie," she said, and I could tell from her tone that I was about to be disapproved of. "I can't play that role. You know that. Being the president of the board of trustees means I have to be more careful than other parents—grandparents in this case—not to throw my weight around. It's inappropriate."

"Don't you even care about Noah?"

She raised her chin. "Do you really have to ask me that?"

"Yeah, maybe I do."

"I think I've proven my devotion on a daily basis."

"Most grandmothers would care that kids were torturing their grandchild and would want to do something about it."

"Don't draw one of your lines in the sand," she said. "Don't tell me that if I do this I'm a good grandmother and if I don't,

I'm a bad one. You've done that to me enough as a mother—I can't take another twenty years of being tried and found guilty on a daily basis."

"That's not what I'm doing."

"It's what you *do*, period." She bent down and opened the dishwasher door with a loud creak. "I'm sorry that those boys were mean to Noah. You should call their mothers and let them know what their boys did and suggest they have a long talk with them about their behavior." She tilted her head at me. "That's how adults deal with these things, Rickie."

"Thanks." I headed toward the door. "Thanks for all the support, Mom. I'm so glad that you're willing to help out when we need you."

"That sarcasm would be much more effective if you weren't living under my roof and off of my money."

I whipped around. "You *begged* me to live here. You said it was the best thing for both of us. You said Noah and I should live here and you'd pay for him to go to Fenwick and it would be best for everyone. You said you wanted him—wanted *us*. And now you're throwing it in my face like I'm some kind of parasite?"

"I'm not throwing it in your face." She slammed a dish into the dishwasher rack. "Why does everything turn into a fight with you, Rickie? I *do* want you here. I think I've made that clear. I'm saying that the very fact I want you here should mean something to you. You have no right to tell me I don't care about Noah. It's mean and it's not true."

"I wasn't the one picking a fight. You started it. You said you wouldn't help and then accused me of being ungrateful."

She stood up straight, closed her eyes briefly, then opened them again. "I'm tired," she said in a quieter voice. "And you've had a tough day. So let's take a break. Think about this conversation, Rickie. Think about whether you're being fair to me or not. And once you've thought about it long enough, come back and talk to me again."

"Whatever," I said, and, on that brilliant conclusion, I turned my back on her and left the room. I didn't come back later to talk again.

4.

Melanie came into my room that night. I put my finger to my lips to let her know Noah was asleep, and she nodded and pointed down the hallway. I got up and left the room, softly closing the door behind me. Noah slept on the pull-out part of the trundle bed that my mother had bought for me when I was nine so I could have friends sleep over.

I followed Melanie into her room. She still had most of her stuff in boxes and suitcases, like she was just visiting. But it smelled nice in there: she had another vase of fresh flowers on her dresser, must have picked them when she gathered the ones for the dinner table.

"I had an idea," she said, once she was seated in her desk chair and I was settled crosswise on the twin bed. "You know how you always complain that the other mothers at school don't talk to you?"

"I don't complain about it. I'm relieved. I love that they don't talk to me."

"Seriously," she said, even though I wasn't joking. "You want Noah to have more friends, don't you? At his age, it's not about the kids' being friends—well, not completely about that, anyway. It's about the *moms'* being friends and making plans together. If you get to know more of the moms in your class—"

"I'm like ten years younger than the youngest mom in Noah's class. They all assume I'm his babysitter. Someone even asked me the other day if I was looking for more work."

"If you got to know them better, that wouldn't happen. Anyway, you have to think about Noah. Don't you want him to get included more?" She didn't wait for me to respond. "And it's not just you—I've been bad too. Because of what's been going on with Gabriel, I haven't been very social, but I have to start getting out there again. Feel like I'm part of something." She tilted her head toward one shoulder and then the other, like she needed to stretch the muscles there. "I can't just keep waiting for my old life to come back. I have to get proactive about this, Rickie."

"That's very healthy of you," I said politely. I scooted to the edge of the bed and set my feet down on the carpet. "But why drag *me* into this?"

"Because you're worse than I am. Your son is going to be at Fenwick for the next twelve years, Rickie. And you can race past everyone whenever you need to pick him up, and you can sit by yourself at all his performances, and you can skip every class party. But that's not fair to him or to you. You're both being left out of stuff you might enjoy."

If I had been having the same conversation with my mother—and I easily might have—this would have been the point where I would have said something sarcastic and walked out of the room. That was just how it was with me and her. But it was different with Melanie. *I* was different with Melanie. That didn't mean I was going to agree with her, though. "So what are you thinking exactly? That we walk around carrying little signs that say 'Come play wiz us'?"

"Well since you ask…" She smiled sheepishly at me. "I've already gone ahead and signed us up for the Event Hospitality Committee—they do the food for all the fund-raisers. There's a meeting this Friday. We missed the first couple, but the woman who runs it said it's not too late to join and they could really use the additional help, especially with the Autumn Festival coming up so soon."

I stared at her. "You've got to be kidding."

"Why?"

"Come on, Mel. Me on a *committee*? An event hospitality committee? Do you really think I'll fit in with that crowd? They're probably a bunch of crazy type-A mothers who—"

"Don't judge them until you've met them," she said primly.

"I *have* met them," I shot back. "I see them every day at school."

"People are different when you get to know them one-on-one. Oh, and you know what's really cool?"

I crossed my arms. "Not an event hospitality committee, I can tell you that."

"No, listen. She—the woman I talked to who runs the committee—she said that Marley Addison is actually *on* the committee."

"Bullshit."

Melanie wrinkled her nose. "Don't," she said. She hated when people swore. "Anyway, it's true. She'll be at all the meetings."

"No, she won't," I said. "She's a movie star. Celebrity parents never show up for stuff like that. They'll come watch their kids sing in a Christmas show but they're not going to show up to talk about what kind of sandwiches we should serve at a fund-raiser. They have more important stuff to do."

"Her daughter's in Cameron's class."

"I know. And how many times have you and Marley chatted?"

"None," she admitted. "But once we smiled at each other and another time she told Cameron he was cute. She seems nice."

"Nice or not, she's not going to show up, and even if she *did*, what difference would it make? It would still be an event hospitality committee."

"Please," Melanie said and literally clasped her hands. "Do it for me. You don't have to say a word at the meeting, I swear. Just sit with me so I don't have to go alone."

I rolled my eyes and groaned. "You are so going to owe me."

So there we were a few mornings later, going to a meeting in some stranger's house in the Palisades. I was still grumbling to myself as we got out of the car and headed up to the house, which was too big in proportion to the lot, with a lot of over-sized windows and a slightly fake-looking clapboard front. I thought it was kind of ugly, but it was probably worth several million dollars, given its location and size.

"It's pretty," Melanie said as we walked up the stone path side by side. "Don't you think? I think it's pretty." A pause. "It's really pretty."

I glanced over at her. She had dressed for this event like she was going to an important business meeting, in a pair of tailored black pants, a silk tank top, and a cropped jacket. She had blown her hair dry with a little flip in front and was wearing more makeup than usual. She looked way too polished for a nine a.m. breakfast meeting—or so I thought, until the door opened to our ring and the tall, thin, blond woman of indeterminate age who greeted us turned out to be even more immaculately turned out.

"Hi," she said, holding out her hand. "I'm Tanya."

"I'm Melanie." They shook and Mel introduced me. Then she said to the other woman, "You have such a beautiful house."

"It is lovely, isn't it?" Tanya said evenly. "I wish it *were* mine. Linda was busy getting the coffee, so I said I'd answer the door for her."

"Oh, I'm so sorry," Melanie said, her pale skin turning red the way it always did the second she was embarrassed or anxious. I thought, not for the first time, that the girl could have used thicker skin, both literally and figuratively. "That was stupid of me—"

"It's fine," Tanya said, cutting her off with a shrug that said she never made stupid mistakes but was used to forgiving lesser mortals theirs. She stood back to let us in. "Come in. We're all in the back."

"Man, this is going to be *fun*," I whispered in Melanie's ear as we followed Tanya through a large, slightly cluttered foyer.

"Shh," she hissed, apparently not in the mood for sarcasm.

Me, I'm always in the mood for it.

We entered a cavernous room where a few women were grouped around the biggest coffee table I'd ever seen—it had to be at least six feet by six feet. Two people could *have slept* side by side on that coffee table, although not at that particular moment, since it was spread with plates of muffins, bagels, cut fruit, coffee cups, plates, napkins, and silverware. There was enough food there for the entire parent body of the school, and definitely too much for the small number of skinny women grouped around it.

Heads turned as we came in and Tanya ushered us toward the others. "Everyone, this is Melanie Correa—daughter in fourth and son in kinder, right? And Rickie Allen, who has a son in first." She had done her homework. She probably *always* did her homework. And her kids' homework too.

Tanya pointed to the other women, each in turn. "This is

Maria Dellaventura." Another thin woman with blond hair, longer and more layered than Tanya's, raised her hand briefly. "You probably know her already, Rickie, because she has a son in first"—I didn't—"and also a daughter in sixth. And this is Carol Lynn Donahue"—yet *another* thin blond woman, clad in a tight spandex running tank, raised a tautly muscular arm in acknowledgment—"two in middle school, one in the high school." She gestured to the woman who was just setting a carafe of coffee on the table. "And Linda Chatterjee." This one was thin like the others but at least her hair was dark. She was also strikingly beautiful. "She's got a son in fourth. And this is her house."

"Please sit down and eat something," Linda said. "*Someone* has to eat something." Looking around, I could understand her plea: none of the women had anything on the plates in front of them except a slice of fruit or two.

Tanya sat down next to Carol Lynn, taking up all the easily accessible sofa real estate. I plunked down on the floor, crisscrossed my legs, and reached for a muffin. Melanie studied the sofas hopefully, but the women had resumed the conversation we had interrupted, and no one moved to make room for her. I patted the floor next to me but she shook her head and gestured at her nice pants.

Linda, who was still standing, noticed Mel's uncertainty and said, "Hold on—there are more chairs in the kitchen." She put down the carafe of coffee and ran into the adjoining kitchen. "Here you go!" she said, reappearing and lugging a barstool. She set it down near where I was sitting. It was a very high stool.

Melanie looked slightly horrified but thanked her and climbed up. Once she was seated, her knees were at the same level as the others' shoulders. She was too high to reach the food, so I offered the muffin plate up to her but she shook her head at it.

Too bad for her: my muffin—carrot? zucchini? apple? I wasn't sure—was delicious, moist and warm.

Meanwhile, the conversation we'd interrupted was resumed. Carol Lynn said, "I hear all the sixth-grade girls have huge crushes on him."

Tanya was punching away at her BlackBerry but she looked up briefly. "Is that true, Maria? Are the sixth-grade girls all in love with Coach Andrew?"

That caught my interest.

"Only the ones who've started puberty," Maria said with a laugh. "But forget about *them*—I could name a dozen *mothers* who've invented reasons to go see him in his office. And not just the ones who are divorced, either." She tossed her gorgeous mane of highlighted hair. "Which doesn't leave any space for those of us who are."

"What happened to that coach they had last year?" I asked. "The woman?"

"Coach Brianna? She got 'married,'" Maria said, raising her fingers to make quotation marks, which confused me until Carol Lynn explained with a simple "Same-sex union."

"Her wife moved up north," Maria said. "So they lost Brianna. That's why they pulled Andrew out of the computer lab—he was really hired to teach computers and manage the school network, you know, but then they needed someone to do PE and he took over there."

"Maybe it won't be permanent, then," I said.

"God, I hope he stays," Maria said. "My kids love him. Doesn't yours?"

"No," I said. "And neither do I."

"Why not?" asked Carol Lynn.

I didn't want to launch into the whole story. "I just don't think he's a good coach. Noah hates PE now."

There was a short pause.

"Noah's on the small side for his age, isn't he?" Maria said then, meaningfully.

"Yeah, he's a runt."

She gave a little nod as if something had been explained but all she said was, "He's cute." She crossed her legs, which were sleek in a pair of dark-rinse jeans, and leaned back into the cushions, eyeing me. "I probably shouldn't tell you this, but everyone in our class is dying to know your story. You know, because you look so young."

"I'm not as young as I look."

"Really?" She narrowed her eyes. "So how old *are* you?"

"Thirty-seven."

Melanie said, "Don't listen to her. She's twenty-five."

"And Noah's, what, six?" Maria said. Doing the math in her head, counting back the way people did.

"Something like that." I knew my son's age, but this woman with her perfectly dyed and styled long blond hair and smoothly unmoving skin unsettled me, and that made me turn on my indifferent-mother act.

"So you had him pretty young."

"Right," I said. "He was just a baby."

"Good choice. The older ones hurt more coming out." Maria turned to Tanya. "Should we start? Are we still waiting for anyone?"

Tanya glanced at her watch. "Marley said she would try to come—"

"My son's in the same grade as her daughter," Melanie said. I winced.

"Did she happen to mention to you if she's coming or not?" Tanya asked her, a bit too politely.

Mel flushed. "I don't really know her that well."

Tanya didn't seem surprised. "I'll try her cell, just in case she's on her way." She picked up her phone again.

I reached for another muffin and looked up to discover they were all watching me. Maria said, "Oh, god, girls, remember when we were in our twenties and could eat like that without gaining a pound?"

"Your metabolism just *stops* when you turn forty," Carol Lynn said. She raked her fingers through her two-toned hair. "Nothing will budge that extra inch around my waist. It showed up the week I turned forty and I'll never lose it. I do an hour of Pilates every day and play tennis or run four times a week—and it's still there." What was she talking about? *What* extra inch? The woman was one narrow slab of hard muscle.

Tanya lowered her phone, and Melanie said, "Did you reach her?"

"I got her assistant. Marley won't be able to make it but she's really sorry and said we should sign her up to donate whatever we need to the event." She dropped the BlackBerry on the coffee table and pulled a notebook off of the stack in front of her. "Let's get down to business."

The Autumn Festival was an annual Fenwick School event, a purely celebratory family party with bounce houses, cotton candy, sno-cone and popcorn machines, and carnival-type games. Later in the year there would be a serious fund-raiser, but the goal of this one wasn't to make money, just to have fun and make the kids feel enthusiastic about being back at school. Costs were covered by the Parent Association, which made me wonder how much my parents donated in addition to paying Noah's hefty tuition, but it wasn't the kind of thing I thought about for long.

The Event Hospitality Committee, I learned, was responsible

for supplying lunch that day (hot dogs, hamburgers, and chips) and drinks (soda and water) and for serving them. By the time the meeting ended about an hour later, various exciting topics, like whether or not we should have tofu hot dogs and whether Heinz really was the *best* ketchup, had been debated and hastily resolved, since time was running short: the festival was only two weeks away.

As we got up to leave, Linda begged us all to take some food home. The pastries had hardly been touched. I would have been more than happy to score some of those carrot muffins, but Melanie cut me off with a shake of her head and a "Thanks, but we better not."

"Why couldn't we take any food?" I asked her when we'd left.

"I didn't want them to think we were pigs."

"You should have told me that before I ate three muffins in front of everyone."

We got in the car and she said, "So what did you think? That was kind of fun, wasn't it?"

"Well, it was better than taking Noah to have his blood tested . . . but not by much."

"Really? I thought they were nice."

"They were scary," I said. "So blond and blow-dried and Botoxy—"

"Linda wasn't blond." She carefully aimed the car out onto the road. Melanie was a painfully cautious driver. "Don't be so judgmental. Maria has a kid in your class. How lucky is that? Now you'll have someone to say hi to and sit with at class parties and stuff."

"Oh, yeah!" I said. "I can already tell that we're going to be BFFs!"

"Didn't you think she was beautiful? Maria?"

I rolled my eyes. "Who even knows what she really looks like? She's had so much work done."

"I think she looks great."

"You're prettier," I said. "By far."

"No, I'm not. Did you see how thin they all were?"

"For god's sake, Mel, don't admire them for *that*."

"I wish I could lose five pounds," she said, glancing down at her stomach, which barely curved above her seat belt. "Just five pounds. That's all."

I let out a strangled moan. "Stop. Thinness isn't a goal. Or a virtue. Or a sign of beauty. It's just thinness."

"Easy for you to say. You're thin."

"Not as thin as those women," I said. "But you don't hear me complaining about it."

"It's the kids' fault. I had a flat stomach before I had them."

"Yeah. They really weren't worth it, were they?"

"Shut up," she said, but at least it got her off the subject.

5.

My mother had been dragging me to the Autumn Festival every year for as long as I could remember. The only time I missed it was the fall of my freshman year of college. But since I got pregnant later that year and moved back home that summer, I was around for the next festival—only that time I had an infant Noah with me.

I didn't want to go that year, but Mom insisted.

Her smile was a little brittle that day, but she held her head high. My teenage pregnancy gave her something to be strong about, and she liked to be strong. As soon as we arrived, she snatched Noah out of my arms and carried him around the entire field, introducing him to all her fellow board members and declaring over and over again that the whole family was deliriously happy to have him in our lives. While she showed him off like Baby Simba, I found a place to sit in the shade and thought about how I was right back where I'd started, living in my parents' house and going to the Autumn Festival because my mother wanted me to—the things I thought I'd left behind forever when I went off to college. And I had only myself to blame.

It helped when she brought Noah back to me to nurse. Holding him helped it all make a little more sense, or at least made making sense irrelevant.

The festival was always held on the high school PE field—not the football field or the baseball diamond, of course, because those were sacred to their sports. Fenwick was huge, three schools (primary, middle, and high) spread out on one campus, having patiently and gradually bought up any available neighboring land over the previous few decades. It was an institution on the Westside of LA, beloved by the several generations of residents who'd gone there and hated by everyone who lived nearby who couldn't afford its outrageous tuition or whose kids had been rejected, but who still had to deal with the insane amount of traffic it generated during pickup and drop-off.

Disgruntled neighbors weren't invited to the Autumn Festival: it was only for members of the school community. In addition to the bounce houses, mountain climbing wall, and petting zoo, there were several carnival-type games, usually manned by faculty members. I still remembered my childhood thrill at seeing the usually conservatively dressed faculty in jeans and T-shirts. Except for Louis Wilson, who of course always still wore a jacket and tie, merely switching his usual formal wool for some light, linen-y fabric, which in his universe probably counted as wildly casual, verging on indecent.

The morning of this year's festival, Mom and Noah and I were all ready to leave the house at 10:30, but when Mom called to Dad to come join us, he came downstairs still in his pajamas.

"You're not ready?" Mom said.

He looked blank. "For what?"

"The Autumn Festival! I've told you five times already." She sounded exactly like I did when I was exasperated with Noah.

"Oh, is that today? I forgot." My father sighed. "I was looking forward to a quiet morning. I have that article to write..."

My mother said wearily, "You want to stay home?"

His face lit up. "Do you mind?"

"I don't suppose you'd let *me* skip it?" I said.

She didn't even bother answering, just gave me a gentle push in the direction of the garage. And the truth was that now that Noah was a student at Fenwick he got totally excited about going to the festival, so I had to go for his sake, anyway.

As we started to get into Mom's car, I asked her if I could drive.

She warily handed me the keys and got into the passenger seat.

There wasn't a lot of traffic on Sunset because it was Sunday morning.

"You're going a little fast," my mother said about a mile into the drive.

I accelerated.

"Seriously, Rickie," my mother said. "Slow down."

I darted into the left lane to pass a car.

"Slow down," Mom said sharply. "It's not funny."

I nodded and sped up a little bit more, whipping through an intersection before passing another car by moving to the right.

I stole a glance at my mother. Her face was taut with anger but this time she kept her lips tightly pressed together and remained silent.

The light ahead was turning yellow. I slowed to a stop at the intersection and when it turned green again I went through at a reasonable speed, which I maintained all the way to the school. My mother didn't say anything for the rest of the drive, but when we had parked and were getting Noah out of the backseat, she held her hand out to me.

"Give me the keys," she said. I handed them to her. She threw them into her purse and walked away from me.

Once we reached the field, she transformed back into her usual outgoing self, hailing and kissing tons of people and gaily introducing Noah to anyone who might, by some crazy chance, not be aware that her grandson now attended the school where she'd been on the board for well over a decade.

Noah barely acknowledged the people he was introduced to, sometimes nodding briefly, sometimes just staring off into space, occasionally picking his nose before I could stop him. I didn't enjoy the social stuff any more than he did, although I like to think I smiled a little more and picked my nose a lot less. When I felt we had paid our dues, I told Mom we were going to go check out the fun stuff and let Noah pull me across the grass toward the carnival games.

"Oh, hey, Rickie!"

I turned. It was Maria Dellaventura, wearing a lacy tank

top and skinny jeans with high spike heels, and flanked by two boys the same age as Noah.

I could tell they were the same age because they were a head taller than him.

Plus I recognized them from his class: one was her son, the other his good friend.

"Hi, Noah," she said, smiling down at him. "Austin and Oliver are going to go try the Velcro wall. You want to join them?"

"No," he said, staring shyly down at the grass. Good thing, too—if he hadn't, he might have seen the two boys rolling their eyes at each other. Unfortunately, *I* saw it. I felt my whole body tighten up.

"You sure?" Maria said brightly, as if the boys were the three best friends in the world. "I hear it's really fun."

Noah just shook his head and clutched my hand tightly.

"You guys go on ahead," she said to the two similarly blond, tall, and stocky kids. "I'll find you later." They raced off. She turned back to me. "When are you doing your food shift?"

I looked at my watch. "Half an hour."

"I'm doing the desserts booth later." She put a hand on her concave stomach. "I'm dreading it—being around all that sweet stuff kills me. I can't resist it."

I was tempted to roll my eyes and say "Oh, please!" but I refrained.

She turned to Noah. "Are you going to help your mom when she's working?"

"I don't know," he said and pushed his body against my side. He often did that when he felt uneasy, like he needed to anchor himself against me.

"Austin never helps me," she said, "but Eloise likes to get back there and hand the food out. I don't know where she is right now—she went running off with a group of girls. Probably to giggle about the boys. It starts early," she added in a low voice to me.

"Oh," I said intelligently.

A short pause. "Well, I guess I should go talk to people." She sighed. "It always feels like work, you know?"

"Yeah." God, I was a brilliant conversationalist.

"Plus," she said, "I wore these stupid shoes. I don't know what I was thinking, spike heels on grass? But I was rushing and trying to get the kids ready and"—she raised her foot and looked ruefully down at it—"I've destroyed them. And I sink like two inches every time I take a step." She put her foot back down and glanced at my cruddy old Vans. "You were much smarter."

"I guess. It's hot, though." I was wearing a long-sleeved black top and the sun was crazy bright. "I should have worn something lighter."

"It was cold this morning," she said sympathetically. "Hard to know how to dress." She turned to Noah. "Listen, if you change your mind, sweetie, feel free to join Austin and Oliver. I'm sure they'd like another pal with them."

I didn't get why she kept pushing it. Austin and Oliver clearly didn't want to play with Noah, and he clearly didn't want to play with them. But I guess she meant well. "Thanks," I said. "We'll see you later."

"Bye, Rickie," she said and moved past us, weaving unevenly as her heels got sucked into the muddy grass.

All around us kids were running and playing together, the girls grabbing each other and giggling as they moved around in small groups, the boys shoving each other and shouting. But Noah stayed close to my side, holding my hand even though he was getting a little old to do that in public. I thought about making him let go, but when I looked down and saw how closed and nervous his face looked, I squeezed his hand tightly instead. He had been so excited about coming—the reality couldn't possibly be living up to his expectations.

Reality never lived up to Noah's expectations.

"Look!" he said with sudden energy, pointing to the dunk tank, the carnival-type game where, if you throw a ball hard enough against the target, whoever's sitting out on the platform gets dropped into a vat of water. "Isn't that Coach Andrew?"

I squinted up at the figure sitting on the plastic seat about five feet off the ground. "Looks like him."

"It would be really funny to see him get dunked."

"I agree," I said. "Let's go watch. Hey, maybe we could even dunk him ourselves."

"That'd be awesome!" He raced ahead and got in line behind a bunch of relatively tall girls who were giggling and whispering to each other.

Coach Andrew sat squarely on the little bench, wearing a baseball cap, sunglasses, a UCLA T-shirt, and a pair of cargo shorts. His bare calves showed, tanned and muscular, above equally bare feet. He was calling down to the tween girl in a miniskirt and tank top who was about to throw a ball. "Come on, Angelica! You can do it. I know you've got a good arm—I've seen it in action!"

Angelica blushed and threw and missed the target by a foot.

The other girls burst out laughing, more in delight than derision. Each of them tried in turn. They all failed to hit the target but lingered nearby, whispering and eyeing Andrew's bare legs with prepubescent delight.

Then it was Noah's turn. "Noah, my man!" Andrew shouted. "Show these girls how it's done!"

Noah promptly threw the ball straight down onto the grass

with the same sort of flailing arm motion you'd use to swat something away from you.

"Good try," Andrew said encouragingly. "Try it again, Noah, only stand a little more sideways, bend your elbow a little, and release the ball when your hand is still at its highest point."

Noah processed that and adjusted his body minutely before throwing the second ball. It stayed in the air a little longer but still hit the ground closer to him than to the dunk tank.

"One more try," said the skinny teenager with a bad case of bedhead who was manning the booth. High-schoolers got community service hours for working at the festival—I had done it myself at that age. He handed Noah his last ball.

Biting his lower lip in concentration, Noah took a deep breath and hurled the ball with all his might.

Unfortunately, his aim was so far off that the ball actually hit the teenager, who grabbed his arm and shouted, "Shit, man, be careful!"

"Hey, hey, watch your language," Andrew called down to him.

"It hurt." The kid rubbed his arm. "That's *it*," he snapped at Noah. "Your turn's over."

Noah slunk to my side, his head down.

The kid said to me, "You going?" and held out a ball.

I hesitated, but Noah said, "Yeah, Mom, do it. Dunk him."

"Yeah," Coach Andrew said, leaning forward. "Dunk me, Noah's mom." He was laughing at me. He didn't think I could do it.

He was the grown-up version of all the athletic jerks— like Caleb and Oliver and Austin—who were going to make Noah's life miserable for the next decade or two of his life. I desperately wanted to wipe the smile off his face.

I grabbed the ball and was already pulling my arm back for

the throw when the teenager stopped me and said I had to back off a few more feet—the adults' throw line was farther back. From that distance, the center of the target looked awfully small. And it had been a long time since I had thrown a ball for any reason other than to give Eleanor Roosevelt something to fetch. But I planted my feet and threw *hard.*

The ball fell embarrassingly wide of its mark.

"Aw, come on," Andrew said. "That's not even close."

I glared at him and hurled the second ball as hard as I could.

It bounced off the edge of the target.

"Is that the best you can do?" The coach made a big show of leaning back and crossing his ankles. "Might as well make myself comfortable. I'm not going anywhere."

I snatched my third and final ball away from the teenager and threw it straight and hard.

It missed by even more than my two previous attempts.

"Shit!" I said, stamping my foot in annoyance.

"You can't say that in front of the kids," said the teenager primly.

"*You* did," I pointed out irritably.

"You know, I could give you guys some private coaching," Andrew called down to me. "You and Noah both. Teach you how to throw a ball so it actually goes where you want it to."

"I *know* how to throw a ball," I said. "He just made me stand too far back."

"Ri-ight," he said. "What about you?" he called over to the young woman standing behind me. "You think you can hit the target?"

"Definitely," she said.

"Good. I'm sweltering here. I'm ready for a nice cool swim."

"Oh, I'd love to see you go down," she said with a laugh. I turned to look at her. She was tall and thin and striking, with long, wavy blond hair, fashionably large aviator sunglasses, and an outfit—a white tank top and faded blue jeans—that made her look both athletic and very sexy. Of course, with her body, anything would look sexy, even a flowered muumuu. I suspected she was an assistant teacher—there were a few new ones every year, and they were invariably young and beautiful.

"May I have a ball?" she asked the teenager, who was staring at her, stunned, his mouth slightly open. I wondered what it would be like to have that effect on people. He shook himself awake and handed her a ball.

"Excuse me," she said to me and I realized I was standing there staring at her openmouthed just like the boy. I moved aside so she could step up to the line. She squinted at the target, took up a pitcher's stance, and let the ball fly.

She missed, but only by a little: the ball bounced off the pole, just south of the release mechanism that would have dunked him.

"Hah!" Andrew called out. "You missed by a mile."

"More like an inch. And I was just getting my bearings on that one. Now I know exactly where to aim." She beckoned to the teenager, who eagerly stepped forward to hand her the next ball. This time she took longer to get into position, tilting her head back, eyeing the target, and adjusting her feet and her shoulders until she seemed satisfied. Then she wound up and threw the ball, hard and straight. There was a sudden "Ping!" and a shout from Andrew as his seat gave way under him and he dropped into the tank of water.

A couple of the girls screamed. Noah cried out, "Awesome!" The teenager and I applauded, and the girl looked around, laughing. "Thanks," she said and took a little bow.

"You're good," I said, and the teenage boy said, "That's the first time anyone's been dunked today."

"I played ball in school," she said, like it was no big deal. She trotted up to the tank, where Andrew was holding on to the edges, shaking the water off his face and fishing around for his cap, which had fallen off during his plunge. "I'm sorry, baby," the girl said with a grin. Their faces were pretty much on a level. "Had to do it. You okay?"

"I'm fine," he said. "Nice job." She leaned forward, over the edge of the tank, and they kissed right on the lips.

"She kissed him!" Noah said with amazement. "She dunked him and then she kissed him!"

"She's my girlfriend," Andrew explained with a grin as the girl stepped back. "It's okay."

There was a lot of whispering from the sixth-grade girls at *that* bit of news. Andrew climbed out of the water and resumed his place on the platform, water pouring from his clothes and hair. He wrung out his baseball cap. "It's soaking wet."

"It'll keep you cool," his girlfriend said.

"I'm plenty cool now. In fact, I'm freezing. That water's like sixty degrees."

"Serves you right," she said.

He gave her an exaggerated scowl. "When I get down from here, you are so going to pay for this."

"Yeah? When's that?"

"I'm done at noon."

She looked at her watch. "Oh, good. Not too much longer. I'm starving."

Noah was a suggestible kid. He tugged on my hand. "I'm hungry, Mom."

"Okay. Let's go get something to eat."

We turned to go.

"Hey," Andrew yelled after us. "Come back later when someone else is up here and I'll help you with your pitching." It wasn't clear whether he was talking to me or to Noah.

I just nodded and we walked away.

6.

S orry I'm a little late," I said to Melanie as I joined her behind the counter at the hot-dog booth. "Noah had to go to the bathroom just as I was heading over and then I had to find Mom so I could leave him with her."

"I just let Cameron and Nicole run off with their friends," Melanie said. "It's totally safe. Every teacher from school is out there."

"It's not a question of my *letting* Noah run off with friends," I said. "It's a question of his not having any friends to run off with."

Melanie didn't respond because someone was suddenly thrusting little paper tickets at her and demanding a hot dog. And then a woman was asking *me* for a hamburger "with no sesame seeds on the bun," which had me completely stumped. Fortunately, Melanie overheard and interrupted what she was doing to lean over and explain that all the buns had sesame seeds.

"My son doesn't like the seeds," the woman said. She was wearing a cropped leather jacket even though the sun was high in the sky and blazing hot. "We go through this every year. I don't understand why you people insist on only having buns with seeds."

"Sorry," said Melanie. "Do you want it without the bun?"

"You can't eat a hamburger without a bun. There's no point."

"My son always eats burgers without buns," I said. "He can't eat wheat."

"Oh, poor thing," she said with sudden sympathy. "I know just what that's like. I went off wheat for a while and I had so much more energy, but it was just so hard to maintain. Don't you think?"

"He doesn't have a choice," I said. "It's a medical thing."

"Mine too."

Sure it was. Some quack doctor had convinced her she'd feel better if she stopped eating bread. A little difference between that and my son's chronic autoimmune disease, but I wasn't going to get into it with her.

Melanie intervened. "Here!" she said, handing over a circular, foil-wrapped package. "I cut the top off—that's where all the sesame seeds were. Ketchup's over there."

"I'll see if he's okay with this." The woman snatched it and walked away.

"You're welcome!" I called after her.

"Shh," Melanie said, hitting my arm. "Go help those people." She pointed to a big family that had just come up. It took a while to get them all outfitted with hamburgers and hot dogs, but it gave me a chance to figure out how the system worked. There were several grills set up on a separate lawn about twenty feet away. For some undoubtedly sexist reason, only men seemed to be doing the actual grilling, but Carol Lynn Donahue was working as a runner, carrying the platters of cooked meat over the grass to us. It was our job to put the dogs and burgers on buns, wrap them in tin foil, and exchange them for the tickets people had bought at a separate booth. Six tickets for a burger, five for a hot dog.

"I went to college for this?" I said to Melanie after twenty minutes of fairly frantic burger-wrapping and hot-dog distributing.

She raised her eyebrows. "You only went to college for a year."

"Good point," I said. "*You* went to college for this?"

Before she could answer, there was a cry of "Mom! Mom!" and Cameron and Nicole came running up to the booth.

Cameron was a gorgeous little boy, tall and thin like his mother, but with his father's light brown curly hair. Right now he was literally jumping with excitement. "Mom, Dad's here! With Sherri! He said he'd come say hi but Sherri had to go pee first."

"Really?" Melanie's voice was suddenly unusually high. "Your father's here? He didn't tell me he was coming."

"We asked him to," Cameron said.

"You're not mad, are you?" Nicole asked, peering up at her mother's face. She looked a lot like her dad, with a round face and gorgeous huge brown eyes that didn't miss a thing.

"Of course not," Melanie said with a strained smile. "It's fine."

Someone came up and asked me for a hamburger. As I handed it over, I whispered to Melanie, "You want to go hide somewhere? I can run interference for you."

"Too late." She gestured toward the field. Gabriel was striding across the grass toward us.

"There you are!" he said as he bore down on us. "The kids told me you'd be here."

"Yes, I'm working here," Melanie said a little too brightly. "It's so nice to be able to help out."

He reached over the tray of hot dogs to give me a warm hug. "Rickie! I've missed you! How are you, darling?"

"Good," I said. "I'm good." I couldn't help smiling at him. That was the thing about Gabriel: he always seemed so genuinely happy to see you that it was impossible not to respond in kind.

He turned toward Melanie. "Hi, Mel," he said more softly. He leaned forward and kissed her on the cheek—softly, but you could see his lips really connect with the skin there. It wasn't an air-kiss. His eyes, so much like Nicole's, were keen as he stepped back to study her face. "You okay?"

"Never better," she said, flushing dark red, which was moderately better than the pale greenish-white she had been a few seconds earlier.

Nicole was looking back and forth between her parents anxiously, but Cameron was grinning ear to ear. "It's nice all of us being here, isn't it?" he said eagerly.

"Very nice!" Gabriel said. He scooped up Cameron and swung him up high before clutching him against his chest. "I love the Autumn Festival! I've been dreaming about these hot dogs for days. I'm going to eat like I've never eaten before."

"You always eat a lot," Nicole said.

"That I do!" He put Cameron down and mussed Nicole's hair.

"Where did Sherri go?" asked Cameron.

"Oh, she wanted to wander around a little, see the sights." He kept grinning down at the kids, but now it felt like it was to avoid making eye contact with Mel and me.

"Naomi told me she was famous," Nicole said. Naomi was Nicole's best friend and occasionally her worst enemy. "She recognized her and said we were so lucky we knew her and she wants an autograph." Then, with a sudden anxious look at her mother. "But I don't have to get one. I mean, *I* don't care if she's famous."

"She asked to come," Gabriel said. It wasn't clear who he was talking to. "I was going to come by myself but she asked if she could come. I thought it would be okay?" He gave a quick questioning look up toward Melanie, who was just standing there like she was frozen, a stiff smile on her tight lips.

"Of course," she said tonelessly. "You're allowed to bring whoever you like. Or is it whomever? I can never remember which is right when it's the object of the sentence, can you?"

I said quickly, "Hey, Gabriel, will you do me a favor and take the kids to go find Noah? He's with my mother but I know he'd rather be hanging out with you guys."

He got it. "Of course. Come on, kids, let's go find your cousin."

As soon as they were out of earshot, Melanie's whole body went limp. I put my arms around her and she let her head sink down onto my shoulder. "I can't believe he brought her here," she whispered. "It's *my* event."

"It sucks," I said. "He shouldn't have done that."

"And they're excited that she's here. She's famous. How can I compete with that?"

I squeezed her tightly. "Your kids are smart—they'll see right through her."

"Everyone will see her here with him." She stood up. Her eyes were swollen but she wasn't actually crying. "It's so humiliating." Someone came up and asked for a hot dog and she handed it over mechanically without even smiling or saying "Thank you," which was very un-Melanie-like.

"It's only humiliating if you let it be," I said. "Act like you don't care. Better yet, *don't* care. Someday soon, you're going to be dating someone wonderful and Gabriel will be sick of Sherri."

"I can't imagine ever being with anyone else," she said.

"That's the worst part. That I still love him in spite of everything."

I remembered what Ryan had said. "Did you ever think about giving Gabriel a second chance?" I asked.

"What would have been the point?" she said wearily. "He is who he is. Even back when we were dating, he—"

"Excuse me?" said a tall man with glasses who had stepped up to the counter. "Is it possible to get a burger that's not beef?"

"We have veggie burgers," I said.

"What brand?"

"I have no idea."

He narrowed his eyes at me.

"Let me go find out," I said with a sigh. I gave Melanie a quick pat on the shoulder and headed toward the grills. Carol Lynn was coming my way with a tin of freshly cooked hamburgers, the weight of it making the narrow, ropy muscles in her arms stand out even more than usual.

"Hey." She nodded in Mel's direction, resting the tin on her hip while she stopped. "She okay? That was her husband, right? And they're separated?"

"Yeah." I had no desire to gossip about Melanie's private life with someone over the age of forty-five who was wearing a baby-doll T-shirt with the word *Juicy* over her chest.

When it was clear I wasn't going to say more, Carol Lynn said, "I feel for her. I remember when I was going through this—school events were the worst. Do you think I should say anything to her?"

"I don't know," I said honestly.

"I just want her to know it gets better."

"That's just what I was telling her."

"Only... it never gets *all* better," she said.

"Yikes," I said. "That's depressing."

"It's just life." She stared down at the foil-covered tin propped against her side. "We all have crap to deal with, right?" She shifted and lifted up the tin again. "Ah, well. Better get this over to the counter while it's still hot." I nodded and watched her make her way over.

Her T-shirt looked normal from the back.

I hailed one of the grilling dads, who wiped the sweat out of his eyes long enough to dig up a veggie burger package and show it to me. I came back to the counter, but the tall guy had vanished. "What happened to Veggie Burger Guy?" I asked, but Mel and Carol Lynn were talking quietly and intently to each other and didn't seem to hear me.

Tanya Bonner came gliding up to the booth. "Why are you all up front?" she asked, an edge to her voice. She was wearing a cotton hat with an enormous brim, which contrasted oddly with her severely tailored outfit but made it clear that the sun wasn't going to get anywhere with *her* skin. "One of you is supposed to be the mover. Two servers and one food mover. I thought I explained that."

"I'm the food mover," Carol Lynn said, a little guiltily. "I just brought this over." She gave a little push at the tin she had set down on the counter.

"You should be clearing away the used ones." Tanya pointed to an empty tin that had been shoved to the side. "That's part of the mover's job. We want the booth to look neat and inviting—can't let the mess pile up like that."

"I was just getting to it." Carol Lynn picked it up.

"Don't forget you're covering the drinks booth next," Tanya said to Melanie.

"Right. We'll be there." She included me with a gesture.

Tanya gave a brusque nod. "Until then, keep things moving. We want the food hot and ready. Hot and ready." She stalked off.

There was a pause and then Carol Lynn, Melanie, and I all looked at each other. I'm not sure who giggled first, but pretty soon all three of us were cracking up like fourth-graders who'd just given fake names to a substitute teacher.

"I'm failing food moving!" Carol Lynn cried out.

"The food's *hot* but is it *ready* enough?" Melanie said. "I just don't think we're getting the 'ready' part right."

Carol Lynn picked up the errant tin. "Lord knows we need people like Tanya to run things and she's great for the school, but honestly, how she can bear to be like that is beyond me."

"You're not moving," I pointed out. "Movers have to keep moving."

"Look at me move," she said and headed back to the grill area.

"See?" Melanie said to me almost accusingly.

"What?"

"She's *nice*. You were all mean about her before, but she's nice. She was telling me about her own divorce, how hard it was."

"She dresses like a tween," I said. "And she's closing in on fifty."

"So? *You're* going to be judgmental about someone's clothes?" She eyed my frayed jeans, my Vans, my long-sleeved old T-shirt with a tear at one shoulder seam.

"It's different—"

A male voice interrupted me. "So did you ever find out what kind of veggie burgers you serve?" Veggie Burger Guy was back. "You were gone long enough."

"I did," I said. And then, realizing, "but now I've forgotten what it was. Oh, wait. Gardenburgers. I think. Or was it Boca burgers? It was a blue package. Or green…"

"Oh, forget it," he said and turned away as someone else

came up and asked for hot dogs and then there was a rush of people that kept us busy until Maria and her daughter arrived to relieve us and Melanie and I fled to the relative calm of the drinks booth.

As the lunchtime mania passed, things slowed down at the drinks booth even more. During a long and boring lull, I pulled out my cell phone and started playing a game on it.

"Hey, I know that music," said a voice. I looked up. Coach Andrew was standing in front of me, on the other side of the counter. "Tetris, right?" I nodded. He said, "Where's Noah?"

I closed the game and slipped the phone in my pocket. "With my mother."

"Oh, you brought your mother? That's nice."

I gave a short laugh of disbelief. There was actually someone at the school who didn't know who my mother was. "*She* brought *me*," I said. "My mom kind of runs the board of trustees."

"Oh, wow," he said. "I had no idea."

I wondered if it was now occurring to him that I had power at the school and he should be more careful how he treated Noah. I hoped so. "So," I said, feeling the need to make polite conversation, "did you enjoy the dunk tank?"

"I wouldn't say 'enjoyed it'—you're either burning up in the sun or sucking in some really nasty water. But the kids love it."

"Your girlfriend has a good arm."

He nodded, pleased. "She played softball in college."

"I'm a little bummed *I* didn't dunk you."

He raised his eyebrows. "Yeah? It wasn't enough you tried to get me fired? You have to try to drown me too?"

"I didn't try to get you fired," I said stiffly.

"I was kidding," he said, but there was an awkward moment where we were both just kind of standing there, not really looking at each other. "Can I have a Coke, please?" he said abruptly and held out a ticket.

I bent down and got a Coke out of an ice-filled tub. As I handed it to him and took his ticket in exchange, I said slowly, "Maybe I overreacted that day. I don't know. It's just... sometimes it's a little rough for Noah here and I want to help him and I don't always know what the best thing to do is. It's hard."

He studied me a moment, his eyes dark and thoughtful. "I'd feel the same way if I had a kid."

It felt like we had both apologized, even though neither of us had.

"How old are you?" I asked.

"I turn twenty-six next month."

He was less than a year older than me. "It's intense," I said, suddenly wanting him to understand. "Having a kid like Noah. You don't know whether you're—"

"Andrew! There you are!" His pretty, athletic girlfriend was coming toward us, moving quickly with the confident strut of a head-turner. "Is that Coke for me?"

"It is now." He handed it to her.

"We can share." She opened it with a quick snap of the ring. Her fingernails were neatly trimmed and painted a pretty light peach color. She noticed me as she took her first sip. "Oh, hi!" she said. "You were at the dunk tank with me! Where's your cute little brother?"

I was confused, but Andrew cleared his throat and said, "That was Noah, one of our first-graders, and this is, um... Noah's mom. I've completely forgotten your first name," he added apologetically.

I told them, and his girlfriend put out her hand and said, "I'm Gracie." We shook and then she leaned back comfortably into the curved part of Andrew's arm. "That Noah's a real cutie."

"Thanks," I said. "Are you a teacher too?"

"*God*, no."

"Gracie works for a big PR firm," Andrew said. "She makes famous people even more famous."

She pushed her hip against his and smiled up into his face. "Speaking of my job," she said, "we have to go home and change for that dinner tonight."

"What are you talking about? It's like six hours from now."

"Guys just don't get it, do they?" she said to me. "They get annoyed that it takes us longer to get ready, but all they have to do is comb their hair and put on a jacket and they're done, right?"

I nodded politely. I almost never went out to fancy events, and even on those rare occasions when I did, there wasn't any guy waiting impatiently for me to finish getting ready. Unless, of course, you counted Noah, who took longer than I did to get dressed, simply because he usually got distracted and forgot what he was doing halfway through pulling on his shirt or tying his shoes.

"I have to help organize the tug-of-war," Andrew said. "After that, we can go."

"Okay." She moved away from his side. "Let's walk around, see if we spot anyone interesting."

He rolled his eyes. "And by interesting, you mean famous?"

"Not necessarily. Come on." She pulled at him, tugging him away from the booth. He tossed out a quick good-bye to me over his shoulder then extricated his arm from her grasp, but only so he could put it around her waist.

They moved across the field together, and I felt a vague stab of something like jealousy. It wasn't specific to them. I just felt lonely. It helped that I had seen Ryan recently, but as much as I liked having sex with him, it wasn't the same as having a boyfriend. A boyfriend would have come with me to the Autumn Festival.

During all this, Melanie had dealt with the trickle of people coming up and wanting drinks. Once Andrew and Gracie had left, she moved closer to me and said, "Look over there," in a low voice, twitching her shoulder to indicate which direction.

"What?" I scanned the field.

"Don't *stare*," she said. "It's Marley Addison and James Foster—how cute is *he*?"

"Super cute," I said, watching with interest as Coach Andrew and his girlfriend headed right for the school's biggest celebrities. Gracie was bearing down on them with a determined square to her shoulders, but Andrew suddenly jerked her around and steered her in the opposite direction. What was that all about?

I turned back to Mel. "Foster's not her kid's dad, though, right?"

"Germaine Longman's the dad. But she never married him." Melanie had an impressive knowledge of pop culture.

"Think Marley will be doing a shift at the hot-dog booth?"

"It's impressive she came at all," Melanie said. "She must be a good mom."

"The bar is set so low for celebrities," I said. "I mean, I hate these things, but when I show up, no one praises *my* mothering skills."

"I do," Mel said and put her arm around me. Then released me as some little kid came up and asked for a Sprite. "That's your third one," she reminded him gently. "Does your mom know you're drinking so much soda?"

He gave a very tentative nod that didn't inspire any confidence. Melanie sighed and handed him the Sprite.

Linda and some friend of hers showed up a few minutes before two to take over at the drinks booth. After two hours of nonstop serving, Melanie was as relieved as I was to be free again. "Don't ever sign us up for that much again," I said to her as we walked away, and she didn't argue.

We found all three of our kids together, eating hot dogs at a picnic table. My mother was there, too, her chair pushed back so she could talk to someone at the next table.

As soon as Noah spotted me, he bounced up and said, "They put my hot dog in a bun even though I told them not to and Grandma had to take it back and get me a new one and I got hit in the nose in the bounce house and Simon called me a crybaby."

"Sounds like I missed all the fun."

"I told Simon he was a jerk," Nicole piped up. "He is too. And I told him to leave my cousin alone and after that he did." She smiled proudly. "He's scared of me."

"Nicely done," I said and high-fived her.

"So where's Daddy?" Melanie asked, affecting nonchalance as she plucked a potato chip off of Cameron's plate.

"He had to go," Cameron said. "Don't eat any more of my chips, okay?"

"He told us to tell you good-bye," Nicole added. "You can have *my* chips, Mommy."

"Thanks, sweetie. So . . . did you guys have fun with Daddy and Sherri?"

"It was okay," Nicole said cautiously. "I missed you, though."

Cameron was a good kid, but he didn't have Nicole's empathy. "We had the best time! Sherri went in the bounce house with us and all these kids recognized her and wanted to play with us. It was so cool!"

"That was nice of her." Melanie's voice was doing that thing where it got all high again.

"I don't like her," Noah said suddenly, looking up from his hot dog. He had a smear of ketchup on his chin. "She smiles like she wants us to brush her teeth for her or something."

Melanie stared at him with a kind of delight. "I know *exactly* what you mean," she said.

I reached over to give Noah a grateful hug. He submitted to it and then said, "Mom? I need to go to the bathroom like *right now.*"

On the way back from the bathroom, I stopped to get him a sno-cone. He couldn't make up his mind which flavor he wanted and asked if he could get four different flavors on one cone. The high-school girl who was manning the booth went ahead and gave them all to him, in neat little colorful rows. I had to remind him to say thank you. I always had to remind him to say thank you.

We were barely five steps away from the sno-cone booth when Noah suddenly bobbled the paper cone, spilling its contents right down the front of his shirt.

"Noah!" I brushed roughly at the rainbow-colored ice bits on his chest. "Why can't you be more careful?"

His face screwed up. "It's not my fault! Why do you always yell at me?"

"How can it not be your fault?"

"Someone must have bumped me—"

"No one bumped you. No one came near you."

"I didn't mean to spill it! You act like I meant to!" He clutched at his chest. "It's cold!"

"Of course it's cold!" I snapped. "It's ice, genius!"

Dr. Wilson picked that moment to walk right by us. His eyes flickered briefly over in our direction. He just kept going, but I knew that my moment of bad parenting had been noted and would be remembered.

With Noah's shirt ruined, it was definitely time to leave. Mom wasn't ready to go yet, so Melanie offered to drive us, but just as we were all heading toward the parking lot, Tanya came sailing toward us. "There you are!" she sang out. "We need help at the dessert booth. One of the moms who signed up for the last shift never showed and they're swamped over there. I need you two to fill in."

"We did two hours already," I said.

"It's okay," Melanie said. "I can do it. I'm happy to help out."

I nudged her elbow. "You were going to drive us home."

She rejected my attempt to rescue her. "You can take my car and the kids. I'll get a ride back with your mom."

"Thank you," Tanya said. "I knew I could count on you."

"But not me!" I said brightly.

She gave a strained smile. "You've helped a lot too," she said and left.

I walked Melanie over to the dessert booth. She stopped and clutched my arm. "No one's bought our cupcakes!" she said with horror.

"You're kidding me!" We'd spent an entire day baking and decorating those damn things. (Nicole had helped, while

Noah and Cameron played video games.) We'd frosted them with thick chocolate frosting and sprinkled colored sprinkles on top. They looked homemade but not *too* ugly. Cameron and Nicole had split one and begged for more, but Melanie had insisted we save the rest for the festival.

Noah hadn't been able to sample them because they had wheat in them. Gluten-free mixes were too expensive to waste on a crowd. "They look good," he had said, a little wistfully but not angrily. He was a pretty good sport about his diet.

But it wasn't hard to figure out why our obviously home-made cupcakes were being passed up: several other people had brought boxes of bakery cupcakes, which were easily twice the size of ours but cost the same number of tickets.

Maria Dellaventura was working at the booth, busily handing out the desserts in exchange for food tickets. She waved at us. "Good! Reinforcements. We went from having no one here to being mobbed. Cookies are one ticket, a slice of cake or a cupcake is two, and the croissants from Belwood Bakery are three."

Melanie handed me her car keys and then circled round to join Maria on the other side of the counter. "You're not staying?" Maria said to me.

"We already did our time. I'm not as scared of Tanya as she is."

"Fight the power," Maria said with a wink as she handed someone a cookie.

I took the three kids back to my parents' house. They were so fried from running around in the sun and eating junk food that I let them collapse in front of the TV while I sat with them and fooled around on my laptop. A friend of mine had sent out a mass e-mail describing her first week as a graduate student in Australia, and I felt my second big jolt of jealousy of the day.

I owed a bunch of friends e-mails, so I spent a while composing ones that were funny and sounded like they had been quickly dashed off. Lately it felt like I had to work harder and harder just to sound casual and upbeat.

Maybe because I had nothing new to say about myself or my life. Oh, wait—I could tell all my cool friends I now belonged to an Event Hospitality Committee. Yeah, I'd rush to do *that*.

After about a half hour or so, my dad wandered by the TV room. "Oh, hi," he said, peering in with mild surprise. "Look at all my handsome grandchildren."

"Hi, Grandpa!" Nicole said, blowing a kiss to him.

Noah reached out and grabbed at the air like he was catching something. "Got it!" he said and pretended to chew and swallow Nicole's kiss.

"Stop it!" she said with real irritation. "Grandpa, that kiss was for you."

"Don't worry," he said. "I got it. I'm not sure what Noah just ate, but I definitely felt your kiss on my cheek. Where's your mother, Rickie?"

"Still at the Autumn Festival."

"Oh, yes," he said. "Do you think I should go meet her there?"

"Probably not, since it ends in five minutes."

"Have you eaten lunch yet?"

"It's four in the afternoon, Dad. Of course we've eaten lunch. You want me to make you something?"

"I'll scrounge," he said and went on into the kitchen. He wandered past the doorway a little while later with a cup of coffee in one hand and a couple of Oreos in the other. Mom would have made him eat something healthier, but my dad and I tended to leave each other alone about stuff like that.

I heard the garage door soon after that and put my laptop on the table so I could go greet Mom and Mel. They came into the kitchen carrying platters that were still loaded with our cupcakes.

"Oh, boy," I said. "Should we freeze them?"

Melanie put hers on the table. "No, Tanya suggested we drop them off at school tomorrow afternoon. The fourth-grade boys' basketball team is playing a home game and our side is supposed to supply the snacks. You can do it when you get Noah, right? I won't be there—it's Gabriel's day to pick up the kids."

"Sure. Where do I leave them?"

She rearranged a couple of the cupcakes to make the display neater. "Just give them to Coach Andrew. He'll know what to do with them."

"You really can't do it?" I said with sudden reluctance.

"Why?" She looked up at me. "What's the problem?"

"You know. The whole Noah and PE thing. When I complained about Coach Andrew to Dr. Wilson. Makes things kind of awkward."

"Oh, please." Mel waved her hand dismissively. "Parents are in there complaining about god knows what all the time, Rickie. I'm sure he's forgotten all about that already."

"Hardly—he brought it up today."

"Oh." She digested that. "Was he mad?"

"I think he's over it."

She smiled. "Well, then. And you know what will really make him see that you're a nice person?"

I sighed. "Cupcakes?"

"Cupcakes," she sang out in happy agreement.

7.

The lower-school courtyard was deserted when I walked through it the next afternoon. I knocked on Coach Andrew's office door, which was in a hallway off the gym.

He called out, "Come on in."

I called back, "I can't," because I was holding the platter of cupcakes with both hands.

A moment later, Andrew flung the door open. "Noah's mom!" he exclaimed with genuine surprise. "Wearing cupcakes!"

I handed the platter to him. "I have another one in the car. Hold on."

When I came back, he took the second platter from my hands. "You have a sec to talk? Believe it or not, I was just going to call you. I've been thinking about Noah, and I have an idea."

"What about?" I asked, a little warily.

"Come in and I'll tell you." I followed him in. He put the platter on the desk, next to the first one. "Before I forget, what should I do with these plates when we're done?"

"Can you send them to Noah's classroom? I'll grab them tomorrow." A framed photo on the desk caught my eye: Andrew and Gracie were in bathing suits on a sailboat. She was wearing a bikini and looked model-fantastic in it. He was wearing board shorts and looked a little round-shouldered, but otherwise not bad. She was leaning back against him and smiling at the camera while he looked down at her, his face mostly in shadow. "I like the picture," I said.

He glanced at it. "That was from this summer. Gracie's family has a place in the Hamptons."

"Wow. Nice."

"You have no idea."

"You both from the East Coast?"

He shook his head. "I grew up in the Valley."

"And then UCLA?"

He nodded toward his diploma on the wall.

"Ever live anywhere other than Southern California?" I asked.

"Nope. You?"

"I was up north for a year. Berkeley."

He gave a low whistle. "Impressive. Why just a year?"

I looked down at the tattoo on my wrist. "Noah."

"Which brings us back to what I wanted to discuss," he said, a little too quickly. People always got uncomfortable when I talked about dropping out of school to have a kid.

Only it was my life.

"Did something happen in PE today?" I asked, trying to sound calm about the possibility.

"No, no. Everything's fine. I was thinking more generally about Noah and school and stuff." He hesitated. "You know, yesterday you said things can be rough for him—"

"Yeah." I was embarrassed he had remembered that. "The poor kid lives in a nice house on the Westside of LA and is forced to go to a really good private school. Get out your violin, right?"

"You meant it." He had the calmest voice, this guy. I hadn't noticed before how low and mellow it was when he wasn't shouting from a platform above a dunk tank—or defending himself against the accusations of an angry parent. I wondered if he sounded like this when he was teaching the kids. It didn't fit with the image Noah had painted of an impatient, vengeful teacher. "Anyway, I've seen with my own eyes how hard it is for him to join in with the other kids."

"He's just different." A sudden and intensely loud buzzing sound made me jump. "Jesus, what was that?"

"School's out. Sorry—there's a speaker right outside my office."

"I should go get Noah." I edged toward the door. "I'm meeting him in the classroom and he'll freak out if I'm late."

"I'll walk you over there. I wanted to include Noah in this conversation, anyway."

"Don't you have a basketball game to get to?"

"It's a home game, and the other school won't be here for a half hour or so."

"Don't you need to get our team warmed up?"

He cocked his head at me. "I get the feeling you're not all that eager to talk to me, Noah's-mom-whose-name-I've-forgotten-again."

"It's Rickie," I said. "And, to be honest, I'm not all that into having another conversation about how my kid needs to try harder."

"That's not what this is going to be. I promise." He followed me over to the door. "I actually think I'm beginning to figure Noah out."

"Really?" I said. "Because I'm completely lost."

He laughed. "Well, I'm still working it out, but my theory is that he's basically terrified of being bad at anything so he'd rather not try at all than fail. Especially when it comes to sports—he has zero confidence in his athletic ability. But if we can boost his self-esteem, give him a reason to feel confident—" He held the door open and gestured to me to go through it. He followed me out and shut the door. "Like just today, in PE, we were playing Capture the Flag and I made him captain of one of the two teams. Everyone was begging him to pick them. He definitely enjoyed the power."

"How'd he do once the game started?" I asked as we went down the hallway.

"He lasted longer than usual."

"I'm guessing that's still not very long."

He opened the door to the courtyard and held it open for me. "You wouldn't be wrong," he said as I went through.

We walked across the courtyard. Kids were dashing all around us on their way to buses, car pools, and team practices. A lot of them called out an enthusiastic "Hey, Coach!" as they passed Andrew. Noah was clearly in the minority in not liking him.

As we entered the lower-school building, I almost got knocked down by a pack of older boys. "Slow down!" Andrew yelled after them, just as another group of boys in basketball uniforms came running up to him.

"Where are you going?" one of them demanded. I knew he had to be in fourth grade, but the kid was probably as tall as I was and definitely weighed more. The way he was talking to the coach seemed pretty arrogant to me. "We have a game today."

"I know," the coach said calmly. "I'll meet you guys in the gym in five minutes. Do some stretching till I get there."

"Don't be late," the kid said and then he led the others toward the door.

We kept going down the hallway. A pretty young teacher was talking to a student outside one of the classrooms. She looked up and waved at Andrew. "Game today?" she called out.

"Yep."

"I'll come cheer!" She went back to talking to the student as we passed by.

"It's good to be a male teacher, isn't it?" I said to Andrew.

"I've never really thought about it," he said uncomfortably.

We had reached Noah's classroom. The door was wide open, but Andrew stopped and gestured me through first. "Who taught you to do that?" I asked as I passed him. "The whole the-girl-always-goes-through-the-door-first thing?"

"My grandmother. She was from the South. You think it's sexist?"

"I think it's fantastic. Oh, good, there's Noah." I mentally took back the "good" part as I realized his teacher was reaming him out for something. She was talking down at him very seriously while he hung his head and stared at his feet.

I suddenly felt very tired. I didn't want to go over and get involved, but I knew I had to.

The really weird thing was that I'd actually *had* Ms. Hayashi back when I was in Noah's grade. That's how long she'd been teaching at Fenwick. As far as I could remember, my year with her had been pretty smooth. I was a confident kid, good at my classwork, well behaved, and eager to make my teachers like me. Which they pretty much did, all the way through. Hayashi had been no exception.

So when I found out Noah was going to be in her class, I assumed he'd have an easy year, just like I did. But over the last couple of months, I'd come to realize that Hayashi must have liked me because I didn't require any special attention or assistance, and that Noah, who frequently required both, wasn't going to have such a smooth year of it after all.

We'd already had several moderately tense phone calls and e-mail exchanges about worksheets that hadn't been finished, tasks that had been abandoned, and tests that were completed in a slapdash manner or not at all.

I took a deep breath and went over to them, leaving Andrew in a press of students eager to greet him. "What's up?" I asked with fake heartiness.

"Nothing," Noah muttered. He pushed his head hard against my side, and I put my arm around his shoulders.

I looked questioningly toward the teacher. The impressive thing about Ms. Hayashi was that she hadn't changed much in almost twenty years. Her hair was more gray than black now, but otherwise she looked pretty much the same, straight-backed and very serious. She seemed shorter than I remembered, but I'd been a lot smaller back then.

She said, "Noah hasn't turned in his spelling worksheet yet."

"I *did* hand it in," he said. "I handed it in with Clark's."

"I've looked through all the worksheets I have and it's not there. I don't mind his not finishing," she added in a lower voice, leaning in toward me. "It's the refusal to admit it that concerns me."

"Noah," I said, peeling him off of me a little so I could look down at his face. "Did you really hand in the sheet?"

"Yes!" he said and I believed him. He was a bad liar.

"You gave it right to Ms. Hayashi?"

He shook his head. "Clark said to put it in the homework box."

"I told you to hand it in to me," Ms. Hayashi said. "Not put it in there."

I gave him a gentle shove. "Go check the homework box, Noey."

Noah ran across the room.

"I wish he'd listen to directions," Hayashi said stiffly. The natural awkwardness of the situation was exacerbated by the weirdness of my having once been her student. She had hugged me the first day I brought Noah to class, but since then neither of us could get back to a comfortable place.

We both watched as Noah rooted through a bin full of

papers and almost immediately gave a chortle of triumph. He raised a sheet high in his hand. "See!" he called out. "It's here. It's been here the whole time. And Clark's is here too."

"Bring them both to me," Ms. Hayashi said, sounding just as annoyed as before. "They shouldn't have been put there. That was the wrong place," she said to me. "That's why I couldn't find it. He didn't listen to the directions."

"Yeah, but Clark's was in there too," I said. "Why weren't you yelling at *him*?"

"I wasn't yelling at anyone. As you know, Noah struggles with getting his work in on time, so I try to keep an eye out for him. For *his* sake." She turned. "Excuse me, some of the kids need my help getting ready to go." She moved away.

"Amazing how quickly she needed to leave once we were right," I said, more to myself than to Noah. I took the worksheets from him and tossed them on the teacher's desk. They looked like stupid busywork, anyway.

Coach Andrew came over to us and said cheerfully, "Hey, there, Noah, how's life?"

"Ms. Hayashi thought I was lying but I wasn't."

"Sounds like there was a misunderstanding." Andrew squatted down. "Listen, buddy, I don't have much time but there's something I wanted to ask you and your mom about. An idea I had. You see, I'm very busy these days running the PE program for the lower school and coaching two teams, and could really use some extra help. So I was wondering: how would you feel about being my assistant?"

Noah eyed him warily. "What do you mean?"

"You'd help me out with my afternoon coaching and do stuff like carry balls out to the field, keep track of the drills I'm running, hold on to my clipboard when I need my hands free—stuff like that."

"And you'd pay me?"

Andrew laughed and stood back up. "Sorry, Noah, I'm afraid this is an unpaid position. But you'd be—"

I cut him off. "I don't think this is Noah's kind of thing." I knew it wasn't a good idea, but I didn't want to explain why in front of Noah. I could already see exactly how this would play out: Noah would start off wildly excited and have incredibly high expectations. Then, half an hour into the first practice, reality would set in: the kids would treat him rudely, he'd realize it wasn't a real job and that the coach was patronizing him, he'd be hot (or cold) and tired, and he'd just want to go home.

That was just how things went with Noah. Life had a way of letting him down, and the more hopeful he got, the more it hurt when he hit bottom. I didn't want to say all that with him standing there, but I also didn't want him to commit to something I knew would end unhappily.

"Let's let Noah decide for himself," Andrew said. "I think he's the kind of guy who'll lend a hand when someone needs one."

"*Sometimes* I am," Noah said carefully.

"So what do you think?"

"Would I have to wear a whistle?"

Andrew folded his arms and considered. "Would you *want* to wear a whistle?"

Noah nodded, his eyes raised up to Andrew's face. "Kids don't listen to you unless you have a whistle."

"Just so you know," I said, "kids aren't so great at listening to other kids even *when* they have whistles."

"I won't be just another kid," Noah said. "I'll be the assistant coach."

Andrew raised a finger. "You wouldn't blow on it unless I told you to, right?"

"No," Noah said solemnly. "I'd wait for your signal."

I suppressed a groan. Noah was falling in love with the idea and taking it way too seriously, which was exactly what I was afraid of. "Maybe the coach and I should talk about this by ourselves," I said.

Andrew turned to me. "It's not a lifelong commitment." His tone was perfectly friendly, but I still got the sense I was being rebuked. "Why not let him give it a try and see how it goes?"

"I *know* how it will go," I said grimly.

"Maybe not." He studied me for one brief moment then turned to Noah and held out his hand. "Is it a deal? You'll give it a try and see what you think?"

Noah put out his much smaller hand and they shook. "When do I start?"

"I was thinking you could help me coach the fifth-grade girls' basketball team. They have practice on Wednesdays and games on Fridays. You can start this week."

Noah turned to me. "Mom? Can I? Please?"

I sighed, shrugged, and finally gave a weak nod.

On the way to the car, Noah said, "We better go buy a whistle now."

"I'm sure Coach Andrew has one you can borrow."

"I'll need my own. I'll probably have to use it a lot."

"I'm a little confused," I said, trying to choose my words carefully. "You don't usually like anything that has to do with sports."

"That's because I'm so bad at them," he said. "Not because I don't like them."

"You're not so bad. You just need to try a little harder."

"Mom," he said passionately, "I *have* tried. I swear. I just suck at sports. But if I'm the assistant coach, I can be on a team without making us lose the game so all the other kids hate me. So can we go get the whistle please?"

We got the whistle.

We also picked up a kids' book on basketball. Noah wanted to study up on it. But once we were home, he didn't even make it through the introduction before he had dropped the book on the table and gone to play on the computer.

Later that evening, he blew his new whistle right next to Eleanor Roosevelt's head and the poor dog squealed and jumped about three feet in the air. I confiscated the whistle and told him he couldn't have it back until game day because he had violated the rules. He screamed that I was the meanest mom in the whole entire world and slammed the door to our room in my face. I muttered a sarcastic thank-you to Coach Andrew for bringing a whole new source of tension into our lives.

The next time I saw her, Melanie informed me there was going to be a "wrap-up" Event Hospitality Committee meeting on Wednesday morning.

"We can skip that," I said.

"But we're not going to."

"We did our part. We were good citizens. Now we're done."

"We're not done until we've celebrated with everyone. It's about community, Rickie."

"You suck," I said.

"I'll pick you up at nine."

This meeting was at Maria's house, a beautiful and enormous yellow Monterey Colonial in Bel Air. There were at least four or five gardeners working in the front yard when we arrived. The noise from their blowers and mowers was deafening.

"Sorry!" Maria shouted when she opened the door to our ring. "I forgot they'd be here this morning." She ushered us in and hurriedly slammed the door. "You'd think after twelve years I'd have learned not to schedule anything here on Wednesday mornings, but I always forget."

She steered us into an airy living room near the front of the house. Tanya waved absently in our direction from a big arm-chair, where she was talking into her BlackBerry. Carol Lynn and Linda were discussing something quietly on the dark blue silk-covered sofa and just nodded at us.

"I'm serving mimosas," Maria said. "To celebrate being done with the festival."

"It's a little early for me," Mel said.

"Just try one. I'm using very good champagne. *Dos mas,*" she told a dark-haired middle-aged woman who had just entered the room from another doorway. The woman instantly withdrew again and Maria turned back to us. "It was my husband's. The champagne, I mean. He had a killer wine collection. I got the house but he stiffed me on almost everything else. Then he asked me to give him back all his wine. Which was in the wine cellar. Which was in the house. *Which I got.*" She grinned wickedly. "I don't think he had thought that one through entirely. Sometimes I'll open a bottle of something that's probably worth three hundred dollars, just to have one glass all by myself. And let me tell you, I enjoy it very much." She nudged Melanie's arm. "You probably have your own war stories, right?"

"It hasn't been too bad," Melanie said faintly. The truth was, she and Gabriel were headed toward the most amicable divorce on record. They still had a joint bank account, and the only argument about money I'd heard so far was when Mel told my mother she thought it was "icky" to demand alimony and my mother said, "You'd be an idiot not to." She'd made Mel meet with a lawyer, but after one meeting Melanie said the lawyer was way too "negative" and refused to go back. I got the sense that neither she nor Gabriel really wanted to deal with divvying things up, so they just limped along, sharing the house and his money. He wasn't the type to cut her off and she wasn't the type to take advantage of his generosity, so it worked out.

"Well, lucky you," Maria said when it was clear Melanie had nothing more to add.

The MHW (maid/housekeeper/whatever) returned with the mimosas and handed them to me and Melanie, who accepted one meekly despite her earlier refusal. "Cheers," Maria said, watching us closely. I obediently gulped at the drink. It *was* good. Melanie took a tiny sip of hers.

"You're going to have to do better than that," Maria said.

"I'm driving," Mel protested.

"It'll wear off by the time you leave."

We joined the others around the coffee table, where there was way too much food, as usual. You'd think they'd learn. Or eat something now and then. One or the other.

"All right, then," Tanya said, punching her phone off. "I don't have a lot of time today so we have to keep things moving. I'm in charge of the fifth-grade campout and that's this coming weekend, plus I'm organizing the faculty appreciation luncheon for next week, so I'm losing my mind with everything I still have to do. I'm sure I'll be getting tons of calls all morning long." She eyed her BlackBerry with a weird mixture of pride and resentment. "Anyway, I wanted to make sure I read you something I got a few days ago." She smoothed out a piece of paper on her lap. "This is an e-mail I received. It's from"—dramatic pause—"*Dr. Sorenson.*" She looked up to gauge our reactions to the mind-blowing news that the head of the entire school had taken time out of his busy schedule to communicate with her.

I yawned. Linda played with a cushion tassel. Maria took another sip of her drink. But Melanie made an encouraging noise.

Tanya cleared her throat. "Okay. So here's what he wrote: 'To the Event Hospitality Committee: The Autumn Festival was a huge success, thanks in large part to your efforts. With gratitude, Mark Sorenson.'" She looked up. "Isn't that nice?"

"Very nice," Melanie said.

"Now, moving on to the next big thing—"

"The next big thing?" I repeated in a desperate whisper to Melanie. "There's a next big thing?"

"Shh," she said, but not before Tanya had heard me.

"There's always something else coming up," she said seriously. "I didn't want to tell you all the big news right away because I needed us to just get through the festival first—"

"What news?" Linda asked.

Tanya sat up even straighter. "At the last Parent Association meeting, they decided to split the fund-raiser into two parts this year. An adult-only evening this winter *and* an outdoor family concert in the spring. They've never done anything like this before."

"Two fund-raisers?" Carol Lynn said. "Are they nuts? It's hard enough to get *one* event off the ground."

"People were sharply divided on which one would be more successful, so a subcommittee was formed." She raised her chin proudly. "*I* was on the subcommittee. In the end, we decided doing both was our best option, but I promise you we did not make the decision lightly." She smiled her tight smile. "I know it's more work, but I think we'll have fun with this." I wondered what her definition of fun was. Definitely something different from mine. "The first thing we need to focus on is the adult event," she continued. "It's going to be a casino night. Doesn't that sound like a hoot? We only have a couple of months to prepare, since it's in January and of course nothing gets done over Christmas break. So there's real time pressure here. Any thoughts about the food? We'll need to give the caterer some direction." Her eyes fell on me. "Any ideas, Rickie? You're young and creative." I didn't know how she came up with the creative part, but I couldn't argue too much about the young.

I fidgeted as everyone looked at me. "Um, I don't know. I guess...well, it's a casino night and casinos make everyone think of James Bond, right? So we should probably serve martinis—"

"Shaken, not stirred," Maria put in.

I spotted croissants on the platter in front of me. "We could serve these," I said, picking one up. "Croissants. That's very European." I bit into mine.

"Too breakfasty," said Melanie, to my annoyance—she wouldn't have publicly disagreed with any of the *other* women. She turned to Tanya. "You know what would be cool, though? Little tiny lamb chops that you can eat with your fingers. I had those at a party once and they were so good. And elegant."

"We'd have to price those out," Tanya said. "We have a couple of caterers we've worked with in the past. Why don't you and Rickie meet with them and let them know the kind of thing we're going for and see what they suggest and how their prices compare." It was phrased as a question but it wasn't a question. It was a command. "You're also welcome to call a few more caterers on your own, of course."

"Us?" Melanie said. "Really?" I was thinking the same thing, only I was thinking "Us, really?" with total dread and horror, and she was saying it with total *delight* like someone had just told her we were going to be starring in the next Leo DiCaprio movie.

"I don't know..." I said.

"We'd love to do it," Mel said firmly. "We'd be honored."

"Honored" was not the word I had in mind.

Maria pulled me aside once the meeting had ended. "I had an idea," she said. There was something imprecise about the way she was talking, and her movements were a little sloppy. I wondered if she often got wasted in the morning. "Austin's birthday party is the weekend after next. He's only inviting a few of the boys in the class, so we've been keeping it kind of quiet, but I think you should bring Noah."

"Does Austin *want* Noah to come?"

"Of course." She waved her hand a bit too extravagantly and accidentally hit Tanya, who was walking by—right in the chin. "Oops, sorry," Maria said with a giggle before turning back to me. "I think it would be good for Noah. He seems like such a sweet kid—he just needs to connect more to the other boys."

"He's weird," I said.

"All boys are weird."

"He's weirder than most."

She waved her hand again but fortunately didn't hit anyone this time. "I'll e-mail you the invitation. You can stay and hang out with me, and if he's not having fun, you can always take him home."

I wanted to be grateful but inside I was groaning at the thought of having to go. I knew Noah would spend the whole time glued to my side while the other boys played together, and history had taught me that we'd return home depressed and more certain than ever that he'd never fit in with his classmates. But I thanked her and said I'd check the calendar.

Carol Lynn caught up to Melanie and me just as we were walking out of the house. "Hey, I need to talk to you two." The gardeners had moved on—you could hear a mower off in the distance, but Maria's property was relatively quiet as we all moved together down the walkway. "So here's the thing," Carol Lynn said. "My adorable little cousin is moving to LA. I love this guy. He was in a fairly serious relationship in Chicago but she refused to move with him."

"That's too bad," Melanie said.

"Oh, she was *awful*," Carol Lynn said. "We're actually all thrilled they broke up. Anyway, his mother—my aunt—asked me if I knew any nice young women in LA who I could fix him up with, to kind of smooth over the whole transition. And I thought of"—she hesitated, looking back and forth between us—"well, both of you, I guess. Mostly you, though, Melanie. No offense, Rickie, you're just a little young for him."

And a little tattooed and pierced, I thought. I could just imagine what her aunt would say if he brought me home and informed her that Cousin Carol Lynn had set us up. "No worries."

"Oh, wow," Melanie said with a forced smile. "That's so nice of you. But I don't know—"

"Come on, Mel," I said. "Why not?"

"He's really cute," Carol Lynn added. "And I'm not just saying that because he's my cousin." The sun was bright and she reached into her Prada purse and pulled out sunglasses, which she settled on her over-straightened nose. "He's also sweet as can be."

"Sounds like your kind of guy," I said to Melanie.

"I think *you* should date him," Mel shot back. "You're the

one who really needs a man in her life—for Noah's sake, as well as yours."

"Carol Lynn thinks you're a better fit."

"I'm happy to set you up with him, too, Rickie," Carol Lynn said with a shrug. "Honestly. Who am I to say what will work? He was crazy about this other woman and I couldn't stand *her*." Then, realizing what she had just said, she added quickly, "Not that you'd be like that or anything. I'm just saying that attraction is a complicated thing."

"Give him our home number," I said. "We'll figure it out from there."

"All right, then," Carol Lynn said. "His name's Matt. Matt Quinn."

"We'll look forward to his call," Melanie said tonelessly.

8.

The sun was blazing hot that afternoon, so when I picked Noah up from his first day of assistant coaching I expected to find a discouraged, sweaty, miserable kid.

I had forgotten that the basketball teams practiced in the air-conditioned gym.

He came running toward me as soon as I came in. "Look at this!" he said excitedly, thrusting a clipboard at me. The paper on it was covered in scribbles and names. "I helped Coach Andrew come up with a new play and the girls totally did it! See? This *X* here is Allison and this squiggle is Pammy, and Allison passed to Pammy who bounce-passed it to Lulu and Lulu threw it in the basket! They totally scored!"

"That's awesome, Noey," I said.

Andrew was surrounded by a group of chattering girls, half of whom were wearing cheap gym pull-on blue jerseys, half in white ones, but he spotted me and extricated himself from them. "Noah did great," he told me as he came over, trailed by the girls. "Completely turned things around for Team Blue."

A girl with long brown hair who was as tall as me said, "Are you Noah's mom? Oh, my god, he is *so* cute."

A smaller girl ruffled Noah's hair. "I am so totally in love with him," she said to me. Her braces gave her a slight lisp. "I just want to take him *home* with me."

Noah smiled a little smile down at his toes.

"He's already made a lot of fans," Andrew said.

"Older women," I said. "Clearly that's the secret to success."

Andrew raised his eyebrows. "I've got to remember that."

"I've seen your girlfriend. You're not exactly hard up."

"I blew the whistle twice!" Noah told me. "Only the first time I wasn't supposed to."

"But we worked out a system, right, Noah?" Andrew said.

"I can only blow it when Coach Andrew tells me to," Noah explained.

"Do you need a babysitter?" the dark-haired girl asked me. "Because I'd totally love to babysit him."

"Me too," said the braces one, and a third girl, who had red hair cut in a bob with a fringe and who had been shyly hanging back until then, took a brave step forward to say, "I want to too."

A mom entered the gym with a small white puppy cradled in her arms, and all the girls squealed and raced over to pet it. One of them stopped and turned and beckoned to Noah, who obligingly trotted toward her. She put her arm around his shoulders and they walked together to join the circle around the dog.

"Wow," I said to Andrew. "He made friends fast."

"I'm glad I put him with the girls' team. It was love at first sight."

"Yeah, it would have been harder for him with boys, I think."

He nodded absently. "Hey, can I ask you a personal question?"

"Those are my favorite kind!" I said.

"Is Noah's father in the picture at all?"

"Oh, *that* personal question." I lowered my voice. "The truth is...there *is* no father. Noah was cloned from one of my eyebrow hairs."

He shot me a look. "I'm fairly certain clones have to be the same gender."

"You'd think, wouldn't you?" I said agreeably.

"Seriously—"

"Seriously, no, he's so much not around that he doesn't exist. Which is fine."

"Have you ever thought about getting Noah hooked up with the Big Brothers organization?"

"The one that tortures people by putting rats on their face?" I said. "He can be annoying but I don't think he deserves *that*."

"I was thinking of the other kind of Big Brother," he said. "The ratless kind."

"Oh, I get it!" I said like it was all just dawning on me. "You think Noah needs a father figure." Then I said, more normally, "Noah has my dad, you know."

"Does he take him outside once in a while, throw a ball with him, stuff like that?"

I grinned at the thought. Man, the guy did not know my father. Or Noah, for that matter. I said loftily, "Don't you think that's a little sexist? Why couldn't *I* be the one throwing a ball to Noah? Or my mother? Or my half sister? He spends time with all of us."

"You could," Andrew said calmly. "Does *anyone* in your household throw a ball with Noah or watch football games on TV with him?"

"No," I admitted. "He doesn't want to do that stuff. But we do lots of other things together—the kid gets plenty of attention. Probably too much. But if he gets a sudden overwhelming urge to play catch, I'll tell him to give Coach Andrew a call. How's that?"

"Good luck," he said. "My home number's unlisted."

"Don't you even *want* to rescue him from his miserable home life?"

He started to say something, then stopped. Then just said quietly, "I'm glad you're letting Noah do this. We have a game on Friday, right after school. Can he come? It's here."

"If he wants to, it's fine with me."

"All right, then." He walked away.

I watched him go, twisting my mouth sideways, aware that I'd sounded pretty snarky. But the whole "you need a man around" thing got under my skin like nothing else. I didn't need a man around. Noah didn't need a man around. We were fine.

"Mom?" Noah said, coming up to me with an uneven hopping skip that was weird even for him.

"What?"

"The dog pooped and I stepped in it." He lifted his foot to show me he wasn't lying. "You need to clean it."

I looked around, but he was right: the job was all mine.

*   *   *

I called Ryan that night and asked him if I could come over. He said it "wasn't a good idea."

"What do you mean?"

"I'm supposed to meet Gabriel and Sherri for dinner and a movie."

"Would that be poor broken-hearted Gabriel?" I said. "Sounds like he's really suffering."

"Give it a rest. I'd invite you to come along, but you'd say stuff like that."

"Forget it," I said. "Have fun." I hung up.

I had already put Noah to bed, so I wandered down the stairs, wondering, not for the first time, what it would be like to be living with a guy who would help me tuck Noah in and then curl up with me to watch TV or read in our own master bedroom.

I heard voices and followed them to the kitchen.

My mother and Melanie were talking at the table, both of them cuddling cups of tea. Mel looked distraught. Mom looked concerned.

"What's going on?" I joined them at the table.

"Halloween," Mel said with the kind of tragic tone one didn't normally associate with a fun holiday.

"What about it?"

"Gabriel's mother is making a big deal out of how she wants to see the kids trick-or-treat. So he's asking if he can have them that night."

Now I understood. That *would* be tragic, from Melanie's perspective. I wondered how I would feel if I couldn't trick-or-treat with Noah, but it was pretty hard to imagine: I never had to fight anyone for time with Noah. I had to beg people to give me time *away* from him. "Can you split up the evening so you can both do it?" I asked.

"It's too hard on the kids. They'd be exhausted."

"I was saying we should just invite Gabriel and Sandra to come here," Mom told me.

"I don't know if I can stand that." Melanie's mouth trembled. "I mean, to be together like we're still together—you know what I mean—and have his mother there and then the kids all excited...It sounds unbearable."

My mother put down her mug. "You have to think about what's best for Nicole and Cameron."

"I know, I know," Melanie said. "I just don't know if I can stand it."

"Then don't do it," I said. "You're the one who's dealing with getting their costumes ready and all that stuff. What right does Gabriel have to start making demands?"

"He's their father," my mother said. "He has every right. And he's asking, not demanding." She clearly didn't like that I wasn't agreeing with her. She turned back to Melanie. "I know it won't be easy. So you'll have a glass of wine first." She shrugged. "Maybe two. But it will make the kids so happy."

"It's *Halloween*," I said. "Free Candy Night. They'd be happy if some crazy homeless guy took them trick-or-treating." Mom gave me one of her looks and I knew she wanted me to back off—and I also knew she was kind of right, that Nicole and Cameron would love to spend Halloween with both their parents. But it still felt to me like she was bullying Melanie into doing something Mel didn't want to do, and she'd done that to me too many times. "You should do what you want, Mel."

"You're right," Mel said, and at first I was pleased because I thought she meant me—but she was talking to my mother. "Go ahead and invite them."

"But I just think—" I was going to continue the argument when my mother cut me off.

"I believe your son is calling you, Rickie."

I thought she was just saying that to make me shut up, but then I heard an unhappy distant voice calling, "Mom? Mom? Where are you? I'm scared."

I went upstairs.

I let Noah climb into my bed and then I lay down next to him. He had had a bad dream and said he couldn't stop thinking about it, so I tried to distract him by reminding him that it was almost Halloween and we still hadn't decided on a costume. We considered various superheroes and characters from books and TV shows and then he bounced up and said excitedly, "I have an idea! I could go as a coach!"

"Lie down. A coach?"

He fell on his back. "Yeah, like Coach Andrew! I could wear my whistle. And a baseball cap. He always wears a baseball cap."

"Sounds nice and easy."

"I *might* need some new sneakers. Mine are the wrong type."

"I think they'll be okay for this."

He pouted briefly. "And sunglasses. Coach Andrew always wears sunglasses outside."

"Yeah, but it'll be night, don't forget. You'd be blind in sunglasses." Then I said, "You like him now, huh?"

"Who?"

"Coach Andrew."

"He's okay. I still hate PE but I like when I'm his assistant coach. Hey, Mom?"

"Yeah?"

"Can I call my dad tomorrow?"

I closed my eyes, suddenly exhausted. "Noah—"

"Please, Mom?"

"I don't even have a current phone number for him."

"You could get it online."

"Says who?"

"You're always getting numbers online."

Whatever else you could say about Noah, he noticed things. Usually things you wished he hadn't noticed. "It wouldn't work," I said slowly. "I'm sorry, Noah. I don't know where he is."

"He's my *dad*," he said. "He probably wants to talk to me."

I was silent a moment. I opened my eyes and stared up at the ceiling. This was a conversation we'd had before. The other kids at school had fathers who cared, even the ones who were divorced. Even the kid with two mommies had a biological father who showed up for his school performances and cheered loudly. Everyone had a father who cared except Noah. It broke my heart. "I'll see what I can do," I said, but we both knew it was an empty promise. "Now go to sleep, Noey. It's late."

"Don't move me," he said. "Don't put me back in my bed, okay? I want to sleep here with you tonight."

"Okay, but if you kick me, I'm going to be tired and mad tomorrow."

"I won't," he said.

He did and I was.

The girls won their basketball game on Friday. It was a close game, and I was glad I got there in time to see the exciting last ten minutes. Whenever a substitute was about to go in, she'd quickly rub the top of Noah's head and murmur something. I asked him later what the girls were saying, and he said, beaming, "'Top of the head for good luck.' Sophia came up with that. And it worked because we won!"

In the car, Noah said, "Oh, hey, Mom? Austin gave me an

invitation to his birthday party. I'm not supposed to tell any-one because most of the boys in the class weren't invited. But it's probably okay for me to tell *you*."

"That's nice," I said. "Do you want to go?"

"Yeah. Except—" He stopped.

"What?"

"It's a sports party. You know how bad I am at that stuff."

"You've got to stop saying that, Noah. You're not that bad. But you also don't have to go to the party if you don't want to."

"I want to," he said. "But don't leave, okay?"

"I promise." So, even though I knew that it was a huge mistake, and that we'd both be miserable and isolated there, I e-mailed Maria Dellaventura later that day and said we'd come to Austin's party.

Melanie arrived at our house on Monday afternoon—Halloween—soon after I'd brought Noah, Cameron, and Nicole all home from school. She was wearing a black sweater dress that was long and clingy.

"Wow," I said admiringly. "That looks great, but it is so not like you."

She blushed. "I know. My mother sent it to me. She thinks I need to 'make more of an effort in the looks department.' Direct quote. I wouldn't normally wear it, but Nicole said it would be a good witch dress and the kids wanted me to wear a costume. I have a hat too." She put the witch's hat she had been holding on her head and struck a pose. "See?"

"Gabriel's going to be very sorry he was such an idiot when he sees you in that dress."

"That's not why I wore it."

I rolled my eyes. "Sure it isn't."

"Are *you* going to wear a costume?" Noah asked me. He was sitting at the kitchen table, eating some GF toast, swinging his legs and looking fairly adorable in a baseball cap that was way too big for him and kept falling down over his ears. I had sent him to school in one that fit, and he had come back wearing Coach Andrew's UCLA cap. The other cap was gone, not in his backpack, although he insisted he had put it in there and that someone must have taken it out and stolen it, which was what he always said when he misplaced something.

"Nah," I said.

"You always look the same," Noah complained. "You never look pretty."

"Noah!" Melanie exclaimed. "Don't say that. Your mom's very pretty."

"But she doesn't ever wear a dress or cut her hair or anything."

"He's got a point," I said. "I mean, look at me." At that moment, I was wearing jeans that were torn at the knees and a men's size-large sweatshirt that my father had gotten for free at some conference. My hair was in its usual messy ponytail.

Melanie diplomatically chose to change the subject. "Do you know what we're doing for dinner?"

"Mom's ordering in pizza," I said.

"What am I going to eat?" asked Noah.

"I'll make you a GF pizza."

"Don't forget to make it so it's ready when the other pizza comes."

"Okay." He was right to remind me: I often forgot to start his pizza on time, which meant poor Noah had to wait for it to cook while everyone else was scarfing down fresh, hot pizza.

"What's for dessert?" he asked.

"It's Halloween, Noah," I said. "What do you think?"

"Oh. Candy, I guess."

"He's a genius," I said to Mel.

"He is," she said with a lot less sarcasm and smiled at him.

That was the last genuine smile I saw on her face that day. An hour or so later the doorbell rang, and Gabriel walked in with his mother and—surprise!—Ryan.

The greetings were awkward. Gabriel gave me one of his patented bear hugs but when he tried to embrace my mother, she stepped back and coldly extended her hand to him. She was still furious at him for cheating on Melanie.

Ryan came over and dropped a casual kiss on my cheek. "Been thinking about you," he whispered. "What are you doing later tonight, when all this is over?"

"Probably talking Noah down from a sugar high."

"And after that?"

I glanced around to make sure no one could hear us. "Coming over to your place?"

"Sounds like a plan." He moved on and shook my father's hand.

As soon as Gabriel and Ryan's mother had bestowed a hostile air-kiss a few inches from Melanie's cheek, Mom took her firmly by the arm and propelled her over to the sofa. "You look younger every time I see you," she said pulling Sandra down next to her on the sofa. "What's your secret?" Sandra, who spent more annually on beauty treatments and plastic surgery than most large families in America spent on food, launched into some absurd speech about how lucky she was with her genes, and Melanie mouthed a heartfelt "Thank you" to my mom for rescuing her from any more interaction with her soon-to-be-ex-mother-in-law.

Gabriel's father had died a long time ago from a heart attack. From the photos I'd seen, he had Gabriel's physique plus another fifty pounds or so, which had made him arguably more grizzly bear than teddy bear. Anyway, since his death Sandra had apparently chosen to devote herself full time to fighting any signs of aging. Her skin was shiny and tight, her eyes tilted ever so slightly up toward her temples, her lips were unnaturally plump, and her forehead was smooth as Lucite. She wasn't young and she wasn't pretty. She was just... not wrinkled.

She had never been welcoming toward Melanie, and had made it clear that she considered her sons her sole property. She had cried at Gabriel and Mel's wedding, and not for joy, although the births of her two grandchildren seemed to have reconciled her somewhat to the marriage. Still, you had to assume that the impending divorce gave her some pleasure. I wondered what her sons had actually told her about the separation and suspected that in their version Melanie had capriciously tossed Gabriel out on his ear for no real reason.

At any rate, it was nice of my mother, who couldn't stand Sandra and had only endured her company in the past for Gabriel's sake, to throw herself on the bomb and keep her occupied and away from Melanie.

The rest of us were still awkwardly standing around the living room, and then Melanie said, "I'll get the kids—they're in the family room," and fled, like the coward she was.

I said, "I'll get the wine."

"I'll help," said Ryan.

In the kitchen, he leaned against the refrigerator and said dryly, "What a fun family we are tonight. Happy Halloween and god bless us everyone."

"I love your mother's zombie mask," I said. "It's terrifying."

"Fuck you," he said, fairly amicably, all things considered.

"Later." I started pouring wine into glasses, carelessly sloshing a little over the side.

He shook his finger at me. "Keep making cracks about my mother and I may change my mind about letting you come over."

"You love when I make cracks about your mother. You don't have the guts to do it yourself."

He watched me lick a drop of wine off my wrist. "You know, it would be nice if some of the wine actually went in the glasses."

"Don't be a backseat pourer."

"I have an idea," he said, coming up close behind me. "We could sneak upstairs for a few minutes—"

"We could." I kept pouring, even though he was making it hard to concentrate. "But we won't."

"Why not?" His breath was warm against my ear.

"Noah might come looking for me."

"I'll be fast." He pushed against me and I leaned back into him for a moment, then sighed and picked up two wineglasses.

"Take these into the other room, will you? And make sure Mel gets one right away. She needs it."

"She looks really good tonight," he said, stepping back and taking the glasses out of my hands. "Better than ever."

"Doesn't she? Your brother is a stupid idiot."

"That's two," he said.

I carried two more filled glasses into the living room. The kids had come in, and Sandra was making a big fuss over how adorable Nicole and Cameron looked (she was a girl pirate; he was Harry Potter) and completely ignoring Noah, who was standing forlornly off by himself, fidgeting nervously. I saw Ryan pass by him on his way to giving Melanie her glass of wine. "Hey, Cameron," he said with an absent nod. "How's it going?"

"I'm not Cameron," Noah said, but Ryan had already gone by and didn't hear him.

Gabriel—bless his generous cheating heart—must have caught that because suddenly he swooped down on him. "My friend Noah!" he roared. "There you are!" He caught him up in his arms in a warm Gabriel-style hug.

That caught Sandra's attention. She deigned to glance at Noah as Gabriel released him. "You should go put on your costume," she said. "What are you waiting for?"

Noah's face crumpled. I rushed over. "He's already wearing it. I think he looks great." I thrust the glasses of wine at my mother, who took them, and I put my arms around Noah's shoulders and squeezed him tightly. "He'll be the only kid out there who's a coach," I said.

"A coach! Of course!" Gabriel said enthusiastically. "It's a fantastic costume, Noah!" Noah's face relaxed. Crisis of self-confidence averted. For that moment.

"He has a whistle," Nicole said, pointing to where it hung around his neck. "But he's not allowed to blow it. He did, though," she added to me in a lowered voice. "Earlier, when we were in the family room. I told him if he did it again, you'd take it away from him."

"Thanks for handling the situation," I whispered back.

The doorbell rang. "That'll be the pizza," my mother said. She handed the wineglasses back to me and hustled out of the room. I gave one of the wineglasses to Gabriel, and since Ryan had already given his two away to Mel and Sandra, I gave him my last one.

"I love this game," Ryan said as he took it. "Musical wine-glasses. Do I drink it or just pass it on?"

I smiled sweetly at him and murmured, "Would you like me to tell you where to put it?"

"That's three," he said. "Now you're in trouble."

My mother called from the hallway. "Come to the dining room! Pizza's here!"

"Mom?" Noah said. "Is my pizza ready?"

I hit my forehead with the palm of my hand. "Shoot, Noah! I'm sorry!"

"Every time," he said more with sorrow than resentment. "Every time you forget."

"I'll make it right now." I ran into the kitchen. My mother was already in there, getting paper plates out of the closet.

"So much for being environmentally friendly," she said with a nod of greeting. "I'm going to hell when I die."

"They don't use paper plates in hell." I put down my glass and ran to the freezer. "They'd burn right up."

"Plus one of the ways they torture people is probably by making them wash dishes for all eternity. An activity I'm well acquainted with." She piled some napkins on top of the plates and glanced over at me. "What are you doing?"

"Making a pizza for Noah."

"Oh, right. Bring a pitcher of water and some cups when you come in, will you?" She hustled out with the plates.

I turned on the toaster oven and was searching for a pitcher when the phone rang. "Hi," said the male voice at the other end. "I'm looking for either Melanie or Rickie."

"This is Rickie. Who's this?"

"My name's Matt Quinn. I'm Carol Lynn Donahue's cousin—she said I could call you?"

"Oh, right." I had totally forgotten about him. "Uh, hi. What's up?"

"I think Carol Lynn told you I just moved to LA? She thought maybe you—or Melanie—that one of you could maybe show me around a little?"

You could tell the guy didn't have kids: no one who did would have cold-called on Halloween night. I was about to ask him to call back another time when the voices from the other room gave me an idea. "Hold on a second," I said into the phone. "Let me get Melanie. She's really the one who"—*Who what?* I wondered frantically. I didn't know how to end the sentence, so instead I said abruptly, "Just a sec" and put him on hold.

I entered the dining room, cradling the phone against my chest. "Hey, Mel?" I called over the noise of people sitting down and doling out pizza and talking.

She looked up from where she was getting Cameron settled at the table. "What?"

"Phone for you. It's that guy." There was a sudden silence in the room.

"What guy?"

"You know. That guy. The one who"—I shook the phone at her—"You know. He really wants to talk to you." I sneaked a glance at Gabriel. He was watching the whole exchange, eyes slightly narrowed.

Melanie came around the table toward me. "I don't know what you're talking about."

"Shh." I pulled her into the kitchen and closed the door. "It's Carol Lynn's cousin."

"Oh. Just tell him I'll call him back." She turned.

"No, wait." I grabbed her arm. "Talk to him. Make a date. Laugh loudly."

"Why?"

"Because Gabriel's in the next room," I hissed. "And I saw the expression on his face when I said a guy was calling you. Make him suffer."

"But I don't really want to talk to this guy."

"Come on," I said. "This is perfect timing. Make a date

with him then come into the other room and tell me about it—very loudly, and in front of everyone."

"It's childish, Rickie."

"Do it for me," I said, and forced the phone on her.

9.

S andra tolerated about two blocks of trick-or-treating before saying she'd had enough and wanted to go home. Ryan came over to say good-bye to me and whispered that he had decided to "let" me come over later, despite the three strikes against me. I thanked him politely and reminded him to remove his mother's mask before he tucked her into her crypt for the night.

"Shut up." Then, lowering his voice even more, he said, "So who's the guy who called Melanie?"

"I don't have to tell you." He couldn't see it in the dark, but I was smirking.

"Gabriel asked me to find out."

"Yeah? I hope the suspense is killing him."

"You have a bad attitude about this," Ryan said. "Isn't the goal to get them back together? I mean look at them." He gestured to where they were both bent over Cameron's bag of treats, exclaiming over the treasures. "Don't you just want things to go back the way they were?"

"You're such a girl," I said.

"Fuck you."

"It's not such a bad insult. Go ahead, call me a girl. I don't mind."

"Wouldn't kill you to be a little more girly," he muttered and stalked away.

I turned back to the others and, in the weird orange glow of a house's Halloween pumpkin lights, I watched as Gabriel said good night to Melanie. He hugged her, and—for just a moment—her body melted into his and she let her forehead drop onto his shoulder. He held her close with real tenderness and didn't seem in any hurry to end the embrace, but then she suddenly twisted away from him and busied herself adjusting Cameron's Harry Potter glasses. She didn't look up again, not even when he walked away.

They all left, and Mel and I continued on with the three kids. My mother had stayed back at the house to hand out candy, and my father had vanished into his study right after dinner.

"You okay?" I asked Melanie as Nicole marched the two boys up to another house.

She shrugged silently, her mouth drooping, and I realized how close she was to crying, so I left her alone. She made a big fuss over the kids' candy when they rejoined us, and that seemed to steady her.

"No one knows what Noah is," Cameron told me as we walked on to the next house, loudly enough for Noah to hear.

"That's because his costume's so original," I said quickly.

"Yeah," Nicole said. "Unlike yours, Cameron. I've seen like twenty other Harry Potters."

"Shut up!" Cameron said.

"It's true."

"Well, at least people know who I am."

Noah tugged at my hand. "I want to go home," he said in a small voice.

"Already? I thought we'd still do a few more blocks."

"No one knows who I am," he said and his voice broke. "I feel stupid."

"I love your costume," I said. "You are so obviously a coach. If other people don't get that, it's because they're stupid, not because it's a bad costume."

"I wish I was Harry Potter like Cameron."

"I like your costume better."

"Come on," Nicole said, pulling on his other arm. "Let's go do this house, Noey. They have Twizzlers."

"I can't eat Twizzlers," Noah said. "They're not GF."

"Oh, sorry. We'll see if they have something else."

He let her lead him up the path to inevitable disappointment.

The next morning, Noah couldn't find the baseball cap Coach Andrew had lent him. He ran frantically around the house searching for it. "I had it when I came home from trick-or-treating," he said. "But now I can't find it anywhere." His face was taut with anxiety. "Is he going to be mad? Do you think he'll tell me I can't be his assistant coach anymore?"

"I don't think so. But you should have been more careful."

"He's going to kill me," he said, and was inconsolable for the rest of the morning. He was a knot of misery when I dropped him off at school. I watched him drag himself slowly inside. I had driven halfway home when I pulled a sudden U-turn at an intersection. A car coming toward me honked and I just waved cheerfully at the driver with deliberate obtuseness.

I made my way back to school and parked on the street outside, since parents were still dropping kids off, then walked through the courtyard, sidestepping the roughly ten million small children who were making their way to their classrooms.

Andrew's office door was open a few inches, so I stuck my head in. "You got a second?"

He was sitting at his computer, but he gestured me in. "Yeah. Not much more, though."

"I'll be fast." I came inside. "I think Noah lost your baseball cap."

"Oh." If he was annoyed, he hid it well. "It's okay. I've got more."

"I just wanted you to know that I'm getting you another one, so you wouldn't be mad at Noah. He's kind of worried about it."

"I wouldn't get mad at a six-year-old kid for losing something."

"I get mad at him all the time for losing stuff."

"That's different—you're his mom."

"He loses everything," I said. "He's so spacey."

"I was like that when I was his age. My mother was always threatening to staple things to me." He got up from his desk. He was wearing shorts and a zip-up sweatshirt. It was a slightly dorky outfit.

"My dad's like that too," I said. "He'll put something down and won't ever remember where."

"Maybe it's a guy thing."

"It's a wonder that your gender rules the world."

"And yet we do."

"Yeah, and look what a great job you're doing." I stood there for a moment, listening to the noise of the kids out in the courtyard, oddly reluctant to leave. "So if you see Noah today, just tell him I talked to you, okay? And I promise you that by this time tomorrow you'll be wearing your brand-new USC Trojans cap."

"Oof," he said. "That better have been an innocent mistake."

I smiled sweetly at him, deliberately tormenting him. "Oh,

I'm sorry—I just thought you might want to wear something from a *good* school."

He waved a finger at me. "Watch it, uh...Noah's mom."

"You still don't remember my name, do you?"

"I know who you are," he said defensively. "That's what matters. I mean, I could pick you out of a crowd of mothers, even without the tie-dyed hair—"

I opened my eyes wide in horror. "Tie-dyed? Tie-dyed?"

"But there's something about your first name. It's impossible to remember."

"You're blaming my name?" I said. "Not your memory, but my name?"

"It's just not memorable."

"And I suppose Andrew is?"

"You remembered it."

"Because I'm a caring person who takes the time to learn people's names," I said airily. I turned to go. Then I turned back. "Oh, wait. About your hat size: am I correct in noting that your head is extremely big and swollen?"

"Sure, criticize other people's heads, girl with the tie-dyed hair."

I was laughing as I left his office.

I got to the UCLA student union store as soon as it opened and spent an hour sorting through the baseball caps. I couldn't find the exact one Andrew had lent Noah, so I just picked out the one I liked best and sent it with Noah to school the following morning in a bag marked *Give to Coach Andrew*. I thought about hand-delivering it, but I felt a little funny about dropping by his office two days in a row.

He was busy talking to a parent after practice on Wednesday, so in the car on the way home I asked Noah if he thought Coach Andrew liked the cap we'd given him.

Noah wasn't helpful. "I don't know. I guess."

"Did he say anything to you about it?"

He shrugged. "I think maybe he said thanks."

"Anything else?"

"No. Oh, he did say I should tell you we're playing an away game on Friday."

"Yeah? Where? Do I pick you up there?"

"I don't know. Can we go get ice cream?"

An e-mail to Andrew Fulton scored some more helpful answers to my questions. He said I could pick Noah up at the other school at five on Friday.

That freed up the whole afternoon, so I went with an old high-school friend to see a movie at the Third Street Promenade. It ran long, over two hours, and as soon as it was over I dashed to the parking garage feeling a little panicky. The school was in Culver City and I'd only make it there on time if I didn't hit any traffic.

It was after 4:30 on a Friday afternoon. Of course I hit traffic. Tons of it.

I was horribly late. The sun had set and it was getting cold by the time I finally drove into the school's lot. The one lone parking guard left informed me that the school's basketball court was outside, around the back of the school. I ran around the building and felt awful when I saw that there were only two people left waiting there: Andrew and Noah. And Noah didn't have a sweatshirt.

He hurled himself at me. "Where were you?" he sobbed. "Everyone else got picked up ages ago!"

"I'm sorry!" I appealed to Andrew. "I didn't realize how far this was and the traffic—"

"It happens," he said brusquely. "I've got to run. I'm late for an appointment. Bye, Noah. Thanks for your help."

"We lost!" Noah wailed.

"Unfortunately, that also happens. Good-bye." Clipboard and net bag in hand, Andrew sprinted toward the parking lot.

"Why did you have to be so late?" Noah said as we gathered up his backpack and headed toward the car. "You ruin everything. Don't ever be late again."

"I'll try not to be."

"That's what you always say about everything. That you'll 'try.' That's your way of not really promising."

I sighed. He had a point.

By the time we actually got home, it was dark and Melanie was on her way out the door. She was meeting Carol Lynn's cousin at the Grove—her first date since she and Gabriel had separated.

"It'll be a mob scene there," my mother warned.

"I know," Melanie said. "But he said he wanted to go somewhere quintessentially LA and I panicked. I couldn't think of anything else."

"The traffic will be horrific at this hour on a Friday."

"I'm leaving myself two hours to get there. I'll probably be early, but I don't mind wasting time there."

"Yeah and I know how," I said. "But Nicole does *not* need another American Girl doll."

Melanie smiled sheepishly. "Not another doll, but maybe a little nineteen-forties pajama set? They're so cute, Rickie, you wouldn't believe it."

I rolled my eyes. "Just don't have a bunch of American Girl bags in your hands when you meet up with him, okay? He'll run away screaming."

"Actually, I think she should," Mom said. "If he's a good guy, he'll be thrilled she has kids."

"God, Mom, you so don't know what it's like to have a kid when you're dating."

"Maybe not," she said, "but I did date a man who already had a daughter and from the very beginning I considered her a wonderful bonus." She touched the back of Mel's hand lightly.

"You were always so nice to me," Melanie said. "I always get mad when people say stepmothers are evil. And now, letting me live with you..."

Oh, for god's sake, now the two of them were hugging each other. It was enough to make you puke. I left the kitchen, the odd man out as always.

I never understood why Melanie adored my mother so much. Melanie's own mom was a lot more hands-off, which I thought would be kind of nice in a mother. Mom had told me that back when Dad and Colleen first got divorced, Colleen spent all her time either working at her nursing job or taking care of little Melanie. She never went out, never had fun, never dated, and looked older than she was. But once Melanie went off to college, Colleen had some kind of midlife rebirth. She dyed her gray hair brown, joined a health club and lost twenty pounds, started wearing tight, youthful clothing, and signed up for every online dating site she could. Her life became a whirlwind of social engagements and trips to exotic places.

Melanie always joked about how busy her mother was and how she had to schedule an appointment just to see her, but I think it genuinely hurt her feelings that Colleen had so little interest in her own grandchildren. She never babysat for Nicole and Cameron, and when she came by to see them, she was usually in a rush, on her way to doing something else.

My mother had her own theory about it all. "She sacrificed too much early on," she said to me once. "She did the martyr thing after the divorce, and once she didn't have to take care of Melanie, it was like a spring that had been wound too tight. She just popped, went the other way."

"I think it's good she's learned to enjoy herself," I said. "Seems healthy."

"Yes, well, believe me, I expected to be doing a bit more of that myself at this stage in my life," Mom said, a little acidly.

"Feel free to do whatever you want. No one's stopping you."

"No one except the three generations of Allens living under this roof who all expect me to cook dinner and keep the fridge stocked and the house clean," she said.

I waited up for Melanie, who got back from her date around eleven-thirty.

"Well?" I said.

"Well, what?" She dropped her bags on a chair. Predictably, they were from the American Girl store and Pottery Barn Kids.

"How was he?"

"Okay. Cute in kind of a metrosexual way." She wrinkled her nose. "But he wore a ton of cologne. Do guys really think women like that? Do you know any woman who does?"

"No," I said, but I suspected her of looking for reasons to reject him, and that one seemed pretty flimsy to me. "So are you going to see him again?"

"I don't know." She yawned. "He was fine, but he wasn't Gabriel and I'm not sure I'm ready to be with someone who's not Gabriel."

"Then maybe you should be with Gabriel."

"He hurt me so much," she said and her voice broke, so I dropped the subject and busied myself poking through the bags to see what she had gotten her kids.

10.

O h, good, you came!" Maria said when she opened her front door to us the following morning.

"Noah's so happy you invited him," I said.

He hip-checked me angrily. "Don't say that, Mom! It's embarrassing."

Maria laughed. "The kids are all out back. They're just running around now, but we have a special guest coming soon who's going to organize some sports."

"Sounds great," I lied. I gave Noah a little nudge. "Go on back, Noey."

"You have to come with me." He took my hand and dragged me toward the back of the house, past some moms who were sitting talking in the family room and who didn't even bother to greet us.

It was going to be a long morning.

Maria's backyard was incredible. There was a fenced-off pool, a large grassy area, an enormous play structure, and a small basketball court. It was total kid paradise.

A bunch of boys were already chasing each other around on the grass and some other mothers were standing around a table of food and drinks that was set up in the shade. They seemed comfortable together, talking and laughing and poking through the snacks. The boys all seemed pretty comfortable together too.

I wondered what it would be like to show up at a school party and know everyone, to feel like I fit in—like Noah fit in—to not always be pressing our noses up against the glass gawking at the insiders.

Noah was still clutching my arm as we halted uncertainly on the edge of the grassy area.

"Look, there's Austin." I pointed across the yard. "Why don't you go say happy birthday?"

"Come with me."

"I'm not coming with you. There are no mothers over there, just kids."

"I want to stay with you."

"Noah, it's stupid to come to a birthday party and cling to me. The point is for you to hang out with your friends."

He glanced at the boys out on the yard. "They're not my friends."

"Noah—"

"They're not *not* my friends," he said quickly. "They're not the bad boys or anything. But I don't—"

"Want me to ask Austin to come over?" I hadn't heard Maria come up behind us. "Would that help, Noah?" she asked, bending down a little toward him. "If Austin came and got you?"

"No," Noah said and I could feel the panic trembling in his body as he pushed it hard against mine. This was what fun little birthday parties did to him. "Don't do that. I'm fine."

"It's okay," I said to Maria. "He just needs to warm up."

"Well, let me know if I can do anything to help." She crossed over to the other women, who greeted her with quips and smiles.

I thought about how much I didn't want to go over and talk to those mothers who knew and liked one another much more than they knew or liked me. It made me feel less impatient with Noah. He was in exactly the same place I was.

I hugged him against my side. "You and I can just hang out together for a little while," I said. "You hungry?"

"A little. Is there anything here I can eat?"

I moved us closer to the table and pretended to be so busy

scanning its contents and describing them to my son that I couldn't possibly make eye contact with anyone standing around it. "There are grapes. And some chips. That's about it." There was tons of other food, of course—mini bagels, and pita bread, and crunchy Chinese noodle things—but Noah couldn't eat any of that.

"I'm okay," he said.

We stood there for a while, watching everyone else have fun. I checked my watch a few times and wondered at what point we could leave without seeming too rude. Maybe I could say I had a headache? Or that Noah did?

From far away inside the house a doorbell rang, and Maria ran inside.

A moment later she reappeared at the back door. "Look, everyone!" she called loudly, and the kids and mothers all turned. "It's Coach Andrew! He's here to play some games!"

Sure enough, there was Andrew Fulton, wearing sweat-pants, a whistle, and, I realized—with a sense of pride that was totally out of proportion to what was inspiring it—the baseball cap we had given him. He was also carrying an enormous mesh bag of balls and had a bunch of plastic cones and rubber baseball plates under his arm.

The boys *and* the mothers whooped and cheered.

"Look, Mom!" Noah said, tugging on my arm excitedly. "It's Coach Andrew! Did you know he was coming?"

"I had no idea."

"I'm going to go see what he's doing. Want to come?"

"You go ahead. I'll be right here."

"Okay." He trotted over to the knot of boys around the coach but hesitated at the edge of the group, eyeing with a certain amount of apprehension and uncertainty the taller boys who stood between him and the coach.

Andrew spotted him. "Noah!" he called out. "My assistant! Come over here, man. I need your help getting organized. I was hoping you'd be here!"

The boys shifted aside to let Noah through, watching with envy as the coach high-fived him enthusiastically.

Andrew set the kids to work making the goals and marking the field. He kept leaning down to "consult" with Noah, who stayed close by his side.

Maria tapped me on the shoulder. "Come join us," she said, pulling me toward the mothers who were grouped around the snack table. "Noah's fine."

"I didn't know Coach Andrew was coming."

"Isn't he the best?" She appealed to all the other moms. "Who here thinks Coach Andrew is just the *best*?"

"Is he as good-looking as I think he is, or is it just that he's the only male in the lower school?" asked one of the moms, who looked vaguely familiar but whose name I didn't know. Actually, they all looked vaguely familiar and I didn't know any of their names.

"He's not the only male," another one said. "There's the assistant teacher in third grade and the science teacher."

"They're both gay," Maria said.

"Are they?"

"Oh, who knows? Odds are good, right? They're certainly not like *him*." We all watched Andrew a little while longer. "Anyone want a glass of wine?" Maria said. "Now that the kids are distracted?"

A couple of the women said yes, and Maria took them inside. That left me at the table with a bunch of women I didn't know. I felt tense and wary.

"You're Rickie, right?" one woman said. She was on the younger side for a Fenwick mom—still at least a decade older than me, of course, but not much more than that. She was wearing jeans and a cardigan sweater and had her brown hair pulled back in a sloppy ponytail. I liked that she wasn't all Stepfordy. "You're Noah's mother?" I nodded, and she said, "And Melanie's sister? I have a daughter in Nicole's class, too. They're such a nice family."

That I could agree with. And did.

"My son's Joshua." She pointed to a smallish boy standing by second base, gazing dreamily down at the grass. "That guy. The one who would rather be picking clover than actually catching a ball. And there he goes." Sure enough, the kid squatted down and plucked at the grass, oblivious to the shouting and racing going on around him. We all laughed.

"Did you ever resolve that bullying thing with those other boys?" another woman said to her. She had copper red hair—obviously dyed, but it looked good on her. Made me want to try dyeing mine that color.

"I wouldn't say we *resolved* it. Things are moderately better." She turned to me. "Joshua was getting picked on by some of the boys in the class, and I didn't feel like Ms. Hayashi was staying on top of it."

"Noah's been dealing with the same problem," I said. "I mean, I assume it's the same problem. Caleb and his crew?" Joshua's mom nodded ruefully. "They gave him something to eat that made him sick—he has this disease so he can't eat wheat—and laughed when he threw up."

"Oh, my god," Joshua's mother said. "That's horrible. What did you do?"

"Nothing. I thought about talking to Dr. Wilson about it, but…" I shrugged and a third mother in the group snorted. She was wearing a huge sunhat and sunglasses, and her skin was white with a layer of sunscreen that hadn't been rubbed in all the way.

"Not worth the bother, right?" she said. "He'd tell you he'd take care of it and nothing would change."

Joshua's mother said, "We've all been down that road."

I nodded. "Yeah, I went to see him about something else and that's pretty much what I got."

"Sometimes I think he was hired just to sit in that office nodding and smiling and making us feel listened to," said Joshua's mother. "But he's not actually hearing a word."

"And for this we pay twenty-four thousand dollars a year," said the sunhat mom.

The sum shocked me. Since my parents took care of the tuition, I just passed the bills on to them without even opening the envelope. I didn't want to know how much it cost.

"It's a good education," Joshua's mother said with more hope than conviction. "And the high school is supposed to be amazing. If Joshua survives until then."

"Hey, whatever happened with that playdate?" the redhead asked her. "When Hayashi told you to invite Caleb over, see if the boys could connect?"

"Oh, that. It never even happened. Joshua hated the idea, of course, but I was willing to give it a try—at our house, though, so I could supervise and make sure Caleb didn't actually murder him or saw off his arm or anything. Anyway, I called up Caleb's mother and asked if he could come over to our house, and there's like this pause and then she says, 'Oh, his schedule's so busy, we don't really do playdates.'"

The redhead raised brown eyebrows. "But he's always going home with other kids."

"Believe me, I've noticed."

"You're not rich enough for them," the sunhat mother said. "All his friends are rich or famous or both."

There was some general agreement about that, and then the

baseball game started and we all turned to watch, laughing at the boys' attempts to look like professional baseball players by sticking out their tiny butts and raising their bats high when hitting. Andrew was pitching, and you could see him adjust his pitch for each kid: slow and easy for the smaller, less athletic ones, harder and faster for the stronger guys. I wondered if there was a pitch in the world slow and soft enough for Noah.

Maria and the other two moms returned with their glasses of wine, and for a while I felt almost relaxed.

And then Noah came up to bat. Up until then, he'd been either on the bench or in the outfield, and none of the boys hit the ball far enough for an outfielder to have to do anything but stand there with a mitt looking interested. But when he came up to home plate, I felt a familiar sick feeling. He was so small...and so weak...he could barely lift the bat...and he looked swamped by the helmet...and nervous and uncertain. Could he even hit a ball with a bat?

As I watched, Coach Andrew approached him and moved his arms and legs a little to put him into more of a hitter's stance. He got behind Noah and put his arms around him to show him how to lift the bat, then did a couple of slow, practice swings with him. Then he clapped him reassuringly on the shoulder and walked back to the plate that subbed for the pitcher's mound.

"Ready?" he called to Noah.

Noah nodded. But the bat was already sagging in his weak grip.

"Lift the bat a little," Andrew said. "Good job." He leaned forward and very gently and carefully threw the ball right at Noah's bat. It touched it and fell straight down, because Noah hadn't swung at all.

There was a general call of "Foul," and the boy who was

the catcher picked up the ball and tossed it to Andrew before resuming his crouch.

"Remember to swing this time," Andrew called to Noah. He threw again. Noah swung the bat too soon. This time the ball didn't touch the bat at all. A strike was called.

The third time wasn't that different from the second. "I think that was off the plate," Andrew lied as he neatly caught the ball the catcher threw to him. "We'll call that a ball. One more try, Noah."

He could have given him a hundred more tries: the kid wasn't going to get any lift out of the ball, not the way he was barely moving the bat. Andrew geared up to pitch—

"Oh, just let him get a hit," I heard someone murmur. It was so completely what I was thinking that it startled me. I looked over my shoulder: Joshua's mom was watching Noah as intently as I was.

Andrew pitched, Noah barely moved the bat, the kids all shouted, "Strike three, you're out," and Andrew said, "Good try, Noah. Next batter up!"

Noah handed the bat off and slumped back to the bench. I saw him sitting there, all hunched up and disappointed, and wondered why just this once a miracle couldn't have happened so he could have hit the ball right across the yard. Who would it have hurt?

The next kid hit the ball hard and sent it soaring. I wondered what it would be like to be the mother of a kid who could do that.

Still, Noah stayed in the game and I was proud of him for that. The kids played several innings, and then there were cries for some game called Fenwick Ball, which I'd never heard of and which seemed to be a sort of cross between dodgeball and soccer. They played in two even teams at first, and then it was the coach against all the kids, which delighted them no end as he called out good-natured taunts and sprinted around, trying to avoid their balls and kick his own. Even Noah was laughing and running around happily during that one, not necessarily helping his team but not noticeably hurting it either.

Then Maria sang out that it was time for cake and ushered everyone inside.

"Hey, Noey!" I said as he came running up with all the boys.

"I struck out," he informed me.

"I know, but you stayed in the game and that's what matters."

"Only to you," he said. "Did you bring cake for me?"

I groaned. "I forgot."

"Mo-om!"

"I'm so sorry, Noah. Maybe there'll be ice cream."

"Why don't you ever remember?"

"Why don't you ever remind me?"

He shot me a look and pushed past me into the house.

On the dining room table there was an enormous cake that was decorated like a baseball diamond with a bunch of plastic baseball players arranged on top. On the outfield it said, *Happy Birthday, Austin! You're the best!* in blue frosting. Everyone sang "Happy Birthday" and Austin blew out the candles. Maria sliced the cake and her housekeeper handed out the slices to the kids crammed around the table.

Noah came over to me. "There's no ice cream, Mom. There's nothing I can eat."

"Sorry. We'll get some on the way home."

The housekeeper overheard us. "He doesn't like cake?" she said to me.

"He can't eat it."

"We have Popsicles in the kitchen." She pronounced it "pope-see-cules." "He likes pope-see-cules?" I nodded and thanked her. "Come," she said to Noah. "We'll get you a pope-see-cule." He willingly trotted off with her.

I took over her job of handing out the plates. The kids all had theirs, so I offered slices to the mothers, all of whom declined, and then I spotted Coach Andrew standing in the doorway. He had been packing up his equipment when we all came inside, but he must have finished. I went over to him. "Cake?" I asked, offering him a plate.

"Am I allowed? None of the other adults are having any."

"They're Fenwick moms," I said. "They don't eat. But there's more than enough for twice this many people."

"Good, I'm starved." He took the plate from my hand. "I didn't know you were coming," he said. "I was really happy to see Noah here."

"I think it was a pity invite on Maria's part. But it's been nice." I decided to eat the slice I was still holding. I cut and speared a heavily frosted chunk. "I wanted him to hit that ball so badly."

"I know," Andrew said. "If sheer force of will could move objects, I promise you I would have willed him a home run."

"Really? If sheer force of will could move objects, I'd go for flying," I said. He laughed. "I didn't know you did birthday parties," I added.

"For parents I like. Frankly, I can use the money."

"The kids love you."

"They're used to me," he said with a shrug. "Hey, you know what else I do on the side?"

"Chippendales?"

"Thought I recognized you from somewhere," he said with

a quick grin. "Seriously, sometimes I coach kids privately—you know, to help them get ready for soccer season or T-ball or whatever."

"Cool," I said politely.

"You know, I've been thinking..." He had already wolfed down his cake and now he dropped the fork on the plate and put it on a side table next to us.

"What about?"

"About Noah. He really liked playing baseball just now—he was totally into it, just frustrated that he couldn't hit better. I think if he felt more confident about his game skills, he'd be more enthusiastic about PE and birthday parties and stuff like that."

"Uh-huh," I said cautiously.

"I'd be happy to do some private coaching with him."

"That's nice of you. But—"

"You don't have to pay me," he said quickly. "Just bake me some more of those amazing cupcakes, and we'll call it a deal."

"I thought you needed the money."

"I'd just use it to buy cupcakes," he said with a smile.

"Anyway, the money's not really the issue." The truth was, my mother would happily pay for Noah to get some extra coaching help. She wanted him to play more sports. "It's just... what's the point? The kid's never going to be an athlete."

"Don't write him off so quickly."

"Come on," I said. "*Look* at him."

Obediently, he turned and looked at him. Noah was sitting at the table licking his grape pope-see-cule, a quiet, isolated island, while all around him kids laughed and talked to each other and shoveled bites of chocolate cake into their mouths. "You never know," Andrew said, turning back to me. "Things change. Anyway, no matter what, he has a lot of years of PE ahead of him. Why not make them more fun for him by increasing his confidence?"

"Why do you want to help him so much?"

He didn't answer right away, just studied me thoughtfully for a moment. Uncomfortable under his scrutiny, I ducked my head and poked at my piece of cake with the fork. "Because," he said finally and I looked up again, "I think it would be time well spent."

I didn't even know what he meant by that, but before I could ask him, Joshua's mom had come up to us. "I know you're off the clock here, Coach," she said, "but can I ask you a school-related question?"

"Shoot," he said genially.

"Thanks. Some of the boys have been a little rough on Joshua lately and I'm just wondering how that's playing out in PE."

I slipped away while Andrew was still thinking it over, in that never-rush-into-anything way of his. I figured Joshua's mom had a right to some one-on-one time with the coach.

11.

A couple of days later, when I got back from dropping Noah off at school, I found a brand-new pair of dressy wool pants lying on my bed. I brought them downstairs to show Melanie. "Do you know where these came from?"

"I think maybe your mom got them," she said, her voice a little too casual.

"You *think maybe*?" I repeated.

"I helped her pick them out," she admitted.

"Why? I don't need pants."

She eyed the torn jeans I was wearing, which were older than Noah. "Yeah, you kind of do."

I scowled. "And I *really* don't need my mother buying clothes for me like I'm two years old."

"Right," Melanie said. "She's such a jerk—buying you nice clothing because she thinks you might like it. How dare she?"

"Shut up," I said. "You don't get it because she's not *your* mother." I shook the pants at her. "You don't even see that this is all about control."

"Really, Rickie?" Melanie said, eyebrows raised. "Control?"

"You don't get it," I said again and, grimly clutching the pants, went in search of my mother.

She was drinking coffee in the kitchen. Eleanor Roosevelt was curled up against her leg, and, as I walked in, I saw Mom tear off a piece of her bagel and toss it to the dog, who gulped it down happily and then stared at her hungrily, waiting for more.

"You shouldn't do that," I said sharply. "You're just teaching her to beg."

Mom started at the sound of my voice and then laughed sheepishly. "You caught me."

"That's why she bugs us during dinner, you know."

"I know. I'll try to stop."

There was silence while I poured myself a cup of coffee and Mom went back to reading the newspaper. My parents were probably the only people left in the greater LA area who still got the newspaper delivered instead of reading it online. "So I got the pants," I said abruptly. "The brown ones you left on my bed."

"Do you like them?"

"No," I said.

She frowned. "No, thank you?"

"Even if I liked them, I wouldn't like them."

"Meaning?"

"I don't need you to buy clothes for me. I'm sick of you treating me like a little kid."

She leaned back in her chair. "I'll stop treating you like a little kid when you stop acting like one."

"Meaning?"

"Grow up, get a job, dress like an adult, stop piercing and dyeing and tattooing yourself—"

"I haven't gotten a piercing or a tattoo in over a year and a half. And I haven't dyed my hair in ages."

"You haven't tried to clean it up, either." She took a sip of coffee, then put the mug down with a definite clack. "Anyway, I'd like a little more from you than just not getting yourself mutilated on a regular basis."

"Are you talking about money?" I said, my voice high and strained and, even to my own ears, whiny and childish. I hated the way I sounded and I blamed her for making me sound like that. "Is that what this is about?"

"Let me make one thing perfectly clear," my mother said. "It is *never* about money. I just want to see you doing something with your life. I don't care what it is: finish up college, get an internship, write a screenplay, whatever. Just find something you love and start doing it."

"And dress the way you want me to. You forgot that one."

She heaved an overly dramatic sigh. "Grow up, Rickie."

"We'll move out, if that's what you want," I said. "I'll send Noah to public school and get a menial job of some sort and we'll live in an apartment somewhere. Would that make you happy?"

"No," she said calmly. "Would it make *you* happy?"

I raised my chin defiantly. "Maybe."

"I want Noah to have a good life and a good education," she said. "The way things are now, I don't think you're capable of providing him with either without our help."

That hurt. I knew I wasn't doing much with my life, but I thought I was a pretty good mom to Noah. There was a pause. I didn't want to say anything because I didn't want her to hear my voice break and I wasn't sure I could control it.

She pushed back her chair and got to her feet. "Rickie," she said gently and started to put her arms around me. I flinched and ducked away from her touch. Then I left the room.

I left the pants in a heap on her bed and neither of us mentioned them again.

When I checked my e-mails later that day, I had a short one from my friend Monica, who had finished law school the year before and now lived in Manhattan, where she worked about a hundred hours a week and devoted whatever free time she had left to doing pro bono work for various civil liberties groups.

She and I had run our high school newspaper together, co-editors-in-chief. When I got into Berkeley, she was a little jealous because she didn't. She went instead to a small private school on the East Coast where she totally kicked ass, which is how she ended up at NYU Law School, where she also totally kicked ass.

In retrospect, Berkeley probably should have bet on her, not me.

I also had an e-mail from Coach Andrew. It was short. "I can come on Sunday from 9 to 11 to work with Noah on some skills. If I don't hear from you, I'll assume the time works for you and that the directory address is correct. Don't forget the cupcakes." It was signed "Andrew."

My finger gently danced on the touchpad, positioning the cursor over the Reply button, but I didn't click it.

Having the school coach come to our house because my kid was a loser was awkward. Paying him in cupcakes instead of money was awkward. Insisting on giving him money when he had already refused it was awkward.

But telling him *not* to come seemed like the most awkward thing of all.

I closed his e-mail without replying.

Ryan called me on my cell that night, right after I'd put Noah to bed.

"So what are you up to right now?" He sounded a little drunk. Not the first time he'd called me in that condition.

"Nothing."

"Then come over. I'll be leaving town again before you know it. We have to get in some quality family time while we can."

"This counts as family time?"

"Sure," he said. "We're strengthening the in-law bonds."

"We're not going to be in-laws much longer."

"We'll always have a niece and nephew in common, right?"

"How old are they?" I asked suddenly.

"What?"

"How old are Nicole and Cameron?"

"Why?"

"I was just wondering if you knew."

"Nicole's older, right?"

"Never mind," I said. "I'll be there in an hour."

"I get the sense you're mad at me," Ryan said later that evening.

"And that explains my driving all the way here to see you... how?"

"Seriously. You seem weird tonight."

"Do I?" I thought for a moment. We were both on his bed, watching *SNL*. We'd already had wine and sex. In that order. And then more wine. "I don't know. I guess sometimes it strikes me that this is a little...you know...pointless."

He shifted his body a few inches away from me. "This isn't going to be one of those talks, is it? About how I can't commit?"

"Have I *ever* said anything like that?"

"No," he said, relenting. "I'm sorry. Guess I'm thinking of someone else." He flashed a brief grin. "A couple of someone elses, actually."

I studied his face for a moment. "Do you ever think that maybe you guys got a little screwed up about fidelity and commitment?" I asked. "You and Gabriel?"

"It *is* one of those talks!" he said accusingly.

"No, really. I'm just thinking out loud. I don't have a problem with your total lack of commitment. I kind of like it. And at least you're consistent. Unlike your brother. He tried settling down and look where that led."

"Are we back to talking about that?"

I slid off of the bed. "We're not talking about anything. And I have to go."

"Don't forget I leave in December," he said to my back as I pulled on my clothes. "We don't have a lot of time."

"Call me."

So I was thinking about all that stuff when I got home: about Ryan and Gabriel and whether their parents had somehow screwed up their attitudes toward women and relationships, and then I was thinking about myself and how, when I was eighteen years old, I thought it would be great to be all settled down with a kid and a lifetime partner but now that I was in my mid-twenties and my friends were all searching for permanency, I was deliberately having sex with the one guy who I could be sure would never want a serious relationship. Which made me wonder if I was living my life backwards, becoming less and less mature, an emotional Benjamin Button.

Anyway, I was musing about all that as I came into the house and was absently heading toward the stairs when I heard voices in the kitchen so I changed direction. I peeked in. Dad was sitting at the kitchen table in his bathrobe, his face settled into tired but peaceful lines. Noah sat across from him, sipping a glass of milk. He was wearing an old pair of pajamas that were like a size four or something. He was so thin and the elastic was so shot that he could still get into them, but they were comically tight and short on him.

Noah was telling Dad about Austin's birthday party. "I wasn't very good at the baseball part," he was saying as I came within earshot, "but I totally ruled at Fenwick Ball." That was a definite exaggeration—I don't think he landed a single shot at Fenwick Ball—but I was happy to hear Noah sound even the slightest bit proud of his athletic ability, so I said, "He did great," as I entered the room.

"Where were you?" Noah whipped around. "I woke up and you weren't there."

"Sorry. I went out. But I told Aunt Mel to listen for you if you woke up."

"I was up anyway," my father said. "I heard him calling for you."

"You should have told me you were going out." Noah had been perfectly happy alone with my dad a second earlier, but now he was working up some tears. "I woke up and you weren't there and I was so scared."

"Noah, there were three other adults in the house with you. There's nothing to be scared of. You know that."

"You should have told me you were going out."

"I didn't know I was going until after you were already asleep."

"Then you should have woken me up. I was scared."

He drove me crazy when he got into these never-ending circles of complaints. I was too tired to argue him out of his misery, so I said sharply, "Look, Noah, you're *fine*. You were sitting here having a perfectly nice time with Grandpa, so don't give me a hard time about this. Just go back to bed, okay?"

"You're mean," he said as he got down from his chair. "And I'm sleeping in your bed and you better not move me!" He left the room.

There was a brief pause. Then "Kids," my father said genially.

"Was he really upset when he couldn't find me?"

"Not that I noticed. I heard him calling and brought him down here and got him some milk. We had a nice chat."

"I wish he'd sleep through the night."

"That would be nice," Dad agreed. "He gives you a run for your money, doesn't he?"

"You have no idea."

"But that's how it is with kids," he said, sounding a little like he was reciting something he'd been taught to say. "They make life complicated. But what would we do without them?"

I leaned against the counter and regarded him. "Do I complicate your life, Dad?"

"Only in a good way. I enjoy having you around. Always have."

"Really?" It suddenly mattered to me that this kind man who shared genetic material with me was glad I existed.

He held out his arms. "You've been a delight since the day you were born, Mel."

I went over and hugged him, although I couldn't help feeling that his praise would have meant a lot more to me if he hadn't called me by his other daughter's name.

Dad went upstairs and I was about to follow him when my eyes fell on the oven and I suddenly remembered I was supposed to bake cupcakes for Coach Andrew.

It was late and I was exhausted. I thought about putting off the baking until the morning, but that would mean I'd have to wake up early, which sounded even worse than staying up a little while longer. I decided to compromise: bake them now, frost them in the morning. Even if I overslept, I could finish them up while Andrew was playing with Noah.

It took me a few minutes of searching through the pantry before I remembered that I was out of gluten-free mixes. I had used up the last box the week before. I cursed myself for forgetting to pick up some more.

Baking from scratch sounded like way too much work at that hour, so I used one of Mom's regular mixes. I mixed the batter by hand so I wouldn't wake anyone up with the Kitchen-Aid, and by the time I had filled the cupcake liners and put the pans in the oven, I was pretty wiped out. I went into the family room and watched TV, fighting my eyelids, which kept trying to close, until the cupcakes were done. Then I pulled out the pans and just left them on the stove to cool. I'd deal with them in the morning.

I saw Eleanor Roosevelt sniffing at that end of the room and hissed at her, "Don't even think of it!" Then I finally, finally dragged myself up the stairs and did a quick and cursory face-wash and tooth-brush before collapsing onto my bed, where Noah was sprawled across the whole mattress. I shoved him to the side and fell asleep within seconds of lying down.

12.

I was still asleep when Noah ran into my room and shook my arm. "Mom! Mom!"

I burrowed my forehead deeper into the pillow and tried to ignore him.

He just shook me harder. "Coach Andrew is here! At our house! He said he's here to play with me and that *you knew about it*!"

That got my attention. I sat up. "Oh, my god! What time is it?"

"Why didn't you tell me he was coming?"

"I forgot." I was only sort of lying: I hadn't told Noah ahead of time because I wasn't sure how he was going to react and didn't want him to have time to decide he didn't like the idea or to get nervous about how he'd do. I had planned to tell him that morning, before Andrew came—but apparently I'd overslept.

I jumped out of bed and looked down to see if I was decent. I had slept in sweatpants, so that was fine. I grabbed the sweater I had been wearing the night before and threw it over my tank top to hide the fact that I wasn't wearing a bra. I shoved my feet into a pair of old Crocs that technically belonged to my mother, who used them for gardening, but that I stole from her whenever mine went missing—which happened a lot.

I took a deep breath and turned to Noah. "Okay, I'm ready. Where is he?"

"I don't know. Outside somewhere. Come on, Mom! Hurry, before he leaves!"

"You mean you didn't let him inside?" I ran toward the doorway and he followed close behind.

"You always say I'm not allowed to let anyone in unless an adult is around."

"I know, but—" I cut myself off. He was right. "Where are Grandpa and Grandma?"

"They went out somewhere. Aunt Mel too."

"Shoot." I raced down the stairs and over to the front door, which Noah had carefully closed, leaving Coach Andrew stranded on the porch. Eleanor Roosevelt was standing sentinel in front of the door, barking at odd intervals, clearly trying to figure out why this person wasn't either coming in or going away.

I kneed her aside and flung the door open. Andrew looked at me quizzically. "I'm sorry," I said. "I overslept."

"Is it too early?" he asked. "Should I come back?" The guy was apparently a morning person: his eyes were bright and he was freshly shaved and he smelled all clean and showered. Unlike me. I probably still had sand in my eyes.

I stepped back to let him in. "No, no, it's fine. I should have set my alarm. I was up kind of late."

"Doing something fun, I hope." He came inside, his big net bag of balls and cones and stuff slung over his shoulder Santa-style.

"Baking cupcakes, actually."

He winced. "Oh, man, I was just joking about those! You didn't really need to make them. And you *really* didn't need to stay up late to make them."

"Well, I did. So what's the plan? Baseball first? Football? Curling?"

"Maybe we should start by getting Noah dressed to go outside?"

That was when I realized that Noah was still in those embarrassingly too-small pajamas. I'd been in such a rush I hadn't even noticed. "Run upstairs, Noah, and put on some sweatpants and a T-shirt—and a sweatshirt too. It looks cold out."

"It's beautiful," Andrew said. "Gracie and I went running this morning up in the hills. It's one of those perfect days."

"Too bad we get so few of those here in LA," I said. "Only about every twenty-four hours or so. You guys go running together a lot?"

"As often as we can. I can barely keep up with her, though."

I realized Noah was still hovering and pointed up the stairs. "Come on, Noah—go get changed."

Noah ignored me and said in a trembling voice to Andrew, "Why are you here to play with me? Is it because I'm such a loser at sports? Did Dr. Wilson say you had to do this or he'd kick me out of school?"

Andrew put his net bag down on the floor then squatted down so he could look Noah right in the eyes. "Of course not," he said firmly. "This is totally my idea. I just thought we'd have fun playing some games together and then you'd have some new skills to show off in PE. What do you think?"

"I don't know," Noah said. "I'm not sure I want to do this."

"Tell you what." Andrew gave him a friendly arm pat as he rose to his feet. "You go up and get changed and then we'll head outside and throw the ball around and play some games—whatever sounds like fun to you. If it's the most miserable experience of your life, tell your mom and she'll let me know I shouldn't come again." He gave me a slightly evil grin. "Knowing *her*, she'll be happy to tell me I failed." He returned his attention to Noah. "But if it's kind of sort of a little bit fun, then maybe we'll keep doing it. Does that sound fair to you?"

Noah nodded slowly. "Only I'll tell you if I don't like it, not Mom. She never listens to anything I say."

"Noah!" I protested.

Andrew laughed. "Women are like that, Noah. Get used to it."

"Just go get dressed, will you?" I said. Noah finally turned and headed up the stairs, slowly dragging his feet to let us know he still wasn't sure about this whole thing.

"So…" Andrew said after we'd watched Noah disappear and the silence was starting to grow awkward. "How's your weekend going? You have fun at that party last weekend?"

"Yeah, actually. There were some nice moms there."

He nodded. "It was a good group."

"Maria Dellaventura kind of fascinates me. When I first met her, I thought she was a total Stepford Wife. But she's nicer and more interesting than she looks."

"There are a lot of moms like that at Fenwick. You look at them and think they're everything that's wrong with the Westside of LA—and then you talk to them and they're actually incredibly nice. Of course, there *are* a few—" He stopped then said, "Wish we teachers were allowed to vote one or two off the island, if you know what I mean."

"Good thing for me you can't. I'd probably make the list."

"Nah. Maybe a few weeks ago. Not now."

I felt oddly pleased. And a little hurt. "So who *would* you vote off?"

He shook his head. "No way I'm telling. Not without being drunk. And Dr. Wilson would have to be in another country. He's like a dolphin—he can hear everything, even from miles away."

"Do dolphins have good hearing?"

"I think so. I saw a special about it once. On PBS."

"How very educational of you," I said.

Noah came clattering back down the stairs. "I guess I'm ready," he said. He was wearing sweatpants that Cameron had outgrown and handed down to Noah, even though Noah was older. He was also still wearing his pajama top and had forgotten all about a sweatshirt. No wonder it hadn't taken him long to get dressed. I decided I didn't care enough about the sweatshirt to make an issue of it. He might get cold, but it was Southern California. He'd live.

"All right, then," Andrew said, hoisting his bag of equipment back up on his shoulder. "Let's check out this so-called backyard of yours."

I glanced out the window every now and then to see how it was going. They looked like they were having fun. Andrew pitched balls to Noah, who would either catch them or hit them with a bat—the game varied from time to time. Every once in a while he would hurl himself at Andrew, who would grab him and spin him around. You could hear Noah's shrieks of laughter even through the closed window.

Melanie and Mom came home while they were still outside. "What's going on out there?" Mom asked, looking out the kitchen window. "Who's that guy?"

I had finished frosting the cupcakes and was passing the time instant-messaging a couple of friends on my laptop. I wrote a quick "gtg" to them both, closed the computer, and explained how Andrew had come to be at our house. "It was his idea. But Noah may refuse to let him come again."

"I think you should insist on it," Mom said. "This is just what he needs. And I'm happy to pay for it." Her enthusiasm made me wonder how awful an athlete she thought Noah was.

I said, "Actually, Andrew's not charging us for this. He said just to bake him cupcakes."

She frowned. "That's not right. He should be paid for his services."

"He said he didn't want us to pay him."

"I'll talk to him."

"No, don't," I said. "Stay out of it."

She briefly pressed her lips together, annoyed. "You should have insisted on it right from the start."

"I did," I said. "That's what you don't understand. I *did* insist and he said no. So get off my back about it, okay? He's a grown man. No one's making him do this."

My mother made an irritable noise and left the room.

Melanie was looking at me.

"What?" I growled.

"Can't you be a little more patient with her?"

"Oh, for god's sake!" I said and reopened my laptop to let her know that the discussion was over.

The boys came in a few minutes later, and I stood up to greet them. "You all done?"

"Water break," Andrew said. "But we probably won't go on too much longer."

"I'm *really* tired," Noah said. But he looked happy.

"Anyone want a cupcake?" I asked. "They're all frosted now."

"Those look great," Andrew said. He and Noah each grabbed one.

Melanie had left the kitchen earlier, but now she came

running back in to greet Andrew. She welcomed him with an enthusiastic hug.

I wondered if that's what mothers were supposed to do: give the PE coach a hug when they saw him away from school. That seemed weird to me. I tried to imagine giving Andrew a casual hug and the thought made me squirm. "I wish Nicole and Cameron were here to see you," Mel told him. "They'd be so excited."

"You should have them come next time," he said. "I could use more kids."

"Really? It wouldn't be more work for you?"

"It would be great—we could play a lot more games." He carefully peeled the paper liner off the cupcake. "Actually," he said to me, "I meant to tell you to invite some of Noah's friends to join us, for just that reason."

I checked to make sure Noah wasn't listening. He had wandered over to the corner of the room, where he was idly leaning against Eleanor Roosevelt's broad back while eating his cupcake. "Don't hold your breath," I said in a low voice to Andrew. "We're not so strong in the friends department."

He considered that for a moment, then said, "I noticed he was really hitting it off with Joshua at Austin's party. They're very similar kids."

"Right," I said. "You can tell because they get beaten up by the same bullies."

"Stop that. No one's getting beaten up at our school."

"I meant metaphorically."

"What's a metaphorical beating?"

"You know."

"Do I?" He bit into the cupcake. "This is good," he said through a mouthful of cake. "Even better than the other ones were."

"Can I have another one?" Noah asked, coming back over to us and handing me the paper liner from his first one.

I looked at the frosting smeared around his mouth and said, "You're covered in—" I stopped and gasped. "Oh, my god, Noah!"

"What?" He stared at me. They all stared at me.

"These aren't gluten free! I totally forgot! I had to use one of the store mixes last night. It was so late and I couldn't find a GF one . . . Did you eat that whole cupcake?"

He nodded. His lip trembled. "I'm sorry."

"It wasn't your fault. It was mine. I can't believe I did that. Oh, Noah, I'm so sorry!"

"I don't feel very well," he said in a little voice and clutched his stomach.

"And thus endeth the baseball practice," Andrew said as I reentered the kitchen fifteen minutes later. "How's he doing?"

"Much better. Lying down." I didn't feel like going into detail about how many times Noah had vomited before feeling better. I slumped into a chair at the kitchen table across from Andrew. Melanie was pouring coffee at the counter. "I suck at being a mother," I said.

Mel came over with a couple of mugs and put one down in front of each of us. "It's not your fault."

"What are you talking about? I baked the cupcakes and served them to him. In what possible universe would that not be my fault?"

"You didn't *mean* to do it. It was an accident."

"Yeah," I said. "Much as I've been tempted at times, I have never deliberately poisoned Noah. I only do it accidentally."

"He'll be fine." Mel poured a mug of coffee for herself and joined us at the table.

"I know. That's not the point." I turned to Andrew. "Sorry about all this. I'm guessing this wasn't exactly the way you wanted the lesson to end."

"Yeah, I prefer the kids to *sprain* something. Anyway, I think this is actually my fault. I asked you to make those cupcakes in the first place."

"You're right," I said. "It is all your fault. You've had it in for Noah from the start."

He cocked his head at me. "Just to be sure, you're joking, right? I mean, you don't still really think I'm out to get him, do you?"

"I don't know. It's not like you've ever done anything nice for him, like coach him privately or anything."

"Rickie isn't good at expressing gratitude," Melanie said to Andrew.

"That's so not true," I said. "But thanks for pointing it out. See how I did that?"

She ignored that. "Can you believe Thanksgiving is coming up so soon?" she asked, cradling her mug in both hands. "Do you have any special plans, Andrew? Are you going away?"

He shook his head. "Normally I go home, but my parents decided to visit my sister this year. She moved to Canada and had a baby."

"What a jerk," I said.

"Exactly. She couldn't have had a baby in LA? Plenty of people do."

I gestured to myself and Mel. "We did."

"Right. So then Gracie said I should join her and her family, but they're going on a Mexican Riviera cruise for the whole week. I don't have Monday and Tuesday off, and anyway"—he made a face—"Thanksgiving on a cruise? Doesn't that sound depressing?"

We were agreeing with him when the garage door banged open and my mother entered the kitchen with Eleanor Roosevelt. "We came back early from our walk," Mom said as she unhooked the leash. "Someone was more interested in chasing squirrels than walking nicely."

"I thought we'd cured you of that, Mom," I said.

"Very funny."

Andrew held his hand out toward the dog. "Come here, you beauty." He whistled and Eleanor Roosevelt came bounding over. He caressed her ears and scratched down her back. "You're a good girl, aren't you? Yes, you are. Yes, you are."

"She's not *that* good," I said.

"Oh, yes, she is," he crooned, tugging gently on her ears. She half-closed her eyes, totally blissed out. "Oh, yes, she is."

Melanie jumped up suddenly from her seat. "There's more coffee, Laurel. Here, I'll help you." She pulled my mother over to the counter. They started whispering. I wondered what they were conspiring about now.

"You have a dog?" I asked Andrew as Eleanor Roosevelt nudged his hand hard and then fell onto her back, inviting him to rub her tummy, which he did, although he had to lean way over in his chair to reach it.

"I wish. God, I wish. But Gracie's allergic."

"Get rid of her."

He gave a short laugh. "I would for one like this." He thumped Eleanor's chest with his hand and she wagged her tail enthusiastically in response.

"You just like her because she's pretty," I said with mock disgust.

"What are you talking about? Look at those eyes—you can tell she's profound."

"She's just a big *stomach*," I said. "With some cute fluff on the outside to make us put up with the fact that she steals our food and chews our shoes and poops all over the yard."

"Typical female."

"Excuse me," I said with great dignity. "I haven't pooped on the lawn in years. Well, months at least."

Melanie and Mom came over to the table. Melanie said, "We were wondering...Andrew, would you do our family the honor of joining us for Thanksgiving dinner?"

So that's what they were whispering about.

He sat upright. "That's so nice of you." He sounded a little uncomfortable. Eleanor Roosevelt waited for a moment on her back, then, realizing he was done patting her, righted herself and rose to her feet and looked around to see who else might pay her some attention. "I hope I didn't sound like I was hinting for an invitation."

"Not at all," Mel said. "It's just that we'd like to have you."

"We really would," my mother said. "Thanksgiving's going to be smaller this year than it's been in the past." She glanced at Melanie, who flushed.

"It's so nice of you," Andrew said again. "But I feel like I'm imposing."

"You'd be doing us a favor."

"I'm honored," he said. "And touched." He looked at me. "You're awfully quiet. What do *you* think?"

"That if you come, I want to be on your team for the football game."

He perked up at that. "You guys play football on Thanksgiving?"

"Only when the Kennedys visit."

"I'd like to see you playing football," he said. He glanced at Mom and Mel. "All of you." But he had meant me.

"I've never played in my life," I said. "But I will if you come."

"That may be an offer I can't refuse."

It must have been: a few more minutes of coaxing and he agreed to come.

13.

After Andrew left, Melanie said, "I was thinking of going to Floyd's today to get my hair cut. You want to come, Rickie?"

I was already reaching for my computer again. "Nah, I'm good."

"Really? Because your hair looks like it could use—"

I cut her off. "I know how it looks."

"Come on," she said. "Please, Rickie. Just get the color evened out and maybe a trim. I'll pay for it." She flicked at my multicolored ponytail. "Please?"

Normally I would just say no to something like that. I hated when she and Mom tried to pretty me up. But I was starting to resent my reflection in the mirror. Looking pretty didn't seem as wrong as it had a year or two ago when for some reason it had been important to me to look hard and dirty and angry and anything but maternal.

She seized on my hesitation. "Come on," she said. "I'll ask Mom to watch Noah. Maybe we can sneak in a little clothes shopping too—have a fun girly day."

"Have you *met* me?" I asked.

"Be nice to me. I hate these weekends without the kids. They're endless."

She knew how to get to me. "Fine. Let me just go tell Noah I'm leaving." I went upstairs to my parents' bedroom, where Noah was curled up on the bed watching TV. My father was lying next to him companionably, his laptop resting on his thighs. He looked up and nodded to me when I entered.

"Our patient seems to be improving," he said.

I bent down toward Noah, who immediately moved his head to the side so he could still see the TV screen. "How're you doing?" I asked.

"Fine. Can you turn the TV up?"

"The remote is right here," I said. It was lying on the bed two inches from his hand. I picked it up anyway and turned up the volume. He was watching *MythBusters*, which was one of his favorite shows. It was still TV and I probably shouldn't have let him watch it as much as I did, but I figured I should just be grateful he preferred that particular show to Disney dreck. "I'm going out, Noah. Grandma and Grandpa will be here if you need them. That okay, Dad?"

My father was peering intently at his computer screen. "Sure, fine," he said absently.

"He can watch TV the whole time if he wants."

"That's probably what he'll do, then."

As I left the room, I took one last glance back at them. They were both completely absorbed in their separate screens, their mouths slack, their eyes glazed.

The haircutter I got at Floyd's, a girl inexplicably named Harlan, had even more tattoos than I did, including one of Tinker Bell (copyright infringement and all) on her upper arm. More piercings too. I found all that reassuring. "So what are we doing?" she asked as she undid my ponytail and fluffed the hair out around my shoulders. Man, it had gotten long. It fell halfway down my back.

Melanie had followed us over to the chair without being invited. She said, "It should be prettier and softer. And she needs the color evened out."

"Excuse my mother," I said to the haircutter. "She likes to butt in."

"Wow, this is your mother?" Harlan said. "You look great," she said seriously to Melanie.

I cracked up.

"I'm her sister, not her mother," Melanie said. "Shut up, Rickie."

"The point is don't listen to her," I said. "I don't want to go all soft and pretty and housewifey. Know what I mean?"

Harlan reassured me that she didn't do "housewife" cuts. "I like a little edge myself." She flicked at the ends of my hair. "How short do you want to go?"

"What do you suggest?" Mel asked.

"Well, she's pretty small." Harlan took a step back to get a good look at me from the side. "And she's got good bone structure."

"Thank you."

She nodded, circling around me. "You could actually go short, if you wanted to. Really short. Like cropped short."

Melanie immediately shook her head. "Just a nice shoulder-length layered cut is what I was thinking."

"That would be great," I said. "And then I could dye my hair honey blond, and look like every other mother at Fenwick."

"Don't go blond," said Harlan, who apparently didn't recognize sarcasm. "Too much maintenance with your base color. Actually, if you go short you won't have to re-dye your hair at all—unless you want to just for fun."

"Don't cut it short," Melanie said.

I grinned wickedly at her reflection in the mirror, and I saw her eyes widen with the realization that she had just said the one thing that was likely to make me cut all my hair off.

I kept running my hand over the top of my head afterwards, trying to get used to the way it felt. Harlan had used some kind of pomade to rough up the hair and make it look piecey. It felt rough and foreign to my fingertips and my head felt way too light.

Melanie had gotten her usual prettily layered cut and had her hair blown dry. She joined me at the cash register and, without even asking, rubbed her fingertips up the nape of my neck.

"Well?" I said as she handed them her charge card.

"It suits you," she admitted reluctantly. "I wouldn't do it in a million years, but your features are so delicate. It's better than I thought it would be."

"I think you look fantastic," said the cashier. "Like a young Winona Ryder—you know, back before she got sticky fingers."

"I think it's very Natalie Portman," said a male haircutter who was coming up with a client and pay slip. "Not everyone can pull that off but you're rocking it, honey."

"No one said anything nice about *my* haircut," Melanie complained as we walked out.

"What were they going to say? 'You look like you did when you came in, only with slightly shorter hair'?"

She checked out her reflection in the window as we walked past the shop toward our car. "Next to you, I always feel like a boring old drudge."

"What are you talking about, nutball? You're beautiful."

"I look exactly like the kind of dull housewife you're always so terrified of becoming." She sighed. "You should be grateful to me, Rickie, because no matter what, you'll always be cooler than me, even when we're both old and living in some assisted-living home together."

"I'm going to get a lot more piercings when I'm old," I said. "My skin will be all loose by then, so it'll be easy to find extra folds to pierce."

"That's the most disgusting thing I've ever heard."

"Oh, I think I could top it. Shall I try?"

"God, no." She took my arm and steered me toward the car. "We're going to the Promenade and I am going to make you buy a whole new wardrobe to go with this haircut. It's one thing to slob around in old jeans when you're wearing a pony-tail, but now you *have* to be chic."

"It's just a haircut," I said.

"No. It's a whole new look."

At H&M and then Urban Outfitters, Melanie pulled out tons of clothes for me to try on, and in the dressing-room mirror, wearing tight new jeans and even tighter sweaters, my eyes bigger with no hair hiding them, my cheekbones suddenly prominent in a way they hadn't been before, I actually *did* see someone who had a "look," not just a kid hiding behind weird hair and loose clothing, but a woman who might draw a second glance from someone passing by.

I came out of my cubicle to consult Melanie about an outfit.

She stared at me. "You really do look great, Rickie. You were right to get that cut."

"I only did it to annoy you."

"I know. That's why it's so maddening you look so great. I hate you."

"What about these?" I plucked at the pants and top I had on.

"Fabulous. Get them both. I'm paying."

"You don't need to pay for my clothes."

"I know. But since you're not earning any money, anything you spend comes from Dad and Laurel. And anything I spend still comes from Gabriel. I figure he owes me. Whereas I owe Dad and Laurel for taking me in. You see what I mean?"

"Not really. Whatever." But as I went into the dressing room to take off the clothes, I felt vaguely uncomfortable with Melanie's saying "anything you spend comes from Dad and Laurel." She was right, of course: I had no money of my own, just a charge card that was billed to my mother. It was slightly shameful and I was slightly ashamed.

Mom, Dad, and Noah were all in the kitchen when we got back. Dad was eating a sandwich even though it was the middle of the afternoon, and Noah was nibbling on a piece of GF toast. Mom was mixing something at the counter.

"Hey!" Noah said when we came in and dropped the bags we were carrying on the floor. "I don't feel sick any—" He stopped mid-word. He stared, his mouth open and noticeably filled with half-chewed bread. "Mom?"

"Ta-da," Melanie said.

My mother turned. Her eyes widened. "Oh, my god," she said, coming closer. She tapped my father on the shoulder. "Look at Rickie."

He looked up from the journal he was reading. It had crumbs and bits of tuna all over the pages. "What?" He squinted at me. "Something's different."

"Of course something's different," Mom said impatiently. "She cut all her hair off. All of it."

"There's a *little* left," Noah said.

My father said, "Lovely, Rickie. You look like Audrey Hepburn."

"You think? The woman at the barbershop said I looked like Winona Ryder."

He shrugged. "I don't know her. But you're pretty the way Audrey Hepburn was pretty—those big eyes and long neck and all."

"Did you have to cut it *all* off?" my mother asked. I shifted under her gaze. How many times had she studied me like that? How many times had she sighed and then turned away, her disappointment plain to see? Sure enough, she sighed and moved back toward the counter. "At least all that awful color is gone," she muttered.

"I'm thinking about putting in some streaks." I hadn't been until that moment. I mean, there was a period when I was doing crazy stuff to my hair but I'd stopped a while ago and didn't really want to do it again.

"Don't," she said.

Which of course instantly made me want to paint my hair all sorts of bright colors and make myself look like something out of a punk rocker's wet dream.

Maybe I was getting older, though, because as soon as I had that thought I also thought, *But then I'll look like an idiot.*

At some point I had to stop doing things to annoy my mother.

No, wait—I had to stop doing things to annoy my mother that I didn't *want* to do. No reason to stop doing the ones I enjoyed.

"What do you think, Noey?" I asked, turning to him.

"You don't look like you," he said thoughtfully. "But you look kind of cool."

"I like that," I said. "I like looking cool."

"We got lots of new clothes for her too," Melanie said.

"Oh, thank god," said my mother. I glared at her, but she either didn't notice or didn't care.

Melanie and I had to report back to the Event Hospitality Committee about the caterers we'd called and met with over the previous couple of weeks—or, more accurately, the caterers *she'd* called and met with and then told me about. But I figured I had done my part by listening to her go on about it all.

To my amazement, the next meeting was scheduled to take place at Marley Addison's house.

"Really?" I said to Melanie when she told me. "Really? She's never come to a single meeting but she's hosting one?"

"I can't wait to see her house, can you?" Her eyes were bright with excitement.

"Where is it?"

"On Maple Drive, one of those huge mansions with the gates that you need security clearance just to drive by." Her face fell. "Actually, Gabriel said Sherri just bought a house on that same street. A smaller one—she's not as successful as Marley."

"Not as talented, either."

"I hope this is the last steady job she gets," Melanie said with a viciousness I'd never seen from her before. "I hope her house goes into foreclosure."

"I hope she gets an STD and it goes into her brain and she dies," I said.

She touched my arm. "You're a good sister."

"I know."

We didn't actually need security clearance to drive down Marley's street, but we did get stopped at the gate, where a guard asked to see Melanie's driver's license. Funny how nervous that kind of thing can make you—both of us were tense and silent as we drove up the long driveway to a huge flat parking pad where a few other familiar cars were already parked. The house wasn't as enormous as I expected, but the landscaping was stunning.

"This is so exciting!" Mel said, clutching my arm as we walked up to the front door.

"Really?" I said. "Just because she's a celebrity? So is Sherri, you know, and she's a jerk."

"I don't care. I'm still excited about being in Marley Addison's house."

"Yeah, me too."

A beautiful young woman with perfect hair wearing linen pants and a silk tank top answered the door and for a moment I actually thought it was Marley herself—she had the same fair coloring and long layered haircut and even similar features—but then she held out her hand and said, "Hi, I'm Cori, Marley's assistant. Come on in!" I wondered if Marley had hired her because they looked so much alike, or whether it was some kind of creepy stalker thing where Cori was transforming herself over time into looking more and more like her boss and would one day kill her and take her place and no one would even notice except for Marley's kid, who would tell people "That's not really my mother!" and no one would believe him.

Or maybe it was just a coincidence.

Cori led us down a huge hallway lined with paintings. "Marley's been stuck in a meeting all morning and still isn't back. She said you should all go ahead and enjoy the snacks and get started and she'll get here as soon as she possibly can."

Gee, what a shocker. The A-list movie star hadn't cleared her schedule for the Event Hospitality Committee after all.

Tanya and Carol Lynn and Maria were already in the living room.

"Wow," Melanie said as we entered. And wow it was. All of the houses that we'd had meetings in had been nicely decorated. But this room was *perfect*: someone with an impeccable eye for color and design had put together that bright pink ottoman and dark green chair because they shouldn't have gone together but they did, in some profound and soul-delighting way. The whole room was like that. In a million years, I couldn't have mixed the fabrics, colors, and styles the way they were mixed, and knowing that I would never have the guts or knowledge to decorate like that made me feel strangely sad, like a door was shut to me that would never open no matter how long or hard I knocked at it. This was how famous and powerful people lived, the ones who were richer than 99.9 percent of the world, and normal folk like us, who were merely richer than 99.6 percent of the world, could only envy them.

Maria was hovering over a sideboard covered with platters of food and dominated by a large silver coffee urn. "I can't get over this spread."

"I'm so glad you like it!" Cori said. "Marley left the choice up to me and I just love Clementine's pastries, so that's what I got. Is there anything else I can get you ladies?"

"We're great, thank you," Tanya said. She was already seated and, as usual, peering at her BlackBerry screen like it held the secrets of the universe. "We really appreciate this."

"It's our pleasure," Cori said. "Go ahead and start your meeting—Marley will be here soon. And don't hesitate to give a shout if you need anything. I won't be far." She gave a little wave and left the room.

"Oh, my god!" The exclamation came from Maria, who

had just turned around, plate in hand, and was staring at me. "You cut your hair! I thought it was just pulled back at first. But you chopped it all off!"

Now everyone was looking at me.

"Oh, my god, that takes courage," said Carol Lynn from the sofa where she'd been scrolling through some application on her iPhone. "I mean, it's *adorable*, but..." She gulped theatrically.

"You should wear more makeup now," Maria said, squinting at me thoughtfully. "Outline your eyes, make them really stand out. That would totally work with this. And you're still young enough to use color on your eyelids."

"She looks great," Tanya said with an air of summation, clearly more interested in the conversation's ending than in the haircut. "Let's start the meeting."

Melanie settled in the other armchair. I stayed on my feet to study the food options. There were a lot of them.

"So how was the fifth-grade campout?" Maria asked Tanya as she sat down on the sofa next to Carol Lynn.

"Wonderful."

"Really? I heard two boys threw up." Carol Lynn was wearing running shorts. You could literally see her thigh muscles contract every time she crossed her legs or uncrossed them—there was no fat to obscure them. "I also heard that a girl had some kind of middle-of-the-night freak-out and was screaming in her tent so loudly she woke up all the other kids."

"It was just a bad dream," Tanya said.

Carol Lynn's eyes widened. "So it's all true?"

"There are always a few hitches," Tanya said stiffly. "Overall, it was a lovely weekend."

"God, I'm glad I wasn't there," Maria murmured audibly to Carol Lynn, who laughed.

Tanya cleared her throat and shuffled some papers. "Okay, so...The good news is that I think we've figured out the napkin situation, thank you, Carol Lynn. Now for the biggie. Food. How'd you two do?" She looked at Melanie, well aware which of us was the responsible adult.

Melanie had printed up the menus that all three caterers had e-mailed us and made copies for everyone, which she now quickly passed out. "These are on recycled paper," she said.

"Good girl," said Tanya approvingly. She studied the pages, flicking each one aside after she had read it. For a few moments, the only sound in the room was the rustling of the pages—and the noises *I* made as I poured myself some coffee and heaped my plate with scones, fresh fruit, and jams. I didn't need to look at the estimates; Melanie had already made me look at them too many times as she agonized over which one we should recommend to the rest of the committee.

"Only one of them was willing to make the lamb chops for our budget," she explained now to the others once they had finished reading. "But the rest of the meal suffered for that. The others offered more variety but no lamb chops. So I'm a little torn."

"Let's go with this one." Tanya waved a page. "Crackerjack Catering. But tell them to substitute something else for the soup. I hate when they serve soup in those spoons and call it finger food. Soup is not a finger food."

"Hear, hear!" Maria said. "It's time someone stood up against that insanity." Tanya narrowed her eyes, and Maria said quickly, "I'm serious. I hate that too." Tanya returned her attention to Mel, and Maria gave me an amused *got out of that one* look behind her back. I grinned at her.

"I actually kind of liked the third menu best," Melanie said to Tanya. "From Spicy Girl Catering. I thought she was offering us more for the money and the food seemed a little more interesting and sophisticated."

Tanya shook her head. "We need to go with Crackerjack. They know the school and everyone was happy with what they did last year."

"But this could be even better," I said.

She shot me a look. "*And* the guy who owns it has a nephew at the upper school. His sister is president of the Parent Association and called me last week to make sure we were using him again."

"Why were we checking all those other caterers, then?"

"I didn't want it to look like nepotism. We had to be fair and open-minded about this."

I folded my arms across my chest. "In that case, both Mel and I think that Spicy Girl offers more for the money." I didn't really care, but I was mad she'd wasted our time. Well, Melanie's time.

"I'll take that into consideration," Tanya said flatly.

Marley never showed. Cori apologized for that as she escorted us all to the front door an hour or so later. "Marley just called to say she feels awful that she got held up and hopes you all understand. And she said to please let us know how we can help out with the event." She smiled brightly as she ushered us out the door.

As we strolled toward our cars, sluggish in the midday sunshine, Maria said to me, "I'm so glad Noah came to Austin's party. And you know who absolutely fell in love with your son?"

"Who?"

"Debbie Golden."

"Who?" I repeated, just as blankly.

"Joshua's mom."

"Oh, her! She was really nice."

"She's *great*," Maria said. "And Joshua and Noah are two peas in a pod. I'm surprised they haven't connected before now. But Debbie said Joshua's been talking about Noah ever since the party. You have to get them together."

"Well, now that I know their last name I can actually look them up in the directory," I said. "Thanks."

"And how terrific was Coach Andrew?"

"He was pretty awesome." I felt funny as I said it. Like I had some personal stake in how "terrific" Coach Andrew was. Which I didn't. Did I?

"Bye." Maria gave me and Melanie each a peck on the cheek and then walked briskly toward her car, agile despite four-inch high heels that would have slowed *me* down. She got into a large black Mercedes and drove off.

"Wait a second," I said. "Her license plate—I've seen her car before."

"Yeah, at all the other meetings," Mel said.

"No, I mean—" It hit me. "She's the one who cut me off in car pool a couple of months ago! I was so annoyed—she broke all the rules and then blocked me in."

"A lot of people have black Mercedes."

"No, it was definitely her. The car had that license plate—and now that I think about it, I can picture her driving. I just didn't know her back then, but I remember the blond hair and all." I shook my head. "It was the most piggish thing I've ever seen."

"But you like her now," Mel said.

"I guess. It's weird. I hate so many things about her but I like *her*."

"You judge people too quickly. If you hadn't grown up with

me, you'd probably hate me because I'm so wishy-washy and boring. You'd think I was pathetic and write me off."

"That's not true. I couldn't help but like you. No one can."

She shook her head. "You're loyal to everyone who's close to you, Rickie, and suspicious of everyone you don't know. I promise you, if you had never met me—"

"My life would be a tragic waste." I cut her off in such a mock-dramatic voice that she laughed and thankfully dropped the subject.

The next Sunday, when I opened the front door in answer to his knock, Andrew took a startled step back. "Holy cow," he said.

"That's a stupid swear," I said.

"When did you cut your hair?"

"Last week." I touched it self-consciously. "I know it's extreme." He studied me so intently that I had to look away. "Well?" I said when I couldn't stand it anymore.

"It suits you," he said and came in the house.

I wondered what he'd say to Gracie—she of the long, blond flowing tresses—if she showed up one day with it all cut off. Probably not "It suits you."

Nicole and Cameron were joining the coaching session. Mel had dropped them off earlier and gone on to take a yoga class in Brentwood.

Whenever I looked out the window, the three kids seemed to be having a great time playing with the coach.

At the end of the hour, Noah ran into the kitchen ahead of the others, shouting, "I totally creamed Cameron in the last game!"

"You shouldn't gloat," Nicole said as she and Cameron followed him in. She was wearing a neat ponytail and a yellow sweatsuit that fit her low in the hips and showed off her little-girl belly bulge—which I loved. "That's bad sportsmanship."

"Sorry." He whispered to me loudly, "But I totally did!"

"Who wants a cookie?" I asked diplomatically. I put out the plate of cookies I'd made while they were playing and poured some milk for them and then went out back where Andrew was tossing the last of his equipment into his net bag. "How'd it go?"

"Terrific. They're such great kids."

"Did Noah really beat Cameron at something? Because that would be a first."

The coach grinned. "There may have been a tiny bit of creative scorekeeping."

"You cheated?"

"Not exactly... It's just that Cameron is so much more athletic than Noah but he's younger and that's hard on Noah. He was beating him at everything." He gave me a sly look. "So I may have engineered things a bit on the last game to make sure Noah would end on a high note."

"You seemed so honest."

"It's all an act." He slung the bag over his shoulder, and we walked back into the house.

Mom was in the kitchen. She was removing the plate of cookies from the table, over the kids' protests. "It's too close to lunchtime," she said. "You can have more after you've eaten a healthful lunch."

Cameron appealed to me. "I only had *one* so far, Rickie. Everyone else had two."

"You can have another one." I took the plate from my mother and let Cameron pick out a cookie. Mom made an annoyed sound, which I ignored. I offered the plate to Andrew.

He dropped the bag of balls on the ground so he could take a cookie. "It's okay that Noah's eating one of these, right?"

"I'd like to get annoyed at you for asking me that," I said, "but, sadly, you're kind of justified. This time, it's safe." He took a bite and then I added, "Of course they're deadly for anyone who *doesn't* have celiac disease."

He put his hand to his throat and pretended to choke. Then he stopped pretending and took another bite. "It's good," he said.

"Want something to drink?"

"I wouldn't say no to a glass of milk."

"You're such a Boy Scout."

"Would you prefer it if I asked for a shot of tequila?"

"It would certainly make things more interesting."

My mom was already getting him the glass of milk. "Let's keep it dull," she said and handed him the glass.

"Here's to no one throwing up this morning," Andrew said, raising the glass.

The kids cracked up. Nothing like a barf reference to amuse the under-ten set.

14.

It was really hot on Thanksgiving, which annoyed me since it had been cool and autumn-like just the week before. Even though I had grown up in Southern California, I had watched enough holiday specials to know that Thanksgiving Day was supposed to be brisk, Christmas Day white with snow, and New Year's Eve cold enough to freeze your ass off.

For a big city, Los Angeles was awfully reliant on another coast's holiday clichés.

On the plus side, the hot weather made it easy to get

dressed. A new tank top, a pair of jeans (also new), a couple of Havaianas flip-flops (which Melanie had given me on my last birthday), and I was done. I let Noah choose his own clothes. He ended up with shorts that were too small and a T-shirt stained by some previous painting project, but since we were staying home, I didn't care.

The house smelled good. My mother always started the turkey early. Pretty much every year she told us the story of the very first time she had tried to cook Thanksgiving dinner herself and how the turkey slices had come off the bone dark pink and inedible. So now she overcompensated by starting the turkey absurdly early and roasting it until there wasn't a bit of moisture left in the whole thing.

She and Melanie were both busily cooking when I entered the kitchen, Mom stirring something on the stove, Melanie chopping something at the table. I counted the sweet potatoes lying on the counter. "Fifteen?" I said. "For six of us?"

"I wanted to make sure we had leftovers," Mom said. "And I don't know how big an eater Andrew is."

"I doubt he can eat ten sweet potatoes at one sitting, no matter how big an eater he is."

"They'll be mashed."

"Oh, well, that changes everything." I poured myself a cup of coffee. The great thing about living at home with my folks was that coffee was always already made by the time I got up. I moved over to the table where Melanie was chopping furiously at something pale. "Onions?" I guessed, because her eyes were all red and swollen.

She shook her head. "Celery."

"Oh. Why are you crying then?"

"I'm not."

I looked questioningly over at my mother, who explained

carefully, "Nicole and Cameron called from Hawaii to say hi a little while ago."

"Oh. Are they having a good time?"

"Of course they're having a good time," Melanie said vehemently. "How could they *not* be having fun staying at a resort in Hawaii with a beautiful, famous celebrity and their adoring father who gives them anything they want? Why *wouldn't* they prefer being there to being here, in the same old boring place with the same old boring mother?"

"I'm sure they miss you," I said. "But since they had to go, you don't want them to be totally miserable, do you?"

"No, of course not." She chopped savagely at a piece of celery that had never done her any harm. "But I hate it. I hate being away from them on a holiday. I hate that they're with some other woman who doesn't care about them at all. And I hate that Gabriel gets to have fun with them after all he did to break up our family. I hate it all."

"And a Happy Thanksgiving to you too," I said brightly.

My mother gave me a reproving look. Melanie didn't care, though. She was too busy attacking the Celery Stalk of Evil.

I asked Noah for his help in getting the dining room ready. He drew a picture to put in the middle of the table. (I knew it was a turkey because he told me so; otherwise I might have guessed something altogether different, like an alien, or a football with spines.) Then he made place cards, writing the names in big, uneven print on small pieces of paper.

"Where should I put Coach Andrew?" he asked as he sorted through his slips of paper.

"I don't know. Do you want to sit next to him?"

"I don't care. But okay." He put himself next to Andrew.

"And Grandma goes at this end and Grandpa at the other end. You want to be across from me or from Andrew?"

"You decide."

"I'll put him across from Melanie."

"Actually," I said, "put him across from me. Just in case Mel gets sad and has to get up from the table." That seemed like a real possibility.

Noah trotted around the table, carefully folding the little pieces of paper so they'd stand up on the plates. "It's good Coach Andrew's coming," he said. "Otherwise, there'd be no dads."

"Coach Andrew isn't a dad."

"Well, sort of."

"No, he's not. But Grandpa is."

"Forget it," he said. "You don't understand anything." He tossed the last name card on a plate and stomped out of the room, apparently and inexplicably annoyed with me.

I went back into the kitchen. "He's driving me crazy," I announced to no one in particular.

"What's wrong?" My mother looked up from basting the turkey.

"Nothing. I'm just tired of Noah's always getting mad at me for no reason."

She raised her eyebrows and bent back over the turkey with a little snicker.

"What's so funny?" I said.

"Nothing," she said airily. "Nothing at all."

I left it at that, but I felt even more annoyed than I had before.

The doorbell rang at exactly 4 p.m. I called out "I've got it" and opened the door to Coach Andrew, who held out a bunch of flowers. "For the ladies of the house," he said.

"Oh, shit," I said. "Oops, sorry. I mean, thanks for the

flowers. But someone should have told you we don't dress up for Thanksgiving here."

"Yes, I see that," he said with a meaningful glance at my jeans and tank top. He was wearing a jacket and tie and nice black leather shoes. No baseball cap for once. He looked weird without it, almost unrecognizable. His hair was darker than I had realized—as dark as his eyes.

"Not that you don't look nice," I said. "But maybe a little hot?" It was over eighty degrees out. Sweat was plastering down the hair at his temples.

"Does this mean I can take off the jacket and tie?"

"You can and you should." I let him in and he entered the house, shrugging off the jacket and loosening the tie so fast you'd think they were suffocating him. "Just throw them on the sofa."

He tossed aside the extra clothing then went to work on the top button of his shirt. Once he got that open, he started in on his cuffs, undoing the buttons and rolling the sleeves up over his wrists.

"The pants are staying on, right?" I said, leaning against the sofa back. I was enjoying the striptease. "I mean, we're casual, but we're not *that* casual."

"I'm done." With his clothing all deconstructed like that, he looked like a movie nerd suddenly turned hunky and athletic after a workout montage and a few drinks. To add to the effect, he even ran his fingers through his hair so it looked a little thicker and messier. "Okay," he said with what appeared to be a genuine sigh of relief. "I feel much better. Part of the reason I became a coach is so I'd never have to wear a jacket and tie to work."

"Is Thanksgiving usually dressy at your home?" I asked, leading him back toward the kitchen.

He nodded. "My grandparents are formal people and they

kind of set the tone. Gotten used to your new hair yet?" He brushed his hand across the top of my head.

"Hey!" I said, ducking a little.

"Sorry." He quickly retracted his hand. "It's just so tempting. But I should have asked for permission first."

"It's okay. It's just that people keep doing that to me. I'm starting to feel like a dog."

"Speaking of which, where *is* the First Lady of the United States?"

"Right there." We had reached the entrance to the kitchen, and I pointed to where Eleanor Roosevelt sat, intently watching Melanie put the finishing touches to a pie like she could *will* her into tossing her something to eat.

"What kind of guard dog is she, anyway? Letting a stranger come waltzing in without a bark? Come here, girl!" She looked up at the sound of Andrew's voice and broke her pose, dashing over to greet him. As he petted her, she snuffled her nose right into the crotch of his pants. "Whoa!" he said, backing up.

I hauled her back by her collar with my free hand. "For god's sake, Eleanor Roosevelt, at least buy him a drink first. Look, Mom—Andrew brought flowers." I held them out to her.

"Lovely," she said with a quick glance. "Thank you, Andrew." She went back to mashing sweet potatoes. "Can you put them in a vase for me, Rickie?"

"Where do you keep the vases?"

"You really don't know? You've only lived in this house your whole life." Spending the whole day in a hot kitchen never improved my mother's temper. She gave a curt nod across the room. "That cabinet over there."

I went over and opened the cabinet. The vases were on the top shelf. "I can't reach them." I was casting around for a stool when Andrew came up next to me.

"Here," he said. "How's this one?" He reached up and plucked out a dark green glass vase, his arm brushing against mine.

"That's good," I said, shrinking back a bit, embarrassed.

He didn't seem to notice, just took the vase over to the sink, filled it with water, then held out his hand for the flowers. I gave them to him. He undid the paper they were wrapped in and plunked them into the water. "Ideally you'd put a pinch of sugar in the water and trim the stems, but you can do that later. This will hold them for now." He played with the flowers a bit, tilting his head to see how they looked as he gently angled them this way and that.

"Look at you," I said. "For a macho coach, you're awfully good at this."

"Thank you," he said calmly. "I like arranging flowers. Always have." His strong, slender fingers moved smoothly among the stems. I found myself staring at them, mesmerized. "Do we have teams yet?" he asked with a glance up.

"Teams?"

"For the football game."

"Oh. We haven't really thought about it." Probably because no one in the house was actually planning to play football.

"How about kids against adults?"

"Slightly unfair," I said. "Seeing as how Noah's the only kid here."

"He is?" Andrew glanced over at Melanie. "I thought—"

I cut him off. "Nicole and Cameron went to Hawaii with their dad."

"Oh," he said.

"So, anyway, about the football thing..."

"The football *thing*?" he repeated. "That doesn't inspire confidence."

"It's not like you're dressed for it," I said defensively.

"I was prepared to dirty my clothing in the name of sports-manship."

"How many people do you need to play?"

"How many you got?"

"Well, there's Noah."

"And?"

"No 'and,'" I said. "There's just Noah."

"What about you?"

"I don't know how to play."

"I'll teach you."

"You can't play with uneven numbers."

"Sure, you can."

"I'm pretty sure it's against the rules."

He folded his arms. "Who's the PE coach here?"

"Man, it didn't take you long to start throwing your author-ity around, did it?"

My mother was watching us from over by the sink. She wasn't saying anything, but she was watching us.

"So should we give it a try?" Andrew said.

"I don't know if we even have time before dinner—"

He turned to my mother. "Mrs. Allen, does Rickie have your permission to come out and play for a little while?"

Mom laughed. "Please get her out into the fresh air. You'd think she was a vampire, the way she avoids the sunlight."

"That is so not true!" I protested. "I take Eleanor Roosevelt to the park all the time."

"Once in the last month, if I remember correctly."

"Well, you don't, because it was more than that."

"If you say so." She didn't sound convinced.

"You're just trying to delay this," Andrew said to me. "Afraid you'll be bad at it?"

"I just don't want to humiliate you. I mean, if I go out there to play football for the first time, and I totally wail on your butt—"

"I'm terrified," Andrew said dryly. "Come on, get moving. Where's Noah?"

"Wait," I said. "I'll go out with you and Noah and I'll play whatever pathetic little game you can play with three people and a football. But before I do..."

"Yes?"

"I need a glass of wine."

"Fine. Just drink it fast—the sun's going down."

I opened a bottle—Dad already had a few out in preparation for dinner—and poured us both a glass. "How about one for the chef?" my mother asked. She was now working on the salad, tearing lettuce leaves into small pieces. I handed her the glass I had poured for myself, and she immediately took a big, almost desperate gulp. "God, I needed that." She set the glass down. "Andrew, would you mind helping me get the turkey out of the oven before you go out? It's as big as Rickie, and I'm scared to lift it by myself."

"Of course." He followed her to the stove. She opened the oven door and he peered in then gave a low whistle. "Beautiful."

She handed him the oven mitts. "I just hope it's done."

"It's been cooking for seven hours," I said. I had poured myself a new glass of wine and was watching them over its edge. "It's done. And done. And done."

"I'm always worried about undercooking it," she said. "The first time I ever cooked a turkey, I didn't leave myself enough time—"

"I know," I said. "You tell us this story every single year."

"I was telling him. I haven't told you my turkey story before, have I, Andrew?"

"No, and I'd love to hear it." He squatted down and tugged on the oven rack with his mitted hands.

"Let *me* tell the story," I said. "It'll save us all a lot of time. Mom undercooked the turkey and no one could eat it, so now she always overcooks it. End of story."

"You can be a real jerk sometimes, Rickie," my mother said.

"What? That's the whole story, isn't it?"

Andrew was still in a crouch. "Um," he said uncomfortably. "So where should I put this?"

"Right on top of the stove," Mom said. "Thank you."

He stood up carefully and set the pan down. The turkey's skin was too dark and all shriveled, but Andrew said again how great it looked. "You want me to carve it?" he asked.

"Not yet," Mom said. "It needs to rest awhile."

"So we still have time to go out and play a game?"

"At least half an hour."

I drained the rest of my wine. "Guess I'm ready," I said. "Or will be once the alcohol hits."

"Do you always need to get drunk before engaging in any physical activity?" Andrew asked. "I'm not judging, I'm just curious."

"Before *some* physical activities," I said and then realized how much that sounded like innuendo. But it was unintentional. I think.

"Huh," he said. "Just so you know, I was lying when I said I wasn't judging." He touched my arm. "Come on, let's go." We left my mother poking a meat thermometer repeatedly into the turkey and staring at the dial while muttering to herself.

15.

Noah and I were a team. We weren't very good at passing or catching, so Andrew could easily have stolen the ball from us any time he wanted to, but he let us make a touchdown or two. He made more, though, even with no one to pass to. Noah would frequently try to tackle him. Once Andrew's foot slipped just as Noah grabbed at him, and they both fell down on the grass. Neither was hurt, but Andrew's nice white shirt got covered with dirt and grass stains, while Noah's tee went from Slightly Paint Stained to Very Grass Stained.

The sun was setting, and the heat of the afternoon gave way quickly to a comfortably cool temperature, which was on the verge of turning *too* cold for someone wearing a tank top, when Melanie came to the back door and shouted for us to come in for dinner.

"Light's fading anyway," Andrew said. As we all turned back toward the house, he tossed the ball to Noah and managed to land it right in Noah's curved arms.

"What was the final score?" Noah asked, hugging the filthy ball to his chest.

Andrew tilted his head thoughtfully. "Let me think. Three...plus seven...and then there was the safety...and of course that last touchdown...I'm pretty sure it was zero to zero."

"We suck," Noah said cheerfully as we all fell into step, side by side.

"Speak for yourself," I said. "I rule at this."

"Really?" Andrew nudged my shoulder with his. "So you meant to do all that ball dropping?"

"Didn't want to embarrass you amateurs by looking too good."

"Hey." He stopped in midstride and surveyed me. "How come you're not all covered in dirt like the rest of us?"

"Yeah," Noah said. "How'd you stay all clean, Mom?"

I said airily, "When you're as good at this game as I am, you can play for hours without getting filthy like you two losers."

Andrew caught Noah's arm and whispered in his ear. Noah nodded and carefully laid the football down on the grass.

"I don't like this," I said. "What are you up to?"

"Nothing," Andrew said. He and Noah started walking on both sides of me again, both of them affecting casual attitudes by ostentatiously sticking their hands in their pockets and whistling. Then Andrew said, "Now!" and he grabbed one of my arms and Noah grabbed the other and with a sharp tug, they (well, Andrew mostly) managed to pull me off my feet and down onto my butt.

"There," Andrew said, standing over me and dusting off his hands in a "job well done" sort of way. "*Now* you look like you've played ball."

"I hate you both," I said. "Help me up." I held out my hands and they each took one and hauled me to my feet.

"You're heavy," Noah complained.

"Yeah," Andrew said. "You must weigh—what? Ninety whole pounds?"

"Whoa," said Noah, who weighed less than fifty.

"What's going on out here?" Melanie asked, appearing once again at the back door. "I could have sworn I just saw them tackle you, Rickie."

"You did," I said, swiping at the seat of my pants. "And now my butt is dirty and it hurts."

"She deserved it," Andrew said to Melanie. "I swear I only

do that to people who deserve it. Although"—he turned to Noah—"your aunt looks a little too clean, don't you think?"

Melanie shrieked and ran for the house. "Come in now or Laurel will freak!" she called over her shoulder. "Everything's ready."

I limped exaggeratedly toward the house.

"You okay?" Andrew said. "We didn't mean to actually injure you."

"Just know this," I said solemnly. "I may forgive but I never forget. You better start watching your back, Fulton."

"You couldn't take me down if you tried. I'm bigger than two of you put together."

"That's what you think. One day, when you least expect it…"

"Yeah, yeah, I'm shaking in my boots." He opened the door and held it for me and Noah. As I went past him he said, "That was fun. Thanks for playing."

"Yeah," I said. Noah ran off toward the kitchen. I nodded after him. "Somehow you get him doing things that no one else— What's that sound?"

"My cell," Andrew said, sheepishly snaking a phone out of his pants pocket. "It's my ring tone. I liked *Star Trek* when I was a kid."

"God, you're a nerd."

He nodded amiably and squinted at the screen.

"Gracie?" I asked.

"Yeah. She must be at a port."

"You can answer it if you want."

"No, that's okay." He pressed the button to ignore. "We'll talk later."

"You sorry you didn't go with her?" I asked as we moved toward the dining room. "I mean, I've seen that photo of her in a bikini…"

"You did? Oh, the one in my office." He laughed. "Yeah, I guess I didn't take that into account when I said I'd skip the cruise. But, no, I'm not sorry—I've met her parents. Anyway, I'm very happy to be here. I'm having fun."

"Let's go eat," I said abruptly.

Noah seemed to be enjoying being the only kid. It wasn't a bad gig. Most of dinner was taken up by his recounting, blow by blow and play by play, the entire football game. It made me realize how seldom he and I played outside like that. Most of our free time was spent hunched over computers or watching TV or reading or doing something else that was quiet and indoors and solitary. His cheeks were glowing, and his hair was sticking up in clumps from all the sweat and dirt, and he kept chattering away about how I had thrown the ball to him and then Andrew had grabbed it and then it was his turn to throw to me and it *almost* made it all the way to me but then Andrew got it again, and so on. My father plied him with questions, showing an interest that was either sincere or the world's most incredible deadpan. I could never tell with him.

Andrew supplied some additional color commentary, most of it about how well Noah had played. He was pleasant and convivial around my parents and Melanie, but I kept thinking about how, when we had been alone, he had started teasing me in that mildly cruel and edgy way you tease someone you've become comfortable with.

Or are flirting with.

That was the other possibility. There was something flirtatious in his air with me that day. I could have sworn it.

The thing was, I was liking it. I was liking him. That badly timed phone call from Gracie was probably the best thing for me because I had stupidly been forgetting about her, forgetting that the cute guy eating Thanksgiving dinner with us already had a girlfriend—a very beautiful, tall, and successful girlfriend—and if things had worked out the way he wanted them to, he would have been spending the holiday with her.

So I tried to stop thinking about how much fun I'd had outside and focus on eating Thanksgiving dinner with my beloved family, although the food wasn't exactly helping to keep my attention focused. It was decent, not great. My mother was a decent, not great, cook, and both Melanie and I followed in her footsteps. The gluten-free stuffing wasn't as good as real stuffing and we didn't have biscuits, but otherwise it was your basic Thanksgiving meal. The turkey was dried out and barely warm, but once you piled on the gravy, extremely sweet sweet potatoes (my mother loaded on the marshmallows, to Noah's delight), and cranberry sauce, you couldn't really taste it much anyway.

The wine, though... the wine was *good*. Dad was an oenophile (a word he had taught me to say and spell when I was seven years old) and spent a fair amount of his free time researching and tasting wines from all over the world. He liked to discover good obscure wines from different countries, and he often prowled around some of the dustier little wine stores in LA, buying bottles that the owners and managers recommended and keeping careful track of which ones he did or didn't like. He had a whole computer spreadsheet for the cataloguing of wines we'd tried.

For Thanksgiving he had pulled out several different bottles, announcing early in the meal that we were going to decide once and for all whether a light red or a complex white went better with turkey. He encouraged the adults to try them all, and he didn't need to urge any of us twice: Melanie was drowning her sorrows, I was slightly on edge because of Andrew's presence,

Mom was harried from all the cooking and ready to relax, and Andrew—well, I don't know if anything was bugging him or not, but he managed to keep up with the rest of us.

So everyone except for Noah was a little tipsy by the time we'd finished up the meal. And those of us who'd started drinking before dinner were probably tipsier than the rest.

"Should we have dessert right away or take a break?" my mother asked as she surveyed the wreckage of the meal.

Melanie's cell phone rang before anyone could answer. She always left it right next to her plate during dinner when she was apart from her kids. "It's Nicole," she said after checking. "Do you mind?"

"Go ahead," Mom said. "We'll wait on dessert."

Melanie jumped up and, putting the phone to her ear, left the room.

"Can I watch a little TV?" Noah asked. "Just until dessert?" He looked at my mother, not me, aware that she was in charge of the day's activities.

"I guess so," she said with a little sigh, and he quickly slid to his feet and darted out of the dining room before she could change her mind.

The rest of us started to help clear, but Mom said, "Rickie, do me a favor and take Eleanor Roosevelt for a quick walk, would you? I'm exhausted but she hasn't had any exercise today."

"A walk sounds good," Andrew said. "I'll go with you."

I got Eleanor Roosevelt all leashed up and we headed out into the now decidedly cool night air. It felt good, though, after all that wine.

Eleanor Roosevelt strained at her leash, trotting wildly, ecstatic just to be outside.

"Want me to take her?" Andrew asked as she practically hauled me down the street.

"She'll calm down soon," I said. "She's not as young as she used to be." I felt a bit floaty from all the wine, so the dog's tugging didn't even bother me. I just kind of gave in to it, let her pull me along.

"This is a nice neighborhood," he said, looking around. "Nice and quiet."

"I guess. I'm kind of sick of it, though. I thought I'd be far away from here by this point in my life."

"So what happened?"

"Noah happened."

"No, I know, but how did—" He stopped. Then he said, "Is it rude of me to ask about this?"

"It's just such a stupid story," I said. "It's embarrassing."

"Everyone takes risks, you know. Especially when you're a teenager. No matter how many films they show you in human development..." His voice trailed off.

It took me a second to realize what he meant. Probably because of the wine. Then I laughed. "Oh, it wasn't *that*. You've met my mother, right? I mean, she's on the board of Planned Parenthood *and* NARAL. When I was twelve, she told me there would always be a box of condoms in the bathroom cabinet and I could just help myself whenever I felt I needed to, no questions asked."

"Wow. That's pretty cool."

"No, it isn't. It was awful. I was so embarrassed by the whole idea, by the way she always talked about that stuff." I shrugged. "But I guess it achieved its purpose. I mean, I knew everything I needed to know about not having an unplanned pregnancy." It occurred to me I could never have had this conversation if it hadn't been so dark and I hadn't been fairly drunk and the dog hadn't been dancing around on the edge of the leash. This was not a daylight conversation. But somehow it was okay at night. Or at least this particular night. "The crazy thing about Noah is that he *was* planned."

"Oh." A pause while he digested that. "How old were you when you had him?"

"Eighteen," I said. "Almost nineteen. It was the summer after my freshman year of college. Oh, Eleanor Roosevelt, do you have to do that *now*?" The dog was squatting right there, in the middle of the sidewalk. She gave me an affronted look, with some justification: she was only doing her job. I sighed and pulled a plastic bag out of the holder on her leash. "Excuse us," I said to Andrew. "Feel free to look away."

"I'm not that delicate. Want me to hold the leash while you get that?"

"Please." I handed him the leash and, using the bag as a glove, picked up the still warm poop then pulled the bag so it was inverted and the poop was inside. I tied a knot at the top and looked around. "Oh, good, the Casters have already put their garbage out." I ran over, looked around to make sure no one was watching, and quickly lifted the can lid and dropped the bag inside.

"You look like you're getting rid of criminal evidence," Andrew said when I came back.

"You never know when people are going to come screaming out of their house at you. It's happened to me."

"Jerks. You're being a good citizen just by picking it up. They should be applauding you."

"No one applauds a girl carrying a bag full of shit."

"That's very philosophical," he said. "Can I quote you?"

"I'm saving it for the title of my memoirs." I reached for the leash. Our fingers touched.

"I can hold it," he said.

"That's okay," I said. "I'll take her."

He let go of the leash, the side of his hand sliding along mine. We stood there for a moment then I said, "Should we keep going?"

"I'm in no hurry to get back," he said. "Anyway, I want to hear the rest of the story." We started walking again. "So you did this unusual thing. You had a baby at eighteen. On purpose."

"Yes."

"Why did you want to have a baby so young?"

"There was this guy," I said. "That's the short answer, anyway."

"Lots of people fall in love, but they don't necessarily start having babies right away—or at least not if they have access to a medicine cabinet full of condoms."

"Yeah but most people aren't obsessed with human biology the way we were."

A short pause. "Okay, you're going to have to explain that one."

"We were both biology majors. I mean, I wasn't yet but I was planning to be one, and Duncan was in his senior year but he was going to go on to graduate school to get his Ph.D. in human evolution. He had this theory—" God, it was hard to talk about this without feeling the self-loathing and bitterness and embarrassment rising out of this knot of poison in my gut. "I mean, it wasn't just a theory, it's true, I guess. That humans were meant to have babies much younger than people do these days. That an eighteen-year-old girl was likelier to have an easy pregnancy and a healthy baby than a thirty-five-year-old. I mean, biologically it's all true, right?" Eleanor Roosevelt had settled down to a steady walk. Her nails made a quiet clopping sound on the pavement.

"So he said you should have his baby right then and there?"

"It was all much more complicated than that." I flicked the leash lightly on Eleanor Roosevelt's back, the way you'd giddy-up a horse. She turned and looked at me questioningly but then continued placidly on her way. "We had a *plan*. We were going to live together in the school housing for families and have a couple of babies while we were young and take turns going to classes and caring for them—we figured we could stagger our classes so we wouldn't even need babysitting— and then by the time I was done with college and he had his doctorate, the kids would be in school and we'd both be able to have full-time careers and then of course they'd grow up and leave the house and we'd still be young enough to travel and have tons of adventures, unlike people who have their kids later in life and then are too old once the kids are grown to do anything fun." I flicked the leash again, more irritably this time. "You can see how it all made sense, right?"

"Sure," Andrew said, his voice as quiet and dark as the night around us. "If you overlook the part where an eighteen-year-old college freshman has a baby."

"Technically I was a sophomore." I stepped over a tree root that was breaking through the cement of the sidewalk. "Or, more accurately, a dropout, given the way things turned out. I thought I was a very mature eighteen-year-old, by the way. Perfectly ready to settle down." I remembered how Ryan had told me not to be in such a rush to grow up when I was fifteen. Where was he when I needed him?

Andrew's thoughts had gone in a different direction. "What did your parents think of all this?"

"Mom briefly freaked but then she got all 'We can make this work' about it. That's how she operates."

"And your dad?"

"He was pretty nice about it. I mean, compared to how

most fathers probably would have reacted, he was incredibly calm. Just said it sounded like I knew what I was doing, and he'd support me. He liked Duncan. He'd only met him once or twice, but they talked biology and kind of bonded."

"So what happened to Duncan? And the plan?"

I kept my voice flat and emotionless. It was the only way I could actually talk about this stuff. "A couple of months before I was due, Duncan scored a three-year fellowship to go study with some world-famous biologist in South America. I didn't even know he had applied. He said he didn't think he'd get it so didn't see the harm in applying."

"What? That's crazy."

"He said he'd come back soon and join us."

"Did he?"

"He's never even met Noah."

You could hear the disgust in Andrew's voice. "How could he do that?"

"I don't know. He was so far away, living this crazily different life. Maybe the whole idea of Noah seemed unreal to him. I know *he* started to seem unreal to me pretty quickly— Duncan, I mean. Not Noah." I gave a short laugh. "Definitely not Noah."

"But he knew you were going to have a baby, right?"

"Are you kidding? It was completely his idea. For months he was beyond excited about the whole thing. He had this ability to believe in something so totally that he kind of swept you along with it." I found it hard to explain Duncan to someone who had never met him. He had been so compelling in person but now that I hadn't seen him in years, it all felt vaguely hallucinatory. "I thought he was so intense because of how he felt about me, you know? That it was all personal—that he was just so into the idea of *me* and our having a baby and then this

future together...that his whole life had become about that."
I didn't tell Andrew—couldn't tell him, couldn't really tell
anyone—how it made me feel when Duncan's light blue eyes
had burned with desire and passion and certainty and all that
burning was for *me*. When he said he wanted to impregnate
me, I had felt so special, like I was the Chosen One, like I was
some goddamn fertile female Harry Potter.

That was the part I couldn't forgive myself for...that I had
bought into the whole thing and believed him when he said
that I was his future.

Not that Duncan had been lying when he said the things
he said. He had meant every word--for that moment. I just
hadn't known him long enough yet to realize his nature was as
mercurial as it was passionate.

His intensity was like the sun: warm and satisfying and
bright. As long as he had directed it at me, I was sure I was
doing the right thing because nothing in my life had made me
feel as special or wonderful or privileged.

And then it all went away. The warmth, the certainty, the
attention. Our future together.

Sometimes I wondered if there had been other women since
then who had discovered what it was like to feel that unbeliev-
able glow on them, to feel chosen and special because Duncan
had singled them out from all others. Not that Duncan was
likely to have asked anyone else to bear his baby. He *had* to
have learned he didn't want that, right? Plus the odds were
slim he'd have found anyone as willing to follow him into Cra-
zyland as I'd been, anyone else who was young and innocent
enough to think she was old and mature enough to do *that*
before she really was.

I closed my eyes briefly and forced myself to shove all those
thoughts away. For the moment, at least. Then I said, as lightly

as I could, "Turns out Duncan was just intense about whatever he happened to be into at the moment. Once he switched to something else, he just switched completely."

"But you can't get a girl pregnant and then just head off into the sunset," Andrew said.

"For a while he'd call and check up on us. And he always said he'd come join us as soon as he could." Every time the phone would ring in the months right before and then right after Noah was born, I'd run for it, hoping it was Duncan calling me to say he was coming back. I could still remember the look on my mother's face whenever she saw me dive for the ringing phone. I couldn't stand it—the pity and the anger and the confusion that battled in her expression, none of which she ever voiced but all of which I felt radiating from her in waves. I hated her for watching me like that, hated her for being right when she said she didn't trust Duncan. "He kept postponing when he was actually going to come back," I said. "Then he stopped saying he was coming back anytime soon. Then he just stopped calling."

Andrew was silent for a moment. Then he said, "Does he help with child support?"

"I haven't asked him to."

"He should."

"Well, money's not an issue with my parents helping out." I stared at the dog's ears, bobbing gently in the glow from the streetlights. "And I don't want to give him any excuse to butt into our lives. Noah's mine now," I added with an edge of fierceness. "Not ours. Mine."

"The law would see it differently. I mean, legally he has rights. And obligations."

"Believe me, I'm aware of that. You should hear my mother on the subject. If Duncan ever comes looking for us, I'll deal with the legal stuff then. But I don't think he will."

"Noah might want to find him when he's older."

"I know," I said shortly.

A pause. Then, "How was it?" he asked. "After Noah was born?"

"I dropped out of school, cried a lot—so did Noah, he was an awful infant, constantly crying and colicky..." I trailed off and we walked a few steps in silence. "I don't know," I said finally. "We survived. My parents helped. Melanie helped. It wasn't so bad."

"You're lucky to have the family you do."

"Yeah, I am."

"And Noah's great."

"He's great," I said. "But not easy."

"He's still figuring stuff out. He's going to be okay. Better than okay. I can tell."

"How about me?" I asked, only half joking. "Can you tell about me? Am I going to be okay when I grow up?"

"I think so." He gently knocked my elbow with his. "You might want to run around outside a little more and criticize teachers a little less."

"Fuck you," I said amicably.

"And watch your language. And maybe grow your hair out. But you should grow up to be a fine young lady someday."

"Grow my hair out?" I repeated with genuine distress. "You said it suited me!"

"That's the problem," he said. "It *does* suit you. But what's with all that? The nose stud and the tattoos and the torn jeans and all that? You come from this nice upper-middle-class home and you have a kid. You don't exactly look like who you are."

"Who do I look like, then?"

"I don't know." He considered the question for a moment, then said, "A little like the girls who used to hang out in the back alley behind my high school and smoke and scare the shit out of anyone who accidentally got in their way. Only prettier," he added quickly. "And nicer, of course."

"I don't scare the shit out of you?"

"Not so much."

We had circled around the block and were back at my house. I put my hand on the gate latch but didn't open it. Eleanor Roosevelt watched me intently, panting, eager to get inside to her water bowl. I stared absently down at her, wondering why I was telling Andrew stuff I hadn't told anyone else. It was because I was drunk, I thought, and the night was so dark. "I went through kind of a weird phase," I said slowly. "A couple of years after Noah was born. I just—" I shook my head. "It was like I couldn't believe where I was, what my life was, that I was back to living at home only now I had this kid. I had been a good girl for so long. Always getting good grades, always behaving the way I was supposed to . . . And suddenly all these strangers were staring at me like I had done something I should be ashamed of. So I guess I kind of felt like if people were going to stare at me because I'd had a kid too young, then I'd make them stare at me for my own reasons, on my terms—that I'd give them something to stare at. And if it made me look like those tough girls at your school, all the better. I figured I could use a little toughness." He was silent. "Does that make any sense at all?" I said. "Or do I just sound nuts?"

"Of course it does." He leaned against the gate, his face in shadow. "I'm sorry you've had it so rough."

"This isn't rough." I gestured to my parents' gracious two-story house. "Teenage mothers in Compton, they have it rough. I have it easy."

"Okay, so maybe they have it rougher." A pause. "Did you get a college degree?"

"No. I'm still working toward it."

"Where?"

"I take some courses online."

He digested that for a moment. "Do you know what you want to be when you finally graduate?"

"Yeah," I said. "Six inches taller."

"Seriously. Do you think about that stuff?"

"Sometimes. I think about it and then I stop thinking about it." I wished I had a better answer to give him, that I could honestly say I was planning to do something worthwhile, that I didn't sound like such a loser.

"Maybe you should—" A sudden burst of music cut off whatever he was about to say. "Shit, sorry." He hesitated, then reached for his pocket. "I better just check…"

Please don't answer it, I thought.

He checked the screen, flipped open the phone, and hesitated—then raised it to his ear. "I better get this one. I'm sorry."

"No worries." I unlatched the gate. Eleanor Roosevelt waggled with joy. She was always happy to leave and always happy to come home.

"Hi," Andrew said into the phone. "Oh, that's great… Yeah, me too… Listen, can we IM later, at the usual time? We're all here talking and… okay. Love you. Bye." He slipped the phone back in his pocket. I wondered why he said we were "all" here talking. It was just the two of us. Unless he was including the dog?

"We should go in," I said, breaking the suddenly awkward silence. "There's pie."

"Mmm," he said jovially. "Pie."

I started to push the gate open, but stopped. Poor Eleanor Roosevelt, who had waited patiently up until now, nosed at it desperately, confused and eager to get inside. "I just need to tell you one last thing," I said. "So you don't think I'm horrible."

"I don't think you're horrible. Not even close."

"Whatever. But you have to know. I complain a lot about Noah. And if I had to do things over again, I'd probably do them differently because I made a lot of dumb choices. But that isn't to say..." I didn't know how to put it, but I *had* to say it somehow. I had to make this one thing clear. "It's just...I *do* love him, you know. I did from the moment I first looked at him. No, even before that. It's not ever about not loving him. All my complaining and moaning and wondering about the past—it's not because I don't want him around. I'd—" What could I say that didn't sound stupid and sentimental? "He's my son, you know?"

"I know," he said. "You can tell. And not just because you almost got me fired out of concern for him. It's just...you can tell."

"All right, then," I said. I unhooked the leash, and Eleanor Roosevelt dashed up to the house as happily as she'd dashed toward the gate a half an hour earlier.

16.

I sneaked a glance at Andrew as we came inside. I had thought I couldn't read his expression because it was so dark outside, but even in the brightly lit foyer I didn't have a clue what he was thinking.

I felt a little like I'd just peeled off all my skin, exposing everything that was soft and vulnerable and private underneath. It was too late to regret it.

I hung up Eleanor Roosevelt's leash and then Mom called

us into the dining room, where the others were already seated and waiting for us to eat dessert.

She'd just served us all slices of pumpkin and pecan pie when a cell phone rang.

"Sorry," Melanie said, snatching up her phone. "Be right back." She left the dining room, phone clutched to her ear.

"What *did* we do before cell phones?" my father said dryly. "Meals must have been so boring with everyone actually sitting and eating and talking to one another." He appealed to my mother. "Am I allowed to go ahead and eat my pie or would *that* be considered rude?"

"Oh, go ahead," she said, waving her hand with a resigned sigh.

Another phone buzzed audibly. Andrew gave a little uncomfortable laugh. "Sorry," he said. "That's me. But it's just a text."

"You can check it if you want," I said. "Don't let my dad scare you."

He pulled the phone partially out of his pocket, glanced down at it, then pushed it back in. "It's okay," he said. "Just Gracie again."

Mom's head kind of snapped around at this. She studied Andrew for a second and then turned expressionless eyes on me.

"Can I get my own cell phone for Christmas?" Noah asked. He was shaking the can of whipped cream vigorously.

"You're six years old," I said. "What would you do with a cell phone?"

He upended the can over his plate and pressed against the neck so a thick ribbon of whipped cream spurted out. "Call people."

"Who do you need to call? That's enough whipped cream."

He kept going with the whipped cream. "You, when you're late picking me up."

I snatched the can away from him and set it upright on the table. "That's way too much. I told you to stop. And I'm almost never late."

He picked up his spoon. "Well, you *could* be, if I had a cell phone."

My father laughed. "I like his logic."

"Don't encourage him."

My mother said, "Noah, pass the whipped cream to Andrew."

"*Coach* Andrew," I corrected. The last thing I needed was for Noah to start tossing around a teacher's first name at school. Dr. Wilson would love *that*.

Melanie came back in.

"Everything okay?" Mom asked.

"Fine. It wasn't the kids." She sat down. "It was my mother."

"Oh, we should have called her earlier!" said *my* mother, who had a strong—and to me inexplicable—sense of duty toward Colleen, who clearly felt that her life was sufficiently fulfilling without any additional attention from her ex-husband's second wife. "We invited her to join us, you know, but she had other plans."

"You've told Melanie that seven times," I said. "In my hearing, anyway. Probably a few more when I wasn't around."

My mother cleared her throat slightly. "I'm sorry if I repeat myself sometimes."

"Sometimes?"

"Hey, go easy on your mother," Andrew said. "She's a nice lady."

"Thank you," Mom said to him and they shared a smile.

"I go easy on her," I said, annoyed. "But that doesn't mean I don't notice things."

"So what's next on the list of activities?" Mom said, a little too brightly. "Anyone up for a game of Scrabble?"

"And here you thought we'd be boring," I said to Andrew.

"No, I didn't. And Scrabble sounds like fun." He glanced at his watch. "If I'm not overstaying my welcome."

"Not at all. We'd be insulted if you left this early." Mom rose to her feet. "Rickie and I will clear the table and make some decaf. The rest of you go into the family room and set up the game. We'll be right in."

Noah said, "I don't want to play Scrabble. Can I watch TV?"

"No," my mother and I said at the same moment.

In the kitchen a moment later, Mom said to me, "Get the coffee started while I load the dishwasher."

"Yes, sir." I gave her a mock salute.

She bent down and opened the dishwasher door. "So who's Gracie?"

"Andrew's girlfriend." I eyed her warily. "Why?"

"I just didn't know he had one. Is it serious?"

"How should I know?"

Her back was to me as she shifted steadily between the sink, where she was scraping dishes, and the dishwasher, where she was inserting them.

"And why do you care?" I asked.

She didn't answer.

I got the can of coffee grounds out of the freezer and poured some directly into the filter without bothering to measure. "If you're trying to imply something, just *say* it."

"I'm not implying anything." She kept moving back and forth, scraping and loading, scraping and loading.

"I'd like to remind you that *I* didn't invite him here tonight. You and Melanie did."

"I know." More scraping and loading.

I went to the sink. "I need to fill the pot." She moved aside, keeping her wet hands suspended over the sink while I ran water into the carafe.

"You should use the filtered water," she said.

"This is faster."

"It makes better coffee."

"You want to do this?" I held out the pot to her. "Be my guest."

"Oh, for god's sake," she said. "I'm just giving you some advice."

"If you're going to ask me to do a job, don't criticize the way I do it."

She didn't say anything. As I turned away, pot filled, I could see she was pressing her lips together tightly, the way she always did when I didn't agree with every word she said.

I poured the water into the coffeemaker and punched it on. "I'm going to the family room."

She didn't reply.

I think all the wine I had at dinner actually helped my Scrabble game: good words seemed to come more easily. Or maybe they just *seemed* like good words. Because there were six of us, Melanie and I doubled up. Noah was supposedly my dad's partner, but he mostly just sat on the sofa and yawned and fidgeted. Mom and Andrew played alone and were easily the strongest players.

"You're kind of smart for a dumb jock," I told Andrew after he scored forty-five points on one word.

"I don't know how to respond to that."

"Thank you?" I suggested.

He shot me a look.

It *seemed* like he was flirting with me.

Was he?

It was actually *my* phone that rang next. Ryan.

I said to Mel, "Go ahead and play for us." As I put the phone to my ear and left the room, I saw that Andrew was watching me. Well, good. He had taken Gracie's phone call. I had a right to take this one.

"Hey," Ryan's voice said. "Having a nice Thanksgiving?"

"Yeah." I relaxed against the hallway wall. "You?"

"Delightful. Since Gabriel managed to escape to Hawaii, it was just me and Mom and a couple of turkey dinners from Koo Koo Roo."

"Your mother eats turkey? And here I always thought the undead dined exclusively on blood."

"Shut up."

"If your brother hadn't cheated on Melanie, you would have been here with us, you know."

"I was going to invite you to come over, but you're making me wonder if that's such a good idea."

"I can't, anyway." I glanced back through the doorway to the family room. Noah was leaning against Andrew's knee, studying Andrew's tiles, while Andrew whispered in his ear and pointed to the board, clearly conferring with him on the next word. "It's Thanksgiving," I said into the phone.

"So?"

"I can't just leave."

"How about later?"

"Maybe. I don't know."

"Well, call me if you decide you can."

"Yeah, okay." We said good-bye and I hung up.

"Who was that?" Mom asked as I came back into the family room.

"A friend."

"Anyone I know?"

I didn't answer, just perched on the arm of the upholstered chair Melanie and I had been sharing and watched as Andrew arranged some tiles on the board. "Pill," he announced.

"Four points," Mom said.

"Noah came up with it," Andrew said cheerfully. "I was completely stuck, but he saved me."

"Well done, Noah," Melanie said. "You want to help us with ours?"

"Okay," he said and came over to us and peered at the letters while Mom played her turn.

She got "query," ending on a triple-word box. "Thirty-eight points," she said with satisfaction.

"Mom always wins," I informed Andrew.

"Wait until Noah's older. He'll take her down."

I was a little skeptical about that, since Noah's brilliant idea for me and Mel was for us to make the word "ear" using the "r" from "query," which gained us exactly three points. I would have said no since there were plenty of better options, but Melanie was the kind of adult who liked to encourage kids' confidence, so she immediately plunked down the tiles.

My dad said, "I seem to have lost my teammate."

"I can help you too," Noah said and went over to him.

"It's good to be the only kid," I observed.

Once the Scrabble game was over (to no one's surprise, my mother won), we played a couple of other games: Apples to Apples, at Noah's request, and then a simple parlor game that

Andrew taught us where you had to guess which adverb people were acting out.

My parents were in heaven; they loved playing games like this. When I was little, we'd play hours and hours of board and parlor games, but once I was a teenager I just wanted to go online or watch TV and couldn't imagine anything dorkier than playing games with my parents.

Tonight, though, even I was having a good time.

At around nine-thirty, Andrew looked at his watch and said, "I should go."

"But I wanted to play Quelf," Noah said.

"Another time." Andrew rose to his feet. "You guys wore me out with all that football. Which reminds me"—he turned to me—"should I come play with Noah on Sunday?"

"Isn't Gracie getting back then?" I asked.

"She won't be in LA until midday. There's plenty of time." He shook Dad's hand, kissed Mom on the cheek, thanked them both, hugged Melanie and gave *her* a kiss on the cheek, bumped fists with Noah . . . and then just kind of nodded at me. "See you Sunday," he said and headed toward the door.

Why hadn't he kissed me too?

"I'll walk you down to your car," I said suddenly.

My mother turned to look right at me when I said that. I pretended I didn't notice.

I followed Andrew to the living room, where he retrieved his jacket and tie, and then we left the house. I closed the front door behind us and we walked down the gravel path.

Andrew said, "That was a nice evening."

I glanced sideways at him. Why hadn't I thought he was cute that first time in Louis Wilson's office?

Because I'd been angry at him. I tried to remember that anger and it seemed an eternity ago.

I liked his face now. He was cute in a way that grew on you.

We were already at the car. "Well, thanks," he said and unlocked it.

I rubbed the short hairs on the back of my neck. He had said I should grow my hair out. Why had I cut it so short? Just to prove something? I was an idiot. "Thanks for coming," I said.

He nodded and opened the car door. "See you."

"Wait," I said. He waited. "What do you want?" I asked abruptly.

"Excuse me?" He looked a little startled.

"I mean for Sunday. Cookies? More cupcakes?"

"Oh. You really don't have to make me anything."

"I'm going to anyway, so you might as well choose something."

"Well, then..." He thought a moment. "How about brownies?"

"Brownies it is."

"Make them safe for Noah."

"Yeah, I will."

He opened the car door and stood there a moment, sliding his hand idly along the door edge. There was this weird moment. A pause. Neither of us was moving or saying anything, but it felt like one of us should. Like the evening had changed something and we needed to acknowledge it before he left.

Or at least that's what it felt like to me. For all I knew, *he* was thinking about having a mug of cocoa when he got home.

He broke the silence. "Well, good night, Noah's mom."

"You still don't know my name?"

"I just like calling you that."

"Fine," I said. "Good night, Noah's coach."

Another pause. He looked down the street, absently, and then swung his head back toward me. "Okay," he said. "Good night."

"Again with the good night?"

"Sometimes it takes a few of them to get me to actually leave. Especially if I had a good time and don't want to go."

"So...you had a good time?"

This time he didn't look away during the pause. He studied me for a moment, thoughtfully. "Rickie—"

"Ha—so you *do* know my name."

"Just a lucky guess." He grinned, but then his body gave a sudden, convulsive jerk.

I stepped forward, concerned. "What's wrong?"

"Nothing. My phone. Startled me." He pulled it out of his pocket and punched a button. "Oops. I was supposed to be home by now. Gracie goes online on the ship's computer at the same time every night so we can IM. I'm late." He looked up but his thumbs hovered over the keypad. "Sorry. I better—"

"No worries." I retreated. "See you on Sunday."

"Yeah. Bye. Thanks again." He ducked into the car and closed the door. As I entered the house, I glanced back and saw him texting away in there, his face lit up only by the glow of his phone, his brow furrowed in concentration.

17.

He canceled for Sunday morning.

There was a voice mail waiting on the home machine when we got back from seeing a movie Saturday night. Mom hit the Play button and Andrew's voice said, "Hey, first of all, thank you all so much for a terrific Thanksgiving dinner. I had a great time. So it makes me feel especially bad that I have to cancel for tomorrow. Turns out I was wrong about when the ship docks and I have to pick up Gracie at ten. Tell Noah I'm sorry and that I hope he's up for the last week of basketball season."

"Gracie. That's the girlfriend, right?" Mom said, turning to look at me.

I shrugged and left the room before she could see how disappointed I was.

I had already made the brownies.

When I went to pick Noah up from the last basketball game on the following Friday, Andrew spotted me and called out, "Hey, Noah's mom—hold on." He pushed his way toward me, through the gaggle of girls who always surrounded him at the end of practice or games.

"What?" I said brusquely. I was annoyed at him for canceling the previous weekend. It wasn't a fair annoyance, given the fact he was working with Noah for free in the first place, but I wasn't feeling very fair at that moment.

"Two quick things. First of all, I brought this for you guys." He unclipped a piece of paper from his clipboard. "It's an application to the winter session of T-ball at the Westwood rec center. I think Noah should do it."

"I don't know," I said. "Being on a team like that is really hard for him."

"Don't worry. I'm coaching. I'll make sure Noah's on my team and help him along." I accepted the flyer he held out. My irritation was rapidly evaporating. He was standing in front of me in his baseball cap and coach's sweatshirt, all earnest and wanting to help, and it wasn't irritation I was feeling anymore.

It would have been better for me if it had been. This other feeling was worse.

"Please do it," he said. "I think it would be good for Noah. I *know* it would."

"What's the other thing?" I asked, studying the flyer like it was fascinating even though I wasn't actually taking in any of the information.

"Friday night one of the moms is throwing a pizza dinner to celebrate the end of the basketball season and all the girls specifically requested that Noah be included. Can you make it? I'll e-mail you the details."

"Yeah, okay." Oh, god, another event surrounded by parents I didn't know, but Noah would want to go. He loved these girls.

And Andrew would be there.

"Great." He clopped me on the upper arm in a fraternal, friendly way. "Make sure you sign Noah up for that team, okay? I have big plans for him." He started to move away, but then he stopped and turned back. "Oh, and sorry about Sunday. I felt awful I had to cancel. Was he okay with it?"

"He was fine," I said, which was true. It hadn't bothered *Noah* at all. "So, uh, how was the cruise?"

He shrugged. "She claimed she missed me too much to have fun. But what else is she going to say?"

"Ha," I said. "Good point." I stepped away. "Come on, Noah, let's get going!" There was an edge to my voice, something a little too high and harsh. I hoped I was the only one who heard it.

Noah totally broke my heart the evening of the pizza party when he came downstairs all ready to go in a tie and button-down shirt. "Do I look okay?" he asked anxiously. "I wanted to dress up for the party."

"Very handsome." I just hoped there wouldn't be any boys at the party who might make fun of him. "How'd you know how to tie the tie?"

"Grandpa showed me how but I did it myself."

The ends were wildly uneven and the knot was one big lump. "If you want me to smooth it out—"

"Why?" he asked. "Did I do it wrong?" He tried to look down at his own neck.

"No," I lied. "It looks great."

"*You're* not very dressed up," he pointed out.

"This is a new top," I said. "I've only worn it once before." I didn't tell him that it had taken me half an hour of trying things on to choose it. It was black of course, but more girlish than most of my tops, since it was cut in a baby-doll shape, tight at the bust and hanging loose down from there. I had spent extra time playing with my hair, too, getting it to wave in the right ways and not the wrong ways. It didn't look as good as it had that first day when Harlan had styled it, but it was okay.

Noah was still studying me with a critical eye. "Why do you always wear jeans?"

"They're comfortable."

"I think you should wear a dress tonight."

Yeah, right, that was all I needed—to show up in a girly dress and high heels at the fifth-grade basketball pizza party. Talk about looking desperate. "Forget it," was all I said. "Let's go."

"Did you chip in for the gift?" he asked once we were in the car and on our way.

"What gift?"

"For Coach Andrew."

"Nobody told me about a gift."

"Ask one of the moms, okay? Ask them. I want to be part of the gift. You should ask them." His voice was strained with sudden anxiety.

"Okay, okay. I'll ask."

"Don't forget," he said and played with the ends of his tie, flicking them lightly against his cheek and lips, until we arrived at the address I had been given.

The girls swooped down on Noah and whisked him away to play with them the moment he arrived. They treated him like a pet dog: they patted him and called to him and hugged him and exclaimed over how cute he was (the tie was a big hit). He ducked his head a lot, shy but smiling.

That left me a little stranded, without my usual armor of Noah's clinging to me, requiring attention. Andrew wasn't there yet and I didn't know any of the mothers. I recognized them all from picking Noah up after practice but I'd never hung around long enough to talk to any of them. There were some dads there, too, for once.

The hostess eventually spotted me and introduced herself and told me how cute Noah was and how much her daughter adored him. She introduced me to the other moms, who all seemed to know who I was.

Then again, Noah and I kind of stood out.

I asked the hostess mom about the coach gift, and she told me they were all chipping in on a restaurant gift certificate for him and his girlfriend and if I wanted to contribute I could but I didn't have to. As I handed her a ten, she added that she'd chosen Il Cielo because it was "the most romantic restaurant in LA."

I would have steered them in a different direction.

There was a sudden clamor at the door: the coach had arrived, and the girls were all racing over to greet him.

"Oh, look!" said the hostess. "He brought his girlfriend! That's so sweet."

And there was Gracie, looking undeniably stylish in a long, narrow cardigan over a pair of tight jeans and a light linen scarf that was tied artfully around her slender neck.

She was beautiful. The sun had been bright at the festival, and I had been wearing sunglasses, so I hadn't appreciated how perfect her skin was or how golden her hair. Probably highlighted, but so well done that if it had been possible for an adult woman to have hair that clear and bright, you would have believed that it was natural. I touched my brutally short, plain brown hair. What had I been thinking?

In what conceivable universe would a guy who had a girl-friend like Gracie look twice at a loser like me? A single-mother college dropout who was short and ratty-looking and dependent on her parents?

I slumped back against the wall, hoping to fade into the background and not be noticed. A couple of minutes later, though, one of the dads approached me. He was sipping at a can of Diet Coke and wore a pair of loose jeans and a worn-out T-shirt that would have made more sense on a teenager than on someone with a receding hairline and saggy jowls.

"Hey," he said. "I don't think we've met." He held out his hand. "I'm Dane Miller. Pammy's dad." We shook and I explained who I was, while he totally looked me up and down. I was used to getting the once-over by parents at Fenwick but usually by moms who wanted to check out the tattoos and the piercings, and they tended to sneak discreet looks. This guy just put his head back and checked me out, top to bottom. I didn't like it, but it wasn't the first time a guy had assumed that the piercings and tattoos meant I was potentially some kind of sexually available freak.

He realized I was staring stonily back at him and smiled at me, unembarrassed. "Thought you were a babysitter at first," he said lightly. "So you're Noah's mom? He's a cute kid."

I relaxed. He was just your garden-variety doofus, nothing threatening.

"How old are you?" he asked.

"Seventeen," I said with a straight face.

"Wow." He glanced over his shoulder to where Noah and the girls were all vying for the coach's attention. "And your son is—how old?"

"Six," I said. "It's a very complicated story."

"I'll bet. I'd like to hear it sometime."

"I'll make sure I tell it to you," I said, laughing a little.

He drew closer. I think he thought I was flirting with him as opposed to making fun of him. I mean, couldn't the guy do math? No one has a baby at *eleven*. "Does that hurt at all?" he asked, flicking his finger in the direction of my nose stud.

"Only when I sneeze" was my automatic response.

"You must dread the cold and flu season. But it's cool. I like it." I would have bet this guy was some bigwig in the entertainment industry. He had that weird mixture of arrogance and cultivated boyishness that those guys always had. He took another pull at his Diet Coke. "You act at all? You look like you could be an actress."

I shook my head and said, "Oops, looks like my son needs me," which was a complete lie but gave me an excuse to wander off.

I managed to avoid the guy for the rest of the party.

After the pizza was eaten, Andrew handed out certificates to all the girls, saying something funny and sweet about each one in turn. Then, amid all their applause and chattering, he held up his hand and said, "I'm not done yet. I couldn't have coached this team so successfully without the incredible support of my ever-enthusiastic, ever-ready, ever-able assistant, Mr. Noah Allen. Come on up here, Noah!"

The girls cheered as Noah shuffled his slow way to the head of the table where Andrew was standing. Gracie was sitting next to him, smiling her big gracious smile at everyone. "Thanks for everything, buddy," Andrew said to Noah, cuffing him on his shoulder and handing him a certificate all his own.

Noah accepted the certificate without even saying thank you, but I could tell he was just too overwhelmed to remember to be polite. He ran back to where I was lurking at the far end of the table, and I admired the award while he bobbed from foot to foot, excited.

Now the hostess was calling for attention. She thanked Andrew for being such a great coach and handed him a large envelope, explaining that inside was a restaurant gift certificate from all the families on the team.

Andrew thanked her warmly and said he and Gracie couldn't wait to use it.

Gracie took that as her cue to speak. "This is so great," she said, gesturing at the envelope. "Thank you all. He'll finally take me somewhere nice!"

"Hey!" he said and they smiled into each other's eyes.

"Come on," I whispered to Noah. "Let's go." We sneaked out quietly.

That night I went to Ryan's apartment: my idea, my call.

I threw myself on him the second we were inside, slamming my body up against his and plastering my mouth hard against his lips. He responded with a mixture of amusement and enthusiasm, and we were on his bed in record time.

"I feel so used," he said, as we lay back, panting a little, most of our clothes still on, only undone enough to be pushed out of the way. "It's just 'wham, bang, thank you, mister' with you these days."

"Sorry," I said. "I needed that."

"Clearly."

We were silent a moment. Then I said, "When do you leave?"

"In four days."

"Shit," I sat up. "That's soon."

"I know." He pulled at a hank of my hair.

"Ow!"

"Why'd you cut it all off?"

"It was Melanie's fault."

"How so?"

"She told me not to."

He laughed. "Yeah, she should have known better."

"Don't go," I said suddenly.

"What?"

"Don't go. To Turkey. Stay here."

He scooted up in the bed and put a pillow behind his back. "Rickie." Just the one word, but there was a world of disappointment and weariness in it.

"I know," I said. "I know that's not how it works. But things can change, right?"

"They're not going to." He took my hand. "And you know that." I didn't say anything, just sat there, staring at our hands. "Is everything okay with you, Rickie? You don't seem happy."

I pulled my hand away. "When have I ever seemed happy?"

"Sometimes you're less *un*happy."

I flopped onto my back. "I'm sick of my life," I said. "I want to change it, but I don't know how to."

"Get a job. Go back to school. Start dating. Do some charity work. Make a difference in the world."

"Oh, just shut up," I said wearily.

"I'll miss you when I'm away," he said. "For what it's worth. I always do." I didn't say anything to that, just stared up at the ceiling. He flicked at my hair. "The good news is that by the time I'm back, you may actually have some hair again."

"I'll shave it all off the second you're in town."

"That'll show me." He put his arm out and I moved into its embrace, resting my head on his shoulder. "Seriously, Rickie. Move forward. You'll be happier if you do."

"When did you get so preachy?"

He sighed and I could feel his chest move under my ear. "Someday you're going to realize that when people give you advice, they're not doing it to piss you off. They're trying to help you."

"I don't need anyone's help."

"Says the girl who sponges off her parents."

There was a pause. "That was mean," I said and moved off of him.

He shrugged. "The truth hurts."

"I *had* to move back in with them and you know it. Because of Noah."

"That was years ago, Rickie."

"You try taking care of a baby, see how easy it is."

"He's not a baby anymore."

"You can't possibly know what it's been like for me," I said, sitting up, my voice rising. "You've never taken care of anything, not even a fish. You don't even have a fucking plant in this place."

He regarded me calmly, his arms lying quietly at his sides. "Nope," he said. "I don't. Because I've made a choice not to be responsible for anything other than myself."

"How wonderful for you," I said. "How great that you don't ever have to care about anyone other than yourself."

"Yeah, it's nice," he said and laughed.

"God!" I said, half furious, half wanting to laugh too. "I kind of hate you."

"I kind of hate you too."

It occurred to me that that was the closest thing to "I love you" Ryan and I were ever likely to say to each other.

It was the last time I saw him before he left the country again.

18.

For the winter school break, we all left town—Mom, Dad, Mel, her kids, Noah, and me—to go to my mother's ocean-front condo in Laguna.

My mom had been an only child and her parents had died fairly young, leaving her a lot of money, but she didn't throw it around much. If you thought about it, you knew she was rich

because she and Dad had a good-sized house in a nice neighborhood and could afford to support me and Noah without
any difficulty, but she never wore expensive clothes or jewelry
or anything flashy. Her one huge indulgence was this beach
condo, which was big enough to fit us all, so long as Noah
bunked with Nicole and Cameron, and Melanie and I shared
the third bedroom. In the past, Mel's family would just come
down for a couple of days at Christmas and stay at a nearby
resort hotel, but things were different this year with her and
Gabriel separated, so she and the kids were joining us for the
whole first half of break. After Christmas, Gabriel would get
the kids.

We spent a lot of that vacation walking on the beach,
Melanie and I, letting the kids run ahead of us, talking and
sometimes just being quiet together. It was fairly cold out there
that time of year, and we had to wrap up in scarves and hats
and gloves, but the kids never wanted to wear more than a
sweatshirt and often had bare feet on the cold sand. "They run
hotter than we do," Mel said.

It was during a mile-long walk along the deserted beach—
just the two of us that time, because the kids were back at the
condo helping my mother decorate the small Christmas tree
we had just lugged up to the apartment—that I finally told
Melanie I was going back to school after the holidays. "Just
at SMC, but I can apply to UCLA after I've done a couple of
semesters there. I can take three full-credit courses and still be
out in time to pick up Noah from school."

"Oh, Rickie, that's wonderful!" She threw her arms around
me. "I didn't want to nag you about it, but I'm so glad. Did
you tell Dad and Laurel yet?"

I kicked at a rock. "I can't bear to. Mom'll be way too happy
about it."

She stepped back. "Is that such an awful thing? Making her happy?"

"I just can't stand the way she always has to be right about everything."

"I don't understand why you're so hard on her, Rickie. Do you have any idea how lucky you are to have a mother like her? She's generous and kind and smart and she's taken care of you and Noah without ever even criticizing you for—" She stopped.

"For being an idiot?" I filled in for her. "For having a kid when I was too young?" I dug my heel deep into the sand. "You just don't know what it's like, Mel. You have a different relationship with her than I do. She respects you. She doesn't respect me."

Melanie was silent. We started walking again. "Don't get mad at me," she said finally in a small voice that I had to strain to hear above the ocean noise. "But respect is a two-way street. Maybe if you were more respectful toward her..." She trailed off.

"Whatever," I said. "Not in the mood for a lecture, okay?"

"Okay," she said. We turned around and headed back down the beach.

I had made the decision to go back to school a couple of weeks earlier, on the night Ryan called me from the airport to say good-bye. I'd said, "Call me when you get back."

"Change something before then," he'd said. "Surprise me."

As I looked around the bedroom I'd lived in for all but nine months of my entire life, it struck me that that wasn't a bad idea.

Besides, if Andrew Fulton ever asked me again what my plans for the future were, I wanted a better answer than "I don't know."

*   *   *

On Christmas Day the kids got way too many presents and my mother made way too big a ham. Both were Allen family traditions.

Mom gave me a few gift cards to different stores—"I didn't dare pick anything out for you," she said—but she'd gotten Melanie a beautiful necklace. "It's from that jewelry designer in Bergamot Station you love so much," she told her, which made me wonder how many conversations she and Melanie had about things they loved when I wasn't around. Maybe I just tuned them out.

My big gift for Noah was a baseball bat and mitt. A couple of weeks earlier he had gone rooting for a stick of gum in my messenger bag and discovered the form that Coach Andrew had given me about the T-ball league. "Hey!" he said, shaking it at me. "You never told me about this!"

"Oh, sorry. I forgot." It wasn't a lie. I *had* forgotten about it. But I also hadn't really wanted to show it to him in the first place. It had been a convenient lapse of memory.

"Where'd you get it?"

"Coach Andrew. He's coaching one of the teams and thought you'd be interested."

"I want to do it."

"It's a pretty big commitment, Noey. And you haven't played a lot of baseball in the past."

"I want to do it."

"I'll look into it," I said with a sigh. I knew exactly how this would play out: he'd be all excited and enthusiastic ahead of time then he'd go to the first practice, which wouldn't be anything like he'd imagined. He would hate all the hard work and running and would complain about fake injuries and exaggerated exhaustion. After that, I'd have to coax and beg and yell at him just to get him to go to the practices. He'd freak out at having to play in a real game, but the coach would insist he "get on out there," and there I'd be on the sidelines, watching the son I loved mess up every time he was on the field and be jeered at by the kids on both teams.

I knew all this because I'd signed Noah up for an AYSO team the year before and that was exactly what had happened until I just stopped taking him to the practices and games altogether, thus imparting to my son the invaluable lesson that he should quit whenever things got tough.

"Tell him I want to do it," Noah said stubbornly.

What could I do? I surrendered. "Okay."

I had managed to busy myself in other parts of the house when Andrew had come to work with Noah the last couple of weeks before break. I'd stay upstairs while Noah answered the door and just call down my greetings and later my good-bye like I was too busy to come down at all. It just seemed... easier.

That pizza party had made something very clear to me: Andrew was perfectly happy with his present romantic situation. It just felt simpler now to avoid him than to keep reminding myself how cute and nice and funny and unavailable he was.

So when Noah said he wanted to play T-ball, I sent Andrew a short e-mail about it.

"Great," he wrote back. "I look forward to seeing you both at practices and games."

So much for avoiding him.

Anyway, Christmas Day I gave Noah the T-ball gear and he was pretty excited about it, which was probably the first time he had ever shown pleasure in getting some kind of athletic equipment. The rest of his gifts from me and the other members of the family were more traditionally Noah-ish: lots of books, lots of computer and video games, and a chemistry kit from my father, who said he'd help him use it.

I gave Dad a two-year subscription to *Wine Lovers* magazine and I gave Mom a state-of-the-art meat thermometer that worked remotely so you left part of it in the meat and carried around the digital readout. "Now you don't have to worry about when to take out the turkey," I said.

"Thank you." She gave me a big hug. I hugged her back. It was Christmas, after all.

Melanie nudged me. "Don't you have another present to give your mother?" she said archly. I stared at her blankly. "Tell her your news," she said. "It's the perfect holiday gift."

"What news is that?" Mom asked.

"I'm pregnant again!" I said gaily.

For a moment, her jaw dropped open. Then I saw that patented steely Laurel Allen "I can deal with this; I can deal with anything they throw at me" look come across her face as she drew herself up into battle stance. But before she could actually say anything, Melanie broke in. "Shut up, Rickie! She's not pregnant," she told my mom. "She's going back to college after the break—she's enrolled and everything."

My mother put her hand to her heart. "Oh, thank god," she said.

"Overreact much?" I said.

"Shut up, Rickie," Mel said again.

When all the gifts had been unwrapped, my mother said she had another Christmas present for both Mel and me but we'd have to wait to get it. "A friend of mine was raving about how good her masseuse is, so I scheduled her to come to the house and give both you girls a rubdown after we get back to town."

"You'll have one, too, won't you?" Melanie asked.

Mom shook her head. "It's not my kind of thing."

"She'd have to relax for an hour," I said. "She'd probably explode."

"I'm capable of relaxing," Mom snapped.

I rolled my eyes.

"You're welcome," she added pointedly.

The next day Gabriel came to pick up the kids and ended up staying with us at the beach for most of the afternoon. He had brought extravagant and wonderful gifts for everyone. Mine was a portable photo printer that connected to your cell phone. He insisted on running out to pick up lunch, coming back with bags and bags of take-out Mexican food—way too much for the number of people, but the kids were beyond excited as they unpacked it all and tore open the containers of quesadillas, tacos, and nachos. Noah was especially happy because Gabriel had remembered to get corn tortillas instead of flour, so it was all gluten-free and for once he could eat everything his cousins could.

I was just relieved Gabriel hadn't brought Sherri with him. That would have killed Melanie.

She was pretty tense at the beginning of his visit but became visibly more relaxed as the day went on. The thing about Gabriel was that he was always so much fun to be around. Even with all their history, Melanie couldn't help laughing at his stories and smiling at his compliments, which somehow managed to be both over-the-top and oddly sincere. He gave her the most gorgeous Hermès purse I'd ever seen. (I went online later to check out the price and my slight shame at doing so didn't reduce my awe at the fifteen-hundred-dollar price tag.) You could tell Mel loved it and that it was killing her that she loved it as she unwrapped and looked at it.

She had framed a beautiful photo of their two kids for him, and he hugged her close after he'd opened it, dropping a kiss on the top of her head so gently that I'm not sure she even felt it.

When he took all the kids for a walk on the beach, I pulled Melanie aside to see how she was holding up. "I'm good," she said in a reasonably steady voice. "I really think I'm past the worst of this, Rickie. I think I can be with him now and not care all that much."

"Uh-huh," I said. "You took a Xanax, didn't you?"

"Only a half of one."

Later, when I was saying good-bye to Gabriel, I said, "It's not the same around here without you." I didn't even say it in a bitter, look-what-you've-done way; it was just a statement that we both knew was true and sad. Then I left so he and Melanie could say good-bye alone.

When she came back in, she walked swiftly and silently past all of us, straight to the room we shared. She closed the door. I left her alone for a while and then I knocked and went in. She was lying in bed, staring at the ceiling and listening to some melancholy song on her iPod, which was plugged into the clock/stereo dock.

I came in and sat on the edge of the other twin bed. I didn't say anything, just waited for her to speak, which she eventually did.

"He broke up with Sherri."

"Wow," I said.

"Or *she* broke up with *him* but he's saying he did it."

"Either way, it's got to feel good."

"It's better," she said. "Good is an overstatement."

"Does it change anything for you?"

She shook her head. Then she nodded. Then she shrugged

and shook her head again. "Oh, lord, I don't know," she said wearily. "I'd forgive him if I could, Rickie. But I can't. What he did hurt me so much."

"Maybe you don't need to actually forgive him," I said. "Maybe you can still be mad he did what he did but give him another chance anyway."

"He'd cheat on me again."

"You really think so?"

"I'll get older and my body will deteriorate and there'll be a new pretty young actress with perfect boobs and he'll cheat on me again."

"Maybe not. Now that he knows what a huge price he'd pay for something like that."

"And anyway, I won't trust him anymore so I'll be waiting for him to cheat on me whether or not he actually does. And that alone will make me miserable and ruin everything."

I couldn't argue with that, so I just lay down and listened to her funereal music until I realized it was way past Noah's bedtime and he was still up watching TV.

We came back to the LA house the day before New Year's Eve. My mother threw an annual New Year's Day open house party, and so the next couple of days were a whirlwind of food shopping and cooking and cleaning. Her temper, never particularly slow to rise, got sharper with every passing hour, until she was yelling at everyone who crossed her path to "stop wasting time and at least help me get this house in shape!" The house looked clean enough to me, so I just stayed out of her way.

On New Year's Eve, just another day of party preparation as far as my mother was concerned, she came across some cooked chicken that she had asked Noah to cut up for her that he had left out on the counter. "How long has this been out?"

she asked, carrying the bowl of chicken pieces into the family room where the rest of us were watching East Coast coverage of the countdown. It was past eight and the party in Times Square was in full swing. "Noah, do you know?"

He shook his head, eyes on the TV. "I don't remember."

"The chicken feels warm," Mom said. "I don't know if I can use it now."

"I'm sure it's fine," I said. "Just stick it in the fridge."

"I can't risk giving my guests food poisoning."

"Worse that happens is they lose a pound or two. It's all good."

She wasn't amused. "You need to teach your son to finish what he begins. Wouldn't kill you to remember that, either."

"Why are you yelling at me?" I said. "I didn't do anything."

"That's just the point. You don't do anything. I could use a lot more help right around now but all you do is sit around all day, staring at your computer or the TV set."

"Fine," I said. "What do you want me to do? Just tell me and I'll do it."

She shook the bowl of chicken at me. "That tone isn't helpful."

"I'm just asking you what you want—"

"Some help!" she said, her voice rising. "I just told you!"

"What kind of help? I'm willing to do whatever you want, but you have to be more specific."

"You know what I'd love?" she said. "For once I'd love for someone to do something around here without being pissy about it." She turned on her heel and left the family room.

"Did you see that?" I asked Melanie. "You always think I start things but that was all her."

"She's just on edge because of the party. She gets this way every year."

"And yet somehow she never takes it out on *you*."

"She's nicer to me because I'm *not* her daughter. That's just how it works. You're more patient with Cameron than you are with Noah, and I'm the opposite. It's the distance—you don't care so much when it's not your kid, so things don't annoy you as much."

I considered that then shook my head. "I think she just hates me."

"You think Grandma hates you?" Noah said, looking up from the TV.

Rats, he was listening. "Not really. I was just saying that."

"Do *you* hate *me*?"

"Hmm," I said. "Let me think about that."

"Mo-om!"

I grabbed him and hugged him hard against me. "Nah. I kind of love you."

He squirmed away. "I can't see the TV."

"Another beautiful Hallmark family moment," I said. "I could cry."

Gabriel dropped off Nicole and Cameron the next morning, as planned.

"You going to come back for the party?" I asked him as I greeted them at the door. Melanie was in the shower.

"Should I?" He was looking a little forlorn, his big, round face slightly droopy.

"Yeah, you should," I said and hoped I was right about that. "Hey, any news from your brother? He's in Turkey, right?"

"Just a mass e-mail saying he's having fun and is crazy busy."

I had gotten that same e-mail. "Sounds like it's going well. So maybe I'll see you later?"

He nodded and turned to go, then said over his shoulder, "But tell Mel she should just text me if she doesn't want me to come. I'll understand."

"I'll tell her." I said good-bye and closed the door.

Nicole had already joined my mother in the kitchen and was busily rolling forks and knives up in napkins for the buffet. Cameron and Noah were eating cereal at the table together, and my mother was racing wildly around, banging cabinet doors, whisking food violently, checking the temperature of various things that were cooking—and generally freaking out.

I slipped away before she could take some of that frantic energy out on me and went upstairs to find Melanie.

She had just finished showering and I told her about my conversation with Gabriel while she rubbed her wet hair with a towel. When I was done, she said slowly, "I guess it's okay. I don't know. Maybe it's a mistake. But if he wants to come, he should. I'm not going to tell him not to. It just might be weird…and people know we're separated now so that could be weird for *them*…Maybe I should just tell him not to come. But the kids would be so happy to have him here and he knows a lot of our friends at this point. And I want people to see we're still friends. But I'm not sure how *I* feel—"

"It's up to you," I said, cutting her off, and I left to take a shower.

The party guests consisted almost entirely of friends of my parents who wanted to exclaim over how grown-up I'd become and how tall Noah was. As far as I was concerned, both comments simply revealed what liars they all were. I endured it for as long as I could, but when Louis Wilson walked in the front door with his tall, statuesque wife, I fled into the kitchen.

Making polite conversation with Noah's (and my) principal just wasn't something I was at ease with. Maybe in another fifty years or so.

My mother had hired a couple of servers to help at the party. I spent some time comparing tattoos with one of them—she had more, but admitted to regretting a couple—and then lingered in the kitchen, assisting them as they got the food in and out of the oven and onto serving trays.

Noah had escaped upstairs much earlier. My mother always insisted that her grandchildren politely greet the first guests—not that Noah actually said anything, since he became determinedly mute in major social situations—but after that, she got too busy to keep track of them and Noah was able to sneak up to my parents' bedroom and watch TV. Cameron joined him there a little later, but Nicole stayed downstairs for the whole event, eager to help pass food out or chat animatedly with the many adults who exclaimed over how adorable she was in her bubble dress and curled hair.

People stopped arriving after the first couple of hours and started leaving after the third. By five o'clock, all but a few of my parents' closest friends had left.

My mother came into the kitchen then to pay the servers and let them go. She spotted me cramming a broken mini-quiche into my mouth. "So this is where you've been hiding," she snapped at me. "A lot of people left saying they'd been hoping to talk to you but couldn't find you."

"I thought I was more useful in here."

"Well, you weren't. I wanted you out there." She made a big show of handing the servers their check and some cash for tips, just to make her point that she had adequate help. She headed back to the living room after that, barking out a brusque "Come join us!" as she left. It was an order, not an invitation.

Fortunately Melanie came into the kitchen a few seconds later, which gave me an excuse to stay where I was. She dropped down into a chair. "I'm exhausted," she said. "Trying to keep the conversation going with some of Dad's professor friends..."

"I think they only ever leave their offices for this one party," I said. "Their caves, I mean."

"Did you see Professor Orton? He had a big tag sticking out from his shirt collar and there was this orange stain right in the front of his pants."

"Yuck."

"He never showed up," she said.

I looked up from the cupcake I was tearing in half. "Huh?"

"Gabriel. He didn't come to the party."

"Weird. He said he was going to unless you told him not to." I popped a piece of cupcake into my mouth.

"I guess he changed his mind." She twitched her shoulders irritably. "It's probably for the best."

Later that evening, she called me into her room as I was coming up the stairs. She was sitting on the bed, staring at her computer, her half-packed travel bag open next to her, since she and the kids were going back to their house that night.

When I came in, she shifted her laptop toward me. "Read this."

I crouched down so I could see the screen. It was an e-mail from Gabriel.

Hey, Mel. I was going to come today—I was actually in my car, on the way—when I pulled over and thought better of it. Not because I didn't want to come, I did. But because I was worried that it might hurt you, that I might still be hurting you in ways I don't intend. And because it's too hard for me to be with you and not be WITH you. It's stupid to write all this in an email, but it's impossible to say it any other way. This is the point: I'm miserable without you and the kids. I know I screwed up and don't deserve you. But I want you. If you were willing to give me another chance, I'd be happy and grateful beyond anything I can put in words.

I'm so sorry for everything, Mel. Please forgive me and give me another chance.

Love,

me.

P.S. Love me?

I didn't say anything at first, just reread it a couple more times. "Wow," I said finally. "That's quite an e-mail."

"I know."

"Would you consider doing what he wants? Getting back together? You could do the marriage-therapy thing."

"I don't know." She rubbed her temples. "Sitting in some therapist's office, being reminded over and over again that my husband fell madly in love with another woman...not my idea of fun."

"A good therapist might get you past all that."

"Maybe." She dropped her hands. "But then there's the whole timing thing. I mean, if he had just written this right at the beginning, said that he couldn't bear being separated from me, that he realized Sherri was nothing to him. Instead he waits until that whole thing runs its course. For all I know, she broke his heart and now he's coming crying back to me because he thinks I'll take him back in. So, what—no consequences for everything he's done? That's not right, is it?"

"No." I sat down on the edge of her bed. "But"—I stopped and made sure I was going to say it right—"There's the issue of right and wrong and then there's the practical stuff like you miss him and he misses you and that makes me think that maybe you should just forget about right and wrong."

She twisted her mouth uncertainly. "I don't know. I honestly don't know."

"Well, think about it."

She managed a bleary smile. "I can promise you that this is *all* I'll be thinking about for a very long time."

19.

She called me the next day from her house to let me know she had agreed to host Tuesday's meeting of the Event Hospitality Committee. "Do you think I should get the pastries from Huckleberry or Clementine?"

"I don't know or care," I said. "But I think you should shellac them. Since no one actually eats anything, we might as well just keep reusing the same ones."

"You're not very helpful. Oh, my god, you know what just occurred to me? Marley Addison might come! She might actually be in my house!"

"Yeah," I said. "That's likely. Given her attendance record."

"Just promise me you'll come early," Mel said. "I don't want to do this alone."

Tanya, Melanie, and I had all met with the head of Crackerjack Catering right before break to finalize the Casino Night menu, and Tanya was pleased to announce at Tuesday morning's meeting that the meal would be soupless, as she had specified. In addition to no soup, the menu included swedish meatballs, hamburger sliders, puff pastry savory pies filled with spinach and cheese, and crudités.

Maria Dellaventura was in charge of the alcohol. "I've spoken to the bartending company and they'll be mixing pitchers of vodka martinis. We've got a ton of champagne, too—well, sparkling wine, actually, but same difference—and red and white wine. I'm ordering it all from one of those alcohol warehouses—they gave me a bulk discount but because of that, we can't return anything that's not drunk, so we'd better all do our part and drink a lot." She smirked. "Should make it a fun party, right?"

"Ha, ha," Tanya said stiffly. Linda Chatterjee just looked blank. Carol Lynn was checking her cell phone and didn't hear what Maria said. I laughed, Melanie smiled, and Marley—

Marley didn't respond at all because she *wasn't there*. Big surprise.

In an impressive display of hope over experience, Melanie had ordered (and had me pick up on my way) five platters of muffins, scones, and biscuits from Huckleberry Cafe. Five. Count them. Five. Platters. Of pastries. For six women. Six women who didn't eat. "You are certifiable," I told her when I carried the first two into her house. She was too busy fretting about how her house looked to respond to that. "It's so small compared to the other women's houses," she said, looking around.

"And so big compared to the shacks ninety-nine percent of the world lives in," I said. I loved her little house. It was warm and comfortable, and Gabriel had an amazing collection of Mexican art, so every wall and corner was filled with colorful and eye-catching statues and paintings.

As I manfully did my part to eat as many buttery-rich sweets as my stomach could handle, the conversation moved on to a more general discussion of the upcoming event. Tanya didn't approve of the invitation the Event Coordinating Committee had sent out. "Too big and too square—it cost them extra postage on every one, and I just don't think it makes sense to spend money like that in these times."

"But people notice the big invitations more," Carol Lynn said. Today she was wearing a tank top and yoga pants. The woman was always either just coming from or just going to a workout. Possibly both. "They're less likely to just toss them aside."

"I liked the way it was black with silver writing," Melanie added.

Carol Lynn raised her eyebrows. "That was my least favorite part about it. Looked like an invitation to a funeral." Her tone was so pointedly negative that Melanie flinched, hurt, and I frowned at Carol Lynn, trying to figure out what was going on. She had been ignoring or sniping at both of us all morning in a deliberately obvious way.

The reason why became clear later, when the meeting had ended and people were saying their good-byes. Tanya and Linda had already taken off when Carol Lynn suddenly turned to Mel and hissed, "Just out of curiosity, I was wondering what you found so objectionable about my cousin. He said he thought you'd both had a nice time together but then you wouldn't return his calls. He's very hurt. Maybe you could explain it to me so I could explain it to him?"

"Oh, no." Melanie's hand flew to her mouth. "I'm sorry! He's so nice. I thought he was great. Really. I just—it's—"

"You're just not that into him?" Carol Lynn suggested icily.

Melanie's eyes widened with horror. "No, not at all. It's just..." Her voice faltered. "I think I may be getting back with my husband."

Maria had been picking up her bag, getting ready to leave, but her head whipped around at that. "Really?" she said, advancing. "I mean...*really?*"

"I don't know for sure." Mel's face had turned bright red. "At this point we're just talking. That's all. But I don't feel like it's fair to start dating anyone else right now."

Carol Lynn waved her hand at that, the smaller transgression completely overshadowed by the potentially far greater one. "Right, I'll tell my cousin. But...from everything you've said...Are you sure this really makes sense?"

Maria touched Melanie's arm before she could answer, which was good since I don't think Mel had an answer to that. "Just remember how hard this stuff can be on the kids," Maria said. "The back-and-forth stuff. I didn't go through it but I know people who did and in the end the kids were far more devastated by having their hopes raised—and then dashed again—than by the original separation."

"I—" Poor Melanie was trapped between the two bitter divorcées. "I know. I understand. I'll be careful, I promise. And I don't know— It's just—"

"It *seems* so easy," Carol Lynn said, shaking her head. "Like you can just turn back the clock. But you can't. Not ever. And most of the time you shouldn't."

"We're not trying to be negative," Maria added. "Just realistic. We want you to be careful."

"Thank you for the warning," Melanie said faintly.

I rescued her by stepping forward. "It was great seeing you guys! I think Casino Night's going to be fun, don't you?"

They took the hint, said good-byes, and left. But later, when I looked out the window, I saw the two of them still out in front, whispering on the lawn, and, from the way they glanced up at the house periodically, I suspected that it was all they could do to keep from marching back in and making poor Mel even more anxious, all in the name of female solidarity.

"Did you mean that?" I asked her as we carried five almost-full platters of pastries into the kitchen. "Are you really thinking about getting back together with Gabriel? Or were you just saying that so Carol Lynn wouldn't be mad at you about her cousin?"

"Maybe we can freeze some of this," Melanie said, putting her tray down on the counter and heading back toward the living room for more.

Guess she didn't feel like answering my questions.

I wasn't the only one with unanswerable questions.

"What if I don't know anyone on the team?" Noah said. "What if someone I don't like is on the team? What if *Caleb's* on the team? What if a ball hits me in the eye? What if I stink up the place the second I go to bat and everyone laughs at me? What if..."

Anxiety had set in on the way to the first Saturday morning T-ball practice.

I glanced at my son in the rearview mirror. He was dressed in new clothes—sweatpants and a long-sleeved T-shirt—that were way too big for him. I just couldn't go on buying size-fours for my six-year-old son any longer. But he was swallowed up by the sixes, and he looked especially small at the moment, as his terror was making him curl up in a fetal position around his seat belt. He was wearing a baseball hat that came down over his ears and was clutching the bat and mitt to his chest. "It'll be okay, Noey, I promise. Coach Andrew will look out for you."

"What if I hate every minute of it? Can I stop?"

I was tempted to tell him how much happier I'd be if he

quit. I wouldn't have to get up early on Saturday mornings. I wouldn't have to sit in some park for an hour every week, watching my son get made fun of for being the worst player on the team. I wouldn't have to hang out with a ton of sports-obsessed parents who would make it clear they thought that Noah was dragging the team down.

I had my own anxieties about T-ball practice.

Still, I had to push Noah to keep going, for his sake. I had to stop teaching him that quitting was a viable option. So I said, "Let's just think positively about this, okay, Noah?"

"You have to promise me if I don't like it I can leave. Or I'm not going!" His voice was getting shrill.

How could this be the same kid who, before he'd gone to sleep last night, had carefully laid his mitt on the night table beside him "so I can find it first thing in the morning before we go"? How was he able to do a 180-degree turn like this? Why couldn't he just stay enthusiastic about anything? What had I done wrong as a mother that had made him such an anxious little boy? Was it because he didn't have a father? Because I was only nineteen when I had him? Would a forty-year-old mother know the perfect thing to say at a moment like this?

I felt very tired. "Just...let's just get there. Okay? And we'll go from there."

"But what if—"

"Just stop!" I snapped.

He kept quiet then, but he managed to make his breathing sound unhappy.

The good news: Joshua Golden, the nice kid from Austin's birthday party, was there and Noah brightened up considerably when he spotted him.

The bad news: all the other kids were strangers. And most

of them were bigger than Noah and Joshua. I swear a couple of them were bigger than both boys put together.

Andrew was busy making sure all the parents had the right paperwork and the kids had the necessary equipment, so when I walked Noah over he just nodded at me and said a cheerful "Noah! I'm glad you came" and then went back to work.

I left Noah with Joshua, both of them staying close to the coach, and headed toward the bleachers. Joshua's mom came rushing toward me. "Hey!" she said. "Thank god you're here too!" She was wearing sweats and a cardigan sweater that was old and stretched out. Her hair was messy and she had no makeup on. She looked unbelievably normal. "I'm Debbie. Rickie, right?"

"Right. So did Coach Andrew recruit Joshua too?"

"Yep." She laughed. "I think he's going to single-handedly make our little guys into athletes. Even if it kills him."

"It might come to that with Noah."

"Same with Joshua. But if anyone can succeed, it's Andrew. Joshua adores him—I wouldn't have been able to get him here for anyone else. Want to sit down?" I nodded and we stepped up onto the empty bleachers together. "Let's go up high," she said, carefully picking her way up the steps. "He'll come running over to me about every little thing if he thinks he can."

"Noah's the same way."

"They're made to be friends. We have to get them together more often. Where do you live?" I told her. "That's not too far," she said. "We're south of you, closer to Pico." She grinned. "You know, the poor side of town."

"Only by Fenwick standards."

She nodded. "Exactly. My daughter's always coming home and talking about these huge mansions some of the girls in her class live in. Do you know she actually said to me, 'Why don't we belong to a beach club like everyone else?'" Debbie Golden shook her head. "I was this close to calling her a spoiled brat, but I'm happy to say I managed to restrain myself."

"I've called Noah a spoiled brat," I admitted. "I usually apologize afterwards, but I've done it."

"Oh, I've done it too," she said cheerfully. "Just *that* time, I stopped myself."

Andrew was leading the kids onto the baseball diamond. Noah and Joshua walked side by side at the end of the line, lagging way behind the others. Andrew called over his shoulder to them to speed up.

"I don't know..." Debbie said slowly, watching them. "I was so happy the day Josie got accepted to kindergarten there, but sometimes I wonder if Fenwick is the right place for my kids. Between the wealth thing and the way the other boys are all so huge and athletic, sometimes I think Joshua at least would be happier at some loser school where all the kids are small and wimpy like him."

"Plus there's Caleb." It was a weird thing to bond over, but I remembered how she had said Joshua was bullied by Caleb and his friends, just like Noah.

"God, I hate that kid," Debbie said. "I know an adult shouldn't hate a small child, but I can't stand him. On the other hand, there's *always* a Caleb, isn't there? Wherever you send your kid?"

"Maybe. I wouldn't know."

"Noah's an only child, right?" I nodded and waited for the other questions—the you-must-have-had-him-young, huh? kind of questions—but she just said, "I have two, but my other's a girl and it's different with girls. There are plenty of girls in her class who I'd like to throttle, but which *one* changes on a weekly basis. Her best friend one week turns into a viper the next. And vice versa. I can't keep track, so I just stay out of it."

"I remember those days."

"Me too. But the Caleb thing is different: in ten years, Caleb will still be the class bully."

"Unless he's doing time in San Quentin."

"Oh, I like that idea! Think there's a chance?"

Some of the kids were putting on red jerseys. "I hope he keeps them together," I said and just then Andrew handed both Noah and Joshua red jerseys. "Look how he listens to me," I said with a laugh because we were well out of earshot.

"He knows what he's doing," Debbie said. "There's something so trustworthy about that guy." I didn't answer. She shifted her butt on the bleacher bench. "God, these are uncomfortable. We should bring pillows next time. And coffee."

"And food," I said because I was starving. I hadn't had any breakfast.

"We could take turns picking up from Starbucks."

"I think I love you," I said.

"I'm coming tomorrow, right?" Andrew asked when I came over to nab Noah at the end of practice.

"You don't have to," I said. "I mean, Noah's getting coached by you here now."

"I'd still like to work with him privately on his batting."

Noah hadn't exactly managed to get a lot of height on the ball when he was hitting. He had kind of nudged it off the tee with his bat so it dribbled onto the field. I heard one dad in the bleachers say to another, "Hope they keep that kid on the bench during the games" and felt a stab of anger so intense I couldn't move. Then Debbie said loudly, "I hate stupidly competitive parents, don't you?" and I felt better.

"So can I come?" Andrew asked.

"Of course," I said and thanked him. "So," I said to Noah as we headed toward the car. "How was it?"

"Okay, I guess. I kind of sucked but it's okay because Joshua did too."

"He's nice, right?"

"He's okay."

"His mom is really nice. I like her a lot. I said maybe you guys could have a playdate sometime. Would you like that?"

"Maybe." I expected a bit more enthusiasm but realized how tired, and probably hungry, he was when I offered to take him to Cafe 50's, his current favorite restaurant, and he said wearily, "I guess that would be okay."

He just didn't have the energy to be enthusiastic about anything right at that moment.

20.

I was the only adult at home the next morning: Mom and Dad had gone out for brunch with friends, and Melanie was with her kids at her place.

I had learned to set the alarm on Saturday night so I wouldn't be caught half-asleep like that first time. Unfortunately, I hadn't learned how not to *ignore* the alarm, so by the time I finally hauled myself out of bed I only had enough time to brush my teeth and make some coffee before Andrew rang the doorbell, looking all bright and well rested and, yes, kind of cute because at some point I had decided he was cute and didn't seem to be able to change my mind about that as much as I would have liked to.

I worked hard to act like his arrival was no big deal to me: I made Noah answer the door and I just kind of waved nonchalantly at the coach from the kitchen table as Noah dragged him toward the backyard. I overheard Andrew ask Noah if he had had fun at T-ball the day before and then Noah's agonizingly misleading response: "It was okay. Mom promised I could quit if it doesn't get better." Fortunately the door slammed shut so I was spared Andrew's reaction to that.

I baked a pan of GF brownies then leafed through the Sunday *New York Times*, glancing up every now and then to watch the two of them through the window.

I found myself wondering what kind of guy gave up his Sunday mornings to help a kid who never seemed especially grateful or enthusiastic.

He was either very kind or very crazy.

I watched as Andrew played some kind of running game with Noah that involved both of them running sprints from one end of the yard to the other until they collapsed on the ground and rolled back and forth on the grass.

Andrew looked kind of crazy doing that. But he wasn't crazy. That was the problem.

When they came in a while later, they were both sweating and panting. The kitchen was warm from the baking, and they instantly tore off their sweatshirts. Andrew was wearing a dark blue T-shirt. It was a good color on him.

"Hooray!" he said, spotting the plate. "Brownies!" He grabbed one. "You really don't have to bake every time," he said as he tore off a big bite. "Really." He chewed and grinned. "Well, maybe you do. These are great. Even better than the last batch."

"Can I eat them?" Noah asked.

I nodded. "They're safe. But just one. It's almost lunchtime."

He leaned over the plate and studied the brownies, clearly looking for the biggest one.

"Hey, Noah, do me a favor, will you?" Andrew said. "I left all the equipment out on the yard. Will you gather it up and put it in my bag and then carry it to my car?"

"Do I have to?"

"Noah!" I said. "No brownie until you do what Coach Andrew says. He's nice enough to come here and play with you every week—"

"Not *every* week," Noah said. "Just some of them."

I shook my head at him warningly. "The least you can do is help clean up. When you've stowed all the stuff in his car, you can come back in and have your brownie. Not until then."

Noah heaved a dramatic sigh and slouched toward the back doorway and out.

There was a pause. "Got rid of *him*," I said.

"That was the goal," Andrew said. I had been joking, so that slightly unnerved me. He gestured toward the kitchen table. "Let's sit."

"Am I in trouble?" I asked as I sat down. I was still wearing my sweatpants and a tank top—aka my pajamas—although once again I'd thrown a hoodie on top to hide the fact that I wasn't wearing a bra.

He just shook his head as he took the chair opposite me. Then he passed his hand through his hair. He seemed nervous. "I've been thinking," he said.

The nervousness was contagious. My pulse sped up. "Have you ever noticed how often you say that? That you've been thinking? You spend a lot of time thinking."

"Really?"

"It's not a bad thing. It's good to be thoughtful. No one's

ever accused *me* of being thoughtful. Which is how I know it's a good thing." God, I was blithering. "So what were you thinking about this time?"

"Our conversation at Thanksgiving."

"That was a month and a half ago," I said. "You've been thinking about it all this time?" I tried to sound calm. But I felt a little sick. Why was he bringing it up now?

"Yeah," he said. "It takes me a little while to process things sometimes. And you hit me with a lot of information all at once."

"Look, for what it's worth—I was a little drunk."

"So was I. But it was all true, right?"

"Yeah," I said. "How pathetic is that?"

"Here's the thing," he said, ignoring my comment. "It's just...I feel bad I haven't said anything to you about it since then. That was wrong of me." I stared at him, surprised. He smiled sheepishly. "I have a tendency to want to run and hide when things get too heavy. At least that's what every girlfriend I've ever had has told me. And my sister and mother. And my grandmother, but she's a little nuts, so don't count that one."

"It's okay," I said. "I think I owe *you* an apology for talking your ear off."

"No, you don't. I felt kind of honored you confided in me." He leaned forward. "Mostly I've been thinking about all the things I should have said that night and feel bad that I didn't say."

"What do you mean?"

"It's been driving me nuts that I didn't say anything helpful, just stood there like an idiot. What I should have said was you're doing an amazing job with Noah. And that life is—" He stopped, searching for the words. Being thoughtful again. I wondered what it would be like to go through life like that: thinking everything through carefully before speaking or taking action.

You probably don't end up with a kid at nineteen.

Andrew said, "Life just always changes, you know? So where you are at any given moment isn't necessarily where you thought you'd be, but in a few years that could all change again and you might look back and say, 'Where I was then makes sense because it got me to here.'" He grimaced. "That sounded way lamer than it was supposed to. I'm sorry. I'm not very articulate."

"For a dumb jock, you do okay."

He leaned forward. "You know, in a way, that's my point."

"What is?"

"You think I'm a dumb jock because you've only known me as a PE coach."

"I don't really think you're dumb," I said. "I was joking."

He dismissed that with a wave. "The point is, I came to Fenwick because I got laid off at my banking job and so I came to help set up the new computers and teach the older kids some computer skills and then one of the coaches left and they asked me to fill in for her. There was no master plan. It just happened. And the really weird part is I love being a coach. I feel like it sort of is what I was meant to do." He stopped and cocked his head at me. "Am I making any sense at all?"

"I think so. You're basically saying life is random, right?"

"Yeah. Or no. I mean, it *is* random but the randomness can move you forward. We make choices and they lead somewhere. It's just not always in a straight line."

"Yeah, well, I think I took a U-turn a few years ago."

"But maybe you needed to be going in that direction." He made a face. "Okay, now I'm hating this metaphor."

"Let's lose it," I agreed.

"You see?" He looked suddenly young and vulnerable. "I suck at saying things."

"No, you don't. I like everything you just said."

"Really?"

"Really."

"And you forgive me for not being all brilliant and understanding right away, when we first talked about all this stuff? And for being such a coward since then, not bringing it up again until now?"

I shook my head in disbelief. "You've got to be kidding me. You've only ever been nice."

He smiled and it was such a warm and open smile, my heart leaped. "Hey, there," he said. Then I realized he wasn't smiling at me, but past me. I turned and Noah was standing there, his upper body tipping forward in the effort to counterbalance the weight of the coach's big mesh bag, which was slung over his shoulder.

"I think I got everything," he said. "It's really heavy."

"I'll take it to the car," Andrew said. "Go ahead and put it down."

Noah instantly dropped the bag. He hadn't secured the top, and as it hit the ground balls fell out and started rolling all over the floor.

"Noah!" I jumped to my feet at the same moment as Andrew, and we both started grabbing for balls. Meanwhile Noah casually stepped over to the table, selected his brownie, and ate it, idly watching us chase down balls like none of it had anything to do with him and we were very silly people to be scrambling around like that.

My arms full, I approached Andrew, who was slipping a couple of balls back into the bag. He held the bag open and I dropped the balls I'd gathered in there. I looked at his hands as I was letting them slide in—those too-big-for-the-size-of-his-wrists hands—and felt a rush of desire so strong I was terrified he'd see it on my face. I ducked away. "Any under the stove?"

I said and crouched down, pretending to look, just so I could hide my flushed cheeks a little longer.

There was a burst of music. I stood up and turned around. Andrew was answering his phone with one hand, clutching the net bag with the other. "I'm just heading out now," he said into his cell. A pause. "Western Bagel okay?" Another pause. "Onion with light cream cheese. Got it. Be there in twenty minutes." He put the phone in his pocket. "I better run. I'll see you at school, Noah. And I'll see *you* at the next T-ball practice, Noah's mom. You're going to be amazed at how good this kid gets." He hoisted the bag over his shoulder. "Thanks for the brownies."

"No problem," I said and stayed in the kitchen while Noah led him to the front door.

Of course I spent way too much time after that trying to figure out the subtext of our conversation. Had he noticed how I'd been avoiding him and wanted to make sure we were still friends? Was his apology sincere or an act of kindness? What was he trying to accomplish by even having that conversation?

I couldn't ask Mom or Melanie what they thought, because I didn't want to admit to either of them that I was spending time thinking about Andrew's motives.

So I was left trying to figure out the puzzle by myself.

It was only after the next T-ball practice, when I heard Noah say to him, "Don't make me bat. I suck at it," and Andrew gravely, kindly, and patiently replied that he didn't suck, that he was good and getting better all the time, that I realized he was talking to Noah *exactly* the way he had been talking to me, and that our conversation in the kitchen had simply been a coach's pep talk. *You're doing great, don't worry about your past mistakes, get out there and keep going, you're a winner,* etc.

Andrew may have become a PE coach by accident, but, boy, did he have the right personality for it.

*   *   *

My mother had arranged for the masseuse to come and give Mel and me our Christmas-present massages one night the following week.

Eliana the masseuse was big. Not fat, just big. Linebacker big. Shoulders-as-broad-as-a-football-field big.

"You go first," Melanie said with some trepidation as we peeked out the window at Eliana, who was strutting up our front walkway with a folded massage table tucked under her arm as if it were a clutch purse.

Two hours later, after my mother had paid Eliana and she and her table were heading back down the front walkway, Mom closed the door and said, "Well? How was it?"

"Amazing," said Melanie dreamily. She was wearing sweat-pants and a T-shirt, and under her mussed-up hair, her face looked flushed and young. "I told her I didn't get many mas-sages so just to keep it kind of soft. It all felt so good. I haven't been this relaxed in ages."

"What did you think?" Mom asked me.

I sat down heavily on the sofa. "I ache all over."

"Really?" Mel said. "But she was so gentle."

"Not with me she wasn't. I told her I wanted her to go really deep into the muscle. I mean, I kind of figured if I was getting a massage, I should really feel it, right?" They didn't exactly rush to agree with me. "Anyway, she was still being kind of delicate, so I told her that I meant it, that she should really press down hard." I shifted my body, which made me wince. "I think maybe I pissed her off a little because she got kind of rough then. She was digging her fingers so hard into my muscles, it really hurt." I didn't tell them, but I'd actually started panting from the pain.

"Why didn't you just tell her to pull back?" Mom said.

"Are you kidding? That's exactly what she *wanted*: for me to say I couldn't take it anymore, that I wasn't as tough as I thought." I shook my head. "No way I was letting her win."

Melanie said, "So instead you let her *hurt* you?"

"It's fine. I mean, in a way it feels good." As I stood up, I inadvertently let out another small groan.

"You're an idiot," Melanie said.

"Me?" I turned on her. "I'm not the one who invited my on-again-off-again husband to Casino Night so everyone could gawk at us out together. If we're going to talk about idiotic behavior—"

"People aren't going to gawk." She appealed to Mom. "Will they?"

Mom patted her on the shoulder. "Of course not. I think it's a good idea."

"That's not what you told me yesterday," I muttered.

"Shush," she said. But it was true: when we were alone, she had said to me that she was worried Melanie was setting herself up to get hurt again by going out in public so soon with Gabriel. "People will ask too many questions and assume they're permanently back together, which will make it much harder if they ultimately decide it isn't working," she had said. Now suddenly it was A Good Idea? "She's just being Rickie," she told Melanie now. "Ignore her."

"Yeah," I said. "Ignore me even though I'm right." I stumbled toward the stairs, each step igniting a new pain, to go score a couple of Advil from my parents' bathroom.

21.

I had already started my community college classes: Shakespeare, abnormal psych, and economics. I wanted to try out different subjects since I knew I wasn't going to be a bio major when I transferred to a four-year college.

At first I sat by myself in every class, but one day a girl asked if she could borrow a pen, and we chatted for a while when psych class ended. She was twenty-three, not that much younger than me, and was also stuck living at home, although in her case it was so she could take care of her mother, who had been paralyzed in a car accident. From then on we always sat together in psych and sometimes went out to lunch together afterwards.

And there was a friendly guy in Shakespeare who started chatting with me one day. He was only nineteen and had an energetic puppyish quality that was pretty endearing. I kind of liked playing the role of the older and wiser adviser with him. So now I had a seatmate in that class too.

My classes were all on Mondays, Wednesdays, and Fridays, so I was free to have lunch with Mel when she asked me and Mom to join her one Tuesday. She picked us up at home and, saying she had a craving for smoked salmon, took us to Barney Greengrass, the restaurant at the top of Barneys in Beverly Hills.

"I have a confession," she said when we were all seated. "You guys are here under false pretenses. Well, sort of false. We *are* eating lunch. But as soon as we're done—and no stalling, Rickie—we're heading downstairs to try on dresses and we're not stopping until we all find the perfect thing to wear to Casino Night."

"I think that's a great idea," Mom said, but then she added, "For you two. I already have plenty of things I can wear."

"Oh, come on," Melanie said. "When was the last time you bought yourself a new dress, Laurel?"

"It's been a little while," she admitted. "But I haven't changed size in ages, so all my good dresses still fit." I had to give my mother credit: she really hadn't given in to any kind of serious middle-age spread. It wasn't that she was all that thin or buff—she was a solid woman with a slightly thick waist and always had been—it was just that she was consistent, didn't overeat, kept busy all day, and moved briskly around town, taking Eleanor Roosevelt on almost daily walks. She might not have been a size four, but she had been on the thinner side of ten for as long as I'd known her and maybe that's why she always looked so healthy. In a town full of skeletal women with fake tits, she was abnormally normal, and definitely of sound mind and body. Too bad she was so annoying.

Melanie wagged her index finger at Mom. "Well, I want you to look fashionable on Casino Night. You're on the board of trustees, for goodness' sake. And since Rickie and I are the point people for this whole event—"

"If you count picking a caterer who they didn't even use as being 'point people,'" I cut in. "And you just want to look good because you're going with Gabriel."

She picked up a breadstick and irritably snapped it into two. "I just want us all to look our best. Is that so crazy?"

"Not at all," Mom said soothingly. "I'll look for a dress, Mel."

"Me too," I said, and they both stared at me in surprise. I shrugged. I wanted to look nice on Saturday. Sue me.

My mother pulled a dress off of a rack and held it up. "This would look great on you, Rickie."

I glanced at it. "Uh-uh. It's red."

"So? It's a nice color for you."

"Forget it."

Melanie came up as Mom was reaching to hang the dress back on the rack. "Oh, my god, I love that!" she said.

"You want to try it on?" Mom asked, holding it out to her.

She shook her head. "Not for me, for Rickie. It'd be perfect for her."

My mother beamed. "That's what *I* thought."

"Aren't you going to try it on?" Mel asked me.

"It's red," I said.

"Which would look great with your coloring. And it's got that Audrey Hepburn vibe." Melanie took it from my mother and held it up to my body. "It's totally gamine-like or whatever the word is. You have to try it on."

"Okay, okay." I took it from her.

"She'll listen to you but not to me," Mom said to Mel.

"Don't be such a drama queen." I headed toward the dressing rooms with the red dress and several others draped over my forearm. Inside, I tried on the dresses I had picked out myself. They were all black. They all looked okay. None of them looked great.

Then I tried on the red dress.

It had wide red satin straps that revealed the prettiest part of my collarbone and shoulders and a narrow red silk bodice that tapered to an even narrower waist, emphasized by a belt in the same matching satin. The skirt flared out below, becoming unexpectedly full. The cut was kind of old-fashioned, a little girly, and it shouldn't have suited me at all, but it did. Even my crazy short hair looked good with it—the wide straps and low bodice made me realize I had a long and actually kind of graceful neck.

I could hear Mom and Melanie talking to each other from a couple of dressing rooms near me so I called out to them. "You guys want to see this?" We all emerged from separate cubicles, Melanie in a sky blue dress that wasn't zipped all the way up the back yet and my mother in a navy dress with her pants still on underneath. I spun around for their benefit—and the benefit of a couple of other women who were waiting for our dressing rooms and looked like they just wanted us to hurry up.

Mom and Mel were silent as I revolved in front of them, which surprised me. I thought they'd be thrilled with the dress. I stopped twirling. "Well?" I said. "So what do you think?"

"It's fine," Melanie said with a shrug and disappeared back into her dressing room.

I looked at my mother. "She doesn't like it?"

Mom gave an almost identical shrug. "She said it was fine."

"Fine as in you guys hate it or fine as in it's okay?" I looked down at the dress. What was going on? I had on a beautiful and very feminine dress—one they had both liked and wanted me to try on—and they weren't enthusiastic? That didn't make sense. I craned my neck to try to see over my shoulder. "Does it look bad in the back?"

My mother folded her arms over her chest. "Look, Rickie, we're not idiots. It's dawned on us that you only ever ask for our opinion to reject it. So you decide for yourself if you like the dress or not. From now on, we're keeping our mouths shut."

"What are you talking about?" I said. "I bought a ton of clothing with Melanie just a couple of months ago—"

"Right after you cut your hair off because she told you not to."

I flung my hands up in the air and whirled around on my

heel. "I thought you'd be happy I was trying on the stupid dress. Forget the whole thing." I stomped back to my dressing room, where I wiggled out of the dress and left it abandoned on the chair there with the others, a blaze of crimson against all that dull black. I was furious. I had tried it on for them, not for me. I liked the dress, but I wasn't going to let them manipulate me into getting it with their petty mind games.

As I left the dressing room empty-handed, the hovering saleswoman said, "You're not getting the red dress? It looked so great on you."

I just shook my head. I waited for Mom and Melanie to emerge from their cubicles, and when they did, I coldly informed them that I was done shopping and would be waiting in the car for them. I stalked off.

Of course, I had forgotten to get the car keys from Melanie, which left me stranded in the parking garage, where I tried— and failed—to make myself comfortable by leaning against the car. When the two of them finally came out of the elevator, they were walking slowly and chatting with each other. I could happily have killed them both.

"So," I said, nodding at the bags they were carrying. "Guess you guys found something to wear?"

"We did," Melanie said. "Thanks for asking." We got into the car in silence.

"Are you ever going to stop sulking?" Melanie asked me later, when she was dropping us off. Mom had already gotten out of the car.

"I'm not sulking." I swung my legs out. "I'm just being careful about what I say to you and Mom, seeing as how you both totally overreact to every little thing."

"Oh, *we're* the overreacters?" she said.

She drove off as soon as I had slammed my door shut.

Later that afternoon, I went upstairs to get something. As soon as I entered my room, a splash of red caught my eye. The dress I'd tried on at Barneys was spread out on my bed with a note lying on top of it, written in my mother's spiky handwriting:

We liked it.

I stared down at the dress, feeling abused and misunderstood. Feeling annoyed. Feeling ganged up on. Feeling left out.

I gently fingered the satin fabric.

I couldn't wait to wear it.

Debbie Golden brought coffee and muffins to Saturday's practice, and we ate together on the bleachers, watching our boys run more slowly and hit more feebly than any of the others.

It was nice having a companion in discomfort.

"Next week there'll be an actual game," Debbie said with a sigh after Joshua whacked the tee with the bat, completely missing the ball. "I'm terrified. Which is crazy, right? I mean, they're six years old. What does it matter?"

"I'm terrified of *them*," I said, nodding toward the fathers who had been nasty about Noah at the first practice and had done nothing to make me like them any better since then. Mostly they just yelled at their own kids, but through the things they said to them—things like "You're going to have to try a lot harder! You've got to carry this whole team!"—they managed to make their feelings about our less-athletic kids pretty clear. "There's no way they'll be civil through a whole game. Not if we're losing."

"The coach'll keep them in line," she said.

"He'll be a little busy."

She suddenly sat up straight. "Oh, wait! I just realized something. Joshua's going to have to miss the game."

I moaned. "Please tell me you're joking."

"I'm sorry, Rickie. It's my husband's company retreat but we all go. It's at a resort in San Diego, and it's the closest thing I get to a real vacation all year."

"I hope Joshua doesn't tell Noah you're going away. I'll never get him out the door if he knows he'll be all alone out there."

"Don't worry," she said. "Joshua never knows what's going on or what the plan is. He lives in la-la land."

"Yeah? He and Noah should share a condo there," I said and we touched coffee cups in a silent toast.

During the water break, Andrew walked over to us. When he stood next to the bleachers, he was at roughly the same height as we were sitting on one of the top rows. "They're doing great," he said. He was wearing a baseball cap and sunglasses, which left his face pretty much covered up.

"Natural athletes, the pair of them," Debbie said dryly. "Oh, hey, Andrew—Joshua won't be here for the game next week. We're going out of town."

He absorbed that in his measured way. "That's too bad. The first game is always exciting. But there'll be more. Hey—you guys going to the school thing tonight? The casino thing?"

Debbie shook her head. "I'm not, but don't tell Dr. Wilson on me. I hate those things."

"I have to go," I said. "Long story."

"Well, then, I'll see you there." Andrew seemed like he was going to say something else but he stopped. "Better go set up the next drill," he said instead and walked away.

Noah and Joshua came running over right then, which was good because they distracted me from obsessing about what

Andrew might have been about to say. "Can I have a playdate with Noah?" Joshua asked me. Up close, he had the distinctive look of a kid with allergies: he was small and pale with dark circles under his eyes. But those eyes were big and thoughtful and his hair was dark and curly. He was cute. He looked a little like Noah, actually.

Debbie and I promised them they could do something together after practice, so when it was over the four of us went to Baja Fresh. Noah couldn't get anything with flour tortillas and Joshua, who did in fact have a lot of allergies, couldn't get anything with corn, tomato, or cheese.

The boys chose to sit by themselves at a separate table, which meant we could talk freely.

"So," Debbie said as we unwrapped our tacos, "think Caleb has any food allergies?"

I snorted. "Caleb probably eats a virgin for breakfast every day."

"And sharpens his teeth with a file afterwards."

"And then bathes in the blood of innocent children."

"You know what?" she said. "For all that our kids are his victims and he's this great athlete and everything? I wouldn't want to go home with that kid." She gestured toward Joshua and Noah, who were chattering away to each other, their food forgotten in front of them, their cute little faces lit up with excitement at whatever they were discussing. "Those are the ones you want to go home with, snuggle up with at night. Know what I mean?"

"Yes," I said, gazing at Noah and his friend. His *friend*. "I know exactly what you mean."

22.

"My god," my mother said, when I came downstairs dressed for Casino Night. "You look"—she stopped herself—"fine," she finished abruptly.

My father, who apparently wasn't part of the don't-let-Rickie-know-your-opinion pact, said, "What do you mean, fine? She looks fantastic! Rickie, you're a vision."

Noah said, "Why are you dressed like a princess? And where's your nose thing?"

He meant the stud. "I took it out," I said. It just didn't fit with the dress. Neither did the eyebrow ring, which was also gone. The short hair, on the other hand, did, especially after I had used a curling iron to create soft waves with it—it was long enough now to do that—to make it look more old-fashioned, more Audrey Hepburn–like.

Actually, I'd gone so far as to do a Google image search for Audrey Hepburn and model my hairdo on some of the photos I'd found. I wasn't about to tell anyone I had done that.

But I had.

Melanie had helped with my makeup. She'd outlined my eyes so they looked even bigger than usual and used a lot more smoky-colored eye shadow than I was used to, which, come to think of it, any amount would be since I didn't usually wear *any* makeup. It was a little dramatic but, again, it worked with the dress.

The doorbell rang, and my mother strode swiftly toward the front door to greet the babysitter, a grad student of my dad's. Mom's new dress suited her: it was a dark green and very simply cut, but the fabric shimmered when it caught the light. She had blown her bobbed hair dry and was wearing a touch of makeup—just enough to look a little younger and fresher than usual.

Once Noah was settled with the babysitter, we headed toward the garage. Melanie had already left to go pick up Gabriel at their house. She had looked drop-dead gorgeous in a black fringed dress and silk black shoes with stiletto heels that were more overtly sexy than anything I'd ever seen her wear before, except maybe that sweater dress she'd worn on Halloween. She had agonized over how to do her hair, and had settled on an updo that left tendrils curling along her neck. She was wearing dark red lipstick and tons of mascara. She looked incredibly hot, and when I told her so, she whispered, "I'm terrified, Rickie."

"About being with Gabriel?"

"About not knowing what I want to have happen tonight."

"So just get drunk and let things happen."

"That's never a good idea."

"It's always a good idea." It was certainly *my* plan for that evening.

I realized as I walked into the school with my parents that I had never been to an adults-only fund-raiser at Fenwick before. Mom hadn't ever insisted that I go, the way she always did with the Autumn Festival, and it wasn't like I had friends at the school I wanted to spend time partying with, so I'd always chosen to skip them before. So this was all new to me.

The gym had been taken over by gambling tables: roulette, blackjack, poker, and some games I didn't recognize. The party committee had hired croupiers and dealers to man all the tables, and between them and the large number of servers walking around with trays of drinks and the lights that were strung up all over the place, it really did feel like we'd walked into some noisy, crowded Las Vegas casino. There was nothing gym-like about the room at all anymore, unless you noticed the bleachers that had been folded up and pushed into their storage space at the back wall.

"I don't think I know anybody here," I said as we entered and looked around.

"Me neither," said my father.

My mother sighed. "I know *everybody*." A waiter approached us with a tray of drinks. My parents took glasses of sparkling wine. I took a martini. "Those are strong," my mother said, eyeing my choice. "Pace yourself."

I shrugged and took as big a sip as I could without making myself cough.

My mother shook her head but only said, "I should mingle."

"I think I'll try my hand at poker," Dad said.

"I'll go get chips with you." I hooked my arm in his and we started to walk off.

My mother caught at my free arm. "Rickie—"

I halted, bracing myself for some kind of warning or complaint.

"It's killing me not saying anything. You look absolutely beautiful tonight. So beautiful…" She looked at my dad and laughed. "I don't know how it's genetically possible for the two of us to have produced her."

"Well, you never know how the genes will mesh," Dad said.

"You waited until I couldn't change to compliment me, didn't you?" I said to Mom.

"Can you blame me?"

"I guess not." But I smiled and so did she.

*   *   *

I spotted Melanie right after I left Dad happily settled at a poker game: she and Gabriel were standing side by side, watching the roulette wheel spin, their shoulders lightly touching. They both turned when I called her name, and Gabriel caught me to his chest in a big hug. Over his shoulder I mouthed at Mel, "How's it going?" She gave me a noncommittal shrug but she looked happy, so it couldn't have been going too badly.

Gabriel released me, and I said, "How beautiful does Mel look tonight?"

"She leaves me weak in the knees," he said solemnly.

"Oh, be quiet, both of you," Melanie said, blushing. "What do you think of the food so far, Rickie?"

"So far I like the martinis," I said. "Haven't had a bite of food. Is there any?"

"I've only seen a couple of trays go by. Do you think we need to say something to the caterers?"

"I'd check with Tanya first. Have you seen her?"

"Yeah, she's here somewhere." She turned to Gabriel. "Do you mind if I go with Rickie for a second?"

"So long as you come back..." He touched her bare arm tentatively and she shivered slightly.

"Come on," she said to me, and we moved off.

"Well?" I said meaningfully as soon as we were far enough away.

She shook her head a little frantically. "I don't know, I don't know, I don't know, I don't know."

I plucked a martini off of a passing tray and handed it to her. I had finished mine already. "Have one of these."

"You're like a devil on my shoulder. Especially in that red dress." But she took a sip of the drink. "Oh, there's Tanya! But she's leaving."

Tanya was walking out of the gym. "Maybe she's just going to the bathroom," I said.

We threaded our way across the crowded room and out the door and found Tanya inside the girls' PE locker room, which was serving as the official party restroom. She was putting on lipstick in front of the mirror. In a column-like dark blue dress and high-heeled black shoes, she looked dressed up but still businesslike, like a lawyer at a company function.

She spotted our reflections in the mirror. "There you are," she said glumly. "It's all a disaster, isn't it?" She dropped her lipstick into her clutch purse and closed it with a snap.

"What is?" Melanie asked anxiously.

"The food, of course. There isn't enough. Everyone's talking about it. It's ruining the whole event."

"No one seems unhappy in there," I said. "I'm sure it's all fine."

She shot my reflection a look of pure contempt. "Someone has to deal with this, but I can't do *everything.*"

"We'll take care of it," Melanie said. "You just relax and have fun."

She pivoted around to face us. "*Relax?* Do you know how much I'm in charge of here? No one understands how much work something like this takes. I've been here since four this afternoon, setting up. There was a whole thing with the napkins—" She flung out her hand like words couldn't even begin to express the horror of the napkin situation.

"We'll talk to the caterer right now," Melanie said. "Please don't worry about it anymore."

"I'm the one everyone blames when things go wrong," Tanya said. "How can I not worry?"

Melanie didn't bother responding to that, just quickly said good-bye and tugged me out of the bathroom. She led us outside and across the field toward where the caterers' trucks and grills were set up.

"Why does she do it?" I asked as we made our way along the track.

"What do you mean?"

"If it's such a burden to her to run everything, why does she do it? It's not like anyone's forcing her. She volunteers for this stuff."

"Maybe it makes her feel needed," Melanie said. "And she really is helping the school. Someone needs to do it."

"I don't know," I said. "If everyone just said no, what's the worst that would happen? I mean, people would still give money to the school, right? They just wouldn't have to show up to things like this. Is that so awful?"

"I should really be volunteering more," Mel said. Her thoughts had clearly run in a different direction from mine.

Out behind one of the trucks we located the plump, bleached-blond guy who ran Crackerjack Catering. He shook his head irritably when we voiced our concerns. "You said you wanted the food hot and fresh, so we're rolling it out gradually. If you'd wanted a ton of food right at the beginning, you should have made that clear."

"We just want to make sure there'll be enough," Mel said timidly.

"There will be more than enough food," he said tightly, "if you'll all just leave me alone so I can get on with it."

We quickly scuttled away. "To be fair," said Melanie, who always was, "he's under a lot of pressure right now."

"You know what?" I said as we headed back into the gym,

"let's stop worrying about the stupid catering and have some fun."

"Yeah," Melanie said. You could already see her scanning the room, looking for Gabriel. "Let's." She spotted him. "There he is. Come join us, Rickie."

I shook my head. "You guys should have time alone together tonight."

"I feel bad you don't have anyone to be with."

"I have Mom and Dad! What's more fun than partying with your parents?"

"Seriously." She studied me for a moment, hesitating, like something was on her mind. "Rickie—"

"Still standing right next to you," I said helpfully.

"It's just..." Another pause then a deep breath. "Okay. I have to say this, whether you want to hear it or not. I love Ryan. You know I do. He's a great guy. But he isn't exactly dependable when it comes to relationships."

"Whoa," I said. "What are you talking about, Mel? Why are you bringing up Ryan?"

She just looked at me.

"Why would you think that I care one way or the other about your brother-in-law?" I tried to sound genuinely mystified, but the words came out too strained.

"He told Gabriel a while ago that you and he get together when he's in town. And Gabriel told me. But I didn't feel I had the right to bring it up when you seemed to want to keep it a secret."

"It wasn't much of a secret if you guys were talking about it," I said, feeling both embarrassed and annoyed. All those times I thought we were being so sly—and they were just pretending not to notice. "I wish you'd told me you knew."

"You have a right to your privacy. That's why I've never said anything before. But seeing you alone here tonight...I have to tell you that I don't think Ryan, as wonderful as he is, will ever come through for you. He's not worth waiting for."

"I know," I said. "I swear to God I know that, Mel. And I'm not 'waiting' for him—we just have fun when he's around. It's no big deal."

She looked dubious. "Sometimes a bad relationship can keep you from finding a good one."

"Thanks, Dr. Phil," I said. "Now that you've proven yourself so knowledgeable about romance, why don't you go back to the guy you can't decide whether you love or hate? And maybe stop talking about me behind my back while you're at it?"

"That's not what we were doing."

"Oh, right. You were respecting my privacy. Just don't ever respect my privacy like that again, okay?" I turned her around by the shoulders and shoved her gently in Gabriel's direction. "Go." I watched her walk across the room and then made my way wearily toward the bar.

One more martini later and I felt like I was in some Italian movie from the seventies. Unknown people passed by in a blur, with an occasional random, familiar face thrown into sudden sharp focus. From a dreamlike distance I glimpsed my mother talking to Dr. Wilson, my father throwing down a hand in disgust at the poker table, Gabriel walking with his arm tight around Melanie like it belonged there, Maria Dellaventura winking at me tipsily....

And then there was Coach Andrew passing by, laughing, wearing a tuxedo as comfortably as if he were James Freaking Bond himself. Gracie was hanging on to his arm, striking in some long, tight, gray dress that made her look as tall and willowy and graceful as a tall, graceful willow. I tried to sidle by them unnoticed and had almost succeeded when Andrew stopped and looked back at me.

"Noah's mom? Is that you?"

I halted.

"You look"—was it my imagination or did he dart a glance at Gracie before finishing the thought?—"different."

Gracie held out her hand. "Hi," she said. "I'm Gracie."

"I'm Rickie," I said as we touched hands in a mutually unenthusiastic not-quite-handshake.

"I'm Andrew's girlfriend," she said.

"Yes," I said. "I know. We've met a couple of times."

"Oh. Sorry." She didn't look sorry.

"You both look very Casino Nighty," I said. It hurt to look at Andrew. His wavy hair was brushed and almost neat, and the monkey suit made him look taller. I suddenly really didn't want to stand there talking to them. "Excuse me," I said abruptly. "I have to find someone." I ran away.

"Be careful," Maria Dellaventura said, coming up next to me at the bar just as the bartender was handing me another martini. "Those things are strong."

"You say it like it's a bad thing."

"Are you kidding? I'm on my third. The best part is that people are so drunk they're bidding like crazy on the silent auction stuff. It's good for the school, right?" She signaled the bartender, then leaned against the bar and scrutinized me. "You look fantastic, Rickie."

"Aw, shucks."

"I'm serious. I hate you for being so young. Your skin is like fucking milk." The bartender handed her a filled glass and we moved aside. "So tell me, who's the guy with your sister?

The one who looks like Santa minus the beard and white hair?"

"That would be the ex-husband," I said and braced myself for the attack.

Apparently alcohol had a mellowing effect on Maria. She just shrugged and sipped her martini. "That wasn't how I pictured him."

"Fatter than you expected?"

"He looks *nice*."

"He is nice." Having had two martinis, I added, "Too nice to say no to anyone who wants to have sex with him."

"I'm not sure that counts as being nice. Not when you're—" She interrupted herself. "Oh my god! Look who's here!" She nudged my arm and gestured with her glass across the room.

Marley Addison had just entered the gym on the arm of her husband, the not-quite-so-famous-but-still-recognizable movie star James Foster. Despite the fact that people were very carefully *not* staring at them, the change in the energy of the room was remarkable: suddenly everyone was standing a little more erect, voices were a little louder and more enthusiastic, smiles were more animated and heads were tossing like crazy. The party had come alive. It *mattered*.

"A little underdressed, isn't she?" I said. Marley was wearing black pants and a simple linen top. Her body was birdlike, tiny and very thin, and the narrowness of her shoulders made her head look enormous. She was stunningly beautiful on the screen, but in real life she was a little out of proportion.

"*She's* underdressed? Look at him."

Maria was right: James looked like he was dressed for dinner at home in torn jeans and a stretched-out green pullover sweater. His goal may have been to keep a low profile, but his clothes actually made him stand out among all the tuxedoed men around him. Then again, maybe that was his goal. No matter what, the guy was gorgeous. No proportion problems with him: his head and shoulders were perfect.

"He can wear whatever he likes, as far as I'm concerned," I said dreamily.

"He's a good-looking guy," Maria agreed. "Hey, want to place bets on how long they stay at the party? I'll bet you ten bucks it's less than an hour."

"Nah, you'd win."

"Look at them," Maria said. "I wonder what it's like to be that famous."

"We'll never know."

Maria went off to check on her silent auction bids and I was on my own again, which allowed me to discover my martini limit. One sip past two and suddenly things were getting a little *too* out of focus. I put down my drink.

The food had finally started coming out of the catering truck a little more quickly and I nabbed a slider as it went by. I took a bite. It was greasy and not hot enough. That, I thought, was what happened when you hired someone's cousin to do the food. I dropped the rest of it on a tall table. A couple was standing at the other side of the table eating, and just as I was turning away the man said tentatively, "Uh, Rickie? Rickie Allen?"

I turned back.

"It *is* you!" He put down his fork and came around the table. "How are you, my dear?" It was Mr. Greene, my tenth-grade English teacher. He had a bit more gray in his thinning hair, but otherwise he looked pretty much the same: bushy beard, glasses, double chin. At school he had worn a lot of plaid shirts and jeans and kind of reminded me of a lumberjack, but the tuxedo he was wearing that evening lent him an air of old-fashioned and vaguely rumpled professorial elegance.

He gave me a quick hug. "I haven't seen you in ages! How are things going?"

"They're good." I had sat in the front row of his class and argued passionately about how Hester Prynne was a big wimp. It seemed like a lifetime ago. "How about with you?"

"Good, good," he said. "Still teaching at the upper school. My daughter graduates next year—I can't believe it. She's a bit frantic about the whole college thing. But I assume we'll survive it. You remember my wife, Judy?" He gestured back toward the middle-aged woman behind him, who nodded at me with a pleasant smile. I didn't remember her and I doubted she remembered me, but I waved back. Mr. Greene said, "You went to Berkeley, right? That's Arielle's first choice. Did you like it there?"

Did he know I was only there for one year? I couldn't tell. "Yeah," I said. "It was great."

"I hope you majored in English. I still remember that paper you wrote on *Romeo and Juliet.* It was about the girl he's in love with at the beginning."

I remembered that paper. I had been proud of it. "'The Trouble with Rosaline,'" I said.

"Brilliant. Just brilliant. So what are you up to now?" He peered at me curiously. Kindly. Expectantly. Maybe he didn't know the whole Rickie Allen story. Maybe he'd forgotten it for the moment. Maybe he just wanted to let me tell the story my own way.

I didn't know, but it suddenly felt hard to swallow. I jerked my chin up, trying to open up my throat. "Not much. Living with my parents. Trying to figure stuff out. You know."

"Ah," he said. He waited another moment. I looked down at the floor and didn't add anything.

I had nothing to add.

He patted me gently on the shoulder. "Well, if you find any answers, let me know. I'm still figuring it all out myself."

I forced a short laugh and said, "Excuse me. I should—" Should what? "My parents are probably looking for me." Lame.

"Of course, of course," he said. "Don't let me detain you. You look lovely, Rickie. And it's wonderful to see you."

I said good-bye to him and his wife and slunk away.

23.

I was halfway across the room when I spotted my mother and father standing at another one of the tall cocktail tables talking to a guy who I knew was on the board of trustees with Mom. He was some big real estate mogul, but I couldn't remember his name. I also saw Melanie and Gabriel walking from one casino table to another, hip against hip, his arm tight across her shoulder. I got a warm and happy feeling seeing them together and thought how nice it would be if you could change the past with a simple wish. If a genie gave me that power, I'd use it for them, I thought. Not for me.

I was idly and slightly drunkenly watching the roulette wheel spin when I felt something touch my shoulder. Startled, I whipped around. The guy who had just run his fingers down my bare skin looked only vaguely familiar. His thinning hair was too long and he was wearing a skinny black necktie with his tux, which I thought looked weird.

"Hey, there," he said enthusiastically, like we were old friends. "Remember me?"

"I'm working on it." *And wondering why you felt you had the right to stroke my arm without asking.*

"We met at the basketball party. I'm Pammy's dad. Dane Miller."

Okay, now I did remember him. But not fondly. "Oh, right."

He extended his right hand (first transferring a half-empty martini glass to his left) and I reluctantly shook it.

He held on to my fingers too long, and I had to tug my hand away. "You look amazing tonight," he said, his eyes running up and down the length of my body. "I had to tell you. Of all the women here, you're channeling the whole theme like no one else. You look like a brunette Grace Kelly."

"Okay, that one I haven't heard."

"I mean it. You have her delicate bone structure. My father worked with her in the fifties, you know." I had no idea who his father was, but I didn't really care. "Your dress"—he gestured—"she would have worn something like that."

"Yeah?" Plenty of people had told me I looked nice that night. What good did that do me? I was still alone, surrounded by couples. The only man paying me any attention was *this* guy and I just wanted him to go away.

He wasn't done with the personal comments. "Where's the nose ring tonight? I miss it."

"It didn't go with the dress." *And it was a stud, not a ring.*

"I don't know why that kind of thing is so sexy, but it is. Not," he said gallantly, "that you aren't sexy without it."

"Thanks," I said flatly.

"It's the good-girl-gone-bad vibe," he continued. "Guys can't resist it and you have it in spades. Hey, can you act? Are you interested in acting at all?"

"Not really."

"You have the right look for this project I'm working on. A feature. If you wanted to come in one day—"

I was tipsy and tired and depressed and rapidly losing patience. "How dumb do you think I am?" I said.

"I'm serious."

"Sure you are."

"I am. You have that *It* quality. You know what I mean? You have *It*."

"The doctor told me antibiotics would take care of that."

He touched my arm again. "You like to joke around, don't you?"

I recoiled—and stepped back onto the toes of Andrew Fulton, who was standing behind me. Where had he come from? And how long had he been there? "Sorry," I said, hopping off of him.

"No worries," he said. "Hi." He nodded to Dane Miller. "Dane."

I wondered how much he'd overheard. I decided to fill him in, courtesy of the vodka I'd drunk: "Hi, Coach. Pammy's dad misses my nose stud but thinks I'm still sexy without it and also that I have the It factor and should come give him a private audition on his casting couch one day."

Andrew processed that, his eyes flickering back and forth between us.

Dane hastily said, "We were just joking around. This young lady is very funny."

"I'm a riot," I agreed.

"I need to talk to you," Andrew said to me. "Excuse us, Dane." He took me by the arm and propelled me across the gym floor. We didn't say anything until we reached the far wall, where he let go of my arm. "There. Got you away. Sorry about that guy."

I absently rubbed my arm where Andrew had been holding it. It didn't hurt but I could still feel the impression of his fingers there. Or imagined I could. "What's up with him? Does that stuff actually work on anyone?"

"I don't know. I doubt it. His wife is here, so I don't know what he was thinking."

"He's a dick," I said. "Dicks don't think."

"Well put."

"Speaking of wives," I said and stopped rubbing my arm, "where's Gracie the Beautiful?"

"She's not my wife," he said. "But she's over there." He nodded toward the center of the gym. I looked. Gracie was very animatedly talking to Marley Addison and James Foster. Marley was smiling at her with polite detachment, but James was yawning and glancing around the room.

"Does she know them?"

"Of course not. Not personally." Andrew scowled. "Never date a PR person, Noah's mom. They so much as smell a celebrity and they're like dogs on a bone. She probably has some event she wants them to come to, so she pounced." He shook his head irritably. "God, I hate this! It's bad enough when we're out around town and she spots some famous person, but here, at school, where I work...And, you know, Louis Wilson sees all. And he does not like celebrity parents being targeted like that."

I tried not to let him see how delighted I was that he was annoyed at his girlfriend. "Want me to get her away from them?" I said. "I could tell her that her car's on fire or something."

"She'd let it burn," he said grimly. "Just keep me company, will you?"

"Sure."

There was a pause. He shuffled his feet restlessly, glancing quickly and unhappily at Gracie and the celebs again. "I can't watch this anymore. I've got to get out of this room. Will you come with me?"

"Sure," I said again.

He led me out the side door of the gym, swiping a couple of glasses of champagne off of a waiter's tray on the way, and then down the hallway to his office. "Here, take this." He handed me one of the champagne glasses so he could reach into his hip pocket.

"Won't she be mad that you left?"

He pulled out a bunch of keys, selected one, and unlocked the door. "She's already mad at me. What's one more item on a long list?" He opened the door and gestured for me to go in. It was dark, and after I stepped inside I just stood there, enjoying the quiet after the chaos and noise of the casino room. Then Andrew flicked on the light and the spell was broken.

He closed the door behind us with a hospitable gesture toward the extra chair. I sat down and took a sip of the champagne before remembering I had had enough to drink already. I carefully put the glass on the edge of the desk as Andrew circled around it and sat in his chair. Now it felt like we were about to have another meeting about Noah, except the coach was in a tuxedo and I was in a satin dress.

A very formal meeting.

But I didn't want to talk about Noah tonight. So I said, "Why's Gracie already mad at you?"

Andrew put down his champagne glass and leaned forward, yanking at his hair in a comic gesture of despair. "Well, today's big grievance is that I've 'ruined her weekends' by agreeing to coach T-ball. She likes being free to go away and now we're stuck here for the season."

"Are you sorry you said you'd do it?"

"Are you kidding? I love it. Especially with Noah and Joshua on the team—those two crack me up. I love watching them get better every week. And there are some other great kids too." He waved his hand. "And by the way I really don't *need* more nights spent at some dusty bed-and-breakfast in Cambria or some twee place like that, visiting precious little antique stores and eating too much French toast. Don't need them, don't want them, can't afford them."

"Did you tell her that?"

"Yes. Pretty much word for word."

"And?"

"Well, first she pointed out that if I had stayed on my original career track, I would be able to afford it, no problem. So then *I* pointed out that even if I had, I still wouldn't *want* to go to those places."

"And then?"

He slumped back in his seat. "Oh, you know…She said I only care about what I want, not about what she wants. Which I guess is basically true."

I said slowly, "There's the Noah thing on Sundays too. She must hate that."

"I've canceled it when she's asked me to."

"But she *does* hate it?"

He looked down at his hands. "Yeah, she hates it. It 'ruins our Sundays' the same way that coaching 'ruins our Saturdays.'" He glanced up. "And, by the way, this thing tonight? It 'ruined our Saturday night.'" He laughed shortly. "Or at least it did until Marley Addison showed up. I guess I should thank her for making this whole event worth going to for Gracie." There was a pause. When neither of us was talking, you could hear the noise from the casino room but no distinct voices. Andrew said, "I'm sorry. I shouldn't be complaining like this."

"You don't have to help Noah on Sundays anymore," I said. "I mean, he sees you on Saturdays now. And if you didn't have to come to our house, you guys could still get away for at least part of the weekend."

He thought about that for a moment then shook his head. "I don't really want to." He fidgeted, looked away, then looked at me again. "Let's talk about something else." There was a pause. He said abruptly, "I like your dress."

"Can we please not talk about this stupid dress?" I flicked at the skirt, which lay over my knees in satin folds. "I can't tell you how many people have made some comment about how I look tonight. Am I normally such a slob that my wearing a dress is some huge topic of conversation? Don't answer that."

"I won't," he said. "But yes."

"I'm more than happy to discuss your tux. You look good in it."

He glanced down at himself. "Gracie picked it out. I don't know anything about this stuff."

"She has good taste."

"Yes, yes, she does." Another pause. He said, "So we have our first game next week. Is Noah excited?"

"I guess so. I'm terrified."

"Why?"

"All that pressure. Like when he's at bat. And he's probably not going to do well. And I don't know if you can hear them, but there are these dads who sit there and criticize—"

"Those dads are dicks," he said. "To borrow a term."

"Are you sure you're allowed to say that in public?"

"We're not in public." He took a sip from his champagne glass and put it down a little too hard so it clanged on the desk. "God, I hate those guys. They work against everything I'm trying to accomplish with these kids. You know, I actually have the right to ban them from games—I'm just waiting for them to say something bad enough for me to justify it to the head of the rec center."

"Why do there have to be people like that?" I said. "Why can't everyone be relaxed and friendly and get that my kid is trying his hardest?"

"I don't know. There are always a few jerks in every crowd. But I'll do my best to make sure Noah feels good about himself during the game."

"Thanks," I said. "Anything you can do to help *me* get through it?"

"I'd recommend a mild sedative."

"Yeah, that would help." I wondered if he was as aware as I was of how alone we were in that little office with the door closed. I wondered whether he thought of me as just another mom at school whose kid needed extra attention, or as an interesting person in my own right. I wondered if he had been looking for me to keep him company just now, or if he had just stumbled across me by accident. I wondered why men looked so good in tuxes. I wondered—

"We should probably go back to the gym," he said abruptly into a silence I hadn't realized had fallen.

—I wondered if I was boring him.

I stood up, and so did he. He came around the desk. I fiddled with my skirt a bit, fluffing it in back where I'd sat on it, smoothing it down in front. He watched me and said, "Maybe it's a good thing you don't dress like that all the time."

"Huh?" I looked up from my skirt-fussing.

"Nothing." He stepped toward the door. "Come on, Noah's mom. Let's get back to the party."

"Don't call me that," I said with a sudden tipsy vehemence.

"Why not?"

"I'm not just Noah's mom. I know you think that's all I am. But it's not."

There was a pause. Then he said, "It's the opposite, actually. I need to keep reminding myself that you're Noah's mom. Otherwise—" He stopped.

"Otherwise what?" I asked, almost desperately.

He reached out and touched my hair gently and I held my breath. He shook his head slightly and dropped his hand. "Oh, you know," he said casually. "Wouldn't want to send the wrong kid home with you in car pool." He flicked his chin toward the door. "Come on. Let's go." He opened the door and held it for me.

He stayed a foot or two behind me as we walked back into the gym. The belt at my waist felt a little too tight and I could feel the muscles in my calves aching and a blister forming on my right big toe from the unusually high heeled shoes I was wearing. I focused in on those things because it was easier than trying to figure out what had just happened. Or hadn't happened.

You want something bad enough, you start imagining it's a possibility. Was that what I had been doing? Or had he actually looked at me like he wanted to touch me more? Maybe if I hadn't had two martinis I'd have been clearer on the whole thing. But I had and I wasn't.

Marley Addison and James Foster had vanished. Good thing I hadn't taken Maria's bet. But Gracie was still standing near where she'd been when we left. She spotted us the second we walked in—she was *looking*—and swiftly approached, graceful in heels that were even higher than the ones I was wearing. She had to be well over six feet tall in them, which made her a couple of inches taller than Andrew.

"There you are," she snapped at Andrew. "Where were you?" Her eyes darted over to me and back to him. She put her hands on her hips.

"Nowhere," he said. "Just my office. I told you I wouldn't stick around if you were going to go on the attack with Marley Addison."

"I wasn't attacking anyone. We were just talking about some of the charitable events I'm working on—she was very interested and happy to help out. But thanks for your support."

"This wasn't the place for that."

She shrugged that off irritably and turned to me. "Hi!" she said with a big, brittle smile. "So were you hiding away in his office too? What were *you* hiding from?"

"I was just keeping him company." *And he complained about you the whole time*, I thought. Now that she was standing in front of me, it felt like he and I were keeping a guilty secret. I couldn't meet her eyes.

She said icily, "How nice of you."

"Rickie is Noah Allen's mom," Andrew said quickly, like he was in a rush to make that clear. "We were talking about the T-ball game Noah's playing in next week."

"Oh, right—the Saturday morning league," she said, her voice even colder. Sub-Arctic. "Noah's the kid you coach on Sunday mornings too, right?"

"It's really nice of him," I said. "Noah's kind of bad at sports and—"

"Don't worry," she said, cutting me off. "Andrew will take care of that. Nothing Andrew likes better than to spend all his free time helping out little kids who can't play sports. That's pretty much *all* he likes to do on the weekends these days."

"Gracie," he said like it was a warning, but she turned her back on him.

"Would you mind if he missed tomorrow's little session with your son?" she asked me as if he weren't even there. "I was just wondering because we had talked about maybe driving up the coast to Santa Barbara for the day. There's this amazing taco place we both love and it's been a while since we've made it there."

"Oh, of course," I said uncomfortably. "I don't want to mess up your plans. Don't worry about—"

"Hold on a second." Andrew didn't raise his voice, but he sounded angry. "I want to work on Noah's batting a little more before the game. So I'm coming tomorrow."

Gracie raised her chin. "She said it's fine if you don't."

"I *want* to go."

She tossed her head back, and her beautiful golden hair swirled up then settled back into perfect place. "So you care more about some kid's batting practice than about going with me to Santa Barbara?"

"The tacos aren't that great," he said.

"Then maybe I should find someone else to go with."

He studied her thoughtfully, no sign of emotion on his face. I studied him with probably lots of emotion in play across my face, but fortunately no one was watching *me*. "You should do what you want," he said quietly.

She flung up her arms. Her beautiful, slender, pale, smooth arms. Not a tattoo on them. "That's a classic Andrew response," she said. "Helpful as always. So caring. So *invested*. So you."

"What do you want from me?" he asked like he was curious, not angry.

She glanced at me and then looked back at him. "Well, for one thing, I'd like you to walk out to the car with me so we can continue this conversation in private."

"Of course." He inclined his head a little. "Excuse us, Rickie."

She walked away without saying anything to me and he followed close behind.

I watched them go, wondering if I'd see him again that evening. Wondering if this was a normal fight for them. Wondering if they were the kind of couple who fought a lot because they had great make-up sex. Wondering if any part of him was wishing he didn't have to leave with her but could stay there with me.

I was sick of wondering. But there was no one to give me any answers.

Dad was sitting all alone in a corner of the gym. Just sitting there on a folding chair, humming quietly to himself and jogging his knee up and down rhythmically while people bustled past him.

"Hi," I said. I leaned against the wall next to him; there weren't any more available chairs. "How's it going?"

"Fine, fine." A pause. "I'm ready to go home."

"Yeah? How long have you been sitting here?"

"I'm not sure," he said. "I've been lost in thought."

"I bet. Where's Mom?"

He made a vague gesture. "Around. Mingling. She thrives on all this, you know."

"Yeah, I've noticed. What about Mel and Gabriel?"

"They sweep by every now and then."

"They seem happy to you?"

"I'm not the right person to ask. They seemed perfectly happy to me when they were on the verge of separating." He reached up to pat me on the back. "So how are you doing, little girl? Having fun in your pretty green dress?"

"It's red," I said. Dad was color blind but it hadn't occurred to me until then that he had the color of the dress wrong.

"Is it?" he said.

We stopped talking then and just waited there in silence, me standing, him sitting, while other people whirled and moved and laughed around us.

Andrew didn't come back in. I was watching for him.

I was still watching for him when Melanie and Gabriel found us. "I think we're going to head home," Melanie said. Her face was bright and happy above her fringed black bodice.

"Okay." I wanted to ask if she'd be coming back to my parents' place later that night, but Gabriel was right there, so instead I just said good night, and they walked off, arm in arm.

"Oh, god," I said, watching them go. "This is either a really good thing or a really bad thing."

"Huh?" said my father, who wasn't much use at moments like these.

Fortunately, my mother was coming toward us. "What a lovely evening!" she said. Her mascara had slightly smeared under one eye.

"Mel and Gabriel just left together," I told her.

She pulled up short. "Really? That's not a good idea."

"I'm sure it's fine," I said. Now that she was worried about it, I was free to take the opposite view. "I mean, the worst that happens is they have a nice evening together, right?"

"No," she said. "The worst that happens is the kids get their hopes up about having a reunited family and have an emotional breakdown when it doesn't work out."

Yeah, that was worse. "Melanie won't let that happen."

"She's as likely to end up crushed as they are," Mom said. She held out both her hands to my father and hauled him up to his feet. "Come on," she said. "Let's go." We headed back toward the door that led out to the parking lot.

I didn't take my eyes off of the exit as we moved closer to it. Was there a chance Andrew would come rushing back in just as we were leaving? How long did it take to say "This isn't working out"? Was that even what he was saying? Or were he and Gracie tangled up together in the car at this very moment, kissing passionately, promising they'd never leave each other?

In the dark parking lot, my mother grabbed at me because I was so busy scanning the shadows for Andrew's silhouette that I had wandered behind a car that was starting to back up. "Pay attention!" she barked, sounding like me when I was with Noah.

I didn't see Andrew anywhere.

My father opened the back door of our car for me and I slid in, tucking my full red skirt around me. Once we were out on the street I let my head fall against the seat back and just gazed up at the windshield, letting the sky and the road ahead turn into a dark meaningless blur, a little girl in the backseat whose parents were driving her home so she could go to sleep in her narrow trundle bed.

24.

Among the e-mails waiting for me when I turned on my computer the next morning was one that made my heart race with sudden hope—which reading it quickly dashed.

"Have to cancel this morning's session. Tell Noah I'm really sorry. I'll see you at the big game. Andrew."

I sat there staring at the screen, wondering if he and Gracie were having fun eating tacos in Santa Barbara.

Noah came into the room then. "What's wrong?" he asked. "You look sad."

"Nothing." I roused myself and forced a smile as I quickly deleted Andrew's e-mail.

Noah came closer and put his arm around my shoulders, which he could reach because I was sitting and he was standing. "If you need anything, Mom, I can get it for you. Just tell me."

"It's nice just having you here," I said and we stayed like that for a moment or two, his arm across my shoulders.

Then, "Mom?" he said.

"What, Noey?"

"If you want me to sleep with you tonight, I can. If you're sad or scared, I mean."

"Thanks," I said. "I might take you up on that."

"Mom?" he said again.

"What?"

"I kind of came in here to see if you could make me a smoothie. But you don't have to if you don't want to."

I got to my feet. "Sure. Let's go down."

I might not have had a boyfriend, or the slightest prospect of one, but at least I wasn't alone.

I took Eleanor Roosevelt for a long walk that afternoon.

She jumped and waggled ecstatically as we left the house. "Don't you ever get tired of being so happy?" I asked her. She just thumped her tail harder and increased her pace.

Walking fast felt good: I had been feeling slightly hungover all day, and the cool air and movement helped to clear my head. I was depressed, but being out and active was better than sitting around.

I was gone a half hour or so and when I got back Gabriel's car was pulled up to the curb. I could hear his deep, booming voice and laugh as soon as I entered the house. Nicole and Cameron came racing toward me, followed at a slower pace by Noah. "Eleanor Roosevelt!" Nicole cried out. "There you are!" She and Cameron threw themselves on the dog, hugging and petting her as if they hadn't seen her in years, not just a couple of days. I undid her leash so she could run off with the kids, then made my way to the kitchen, where I found Mom and Gabriel having a companionable cup of tea together.

Gabriel beamed at me as I entered and greeted him. "Rickie!"

"Hi," I said. "Where's Mel?"

"Upstairs. She was hoping she'd see you before we left." Both the pronoun and the way he used it so confidently told me the weekend was going well for them.

I ran up and found Melanie in her bedroom, tossing a book and some other stuff into a tote bag. "Hi," I said.

"Oh, there you are. Hi." She didn't meet my eyes, just kept sorting through stuff on the night table with exaggerated casualness, but her face betrayed her by turning bright red.

"Well?" I said, sitting down on her bed and leaning back on my elbows so I could peer up at her. "You going to tell me what's going on?"

"You know what's going on."

"I know you both stayed together at your house last night. But I don't know what that means."

"Does it have to mean something?"

I just snorted and waited.

She gazed absently at a glass of water on the nightstand then shook her head like she needed to clear it. "It feels so good," she said finally. "Us all being together. I just want to let it happen, let everything else go, just be with him and the kids. Is that bad?" Her voice was almost pleading.

"Of course not. I think it's great."

"I don't think I'm being stupid. I mean, I told him we have to see a marriage counselor, make some changes, figure out what went wrong so it won't happen again."

"Good for you."

She hugged the book she was holding to her chest. "I'm going to do what you said, Rickie. Move on and try again, even if I can't forgive what he did. That can work, I think."

"You love him," I said. "He loves you. That's what matters."

"I do love him." She lowered her voice to a whisper. "But I'm not sure I'll ever trust him again." I didn't know what to say to that. She probably wouldn't. Melanie dropped the book into the bag and looked around. "I'm so scared I'll end up back here, even sadder than before."

"You won't," I said firmly. "But I'll miss you, Mel. It's going to be a lot lonelier here without you."

"I only live fifteen minutes away," she said. "And our kids go to the same school. And I was over here all the time even before I moved in. And we'll always have the committee meetings."

I snorted. "Great."

"Speaking of which, Maria and Carol Lynn are going to be so mad at me. I'm doing exactly what they told me not to do."

"Yeah, well, I think you have a better chance of being happy than they ever will."

"I hope you're right. About my being happy, I mean—not about them *not* being happy." She scanned the rest of the room. "I'm not going to take everything here home yet. That feels like bad luck. Just a few things for now, and I'll gradually move everything else back. Over time. If things work out." She picked up her bag by the handles. "Oh, but wait—do you need the room? I mean, Noah could move in here. You want me to clean it out for him?"

"Eventually," I said. "But since he doesn't even make it through the night in his own *bed*, there's probably no rush moving him to his own room."

"Just let me know." She gave a little final bob of her head and took a deep breath. "So that's that, then."

We walked back downstairs together, and a little while later she drove home with her family.

"Still think it's a bad idea?" I asked my mother after they left.

"I honestly don't know," she said. "I worry about Melanie. She goes through life expecting people to be as good as she is, and when they're not, she takes it hard."

"No one's as good as she is."

My mother nudged my arm. "You're pretty close."

I drew back in surprise. "Me? I'm the Anti-Melanie. I'm the opposite of her. She's nice, I'm rude."

Mom just smiled a little. "You're not as different as you think."

I shook my head. "You're just trying to mess with my mind."

"Maybe." She laughed and walked away.

Debbie Golden picked up Noah and Joshua at school on Thursday afternoon and Noah played at their house until I came to get him right before dinnertime.

"They did great," Debbie told me as she let me into their small, slightly shabby, and very cozy West Los Angeles house. "Oh, I hope it's okay—they've been playing computer games almost the whole time. I hope you don't mind."

"Mind?" I said. "They could have dropped acid and I'd be fine with it so long as they were having fun together."

"We usually save the LSD for the second playdate," she said.

Noah and Joshua came floating down the stairs, happily chattering away to each other about some game. Then Noah spotted me and dashed frantically back up the stairs, away from me, shouting, "It's too soon, it's too soon!"

"He definitely had fun," I said to Debbie. I corralled him in Joshua's bedroom and threatened him with an early bedtime if he didn't come with me that minute.

As we were leaving, Debbie said, "Oh, and good luck at the game!" before closing the front door.

"What game?" Noah asked me as we walked down the gravel path to the car.

"Your T-ball game, remember?"

"We're playing a *game*?" The coach had told them like five times the week before but apparently it hadn't sunk in. "Against another team?"

"That's kind of the point of the league." I looked down at him. His face was white with terror. I took his hand and squeezed it. "It'll be fine, Noey," I said.

He didn't answer, just shook his head and stayed silent for the rest of our drive home.

Andrew sent an e-mail on Friday to all the parents on the team, suggesting they make sure their kids ate a good breakfast the next morning and requesting that parents "limit all comments at the game to positive ones and leave the coaching to me."

Early Saturday morning, I told Noah to stop watching cartoons and put on his baseball uniform. He instantly curled up into a ball and said, "I can't go. I'm sick."

"You're not sick."

He forced a cough. "See? And my throat hurts and my head."

I sat down on the sofa next to him. "I know it's scary to have to play a real game—"

"That's not *it*. You think I'm faking but I'm not. I'm really, really sick."

"You're really, really not. And you're really, really going to this game."

"You're so mean," he said. "You don't even care that I'm sick."

I sighed. "Just go get into your uniform, Noah."

He rolled slowly off the sofa and onto his feet like he could barely move and then slouched his way across the floor, hunching up his shoulders and choking out a few more theatrical coughs along the way. "I'm going to die of my sickness out there," he said over his shoulder, "and it will be all your fault because you're the meanest worst mother in the whole world." He fake-coughed again as he left the room.

My mother looked up from her desk in the corner of the room, where she'd been quietly working, and said, "What was that all about?"

I flopped back onto the sofa cushions, already exhausted. "His first T-ball game's today. He's pretending to be sick and he's mad at me for not buying it."

"He doesn't want to go?"

"He's scared. It's a lot of pressure and sports are hard for him. And I swear I'm sympathetic to that—but then he starts taking it out on me, like it's all my fault. It drives me crazy."

"That's kind of how it works with mothers." She swiveled her chair around to face me. "Kids get scared or they make mistakes and get angry at themselves, and you're there, you're *always* there, so they take it out on you because you're the only one it's safe to take it out on." She leaned forward a little. "Kids need to know that there's someone there who won't ever go away or leave them, no matter how horribly they behave. So you give that to your kid."

There was a pause. Then I said slowly, "You think I do that to you. What Noah does to me."

"You're older," she said. "It comes out a little differently..."

"I don't take things out on you," I said. Then, with less certainty: "Do I?"

"Yeah, sometimes. But it's okay." She gave a wry half smile. "Most of the time, anyway." She got up from her chair and came over to me. She was still wearing her nightgown and bathrobe. She wasn't much of a morning person and, if she didn't have a morning meeting, often didn't get dressed until almost noon. "What you've done over the last few years hasn't been easy. And you never take anything out on Noah."

"Just on you?"

"It's the far better choice."

"It's not how it feels," I said. "I mean, I feel like I'm genuinely angry when I'm angry, not like I'm working something out."

She smiled that half smile again. "And Noah has probably convinced himself he's really sick right now."

"Yeah, I'm sure he has." I thought for a moment. "So if I take everything out on you—and I'm not saying I do, but just for the sake of argument—and Noah takes everything out on me, where does that leave you? Who do you get to beat up on?"

"Oh, I probably tormented my own mother when she was alive. In fact, I know I did." She laughed. "And your father's always good for a little verbal abuse when I'm feeling close to the edge."

"He doesn't even notice when you yell at him."

"That's what makes him so good for it." We were both silent for a moment. "Can I come with you?" Mom asked suddenly. "To Noah's game?"

"It's not going to be much fun. He really isn't very good at it and you know how stressed he gets."

"That's why I want to go. I figure you could use a little support."

"Yeah," I said. "I could."

"I'll go get dressed." As she passed by, she gently squeezed my shoulder.

I didn't even flinch.

25.

When I walked Noah over to join the rest of his team, Andrew came toward us. "Oh, hi," he said. It was the first time I'd actually seen him in person since Casino Night. "Hey, listen, I'm sorry about canceling last Sunday."

"No worries," I said, trying to match his casual tone even though my heart was thudding. "You go out of town?"

"No," he said with an almost violent shake of his head. "Just dealing with stuff here."

What did that mean? There were too many kids and parents around to have a real conversation. I squatted down in front of Noah, who was still clutching my hand hard like he wouldn't ever let go. "Listen, guy, don't worry about anything, okay? Just have fun."

"Fun?" he repeated, his voice shrill with anxiety. "Playing ball when I'm sick is not *fun*."

"Is he okay?" Andrew asked.

"No," Noah said. "I'm not. I'm really sick but she's making me play."

"He's not sick." I stood up and tried to let go of his hand, but he was holding on so tightly I literally had to pry his fingers off, one by one. "He's fine. Good luck with the game, Noah. Don't worry too much, okay? You'll do fine." I started to move away.

"Hey, Rickie," Andrew said and I stopped and turned to look at him, but whatever else he was going to say was lost because one of the obnoxious dads came bearing down on him at that moment, angrily spitting out the words, "Did you know the umpire has a nephew on the other team? What kind of bullshit league is this?" and I fled.

My mother was saving me a seat at the top of the bleachers.

"I just want him not to mess up completely," I said as I sank down on the bench next to her. "I don't need him to hit a home run. Just for him not to embarrass himself. That's not asking too much, is it?"

"It'll be fine," she said and patted my leg reassuringly, but then I saw that she was jiggling her own ankle nervously.

The jerky father came over to where his friend was standing on the grass, hands rammed into his pockets, just a couple of feet away from where Mom and I were sitting. "It's bullshit," he told his friend. "He won't do a thing about it. Bad enough we have a crap team, but we had to have a crap coach to go with it."

His friend offered up a few four-letter words that seemed to imply agreement, and then the game started.

Our team won the coin toss and was up at bat first. Noah was fairly far back in the lineup, but our team kept getting hits and he kept moving up. I was hoping they'd get three outs before he came to bat, but he came forward out from the bench under the worst possible conditions: the bases were loaded and his team had two outs.

"Shit," I said. "Too much pressure."

I wasn't the only one who found the situation worrisome. "This kid will blow it for the whole team," one of the evil dads muttered to the other.

"Did you hear that?" my mother said, half rising in her seat to give them a horrified look which they didn't even notice. "I mean, did you *hear* that?"

"Those guys are always saying stuff like that." I watched Noah step up to the tee, dragging his bat in the dirt, his shoulders slumped, his whole body anticipating disaster. *Please*, I thought at him. *Please hit the ball hard enough to get you to first base. Please, little friend. Just do that.*

The telepathy reception must have been lousy there: Noah swung too quickly and too carelessly. The bat hit the tee and the ball dribbled off it and onto the ground.

"Foul!" the umpire cried. "Strike one."

One of the dads groaned. Mom glared at him but he didn't notice.

Andrew darted forward, adjusted Noah's bat on his shoulder, whispered something in his ear, then clapped him on the shoulder. As he stepped back, he looked up into the bleachers. Our eyes met. He raised his hands so I could see his crossed fingers. I showed him mine. We both turned our attention back to Noah.

He opened his eyes wide, sighed so deeply you could actually see his chest heave, and swung. He hit the ball but with an upward motion that sent it straight up. It fell back down about a foot away from the tee.

The umpire called another foul.

"One more and he's out," said one of the dads. "So much for our loaded bases. Hey, Jordan!" he called to his kid, who was on third base. "Whatever this kid does, run for home fast as you can, okay? Don't wait for him to get a hit." The kid nodded.

Andrew was whispering to Noah again and helping him adjust his grip on the bat.

"I can't look," I said and shut my eyes.

I could feel my mother's disappointed sigh even before I heard the other team cheer. "Fuck," I said. I opened my eyes. Andrew had his arm around Noah's shoulders and was walking him away from home plate while the rest of their team came out from the bench. The other team ran in from the outfield.

Andrew looked as crushed as I felt. In the middle of all my disappointment, that gave me a tiny bit of pleasure. Someone else, someone who wasn't my parents or my sister, cared how Noah did and hurt because he did.

I didn't get a chance to enjoy that tiny bit of pleasure: I immediately overheard one of the dads saying to the other, "This is exactly what I was talking about. We could have had three more runs if the coach had put that kid at the top of the lineup. The guy doesn't know how to deal with these lousy players."

My mother rose to her feet and carefully picked her medium-heeled-pump way to the edge of the bleachers, right next to where the men were standing. "Excuse me," she said, leaning toward them.

"What?" one of them said, squinting up at her.

"We'd all appreciate it if you'd shut up."

He took a surprised step back but then recovered enough to say defiantly, "We can talk if we want to."

"Not if you're going to say rude things about the coach and our kids." She raised her chin high. It occurred to me my mother was someone you wanted on your side in a fight.

"You're welcome to emotionally destroy your own children any way you like—I'm sure you're very good at it and will eventually pay the price in drug abuse and therapists' bills. But if you say one more nasty thing about my grandson or the coach, or any other kid on this team, I will get you thrown out of this league so fast and so hard that you won't ever be able to find a way back in."

"Crazy lady," the guy muttered. He and his friend moved farther away from the bleachers, not exactly contrite but moderately subdued.

Mom carefully made her way back to me, the bleachers vibrating gently under her feet. The woman did not tread lightly. "They still don't get it but maybe they'll shut up." She sat down.

"Thanks for saying something."

"Someone had to."

"Why are some guys like that?" I said. "How can they care more about winning some meaningless little game than about hurting a kid's feelings?"

"Just don't ever marry anyone like that," she said. "That's all I ask."

Something about the way she said it made me turn to look at her—like she had personal experience with men like that. Dad wasn't anything like those guys, of course, but Mom had been married once before, for almost ten years. I often forgot about that because she never talked about her first marriage. I was twelve before I even knew she'd *had* a husband before Dad.

"Did you?" I asked. "Marry someone like that?"

"Joel wasn't as bad as them," she said. "But he could be mean." She tapped me on the arm. "Just remember that in the long run it doesn't matter how charming or charismatic a guy is. What matters is whether or not he's nice all the way down.

It sounds corny but it's true." She tapped me again in the same place—a few more times and it would start to hurt. "Your dad can drive me crazy—Lord knows he can drive me crazy—but he's never said or done a cruel thing in his whole life and I know he never will."

"You couldn't have taught me that lesson seven years ago?"

"If I had," she said, "we wouldn't have Noah. So it's just as well I waited."

I looked down at the field in front of us, tears stinging my eyes. "Yeah, you're right," I said, and then we sat in silence, waiting for him to come to bat again, which he did a couple of innings later.

He looked up at me as he trudged to the tee and called out, "My stomach hurts. I want to go home." Someone—a kid—snickered. Andrew squatted down in front of Noah. He spoke to him quietly, his face serious and gentle. I watched him talking to my kid and felt that feeling again: that tiny bit of pleasure that someone else cared about Noah's happiness and dreaded his pain. Then Andrew stood up and helped Noah get into position, moving his arms up into a batting stance and whispering some last bit of encouragement and advice before withdrawing.

Noah swung weakly and the bat just touched the ball. It was a foul.

Mom said, "His swing looked a little better to me this time."

"What difference does that make if he still can't hit it off the tee?" I said irritably.

Andrew darted forward again, whispered to Noah, molded him into place, helped him raise the bat, clapped him encouragingly on the shoulder. "You can do it, pal," he said as he backed away.

And he did.

He hit the ball hard, right off the tee.

It didn't go all that far, but it went far enough, more than the five feet it needed to go to not be a foul. And no one caught it. There was some racing around, some diving, some movement from the other team. Meanwhile Noah was still holding the bat, frozen in place, staring at the ball in play in disbelief. "Drop the bat and run!" Andrew yelled at him and Noah, after one agonizingly long moment of uncertainty, dropped the bat in the dirt and trotted slowly to first base. The second baseman on the other team threw the ball to the first baseman, who dropped it, and by the time he retrieved it Noah had one foot safely on base. I screamed and got to my feet. "You did it!" I yelled down to him. "You did it!"

Mom was on her feet beside me, also hollering away at Noah, who raised his eyes to us with a sort of stunned and bewildered pride.

I'm sure the other parents thought we were crazy, screaming over one small base hit after the other kids on both teams had made dozens of them. I didn't care. The only other person there who mattered was Andrew, and he was smiling this huge smile like he'd just gotten a birthday and Christmas and Chanukah present all rolled up in one quick swing. "That a boy!" he kept saying. "That a boy, Noah! That a boy!" The next kid stepped up to bat, which seemed to bring Andrew to his senses. As he passed the bat to the kid, he glanced up at me. I mouthed the words "Thank you." He grinned. We stared at each other over the kid's head and then I sank back into my seat, my legs suddenly and inexplicably weak.

"Whatever else happens," my mother said as she plunked down solidly on the bench, "Noah got a hit today."

"Maybe something else good will happen today," I said, watching Andrew as he coached the next player.

"Let's not get greedy," said my practical mother.

Noah had two more at-bats during the game, and while he wasn't in the running for MVP or anything, he didn't embarrass himself, either. One time he hit the ball solidly, and even though a kid caught it, so it was an out, a couple of the parents called out, "Nice hit!" which made me want to kiss each and every one of them.

The jerky fathers stayed off to the side and kept their thoughts to themselves. My mother must have made an impression on them.

The other time he was at bat, Noah made it to first base on his first hit.

"Look at him," I said to my mother. "Have you ever seen such a serious look on anyone's face?" He was crouching intently, his eyes moving back and forth between the next batter and his goal of second base.

"He's really focusing," she agreed.

I gazed down at him. "God, I love that kid. Even though he makes me nuts most of the time."

"That's how it works."

I glanced over at her, and she smiled calmly at me. "You're a little smug—you know that, right?" I said.

Noah never made it to home base that morning, but that was okay. Their team won by a couple of points, and he was grinning ear to ear as they filed past the other team to give them high fives. Mom and I made our way to the bottom of the bleachers, and Noah ran over to us.

"Did you see that, Mom?" he asked, his voice high with delight. "We won!"

I hugged him and told him he did great, and then my mother did the same.

"Thanks. Can I get a snack?" He pointed to the other side of the diamond, where a couple of parents were setting out some food and drinks on a picnic table. "Come on, Grandma." He tugged on Mom's arm and she let him lead her toward the food.

I was following them when Andrew called out to me. I moved toward him as he came closer.

His baseball hat was pushed high on his forehead and you could see the red line from where it had rested before. He was wearing aviator sunglasses and his temples were damp with sweat. "Our boy got some nice hits today," he said with an enormous grin.

"Thanks to you."

He shook his head. "He made them all by himself."

"Yeah. The hours and hours you've spent helping him... they probably had nothing to do with it."

He acknowledged that with a noncommittal shrug. "I was hoping I'd get a chance to talk to you today," he said.

"Why?"

"I needed to tell you something." He hesitated then said all in a rush, "I wanted you to know that I didn't cancel on Sunday because I was out of town. I canceled because Gracie and I broke up on Saturday night and had some... sorting out to do." Another pause. "I wanted you to know that," he said again.

I looked down at my feet. Weeks earlier, Noah had taken a Sharpie to my Converse sneakers—with my permission—and drawn stick figures all over them. I studied his drawings now like they were suddenly new and fascinating. "You guys broke up?" I said. "Really?"

"You can't be that surprised," he said with an uncomfortable laugh. "You were there for part of it."

"I kind of figured you'd made up," I said. "You disappeared with her."

"We had to talk. We'd been together almost two years. I didn't want to rush anything."

No, he wouldn't want to rush anything. If there was one thing I was sure of, it was that Andrew Fulton never wanted to rush anything. I risked a glance up at him. He had tugged his baseball cap back down low, so it almost met his sunglasses. He was in hiding. "So what made you decide it was time?" I asked.

"She said something—" He shook his head. "It was just one of those moments when you see something clearly. Made me realize there was no point anymore."

I was desperate to know what she had said. But clearly I wasn't supposed to ask. "I'm sorry," I said, even though I wasn't. I was glad. "It can't be easy to break up after you've been together so long."

"It's certainly time-consuming," he said with another short laugh.

A mother came toward us, but something about the way we were talking together made her hesitate and then move away again.

"I've been thinking," Andrew said after she'd retreated.

"Of course you have."

"I—" He stopped. He seemed stuck.

Another mother came up to us, pulling her kid behind her by the arm like she was towing a broken-down bicycle. "Same time next week, Coach?"

He jumped to attention and seemed slightly relieved by the interruption. "Our game's at nine-thirty," he said. "It's on the schedule. But I want the kids here early so we can fit in a practice first, so try to get here by nine."

"I didn't ever get a schedule," she said.

"Really? I handed them out last week and e-mailed them."

"Not to me." She sounded slightly affronted, like the oversight was personal.

"Hold on, I have some more in my bag." He put his hand on my arm. "Don't go anywhere, okay?"

"Okay."

He took care of the woman and then there was a dad who had a question and another mother who needed something. He couldn't get away but he kept looking over at me and giving me the just-one-more-second raised finger.

Noah and Mom came back over to me. Noah's lips were orange.

"Looks like they had cheese puffs," I said.

"GF ones," Noah said happily. "I took two bags."

"Shall we go?" my mother asked.

I didn't know how to tell her that I needed to wait. That I wanted to wait. "Let me just say good-bye to Coach Andrew," I said instead. I went back over to him.

My hair had grown out so much that I had to shove it out of my eyes as I approached him. I touched his arm and said "Excuse me" to the father he was chatting with. "They want to leave," I told Andrew. "My mom and Noah."

He thought for a moment. "Could *you* stay? Let your mother bring Noah home?"

"I don't have a car."

"I can drive you home."

"Oh. Okay." I wandered back to them. I said, "Mom, do you mind taking Noah home and watching him for a little while longer?"

"Where are you going?"

"Nowhere. It's just...Andrew wants to talk to me."

She studied my face. "About Noah, you mean?"

"I don't know." I avoided her gaze. "Can you just—?"

There was a pause. Then: "All right," she said. "I can take Noah. But, Rickie—"

I cut her off. "It's okay, Mom. Really. I'm not being stupid or anything. It's okay."

She nodded. I couldn't tell if she believed me or not. "Come on, Noah," she said.

"You're not coming with us?" Noah said to me.

"Not right now, but I'll be home soon."

It was a sign of what a good mood he was in at the moment that he didn't object, just said good-bye and let Mom lead him away.

His terminal cough had completely disappeared.

The two teams who were playing next were already moving onto the diamond by the time Andrew got rid of all the parents who wanted his attention. One of the mean dads was the last holdout. He was talking Andrew's ear off about something while his kid stood there listening, his brow furrowed in a Little-League imitation of his father's unpleasant scowl.

I moved closer and heard Andrew say calmly, "If you're not happy with the way I coach, please feel free to find another team."

"He has friends on this team," the father spat out. "The *team* is fine—I just want you to do your job right."

"I have to go now," Andrew said. He clapped the boy on the shoulder in a friendly way. "Bye, Jordan. You played great today." He walked away from them and, scooping up his gym bag, said to me, "Come on, let's go."

"Where to?" I asked, falling into step with him.

"Anywhere away from him." We walked in silence for a

moment and reached the parking lot. "I'm hungry," Andrew said. "You have time for lunch?"

"Sure."

He opened the passenger-side car door first and held it for me while I got in, then carefully closed it behind me before going around to his side.

As he drove, we talked about Noah and the moment when he had gotten that first hit. Andrew said, "I've never wanted anything so much in my life."

"Me too," I said. "The whole world became that one ball."

But I got the sense this wasn't what he wanted to talk to me about, not what he had "been thinking" about.

The sandwich place he picked was noisy and crowded. We ordered at the counter—he paid for both of us—and took our food to a booth where we ate quickly, hungrily. I told him how my mother had shut up the evil dads, and he whistled admiringly. "I love your mother," he said.

"She has her moments."

"She's amazing." Once we'd shoved our plates aside, he looked around the restaurant. People were hovering, waiting for tables to open up. "Let's go somewhere quieter to talk," he said. "I mean, if you have time?"

"I'm good."

We walked out of the restaurant and got back in the car.

"Where should we go?" I asked.

He stuck the key in the ignition. "I don't know. Somewhere quiet. You have any ideas?"

The word "quiet" had given me one. "I do, actually. Only—are you in a hurry to get back?"

"Nope," he said. "I have no plans for the rest of the day."

"Me either." I leaned forward and punched an address into

his GPS, hiding it with my left hand so he couldn't see what I was putting in there. "Follow the directions."

"Seventy-five minutes?" he said, squinting at the screen as it reset. "Really?"

"You said you had time."

"I know, but—" He shrugged. "Okay, but this better be worth it."

"It will be."

"It's a little scary," he said, swinging the car out into the street, "not knowing where I'm going."

"It's good to take risks."

"Just promise me it's not Cambria."

"It's not Cambria," I said. "There's nothing the slightest bit twee about this place." There was a pause. I glanced over at him. "So can you tell me now what you were thinking about that you still haven't told me or do we have to wait until we get to our destination?"

"I guess we can talk now." One hand on the steering wheel, he used the other to pull off his baseball cap and toss it over his shoulder, into the backseat, then he ran his fingers through his hair, making it stick out. "It's just . . . Back at the party—at Casino Night—when you and I were talking in my office—" He took a deep breath. "I didn't want to go back into the other room. I wanted to stay in there, alone with you."

I sneaked another look at him. Without his cap and with his hair all rumpled up, he looked really young. I forgot sometimes that he wasn't even a year older than me. Every other adult I spent time with these days was a lot older than me, but not him. "And that got you thinking?" I said, a little faintly.

"Thinking," he said. "And also agonizing. There was the whole Gracie issue—" He darted a look at me. "Is this okay, that I'm saying this stuff?"

"I'll stop you if I get offended," I said with a stiff laugh. I felt like this couldn't possibly be real: this whole conversation, driving alone with him in the car, everything. It was what I wanted but it didn't feel real so I wasn't letting myself believe any of it yet.

He went on. "And then there was the school thing too—that you're the mother of one of the kids I teach. That seemed... problematic."

"So you were thinking about that?"

"I was *trying* to think about that," he said in a low voice. "I knew that was what I should be thinking about. But mostly I kept thinking about how you looked in that red dress and how much I like talking to you when no one else is around." There was a pause. Then he said, "Before I drive the remaining sixty-seven minutes to this mysterious destination of yours, I guess I should ask you whether, knowing all this, you still want to go there with me."

"How worried are you about the school stuff?" I asked. "That I'm a mother there and all?"

"Not enough to turn the car around because of it."

"Good," I said in a small voice. "I don't want you to turn it around."

"Really? You sure?"

I put my hand—tentatively—on his leg. "Really."

He put his right hand over mine. "I'm glad."

We rode like that in silence for a little while.

Then I said, "Would you have broken up with Gracie anyway? Even if I had worn a black dress that night?"

"It wasn't really the color of the dress that mattered."

"You know what I mean."

"I don't know if it would have happened that night, but eventually, yeah. We've been heading in that direction for a while." He put his hand back on the steering wheel and I pulled my hand off his leg. "When we met, we were both on these high-powered career tracks. But then I went from being corporate and ambitious to being an elementary-school coach—and happier than I'd ever been, to my own amazement. But Gracie couldn't understand how I could be so happy doing something that wasn't ever going to make me rich or famous. Especially since she's so—" He stopped. "Well, you saw her at the party. Practically chewing up poor Marley Addison and James Foster. I mean, I guess that's how you have to be to succeed in her line of work. And here I am just hanging out with kids all day long. Which maybe makes me a loser, I don't know."

"Were you living together?"

"No, we spent a lot of nights together, but we always kept our own apartments."

"That's good," I said. "Otherwise—"

"Otherwise I'd be driving a moving van right now," he said with a little laugh. "Not going god-knows-where with you."

"Trust me," I said. "It'll be good."

A short pause. "I should probably ask you what your situation is. I mean, for all I know you're seeing someone." His fingers flexed briefly on the steering wheel. "Are you?"

I hesitated, not sure whether Ryan counted or not, whether he was worth mentioning.

"I was hoping for a simple no," Andrew said bleakly after a moment had passed. "I can still turn the car around, you know."

"No! Don't do that." I realized my silence had given him the wrong idea. "There's no one. Not really. Just this guy I sometimes see when he's in town. But he travels and we're not serious."

"Hmmph," he said.

"What does that mean?"

"Nothing. When's he due back in town?"

I touched his leg again. "Don't know, don't care."

"Really?" he said.

And I started to let myself feel happy.

26.

Wow," Andrew said when the GPS directions guided us down the road toward the beach. "This is beautiful. Where are we? What is this place?"

"My mother's condo. It's right on the ocean. Should be quiet today—no one comes this time of year." I showed him where to park, and he turned off the car. "I just have to get the keys from the manager."

He waited by the car while I ran into the office. I came out with the keys dangling from my fingers. "Want to go on up or take a walk on the beach first?"

He glanced around uncertainly. "Let's check out the beach," he said, and I gratefully agreed. It wasn't that I didn't want to be alone with him in a room or anything: it's just that the hope and excitement were kind of overwhelming and it was a relief to postpone whatever was about to happen between us.

We had the beach all to ourselves. No surprise, since it was cold and windy out there. I was wearing a light jacket but it felt like nothing with the wind slicing through it, so I squeezed my arms across my chest and tried to hug myself warm. Andrew only had on a T-shirt but if he was cold he didn't show it. He had taken off his sunglasses a while ago and must have left them in the car: the closer we'd gotten to the beach, the cloudier it had become, and here, on the sand, the sun was nowhere in sight.

We walked down to the water's edge. "What is it about the ocean?" he said as we gazed out at the waves.

"It's big," I suggested.

"And it doesn't stop moving."

"And waves are cool, the way they keep coming in." A gust of wind made me shiver, and he looked at me.

"You cold?"

"Freezing."

"Me too. Let's go inside."

We entered the building through the back entrance. In the elevator, we backed to separate walls.

"Hi," he said. "Why do I feel so nervous?"

"I don't know," I said. "I do too."

The elevator doors opened and we headed down the hallway. "It's this one," I said and unlocked the door.

The apartment was pretty much the way we'd left it after winter break, except cleaner. Mom always arranged for a cleaning lady to come through the day after we left. The furniture was old and comfortable, because my mother said you shouldn't have to worry about keeping your feet off the furniture when you're on vacation.

I tossed my jacket on the shabby plaid sofa as we came in. "Come see the view," I said, leading Andrew across the living room to the sliding glass door.

"Oh, good," he said. "It's been thirty whole seconds since I last saw the ocean."

We went out on the balcony, where it felt even colder than it had on the beach. This time, when I shivered, Andrew said softly, "Don't be cold."

I turned to him and he held his arms open and kind of made an uncertain "Well?" gesture with his outstretched hands. I moved into the circle of his arms and he put them around me and held me tight against his chest.

After a moment he said, "Warmer now?"

I nodded, my head moving against his shoulder. I put my face up and as soon as I did, he kissed me. His mouth was literally trembling with nervousness. For such a nervous kiss, it felt pretty good.

When he raised his head again, I whispered, "So what do you think?"

"I wasn't thinking," he said. He slid his hands along my arms. His fingers were warm and rough against my skin. "You're still shivering. Let's go inside." He took my hand and we went back through the sliding door and closed it behind us.

"Now what?" I said.

"I don't know," he said. "Let me think about it." He pulled me back to him and we kissed again, longer and deeper and more confidently this time.

Then we stood there for a while, arms wrapped around each other, my head on his chest, not kissing. "This is nice," I said, a little sleepily. I felt warm all over now. A sudden loud ring from across the room made me jump. "Sorry," I said, pulling away from him. I ran over to where I'd thrown my jacket and fished my cell phone out of its pocket. I answered it and then tried to focus on what Noah was saying. I finally cut him off. "Tell Grandma I say you can watch TV since you played ball all morning. Okay?" He said it was okay. "Bye, Noey." I closed the phone and slipped it back in my jacket pocket.

"Does he need you?" Andrew asked.

I shook my head. "The great thing about living with my parents is that I'm covered."

"That does seem like a good thing." We stood there a moment, looking at each other. "Hi," he said.

"Hi." I moved back into his arms and we kissed again. The taste and scent of him were becoming almost familiar. Our growing confidence was verging on eagerness.

"Let's sit down," he said after a moment, and we sat down together on the sofa. I snuggled right up next to him, my thigh against his, my hand holding his across his lap. He put his other arm around my shoulder and leaned his head on mine. We were all woven together.

"You hated me back in Dr. Wilson's office," I said after a moment.

"*You* hated *me*. You were the one who was angry. I was just trying to defend myself."

"Still," I said. "When did you decide I was okay?"

"I never thought you weren't. You were looking out for your kid. I got it. And you were kind of right. There are kids it's easy to get impatient with and teachers can fall into that trap. But those kids are the ones who usually need you to be extra patient with them."

"You're pretty patient from what I've seen."

"Thank you." He threaded his fingers through mine. "How about you? How'd you go from wanting me fired to . . . this?"

"Well, you're cute," I said.

"Come on."

"You are. Or at least cuter than any other guy at school."

"Which isn't saying much."

"True." I squeezed his hand. "You've been so great to Noah. It's like—there was this moment, at the game today, when I looked at you and you were so bummed he had struck out. And later, you were as happy as I was when he got the hit. Do you know what that's like for me? Having someone care like that? And it was because of you he did okay today, all that extra coaching...and setting him up as your assistant. He loved that."

"I'm glad." A pause. "So, you just like me because I'm nice to Noah?"

"Also," I said, "you're cute. Did I mention that?"

"That's it?" He sounded disappointed.

I put my leg over his and rocked it back and forth. "Every time we talked together, even when it was just about scheduling stuff, I didn't want it to end," I said. "We'd be done and you'd start to walk away and I'd try to come up with an excuse to call you back and make you keep talking to me. I couldn't get enough of you—I know that sounds stupid but I don't know how else to put it."

"It doesn't sound stupid," he said. "I felt like that too."

"Really? Why? I'm kind of a loser. A single-mother college dropout..." It scared me a little, saying it out loud, like maybe he'd change his mind hearing it put like that. But I also needed to get it out or it would feel like this huge unspoken thing.

He shifted so he could look right at me. "You should see your eyes right now," he said. "So big and hopeful and worried. You can read your every thought in your eyes. Did you know that?"

"Rats," I said. "I want to be mysterious."

"I like that you're not." He touched my cheek gently with the back of his hand. "Rickie, I come from a family where everything has to be just right all the time. My mother is..." He shrugged. "Well, she's a grown-up version of Gracie, is the truth. She's never left the house not looking perfect—both her and the house. Always perfect. No matter what happens, she puts on her makeup and does her hair and smiles and says everything is absolutely fine. The day after my father had a heart attack, she was getting on the phone and telling people we were all doing 'wonderfully.' I mean, you've got to admire her but it's tough to be her kid. You can never live up to all that perfection. Gracie's the same way. Everything has to be perfect, even when it's not."

"Yeah, well, I'm definitely the opposite of perfect," I said. "Is that what you like about me? That I'm a total mess?"

"No, it's not that. And you're not. It's the fact that you're willing to say things like that. You're vulnerable, Rickie. Open and honest and able to admit that sometimes things suck."

"If that's what you're looking for in a girlfriend..." I twisted my mouth sideways. "But I've got to say that that perfection thing sounds more appealing to *me*."

"You've never had to live with it." He settled back against the cushions and put his hand back on my leg. "Plus you're cute. Did I mention that?" He rubbed his cheek against the top of my head.

"Don't be so patronizing," I said. "Calling me cute..."

"You started it."

"I have to be honest with you," I said. "I was kind of hating on Gracie a little bit over the last few months. I was jealous."

He said slowly, "That night—last Saturday, after the party— she accused me of deliberately sneaking off with you to my office."

"Why *did* you invite me to go with you?"

"I swear I wasn't planning to. I'd just had a drink or two and I wanted to get away from her and what she was doing with those movie stars, and I saw you standing in that dress with Pammy's dick of a father hitting on you—and I just thought I should take you away somewhere." He pulled me closer. "Preferably far away and forever."

"But you didn't *do* anything. In your office. I wouldn't have minded, you know. Actually, I was kind of hoping."

"Technically I was still going out with Gracie. There are rules."

"For a guy like you, there are." I took my leg off of his and sat up a little. "Will you tell me what she said?"

"Gracie? About what?"

"You told me she said something that night that made you realize it was really over."

"Oh." He hesitated. "She was mad. She didn't mean it."

"I won't hold it against her. I promise. I just want to know what makes a guy like you finally say it's over." *So I won't make the same mistake.*

He looked down at his knees. "She said that there was something wrong with a guy who would keep turning down the chance to go away for the weekend with his girlfriend"— his voice faltered—"just so he could teach some little spastic kid to be less spastic."

"Oh." I just sat there for a moment. Then I said, "I don't think he's *technically* spastic."

"I doubt she was using it in a medical sense." He put his hand on my arm. "She knows better. She's not like that. But she was angry and hurt and said it without thinking."

"I know," I said. "I get that. I'm not mad."

He put his hands up and let them drop helplessly. "But she still said it. And that was it for me."

"Would you have broken up with her anyway?"

"I think so. But that moment just made it... very clear."

"Did you break her heart?"

He looked surprised at the question, like it hadn't even occurred to him. "I don't think so. I certainly hope not."

"But it *is* over, right?" I said. "Definitely over?"

He reached out and took my hand. "I don't do things quickly," he said. "But they tend to stay done."

27.

We were alone together in a rapidly darkening apartment with a view of the sun setting over the beach. Everything felt unreal, like we were moving through an even thicker fog than the one blanketing the coastline at the moment.

We kept doing this dance, coming together to kiss and hold each other, then moving apart again, both of us nervous about pushing things too far too fast. Andrew, of course, was just naturally careful and cautious. As for me, well, given my history and what he knew about me, the last thing I wanted to do was come across like some ravenous, sex-crazed nympho. Even if I pretty much fit that description at the moment.

Anyway, it was nice—no, more than nice, it was incredible—just to be held and kissed as the sun sank lower over the ocean, and while some parts of my body felt inflamed and desperate for more attention, they could wait. I could wait.

"Would it take anything away from this moment if I said I was hungry?" Andrew asked eventually.

We ordered in Thai food and then I called home to let them know I wasn't on my way back yet.

"Where are you?" Mom asked.

"The condo, actually."

"The condo? You mean our condo? At the beach?"

"Yeah."

"I had no idea you were going there."

"I didn't either. Not originally."

A pause. "Remember to turn the lights off when you leave. And unplug any appliances you use. Is Andrew a safe driver?"

"Very. Just like you'd expect. So, are you okay watching Noah for a while longer?"

"And if I said I wasn't?"

"I guess I'd rush back. But I don't want to."

She relented. "It's fine. We were thinking of going out to dinner. We'll take him with us. But, Rickie—"

"What?"

"Be careful."

"When am I ever not?" I said jovially. "Oh and Mom?"

"What?"

"Thanks for babysitting."

"You're welcome."

It wasn't easy to get the words out, but I did it: "I don't know what I'd do without you."

"You don't ever have to find out," she said and hung up.

"What'll we do until the food gets here?" Andrew asked with a smile as I put my phone away.

We managed to pass the time.

The food smelled good and I piled heaps of it on my plate, gooey pad thai and some kind of gingery chicken and lots of sticky rice, and then I took one bite before looking up and catching Andrew's dark eyes watching me...and I couldn't eat any more. I pushed it around on my plate with my fork, waiting for him to finish.

His appetite was apparently unaffected by whatever was destroying mine: he finished off the rest of the food.

Together we tossed the take-out containers back into the bag they had come in, and then I went out into the hallway and threw it down the garbage chute. When I came back, Andrew was washing the plates in the sink. I leaned against the counter and watched him, watched his arms with the too-narrow wrists and the slender forearms and big-knuckled slim fingers as they neatly and efficiently sponged and wiped and propped up the plates in the dish drain.

"You're good at that," I said.

"I've had a lot of practice. You could help, you know."

"Nah. I like watching you."

A minute later, he put the last dish in the drain and wiped off his hands on a dish towel. "Now what?"

"Want to play Scrabble?"

"I seem to remember that you're awfully easy to beat."

"Them's fighting words," I said. We went back into the living room and I pulled the game out of the cabinet where Mom stored it. We set up the board, kneeling on the floor on opposite sides of the coffee table.

Andrew's very first word was "exotic."

"You suck," I said. I made "deluxe," using his "x."

"Not bad." He studied his letters, rearranging them on the wooden rack.

I shifted on my knees restlessly. "You take too long."

"I can play fast or I can play well."

"Is it my choice? Because I know which one I'd pick."

"Here." He put down the letters to make "wreck."

"Huh," I said and played around with my letters, trying out different combinations on the rack.

"Now who's taking too long?" he said.

"Shut up." I reached up absently to stroke my eyebrow; I had a habit of fiddling with the ring there when I was thinking. Only it wasn't there. I hadn't put that or the nose stud back since Casino Night. I ran my finger over the unfamiliar smoothness.

"Why'd you take it out?"

I looked up, startled. I hadn't realized he was watching me. "I don't know. Wanted to look pretty at the party, I guess, and just forgot to put it back in."

"If you didn't think it made you look pretty, why'd you get it in the first place?"

"Because it made me look like I wasn't someone's mother."

"You don't look like anyone's mother," he said. "Even without the hardware."

"What do I look like?"

He stared at me a moment, thoughtfully. Then he swept his arm across the table, sending the board and the Scrabble tiles flying. He got to his feet, pulling me up with him.

"We're done playing Scrabble?" I said, my breath catching in my throat.

"For the time being." He pressed against me and our mouths found each other. His hand burrowed inside my hair, feeling the shape of my head, holding it in place so I couldn't move away. Not that I wanted to.

Our kissing wasn't just eager anymore—it was desperate. "I never showed you the bedrooms," I said against his mouth.

"Show me," he said and released me. I led him down the hallway, into the room Melanie and I had shared last time we were there. "Sea horses," he said because there were patterns of them all around the room, on the blankets and curtains, painted on the walls. "Which one is yours?"

At first I thought he meant which sea horse and was trying to figure out an answer to that, and then I realized he meant which bed. "Does it matter?" I said. "But I usually sleep on this one."

He steered me backwards and gently pushed me down on the bed. I reached my arms up and pulled him down on top of me. For a while that was enough: we kissed and pressed our bodies together, his hard and heavy on top of mine, the weight and the feel of him so delicious I didn't need more. For a while. He moved against me, just a little, maybe even unconsciously, his hips kind of rolling against mine. Then he stopped and lifted himself up onto his elbows. "I don't suppose—"

"No, sorry. Do you have anything with you?"

He shook his head. "What about your mom's medicine cabinet? You said she—"

"Only back home. Not here."

He gave a funny little sigh. "Oh, well . . . it's okay. No rush, right?"

"Right," I said. "This is nice." He lowered himself and we kissed some more, our hands slipping under each other's shirt. Then I pushed at his chest until he raised himself up again and grunted out a "What?"

"On the other hand," I said, my voice also a little thick and hoarse, "there's a drugstore in town. Less than five minutes away."

"I like drugstores." He rolled off of me and onto his feet, then reached out a hand and helped pull me onto mine. "Let's go."

"You might want to straighten out your hair," I said. It was sticking out all over his head.

"You're one to talk."

We shared the mirror over the dresser, nudging each other out of the way so we could see, each of us running fingers through our hair. Mine were shaking a little. "Better?" he asked, turning to me.

"Yeah. Me?"

He tugged on a lock of my hair. "Yeah." He kissed me

again—very quickly, his mouth open against mine and then gone. "Let's go."

In the car, I let my hand linger on his thigh.

"You're not helping," he said. "Unless you want me to limp in there."

"Yes," I said. "I'd like that."

He shot me a look. I snuggled my fingers into the space where his thigh met his hip and left them there.

We went into the drugstore together and surveyed the choices on the "family planning" shelf. "If you're going to be watching," he said after a moment, "I'm going to have to go for the extra-extra magnum size."

"Fine. I'll leave you alone—I want to get some candy for later, anyway."

"Really? That's what you're thinking about right now? Snacks?"

"No," I said. "That's not what I'm thinking about. Hurry up."

We met at the cash register a couple of minutes later. Andrew paid and we headed back toward the car. We were both quiet and tense on the short ride back to the condo, but in a good way.

"Where were we?" he said when we were back in the apartment and the door had swung shut behind us.

"Playing Scrabble?"

He answered that by tugging my jacket down off my shoulders. I pulled it the rest of the way off and he was already grabbing at my T-shirt, yanking it up until I took over and hauled it over my head. I ran down the hallway then—even though we were alone, it felt like we should be in the bedroom, not out in the living room, maybe because it was my parents' place—and he followed close behind. When I turned around, he was naked from the waist up—must have discarded his own T-shirt along the way—and reaching for me. The feel of his naked skin against my stomach and chest and arms was so blissful I closed my eyes and gave a little moan of delight.

"I haven't even done anything yet," he said, amused. But that wasn't true for much longer. We were both in a hurry and it didn't take long for everything else to come off and for us to join the sea horses dancing on the bed.

We didn't make it back to LA that night. I called around nine to see if it was okay for us to sleep over at the condo. I was worried my mother would be annoyed that I wanted them to babysit overnight, but she was just relieved we weren't driving back in the dark.

She put Noah on the phone so I could say good night to him. "I'm staying at the beach place tonight," I told him. "I'll see you in the morning."

"Can I sleep in Grandma and Grandpa's room?"

"That's kind of up to them."

"Grandma said I could sleep in a sleeping bag on their floor if I *had* to."

"Fine with me."

"Is Coach Andrew coming to play games with me tomorrow morning?"

"That's a very good question. Hold on. You coming tomorrow?" I asked Andrew, who was lying next to me. We were kind of cramped in the twin bed, but neither of us was complaining. "To play with Noah?"

"Sure," he said. "Just not too early."

"He'll be there," I said into the phone. "So get a good night's sleep. I love you, Noey."

"Love you too, Mom. Can I watch TV until bedtime?"

"It's already bedtime."

"Can I watch TV anyway?"

"Take it up with Grandma. She's in charge tonight." I hung up and twisted toward Andrew.

"Hi," he said.

"Hi."

He took my hand and raised it to his lips, then lightly traced the tattoo on my wrist with his thumb. "'*Noah*,'" he read. "Were you worried you'd forget his name?"

"No," I said. "I was worried I'd forget to be a decent mother."

"What about this one?" He dropped my hand and nudged my ankle with his toe.

I raised my foot a few feet in the air so we could look at it. "That's a hummingbird. We used to have a lot of them in our backyard when I was little. I don't know what happened— they don't come as much anymore. I miss them."

"And this one?" He touched the snake on my upper arm.

I let my foot drop back down on the bed with a thud. "Ah, that. That one has special significance."

"Really?"

"Yes. It signifies that I was drunk one night and not thinking clearly."

"Why no tramp stamp?" he asked.

"Too trendy." I turned on my side so I was facing him and ran my finger down his chest. He had a good amount of hair, enough so he looked like a guy, but not so much he looked like a *hairy* guy. "You got any tats anywhere I should know about?"

"I think you'd have found them by now."

"They'd have to be well hidden," I agreed.

"I'm not into that whole thing," he said. "Permanently defacing yourself. It seems like something you'd always regret. Or at least I would."

"Yeah, well it's nice to have *small* things to regret," I said. "Makes such a nice break from the big ones."

He rested his arm across my shoulder, letting the weight of it pin me down. "Where does tonight rank on the list?"

"Depends," I said. "Is this a one-night-only kind of thing or something longer-lasting?"

"Rickie," he said in a tone that mingled annoyance and patience. "Do I seem in any way at all like someone likely to be in search of a one-night-only kind of thing?"

I closed my eyes and moved my face close to his chest and breathed in his warm, salty, musky scent. "No," I whispered happily against his skin. "You really, really don't."

"All right, then," he said. I curled my legs up against his stomach and he folded his arms around me and I didn't move for the longest time, just listening to his heart beat under my ear.

Neither of us slept much that night, so we got up pretty early and made it back to my house in time for Noah's lesson. I was glad *I* wasn't the one who had to run around for an hour on only a few hours of sleep, but Andrew rallied Noah with his usual good-natured enthusiasm, and pretty soon they were both tearing happily around the backyard.

My mother had welcomed us a little stiffly when we first arrived, and once Andrew was outside with Noah, she motioned to me to sit down across from her at the kitchen table. "So," she said, crossing her arms. "You spent the night together."

"It was nice." I was too happy to be defensive.

She didn't waste time with pleasantries. "What about the girlfriend?"

"He broke up with her. I mean, he already had when we saw him at the park yesterday." She was raising her eyebrows, so I quickly added, "Really, Mom. I swear."

"You're sure?"

"Andrew's a good guy. He wouldn't have spent the night with me if he hadn't broken up with her. He's not like that."

"He does seem like a good guy," she said. "I've liked him from the beginning."

"Me too. Well, almost from the beginning."

"All right, then. I just wanted to make sure you weren't setting yourself up for being hurt."

"I'm pretty careful about that kind of thing, Mom. These days, at least."

She smiled briefly, then leaned back in her chair and glanced around the kitchen. "Don't you usually bake him something when he comes to work with Noah? I could whip up some brownies..."

I grinned. "I think it's okay to skip the brownies this time, Mom. All things considered."

"Hmm. I guess you're right." She shot me a sideways glance. "But if we should decide to get Noah a math tutor or something in the future—"

"We'll find a more traditional way to pay him," I said. "Promise."

There was a pause and then we both started laughing and we didn't stop for a long time.

28.

Tanya said, "I have the details of the family-concert event right here. Ah, Melanie, there you are. Could you please...?"

Melanie, who had just walked in and was still hovering by the doorway, obediently scurried over to where Tanya was sitting, took the papers she was holding out, and distributed one to each of the women sitting around Tanya's immaculate and vaguely antiseptic family room.

"Our job this time is to provide a picnic dinner for approximately a hundred and fifty families," Tanya said, tapping the paper with a perfectly manicured finger. "I've done a little research, and I think our best approach is to hire one of the local bakeries to make sandwiches and cookies and then buy drinks and fruit at Costco. So I'll need each of you to..." I never did hear what she wanted from us because Melanie had finished her task and come over to the sofa to sit down next to me, and I wanted to talk to her.

"I miss you," I whispered. "I feel like I hardly see you anymore."

She put her purse on the floor and whispered back, "I miss you too. But I love having my old life back."

"And everything with Gabriel is good?"

"So far, really good. And the marriage counselor is amazing."

Maria must have been listening, because at the end of the meeting she grabbed Carol Lynn and they pounced on us. "Did I hear you say you're back with your ex?" she asked Melanie.

"Yes," Mel said. She added, with just a touch of defiance, "And it's been really nice."

The two divorcées exchanged a glance. "Just be careful," Carol Lynn said. "Stay alert."

"There's this computer program," Maria said. "I used it on Jonathan. It keeps track of everything they're doing online. You should try it for a while. Just to make sure—"

"I don't really want to."

Maria rolled her eyes. "Well, of course you don't *want* to. No one *wants* to do stuff like that. But sometimes it pays to be smart instead of trusting."

Carol Lynn put her hand on Mel's arm. "We just don't want to see you get hurt."

"Then don't make me feel like I'm making a mistake," Melanie said. Her voice was quiet, but there was an edge to it I'd never heard before. "I'm doing what's right for me."

"We're older than you," Carol Lynn said. "We've seen things you haven't."

"I can take care of myself," Mel said. She walked off and I followed her with a pleasant shrug at the two older women.

A couple of days later, Maria Dellaventura, Debbie Golden, and I took our three boys out to a build-your-own-sundae frozen-yogurt place in West LA. I had been surprised when Maria stopped us as we were walking out of school and asked if they could join us. I didn't think Austin would want to go anywhere with our uncool guys, but he actually seemed happy to be included. The three boys sat at their own table, scarfing down yogurt and trying to top each other in coming up with disgusting combinations, like mustard and onions on mint and raspberry yogurt. They were six-year-old boys, so this was endlessly amusing to them.

Debbie and I told Maria about the T-ball team. "Wish I'd known about it earlier," she said. "I would have signed Austin up. How did you know they'd get Coach Andrew?"

"He arranged it for us," Debbie said.

"Teacher's pets!" Maria said.

"He just knew our boys needed the extra help."

"Did you hear the gossip about him?" Maria asked.

"What's that?" Debbie leaned forward expectantly.

I looked up sharply.

Maria lowered her voice. "Word on the street is that he broke up with his girlfriend to go out with one of the moms at school. But no one knows who."

"Wow," Debbie said. "If I'd only known he liked older women..."

"I know, right?" Maria said. "But what are *you* talking about? You have a husband. I, on the other hand—well, let's just say that this cougar would have left her cage months ago if I'd thought I had a chance with the guy. But he's so young it never even occurred to me." She turned to me. "Like you, Rickie. He must be right around your age, right?"

I licked my spoon and shrugged. "I guess."

"So who do you think it is?" Debbie asked her. "Any ideas?"

"Well, the person who told me all this said there's this one mom who's always going to talk to him about her kid. She has a second-grade girl. I can't remember her name. And she's even older than I am. But apparently she's always in there with him. And usually wearing something low-cut and very tight."

I concentrated on scraping up the last drops of yogurt.

Debbie said, "Well, you can't blame her. The guy is a sweetie-pie and cute."

"She's married, though. You can blame her for *that*," Maria said. "Plus, you know...leave something for those of us who are actively looking. Rickie knows what I'm talking about, don't you, girl?" She winked at me. "You getting any action these days? Any dates with handsome young men you can tell us about so we can at least have a vicarious thrill?"

"In my dreams," I said cheerfully, and not completely dishonestly. "Does that count?"

"If it doesn't, I'm worse off than I realized." She flipped her hair back over her shoulder. "We should start getting together on Saturday nights, Rickie. We could watch stupid chick flicks and do tequila shots. It's pathetic if you do it alone, but if you do it with someone else it's a party."

I laughed but didn't commit.

"Anyway..." She poked at her yogurt with her spoon. She hadn't actually eaten more than a bite or two of it and the rest had melted into goo. "Since you guys are so buddy-buddy with Coach Andrew, see what you can find out. The universe owes me some juicy gossip."

"He doesn't really seem like the cougar type," Debbie said.

"Oh, who knows?" Maria said. "Who knows what goes on behind anyone's closed doors?"

Behind a closed door, later that same night, I was throwing myself up into the strong arms of my son's PE coach and wrapping my legs around his waist. "I haven't seen you in like *forever*," I moaned dramatically.

"I believe it's been three nights."

"Well, it felt like forever."

"To me too." He held me tight against him, and we kissed long and hard.

He set me down and I stepped back. I glanced up at him coyly. "So someone told me today there's a rumor that you're sleeping with a school mom."

He groaned. "Oh, great. That didn't take long."

"They don't know who. But they all assume she must be at least a decade older than you."

"If they just thought about it...I mean, there's only one mother at the school who's the right age for me."

"There is one suspect. Some mother who's always finding excuses to go talk to you about her second-grade daughter. How come you've never mentioned her?"

"I have," he said. "Therese Paulson. I've complained to you a ton about her."

"Oh, *her*," I said, relieved. "You hate her."

"It's true she won't leave me alone. But I don't think it's an attraction thing. She just has too much free time on her hands and wants to micromanage her kid's school life."

"I bet it is an attraction thing," I said. "She probably totally wants you. You're oblivious to this stuff. You didn't even notice how much I liked you."

"To be fair," he said dryly, "you hid it well. Remember the whole I-don't-want-him-to-be-my-son's-PE-coach thing?"

"Shut up. Anyway, how long do you think we can keep this a secret?"

"Clearly not for long if people are already gossiping about it."

"Will you get in trouble?"

"That's not the right question," he said, advancing toward me.

"What is?"

"The right question is whether you're worth getting in trouble for."

"Oh," I said. "Am I—"

"Yes," he said before I'd gotten any further. "Yes."

Not long after that, Noah informed Ms. Hayashi that he didn't need to go to PE anymore now that Coach Andrew was coming over to his house almost every night.

Dr. Wilson, Andrew, Noah, and I all had a little discussion about that in the principal's office. Noah was made to understand that whatever happened at home was private and in no way affected his school schedule. After he was sent back to his classroom, Andrew and I were made to understand that while Dr. Wilson "could not and would not legislate personal relationships between the faculty and parent body," if we were overly indiscreet or Andrew showed any partiality toward any member of our family in the carrying out of his duties, any subsequent meeting would be less genial. He managed to sound both disappointed in us and resigned to the situation. I wondered how often something similar had happened in the past. I definitely got the feeling we weren't the first couple to be delivered this particular speech.

We slunk out of his office as cowed as Noah, but once I'd recovered from the meeting I actually felt a huge wave of relief. Keeping our romance a secret had been more of a burden than either of us had realized until it was lifted, and, while we weren't about to go around advertising it, I was just happy I could now safely give Andrew a quick good-luck kiss before T-ball games or drop by his office after picking up Noah.

Of course, my living situation kept things complicated, no matter what. There were only so many evenings I could dump Noah on my parents and escape to Andrew's. My mother was often out at meetings for her various boards and causes, and while my father was always happy to have Noah in the house with him, I knew it meant Noah would spend the entire time watching TV and eating junk food and staying up late.

Fortunately, Andrew was a good sport about coming over and hanging out at the house with us. We'd have dinner, watch a movie, maybe play a game, get Noah to bed on time—and save anything more intimate for the nights I was able to go to his apartment.

There was one time, though, when he was over and everyone else had gone to bed, and even though our intention was just to watch TV, our hands met under the throw blanket we were sharing, and then our hands were exploring, and then we were kissing, and then I was pretty much on top of him, and who knows what would have happened next, when the sound of footsteps and some movement beyond the partially opened family room door made us fly apart, frantically settling our clothing back in place.

Luckily it was only my father wandering by sleepily, probably to get a snack from the kitchen. He didn't even notice us in the darkened room. But I was well aware that if it had been my mother, her eagle eyes wouldn't have missed a thing. And Noah would have asked questions.

"I remember this feeling," Andrew whispered as we settled back on the sofa a safe distance apart. "It's like dating in high school all over again."

"I'm sorry," I said. "I know it's weird at our age."

He laughed. "Nah, it's okay. It's kind of fun, actually. Keeps the excitement alive."

I was a little skeptical about that. I felt pretty frustrated at that particular moment. And when Noah came down a few minutes later, right before our show ended, to tell me he had had a bad dream and needed me to go back to sleep with him, prompting Andrew to say a speedy good night before heading back to his place, my skepticism only increased.

But the next night I was able to leave Noah with my parents for a few hours and meet Andrew at his place, where I threw myself on top of him and he responded passionately, and at some point I wondered if maybe he had a point: maybe a little frustration and delayed gratification *did* add some spice to a relationship.

Maybe.

29.

A couple of weeks later, I drove to the Fenwick Family Outdoor Concert with Mom and Dad and Noah. Mom had, of course, remembered to bring a big blanket, which we laid out not too far from the stage that had been set up, but off to the side so we could move around freely without blocking anyone's view. I left Noah with my parents and headed over to the food booth, where I once again had to help out—although this time I had volunteered myself.

I was happy to see Melanie already there, behind the counter. She was handing out the picnic boxes while Tanya was packing and organizing them.

"Hey!" I said to Mel. "Where's the rest of your family?"

"Gabriel dropped me off so I wouldn't be late. He and the kids are still looking for parking."

"I hope they can find Mom and Dad—it's getting crowded out there."

"Gabriel's six foot three," Melanie said. "He'll find them."

Tanya glanced up briefly. "Hurry up and get back here, Rickie—things are going to get crazy soon." I snapped a salute in her direction and Melanie shook her head at me.

This job was pretty easy: there were only two kinds of sandwiches and Tanya had marked which was in which box with a black Sharpie, so we were just grabbing from stacks and handing them out.

Up on the stage, Dr. Sorenson was starting things off with a short introductory speech, thanking the Parent Association for all their hard work planning the event. People were talking and running around and no one paid him any attention. He eventually surrendered the stage to a tall man with a thick, graying beard who started to play the guitar and sing.

"There's something familiar about that guy's voice," I said.

Melanie looked over. "That's John Pudgett, silly. He was huge in the seventies."

"Why's he playing *here*, then?"

"He's got a kid at the upper school."

For a while longer, people continued to swarm the booth like locusts, new hands grabbing for boxes as quickly as we could fill them.

Things were just starting to slow down when a young guy wearing a baseball hat approached the booth. He slouched a little but otherwise he was pretty cute. "This where we get the food?" he asked.

"That's what they tell me," I said.

"How much?"

"It's included in the entrance fee."

"Well, then give me two," he said. "There's this girl I'm hoping to eat dinner with, if she ever has any free time tonight."

Melanie laughed. "Go ahead, Rickie. I can cover here."

"You sure?" I glanced over at Tanya, who was in the far corner, marking boxes.

"Oh, for god's sake," Mel said. "Go now, before she tells you you *can't*."

"Right." Rather than circle around and risk attracting Tanya's attention, I stepped up on a wooden box and climbed onto the counter. Andrew held out his hand and helped me jump down next to him.

"Hi, Noah's mom," he said and smiled down at me.

"Hi." I squeezed his hand, then released it. "Thanks for rescuing me." We moved off, side by side, no longer touching because we were surrounded by kids and other teachers and parents.

"Hey, look," I said, pointing. "There's that guy—Pammy's dad. The one who can make me a star. Maybe I should go schmooze him."

"Why?" Andrew said. "You see an acting career in your future?"

"I have *It*," I reminded him.

"Well, don't go wasting it on *him*. Anyway, I thought you had decided to become a social worker."

"Can't I be both? A Hollywood starlet *and* a social worker?"

"You'd be the first." We picked our way carefully through the spread-out blankets, beach towels, soda cups, and sprawling kids, threading our way back toward my parents. "Who's the guy with your family?" Andrew asked as we drew near.

I sidestepped a plate with a sandwich on it that someone had left on the ground and looked where he was pointing. "Oh. That's Gabriel's brother, Ryan. I didn't know he was coming." He was reclining lazily on the blanket next to Gabriel, and I felt the rush of surprise and pleasure I always felt when Ryan showed up unexpectedly at some family event or another.

Then I remembered that a lot had changed since I'd last seen him.

Ryan jumped to his feet as soon as he saw us. "Rickie!" He put his arms around me and gave me a warmly fraternal kiss on the cheek. I pulled back quickly and introduced him to Andrew. They shook hands. Ryan scrutinized Andrew a little too closely. I hoped Andrew wouldn't notice that, or the way Gabriel was watching the whole thing with frank curiosity and real concern.

"Hey," I said to my mother. "Where's Noah?"

"He ran off with Joshua."

Five simple words but they made me absurdly happy. My kid had a friend to run off with.

Andrew plunked himself down on the blanket, and Nicole and Cameron immediately leaped on top of him. Nicole had already made it clear she was very pleased that the PE coach had become a sort of uncle—she was old enough to appreciate the value of connections in high places. Cameron just liked him.

Ryan tugged on my sleeve. "Come with me to get something to drink," he said.

I hesitated but then Andrew looked up and said, "Get me a Coke, will you?" and it seemed okay, so Ryan and I went the long way around the blankets to get back to the other side, where the food and drinks were.

"It's good to see you, Rickie," he said, letting his arm brush against mine as we walked side by side on the grass. "I missed you a lot on this trip. Did you get my e-mail saying I was back?"

"Yeah. Sorry I didn't write you back yet. I meant to but—" The truth was I had felt overwhelmed by the task of filling him in on everything.

"It's okay. I get it. I told you to change things and you did." He glanced over at me. "Where's the ring and nose stud?"

"I just took them off one night and never put them back in."

He patted my head patronizingly. "My little girl is growing up."

I shoved him away. "Shut up."

"You're even dressing differently," he said. "My god, there isn't a stain on you. And your clothes actually fit."

"Yours don't," I said, having noticed how they hung on him. "You forget to eat in Turkey?"

"I had the stomach flu last week. And no one to nurse me through it. I was sick and all alone." He touched the back of my hand. "Don't you feel a little sorry for me?"

"Not really. The drinks are over there." I pointed.

"I was lying about wanting a drink," he said. "I just wanted to talk to you alone." He pulled me a little farther away from the crowd, into the shadows near the bushes. "So... this guy. Andrew. What's the story?"

"He's nice," I said. "It's good."

He waited, but I was done.

"I'm glad for you, Rickie," he said after a moment, although he didn't sound particularly glad.

"Thanks. We should get the drinks and go back."

"What's your rush?" He motioned with his head back toward where we'd come from. "Is he the jealous type?"

"I don't know. He doesn't have any reason to be." A pause.

"You sure you don't want a drink? They have soda and water. Oh, and juice."

"I'm good," Ryan said. He stuck his hands in his pockets and idly rattled his change. "I think I'll take off, actually. This isn't my kind of thing. All these kids running around and screaming..." He gave a little shudder. "Anyway, I really only came to see you."

"Why?"

"Just wanted to make sure you were okay."

"I'm fine."

He took his hands out of his pockets and held them out toward me. "Then give me a kiss good-bye." I hesitated but he was already putting his arms around me, so I hugged him back, the feel of his body so familiar against mine it freaked me out a little. I tilted my cheek up for him to kiss, but he deliberately bent lower and got my mouth instead. It wasn't a quick peck, either: he pressed his mouth hard against mine and didn't seem like he was going to stop on his own, so I finally ducked away and said good-bye.

"Have a nice time?" Andrew asked in an unusually tense voice when I returned to the blanket with drinks. Cameron and Nicole had moved over to eat with their dad and Noah was still missing.

"Sorry that took so long." I sat down next to him. "I hadn't seen Ryan for a long time. He travels a lot."

"You two always kiss like that when you see each other?"

I drew my knees up to my chest and sat there for a moment, hugging them. Then I said, "I told you there was this guy I hung out with sometimes, when he was in town."

He thought about that. The way he did. Then he said,

"You might have mentioned that he'd be coming here tonight."

"I didn't know."

"Did you have to kiss him on the mouth?"

"He did that, not me."

"And you were just an innocent bystander?"

I shifted toward him and touched him on the arm. "Hey, are you really mad about this?"

He shrugged. In a way that meant he was mad.

"He already left," I said.

"Is that supposed to be reassuring?"

"Well, what *would* be?"

He looked down at my hand, which was still on his arm. My sleeve had fallen back, revealing my "Noah" tattoo. "How about you get a tattoo with *my* name? Right across your forehead where everyone can see it. That would be reassuring."

At least he was joking about it. I gently pushed myself against his side. "I would, only my mother made me promise no more tattoos."

There was a break in the music and some clapping as a singer left the stage and they started setting up for the next performer. A couple of feet away, Gabriel rose to his feet and called out to us, "I'm going to take the kids over to see Mel at the food stand. You need anything?"

"We're good, thanks," I said.

"Did Ryan take off?"

"Yes."

"I'm not surprised," he said with a sigh.

Cameron and Nicole jumped up and the three of them wandered off toward the food booth, the two kids dancing at their father's side, looking like two small pets being walked by their owner.

"It's nice having him around again," I said, idly watching them go.

My mother leaned toward us. "If he cheats on Melanie again, I'll kill him with my bare hands," she said.

"He's a big guy," I said. "I'll help you."

There was a small whirlwind at my side, which turned out to be Noah, Joshua in tow. "Mom? Mom? Can I have a sleepover with Joshua?"

"I guess so. Did his mom say it was okay?"

"Yes! Come on, Noah!" Joshua went running off, but I caught at Noah's arm before he could follow.

"Listen, Noey, you've only ever had a sleepover at your cousins'. You sure you're up for this?"

"Mom," he said, with an edge of exasperation. "It's *Joshua.* He's like my best friend."

"Okay, then," I said, loving his casual use of a term I thought I'd never hear from his lips. "But if you need me to come get you at any point—"

"I won't," he said and went trotting off after Joshua.

I sent Debbie a quick text—easier than looking for her in the crowd—and she immediately confirmed that they were delighted to take Noah home with them. I put the phone back in my pocket and looked around.

The current performer was strumming softly on a guitar and singing a gentle folk song. The quiet music made the darkening twilight feel dreamlike.

I sidled up close to Andrew and whispered in his ear, "You know, if Noah's going on a sleepover, that means I could have one too."

He sat up straight. "I like that idea."

"You want to leave now? We can take the food with us. Unless you want to hear more music?"

He was already rising to his feet and tugging me to mine. "I've heard enough."

Later that evening we were curled up together on his bed, watching a movie, my head cushioned comfortably on the soft pad of his naked shoulder, when Andrew suddenly grabbed the remote. "Hold on." He paused the movie. "Isn't that your phone?"

My bag was lying on the floor next to the bed, so I rolled over, reached down for it, and got out my phone.

"Mom?" said a very small voice on the other end.

"Noah? Are you okay?"

At first there was just the sound of his breathing—the kind of rapid breathing that meant he was trying not to cry. Then he said, "I think maybe I should come home."

"What's wrong?"

"Nothing. I just...I just think I need to come home." A strangled little sigh that wasn't quite a sob. "I miss my room."

I heard Debbie's voice in the background, saying, "Let me talk to her." Then she said into the phone: "Hey, Rickie." She sounded pretty tired. "Noah and Joshua had a great time and they went to sleep no problem, but Noah woke up a little while ago and he's having trouble going back to sleep."

"It's his first sleepover," I said apologetically.

"I think he'd be more comfortable sleeping in his own bed. Can you pick him up? I'd drive him home for you, but Paul's out of town and I can't leave the kids."

"Of course," I said. "I'll be there as soon as I can. I'm so sorry about this."

"Are you kidding?" she said. "He did great. Someday I'll

tell you the whole story of my daughter's first sleepover, but for now let's just say that the other girl's parents still aren't speaking to us. See you soon."

As I sat up and pulled on my jeans, I explained what was going on to Andrew, who instantly hopped out of bed and reached for his boxers. "I'll drive you over there and then drop you and Noah back at your house."

"If it's easier, you can just take me to my parents' and I can grab my car and go on from there." I scanned the room for my clothing and spotted my bra lying on the floor near his dresser.

He turned, holding a sock in his hand. "I don't like the idea of you driving around town by yourself at this time of night."

"It's not that late."

He shook his head and went back to getting dressed. "I'm driving you."

We both quickly finished putting on our clothes and were in the car in less than five minutes. I told Andrew where the Goldens lived, and as he steered us along the quiet, empty, late-night streets, I thought about how I would have been doing this by myself, all alone, if he hadn't said he'd come with me. And then it occurred to me that if it hadn't been for Andrew, I probably *wouldn't* have been doing this by myself, because Noah might not ever have made friends with Joshua.

He glanced over and caught me looking at him. "What?" he said.

"Nothing. Just...thanks for coming with me. It means a lot."

"I'm happy to. Hey," he said, "I was thinking: should we just come back to my place so we don't wake up your parents? Noah could sleep on the sofa or the floor or wherever you think he'd be most comfortable."

I thought about what it would be like to wake up in the morning next to Andrew, with Noah running in from the living room to ask if he could crawl into bed with us and watch TV.

I settled back in my seat with a contented sigh and said, "You know what?"

"What?"

"I like the way you think."

What Mom Gave Me
by Claire LaZebnik

If I could send a letter back in time, there are a bunch of things I'd like to tell my fourteen-year-old self, things like "Think about getting all those baby teeth pulled *now*," because I'd just as soon not have to go off to college in braces again. Also, it would be nice to reassure myself that despite all evidence to the contrary my love life actually *would* work out okay—better than okay—in the long run. But if I only had space to tell my stupid teenage self one thing, it would be a simple "Just be nicer to Mom, okay?"

Like many teenagers, I had a tendency toward sullenness and a profound belief that the members of my family were just supporting players in The Story of My Life. As I got older, and should have known better, I still considered my mother mostly in terms of what she could do for me and didn't concern myself too much with what her own thoughts and fears and hopes might have been. My life seemed more important than hers, and I was often too busy for long phone conversations, took for granted her gifts and visits, and rarely encouraged her to talk about herself.

Then she was diagnosed with Stage IV pancreatic cancer. It was scary and sad, but the sudden tragedy meant we could put the rest of life on hold, and we actually had some amazing talks and shared moments in those ten weeks between her diagnosis and death. The walls I'd spent my adolescence and teen years erecting crumbled pretty quickly under the weight of her illness.

But ten weeks isn't a lot of time, and there were five other members of the family who craved attention and absolution as much as I did. Plus, I had a family of my own to take care of. So plenty of things were left unsaid and a fair number didn't even get *thought* about until later. And some of them didn't come up until I was working on this book.

There's a moment at the end of this novel when Rickie's mother explains to her that kids need someone "safe" to take out their frustrations on, someone who won't leave them no matter how unreasonable or unpleasant they get. "You give them that," she says, meaning that a mother will weather her child's anger and never falter in her love.

I wrote those words thinking about my own kids, about how sometimes they'll come home from a tough day of socializing and academics and just lose it with me, because they *can*. I don't enjoy it when my usually delightful kids scream at me or blame me for things that aren't my fault, but I recognize where that anger's coming from and I understand it. So I took that feeling and put it in this book: both Rickie and Noah tend to explode at their mothers when they're feeling emotionally overwhelmed. But I also thought of my own mother as I wrote it, and how I wasn't always all that nice to her, and I found myself hoping that she understood that it was because I knew it was safe, because I trusted her not to stop loving me no matter how selfish and pissy I was.

I wish I could just ask her if I'm right about that, and maybe also apologize at the same time. I can't.

But she was a smart lady. I'm guessing she got it.

Reading Group Guide

1. There are many mothers in this book—Rickie, obviously, and Melanie and Laurel and Sandra (Gabriel's mother) and Melanie's mother and all of the school mothers. Who does your own mother most resemble? If you're a mother, which mother do you think is most like you? Is that also your favorite mother in the book? If not, why not?

2. At the beginning of the novel, Gabriel and Melanie have just separated because he's been unfaithful. At the end, they've reunited. Do you think they'll make it? Why or why not? Do you think she should have forgiven him sooner? Or maybe not at all? What's unforgivable when it comes to marriage? Anything?

3. Do you know any kids like Noah—kids who just "march to the beat of a different drummer"? Do you think adults should try to make them fit in better or let them do their own thing?

4. If you had to describe Rickie, would you say she's tough or vulnerable? Why? Is she a reliable narrator? Can you think of

any point in the novel when Rickie is absolutely wrong about something and doesn't realize it for a while?

5. Rickie notices how uncommon it is to have a male teacher in the Fenwick Prep elementary school. Have you noticed this to be the case in your community? Why do you think they tend to be rare?

6. In one scene, Rickie watches as Noah gets up to bat, wishing more than anything that he'll get a base hit—or even make contact with the ball. Have you ever wanted something for someone else more than you wanted anything in the world for yourself?

7. What do you think of the way Rickie handles Noah's questions about his father? If you were in her boat, would you demand financial or other kinds of support from him?

8. Rickie's mother says toward the end of the novel that sometimes when things go wrong, kids need someone safe to get mad at and that a mother "gives" them that—lets them get mad at her and forgives them. Do you think that's true? Has that ever played out in your life in some way?

About the Author

Claire LaZebnik lives in Los Angeles with her TV writer husband and four children. She is the author of the novels *The Smart One and the Pretty One* (5 Spot, 2008), *Knitting Under the Influence* (5 Spot, 2006), and *Same as It Never Was* and coauthor of *Overcoming Autism: Finding the Answers, Strategies, and Hope That Can Transform a Child's Life* and *Growing Up on the Spectrum: A Guide to Life, Love, and Learning for Teens and Young Adults with Autism and Asperger's.*

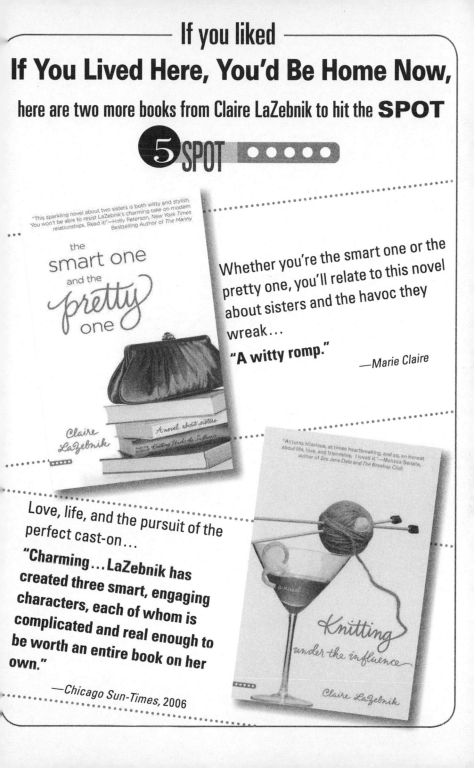